D0049390

PERSONAL
DARKNESS

Also by Tanith Lee

DARK DANCE

HEART-BEAST

TANITH LEE

PERSONAL DARKNESS

SECOND IN THE
BLOOD OPERA SEQUENCE

A DELL BOOK

Published by
Dell Publishing
a division of
Bantam Doubleday Dell Publishing Group, Inc.
1540 Broadway
New York, New York 10036

ISBN: 0-440-21470-X

To
Peter Lavery,
the Godfather of the Scarabae Novels

Personal
Darkness

Now, *here,* you see, it takes all the running *you* can do, to keep in the same place.

Through the Looking-Glass,
Lewis Carroll

CHAPTER 1

 THE GIRL IN THE RAIN:
He had been watching her for about twenty minutes.

Timothy's plan had been to clean his car, but the rain had beaten him to it. He had gone to the window of the room his mother called the Living Room, and his father, obstinately, the Lounge, and was looking out at the water sluicing the street. He did not wonder if it was raining at the country hotel where his parents were spending the weekend. The only second thought he gave them was one of pleasure in their absence.

The Mini Metro shone like blue tinfoil in the downpour. And across the road, between the green cascades of the raining trees, was this girl.

She looked tall, though he thought actually she was not, very, it was her slimness which created the impression. She had a marvelous figure, in her tight-belted raincoat. And plastered all over her was a thick, soaked spillage of jet-black hair. Her face was pale; her eyes were black with makeup, and her lips scarlet. She was just amazing. And wet, she was certainly that, simply standing there under the gushing tap of the rain, staring across at the house.

Timothy assumed she could not see him through the

net curtain. And yet he had the notion she was waiting for him to make some signal.

Finally, after twenty-five minutes, he made it.

He lifted the curtain and waved at her.

He might have been a ghost. She did not react.

"Fucking blind," said Timothy. It was nice to say something like this in the lounge-living room, without his mother going up the wall. He had to be careful at work, too, where Mr. Cummings would come scuttling along the rows of computers like a poisonous woodlouse. "Got those figures yet, Timothy? Mr. Andrews is waiting." And, breathing his halitosis briskly over Timothy's shoulder, "You should wash your mouth out. I don't want that kind of language."

Timothy forgot his mother and Mr. Cummings. The terrific girl was crossing over the street, toward him.

She was past his car, up on the pavement, coming through the gateposts. She had great legs, and weird shoes. Then she was on the steps.

Timothy turned around and stood in the big room with its pallid mother-chosen, satin-finish walls and parent-selected furniture and objects. He, now, waited.

The doorbell buzzed.

Timothy had one curious moment. He felt faintly affronted, assailed. Threatened? Then that went, it was childish, and he told himself that maybe he could be on to something good here.

When he opened the door, he grinned at once, to let her see he liked the look of her. She was sensational, even though her eye makeup was running in the wet, which he wished it had not been. Her clothes were pretty odd, too. The raincoat looked as if it had come out of a dustbin. His grin sagged a little.

"Hi," said Timothy, defensively.

The girl said, "Mrs. Watt?"

"No, sorry." Was he relieved?

"Yes," said the girl. Her voice was clear and quite

flat, like a soft musical chime wrongly played. "Mrs. Watt lives here."

"She doesn't. Never heard of her."

"This is the house," said the girl. She paused. She said, "She lives with her daughter. Liz. Liz and Brian."

Something plucked at Timothy's memory. Had the people Dad bought the house from last year been called Liz and Brian? Everyone had got quite matey when the deal was struck.

"I think—they've moved. The people before us."

The girl stared into his face. Her eyes were not only made up black, they *were* black. Black as black paint. He had never seen a white woman with eyes as dark as that, maybe not a black woman either.

"She's gone," said the girl. There was a note of something after all. Was it regret?

"I'm afraid so." It was fairly obvious no possessive, well-heeled mother had packed the girl off on such a journey. Frankly, she looked as if she had been living rough. Her ankle boots, a glance had told him, were broken, and newspaper protruded soggily from the cracks. She had a split plastic shoulder bag.

"What'll you do?" asked Timothy.

The girl stood and looked at him, and behind her the rain poured as if forever.

And behind *him* was the pale yellow house, with all its rooms at his disposal, open as a hand to Saturday afternoon and Saturday night and all Sunday until ten in the evening, when they would be back.

"Why don't you come in a minute," said Timothy. "You must be wet."

She did not hesitate, neither did she thank him. She walked straight into the hall, where the big mirror reflected her darkly above the wilting flowers his fussy, weekending mother had forgotten to throw out.

He thought of things in horror movies that had to be invited over the threshold. But only for a second. At once she took off her raincoat. She wore a scruffy, skimpy black skirt into which was tucked a gray T-shirt with holes. The rain had got through the topcoat easily and she was damp. Everything clung. She was slender as a bone, with big perfect breasts that had little wicked points. Her hair hung to her bottom in black stripes and waterdrops ran off it. The presage of excitement was fulfilled. He was aroused.

"You'd better have a towel," said Timothy.

He left her in the hall and started up the stairs. At the linen cupboard, out of her sight, he made a joyful gesture to himself. Then hurried back with the big fluffy towel.

Better not leave her alone too long, just in case.

First of all he made tea in the fitted kitchen. As he was doing this she said she was hungry. So he grudgingly put some bread in the toaster. She sat on one of the stools at the breakfast bar, with her hair up in the towel. The eye makeup was in unwiped trickles down her face, but her red lips were pristine, even after she ate the toast, very quickly, as if she were starving. So he had to offer to make some more. She accepted.

He had realized, if she had been living rough, she was probably dirty. She did not smell. The rain must have cleaned her somewhat, but it would not be enough.

"Would you like a bath? You must be cold."

"All right," she said.

He ran the hot water for her into the avocado bath, and put in some of his mother's expensive bath foam. He had always liked the scent of this, although recently not on his mother. She was too old for that sort of perfume, though he still felt he had to give it to her at Christmas.

The girl went into the bathroom with a T-shirt of his own Timothy had sportingly offered her. He hoped she had clean underclothes in her nasty plastic bag. He could hardly give her his mother's, that would be going too far.

He wanted to see his protégée improved. Know she was cleaned up. If she looked all right, he might take her out to dinner at the Italian.

When she came back, she looked wonderful. She had washed her hair and dried it, bathed, and redone her makeup. Her hair, dry, was like frayed black silk, and the new black T-shirt, though it clung rather less, still emphasized her breasts. God knew what he would do about shoes, though. She was now barefoot. Her feet were good, not ugly like so many girls' feet. She must have trimmed her toenails, as she had trimmed the long nails on her fingers, and both sets were now bloodred.

"That's great," said Timothy. "You did look a bit—well . . . What happened? You ran away from home?"

"Yes," said the girl, without faltering.

"You'll have to go back," he said. At twenty-two he was more responsible than she. Besides, he would have to unload her before Sunday night.

"I can't," said the girl. She had not told him her name, although he had revealed his as Tim.

"Of course you can. Parents are bloody awful, I know, but they do have their uses."

She regarded him carefully. Her eyes were even more fascinating now the shadow and mascara had been realigned. She looked like a singer. He wished Rob could get a look at her. For a moment he basked in the future enjoyment of telling Rob all about her. Then he and she went into the lounge-living room and had gin and tonics.

"No, you're going to have to go back. You can phone them, if you like. Tell them you're with a girlfriend, or something. You can stay here tonight. Plenty of room." He thought of rolling with her in his narrow bed, squeezed together. Thank God he had kept stocked up. Like Rob said, you never knew your luck.

The girl sat on the sofa, her long legs—even though she was not tall, she had the right proportions—visible almost to the tops of her thighs. No unwanted hair. No tights. Perhaps no pants?

"I can't go back," she said again.

"Come on. Don't be dramatic. Why not?"

"My father," she said. She drank her gin slowly and steadily, like lemonade on a hot afternoon. "My father abused me."

Timothy put down his glass. He was shocked.

"You mean he—you mean he—what do you mean?"

"I mean he slept with me."

"Jesus," said Timothy. "That's fucking disgusting."

"Yes."

Timothy took both their glasses and poured generous gin and tonics. He would have to remember to get replacements from Viney's.

When he handed the girl her drink she was demure and still, as if she had told him nothing very much.

"Does your mother know?" he asked. Under the shock was a dim prurience, curiosity. She had been broken into, and in unacceptable circumstances. This made her less attractive. And more.

"Yes, my mother knew. And my grandmother."

"Didn't they try to stop it?"

"Oh no."

She was matter-of-fact. Suddenly she said, as if awarding him a favor, "My name's Ruth."

"Yeah," said Timothy, and drank his gin.

Could he still chance her in the Italian? He would have to. He was not going to cook, and already she had had two rounds of toast, a packet of biscuits, and three apples from the fruit stand. Her legs . . . He would have to loan her some jeans. And she could wear his old trainers, the ones he had had when he was thirteen. He had small feet for a man.

Maybe she was lying about her dad.

She was only seventeen. Girls had fantasies. Remember Jean, who said she had slept with David Bowie?

* * *

Later, two or three gins later, when he was wondering if perhaps he need not wait until after the Italian dinner, she sidetracked him. She asked, politely, if she could see the house. The drink had seemed to make no impression on her.

Showing her the house bored him. He was not proud of it, none of it was his, not even his own room, really.

But then, this Mrs. Watt person, who had presumably been her only friend, and not much of one at that, had lived here.

Ruth had already seen the fitted kitchen with its dishwasher, computerized washing machine, ranks of polished knives and utensils, fanged juicers, and endless other gadgets. And the lounge-living room, with china in cupboards, fat TV, *Homes and Gardens* on the coffee table, and the music center. Ruth had actually investigated that. But his mother's seldom-played highlights from *Swan Lake,* Beethoven and Dvořák had not held her interest.

The dining room was small, and superfluously glistened from the cleaner's superfluous attentions.

Upstairs, Timothy showed Ruth bedrooms, and his father's study, quickly. The house had been extended at some time, and there were rooms of various sizes, some now lying fallow. Timothy's was the big room with the inclusive bathroom. Here Ruth paused, looking around at his posters briefly, showing even less interest than before in his music center and discs of Level 42. This room too had been recently decorated, but it was not Timothy's taste. He had let his mother choose, not really knowing what his taste in rooms was.

Ruth did look down from here onto the garden, and she remarked, nearly incongruously, "There's the cedar tree."

Apparently Mrs. Watt had mentioned this tree.

Nothing else was said.

They descended again, and Timothy wondered if Ruth would like to see his car, but she would be seeing it anyway when they went out. That should be soon. He was anxious by now with desire, but also hungry. An early dinner, and they could make a long night of it. Bring back some wine. And a video. Something she would like.

Somehow, she struck him after all as slightly childish.

He lent her the jeans and trainers, and offered her a spray of the scent that went with the bath foam. In his parents' bedroom he felt a touch savage, and also put upon Ruth's milk white ears a pair of large gold earrings. But Ruth, with a peculiar expression, removed these.

Another instant of unease then. She had come to him as a gypsy, but what had she been before? Had the possibly fantasized abusing father been very rich and cultured, hanging on the ears of his courtesan daughter orient jade and priceless pearl?

The blue-for-a-boy car took them neatly down to the Monte Doro, which happily opened at six on Saturdays.

The tables were robed in russet and apple green, and from the ceiling hung a chandelier of ice-green Perrier bottles. It was not crowded yet, and the manager came rustling out and lit their candle hastily.

Timothy was glad he had brought his Visa card. Ruth had a starter of tomato salad with mozzarella and mushrooms, and went on to chicken wrapped in ham, with a cream and brandy sauce, new potatoes, broccoli and carrots. She wanted dessert too, a trifle topped by nuts and cherries, and then some goat's cheese and biscuits. Timothy was used to girls who had to watch their weight. Obviously Ruth did not, or else she was making up for the time lost in the wilds.

They had a bottle of frascati with their meal, and Timothy bought another bottle, with the help of his card, to take away with them.

He drove back carefully. He knew he was over the limit but it was not very far, and he reckoned he was a good driver; the drink had not affected him. Besides, he had had only one glass of wine in the restaurant.

The video he had picked up was *Dragonslayer*. He thought Ruth would like this, although he supposed it was fairly absurd. The photography, landscapes, and animation had not pleased him, but he believed the love scene might do something for Ruth. She was young, and female.

To his surprise, the dragon seemed to concern her most.

He had slipped his arm around her as they watched on the sofa before the big screen of the TV.

She grew tense. She did not like it when the hero attacked the dragon. She said, low and harsh, "He's hurt it," and then, "Shake him *off*. Kill him." She did not mean the dragon should die.

And when it did she was hard, like iron, under Timothy's supporting, barely caressive arm.

He had attempted to kiss her before, at the moment of the kiss in the film, and she had resisted. He did not press her.

When the film was over, he said, "You liked the dragon best."

"It was beautiful," she said.

"How'd you like to be sacrificed to it? Burned up?"

Ruth said primly, "I'd have talked to it. The magician knew how, but he didn't. All the people were stupid. Horrible."

Timothy opened the new bottle of frascati. To his dismay, Ruth asked if she could eat an orange. He was afraid she had an alcohol hunger and might be sick. But she ate the orange, and another, and nothing else happened.

"You know," said Timothy, settling beside her again, "you're gorgeous. You are. And your hair . . ."

She let him stroke her hair, and next her shoulder, but when he brought his lips near hers again, she said, "No, thank you."

Timothy sat up.

"I'm not your father. You have to get over that."

"No I don't."

"Oh, Ruth—"

A car growled, out in the street, a lion returning to its lair. He knew its voice, but this was not feasible. No. He heard the car draw to a standstill behind the Mini Metro.

They could not— They had meant to be gone all weekend. *No.*

Intuitively, Timothy's eyes darted about the room. The strewn gin glasses, the wine, the orange peel not quite on the plate, the video box—and Ruth. Smelling of his mother's perfume, barefoot, red in lip and nail. Black as night of eye.

"Oh, Christ. Oh, fucking shit—"

Feet on the steps.

A rumble of voices.

The key in the lock.

"Timothy?"

CHAPTER 2

KNEELING IN CRIMSON ARMOR BEFORE his shield was a knight. Beside him ran a blue glass stream, at his back lay an emerald wood where a tower burned. The window was more like a tarot card than anything. It reflected all over the polished, deeply scratched round table that stood below. The scratches spelled out a word, but not in English.

The house was quiet and full of heat. And if she closed her eyes, the effect of shuttered hot silence and colored light, the smell of dust and powders, beeswax, cobwebs, damp, evoked the first house.

And yet everything was changed.

Changed—and duplicated. Perhaps not too much. Perhaps only so far as was bearable, or necessary.

She had watched what they do. She had been borne along by it. But she could not really say she had participated. She was still a spectator. That was her role. Witness to the Scarabae.

Rachaela stood in the dark room under the blue, red and green window, and listened.

The sound came, just discernible, the firm summer breeze tossing the tall pines and oaks of the common. Almost, but not quite, like the sound of the sea . . .

Then a car noised dimly by, passing along the road two hundred feet below the house, where the common ended. There was not much traffic. Sometimes, people went that way, and usually stared at the house between the trees. It was quite large, with curious balancing architecture, turrets, and all the stabs of the stained-glass windows. Every one of the windows was of stained glass. All the outer doors were doubled, like air locks. There was a conservatory, and a walled garden. Like the first house. On three sides, the common spread away.

But down beyond the road there was a scatter of big houses, and then clusters of smaller ones, and next one of those villages of London, with its pubs and shops, library, and civic buildings. The steeples of churches sprang from the landscape. On Sundays the bells rang in the distance and an ice-cream van was just audible, playing "The Thieving Magpie."

Michael and Cheta did their shopping in the London village stores, perhaps classed as an eccentric foreign couple.

Books were brought from the library, and punctually returned. Also tapes and discs for Eric's machine. Tapes too were carried from Bonanza Videos. They liked the videos, particularly horror films and thrillers. These they watched with straight moral faces, reminding her of gray hamsters thinking.

Such things were very different from before. There had been no television in the first house. But here there were several. The greater one crouched in the drawing room. Eric, Sasha, and Miranda had each a set in their bedroom. A set had been presented to Michael and Cheta, and one installed in Rachaela's room. They had given her a music center too, and her own video, which she never used. She seldom watched her TV either. But one or all of the other sets were always on the go.

There were electric lights now.

In the kitchen, with its cream and black tiles and the collector's piece, an old, rusted, green mangle, standing by the wall, were now the mod cons: a washing machine, a dishwasher, an electric cooker, food processors, fridge. In the pantry stood a huge chest freezer where the servants inserted enormous joints of meat and the frozen swords of vast fish.

The house was not so large as the first house.

There were more bathrooms, adjoining all the bedchambers and sitting ready on each floor. The bathrooms were white and collectible, like the mangle, having clawfoot baths and brass Edwardian showers. They had green tarot glass windows. Rachaela had found that her bathroom window would open, and also the window in her room. This must have been especially arranged for her. She had a view out across the common. The undulating, heavily treed slopes, like a wilderness, a glade; where only occasionally some solitary walker might go by (staring up). At night, sometimes, an owl called.

The scarred table was in the drawing room.

Rachaela sat down at it. She did not touch the scratches.

Was she trying to understand them at last, the Scarabae, or only herself?

Rachaela, seated on the ground, her back against a tree, had watched the surviving Scarabae, as the house burned to the earth. They stood in a little loose group, at a safe, silent distance. Their clothes were scorched half-off. Bare, skinny witch arms, old, hard, naked legs, holes that showed antique sooty camisoles, withered lace.

In the house, burned, all the rest: Livia, Anita, Unice, Jack, George, Teresa, Stephan, Carlo and Maria. And with them, the already dead, Anna, Alice, Dorian and Peter, stunned by Ruth's hammer and impaled through the heart by hammered knitting needles. The staking of vampires. And, of course, Adamus, Ruth's father, and grandfather.

Beautiful, black-haired Adamus, cold as ice, now warmed through by fire. Hanged from a rope. Suicide.

And Ruth, murderess and arsonist, leaving the house ablaze from her handy candle, had fled across the heath. She had had the mark of Cain on her too. The bruise on her face where Adamus had struck her.

It was hard to dismiss this image of the fleeing Ruth. As it was hard to curtail the other image of her in the blood-colored dress, when the Scarabae betrothed her to Adamus, father, grandfather, and their names were written in the book.

But Ruth was not ready, not old enough, only eleven. She would have to wait for consummation. And Adamus had lost interest in her, vanished back into his dark tower to play the piano alone. And that was when Ruth, disappointed, turned on them with her needles.

The Scarabae were vampires. Or they thought they were. She killed them the proper way. And when she saw Adamus on the rope, she burned the house.

Ruth was a demon. Rachaela had always known. The black and white ugly beauty. The powers of silence.

Probably Rachaela was only too glad to see Ruth disappear into the darkness beyond the fire.

When the fire finished, there was only the darkness. And the Scarabae, all that were left of them, Eric, Sasha, Miranda and Miriam, Michael and Cheta, they stood there in it.

The Scarabae never went out in the daylight. Only Michael and Cheta, that was, muffled up and masked in sunglasses.

And darkness was on the land like mourning, but after that the sun would rise. What then?

The sun rose.

They gazed up into the lightening sky, not fearfully but with a bitter sadness. They had seen it all before, through their two hundred or three hundred years of life. Violence and destitution. Exile. The tyranny of the sun.

She heard Miranda say firmly, "We must go to the village."

Then Michael came over to Rachaela, and his black dusty eyes seemed diluted by the light.

"Miss Rachaela. We must go to the village."

She rose, wearily. There were tiny burns all over her, she could have screamed as if viciously nipped by a hundred miniature beasts.

"All right. How will they—"

But he had turned away.

Like survivors of a plane crash in the desert, they moved out over the heath.

They went the habitual way. The way Ruth had gone?

Skirting the stone like a lightning, going through the gorse and flowers, the dragon places, inland. Stands of pine. Gulls wheeling overhead. Birds loud in thickets, flying off at their approach.

It seemed to take hours before they reached the road. The Scarabae moved out onto it, as onto some desert trail. Rachaela recalled the cars which employed the road, now, but there were no cars.

On the road, she began to see them better.

They moved gaunt and upright. Their faces had been blackened and through the grime, like their bodies through the burned clothes, gaped pale old spaces of flesh. None of them seemed to have received actual burns. Yet material and even hair was singed away. They looked impossible, comic, and this was somehow dreadful. Rachaela felt vaguely frightened. She did not really know why. Was she the child and they the adults, and at their faltering she too lost her grip? That was absurd. She had been away from them twelve years. With Ruth.

She was in her forties. She did not look it. She looked twenty-eight or twenty-nine. Adamus—young, beautiful—had supposedly been in his seventies. No, that too, ridiculous.

Once she stumbled and tumbled on her knees. They

did not wait for her, but they were progressing so slowly she caught them up with ease.

Miranda perhaps cried. If so, she did this very quietly, smoothing her face now and then with a piece of burned stuff. Eric did not cry. He marched in slow motion forward, like a soldier in a dream. Sasha merely moved. Michael and Cheta were possibly more resilient. It was difficult to be sure. They appeared—but it was hopeless to describe them, even to herself. They were beyond all things, fitted nothing. They must all of them be doomed.

But it was Miriam who suddenly fell straight down on the road.

The Scarabae, Miranda and Eric and Sasha, gathered around her. They did not lean to her. Eric said, "Miriam."

Miriam did not stir.

"Michael," said Eric.

And Michael came up at once and raised Miriam in his arms. She seemed like an old valuable doll. She had been wearing a plum dress with beads, and the remaining beads took the sun and flashed cheerfully, as though Miriam might after all be on fire.

They went on, Michael carrying Miriam, Cheta stolidly walking, Eric marching, Miranda and Sasha gliding haltingly as if detached, asleep. Rachaela stumbling behind.

Not a single car. Would a car have been helpful? More likely the driver would have put his foot down.

The hedges, in treacly summer leaf, barricaded off the fields.

They passed the spot where the farm had been pulled down. Two or three black crows picked at the ground.

Every moment Rachaela expected Eric, Sasha, and Miranda to collapse.

The sun had not, seemingly, burned their flesh, just

as fire had not. But in some way, the sun made them transparent, like phantoms, although that, of course, was only a trick of the eyes. Fantasy. Rachaela was herself unwell, shocked. Obviously she must be.

In the end, they were on the hilltop and below was the village, the new village, as it had become over the twelve years.

Everything was shut, naturally. It was very early.

They went down past the estate of brown houses, like lepers past the doors of the feast.

Ignoring the dwellings and the shops, the Scarabae moved without consultation, or hesitation, to the newly built pub, The Carpenters.

It was bright and fresh in the early sun, geraniums in window boxes, bay trees by the door. Above, the rainbow sign of jolly men hammering. *Hammering.*

Michael put Miriam down, among the others.

They waited in the noiseless sunny street and Michael went to a side door. He rang the bell.

Rachaela recollected coming to this village long ago, early, knocking up the publican of the other, shabby pub. He had not been friendly.

Michael only rang once.

After an interval, someone opened the door. It was a young man, collected even brought from sleep, his hair combed, in a green and silver dressing gown and leather slippers.

"There has been an accident," said Michael.

The man stared. He saw the Scarabae. He winced.

"You'll need the police."

"No. We'll take rooms here. We shall need a telephone."

"Well, look," said the young man in green and silver, smiling, "it's just that it *is very* early—" He had a nice London accent. He kept smiling. He meant to do well. He was lovely to the customers and could limit himself to three G and T's a night. He did not stand for nonsense.

Did not expect nonsense, particularly at six in the morning.

"We must come in," said Michael. He sounded barbaric. *Sure.* He produced and held out a wad of notes, twenties, fifties. The nice young man gaped.

"For God's sake—"

"This," said Michael, "is an emergency."

Had Rachaela not said that, years ago? Would this work? Had the green and silver man seen Miriam, lying against Sasha on the road?

He only looked exasperated now.

"Oh—all right. Okay. Just hold on. I'll open up."

The Scarabae waited. Without tension. Without relief. They were not arrogant or insecure.

The pub door was opened a foot.

"Come in. Quickly. Okay."

They stood in the lofty interior now. A fake log fire which would burn in the vast hearth. Old china, perhaps made last week.

Eric said, "We will have champagne."

"Now look," said the young man. "I haven't—I mean, you can't."

Eric said nothing else.

Sasha said, standing by Miranda, whose dark eyes looked clear as forgotten ponds, "In a room."

The young man registered that Michael was now carrying a woman, scorched and hapless as the rest, but also prone and lifeless.

"You want a doctor."

"No," said Eric. "We want champagne."

The rooms were little and chintzy. The beams were not real. False flowers, dyed deep purple and cerise, poked from jugs.

Michael had laid Miriam on a bed, and in this room the others sat. They did not say anything, but Michael had paid the man, and he brought them, grudgingly, two bottles of a good champagne, on ice.

Michael had also apparently used a telephone, for no one approached the telephone in the room.

Who had been called?

Rachaela was given a glass of champagne.

She drank it, and tears flooded her eyes.

No one spoke to her, and she wiped the water from her face with toilet tissue from the bathroom.

They all drank. All but Miriam.

On the chinz coverlet Miriam lay, patiently dead.

In the afternoon, things started to happen.

They had been left alone, with the champagne, and Miriam. Rachaela had eventually got up and gone to the room Cheta said was hers. Here she lay on the bed and slept, the strange daylight sleep of alcohol and fear.

About four—the twiddly shepherdess clock in the room said it was four—she was woken by a sort of soft commotion in the corridor.

She got up and went out, and there in the doorway of the first room, where Miriam was and the other Scarabae, the nice young man who ran the pub was standing. He wore casual fawn slacks, Italian shoes, and a blue shirt and aesthetic tie. He was white as chalk, and, even from her doorway, Rachaela could see that he was shaking.

"It's just—you have to understand—I didn't know. I'm sorry. Please, you must believe me."

Rachaela walked out into the corridor, the carpet furry under her bare feet. Unlike the man, she must evidence wildness from sleep, her torrent of black hair unbrushed, her smoke-grimed face not yet washed.

But he turned to her and gazed at her in terror.

He said, appealing to her, "I'm trying to explain. I must have seemed—rude and unhelpful. It's only—it woke me up. Anything—anything I can do—will you have a meal now? Can I get you anything? Anything at all?"

He was terrified. He had not treated them properly. It would seem someone had put him right. But *who*? *Why*?

He was afraid he had offended the Scarabae.

Rachaela shrugged. Cruelly she watched him flounder. He was sweating. It was Miranda who came, soft, to the door, and said to him: "It's all right, young man. Please don't upset yourself. We have all we need."

Rachaela went in again. She took a bath and washed her face and her hair. The bathwater turned dark. The stink of smoke was now so ingrained in her nostrils it might never go. But the burns seemed to have healed.

As she was sitting in a towel, Cheta knocked and came in. She brought new clothes, which fitted exactly. Pants, bra and slip, tights, a cotton skirt and silk top, all in oatmeal colors. There were even shoes, perfect, they might have been made for her. Some powder came too, in a dainty compact, eye pencil and mascara, the things she used. In addition there was a discreet box of deodorant, toothpaste, tampons, a brush and comb, tissues, an expensive shampoo that made her sorry she had used the hotel soap, a manicure set, a toothbrush.

She emerged again at half-past five, and went to the other room. They were gone. *All* of them. Miriam too. She had heard nothing.

A wave of panic overcame her.

She stood in the room, boiling, a child bereft.

But Miranda—she thought it was Miranda—had left her a note on the hotel pad.

"We have gone with Miriam. We will return before dark."

They had moved out again in the sun. Perhaps it did not matter now. Perhaps it never had. Except to Miriam.

The curtains had been drawn over their windows, it was true.

Rachaela went back to her room, and presently a service trolly came courteously and deferentially to her door. It was the pub's best. Avocado with a lemon sauce, steak and a green salad, strawberries, wine. A rose, real, poised in the vase.

To her surprise Rachaela was ravenous. She ate fiercely, sometimes with her fingers. When she had ended the meal, she buried her face in her hands and wept. She did not know why. She was in her forties. She did not want Ruth. Adamus had been a devil, her enemy. The Scarabae were insane.

They came back after sunset. She heard them, as a child hears in an empty house.

They too wore new clothes, modern clothes that were ageless. They looked like ancient film stars, all in black.

Rachaela went down the corridor, and then she smelled their scent. The odorless inanition of age. Cologne and perfume. And, far stronger, ashes and fire.

They had been at another burning.

It was then, so curiously, that Miranda held out her arms, like a white crystal bird that attempts to fly. And Rachaela went into the arms of Miranda, and together they wept, in the corridor of the modern pub, like ancient sisters in a tragedy.

No one disturbed them. Not Sasha, not Eric. Not Michael, nor Cheta.

Below, the pub made sounds of festival as the village came in for food and drink to drive the dark away. But the Scarabae were the dark, and Rachaela clung to them. Just for a minute. There. That night.

CHAPTER 3

✥ AMANDA MILLS WENT QUICKLY INTO HER bedroom. To immediate scrutiny, it revealed nothing untoward. The teak fitted wardrobes, the plush carpet, the velvet bedroom chair and curtains were undisturbed. But it was the bed which concerned Amanda Mills.

She advanced on it. The duvet and toning pillows were pristine, as she had left them. Nevertheless, she prized them up. Not a ripple on the undersheet.

Amanda sniffed, cautiously, thoroughly. She detected the faint familiar aroma of fabric conditioner, nothing more.

Her sharp shoulders relaxed a little. Not very much. She would go to Timothy's room next.

At her dressing table she paused. A pair of earrings lay on the polished surface, before the jars of cold cream and night cream, the battalion of regimental bottles. Surely she had not left the earrings lying there. Had that ghastly girl—

In her late forties, Amanda Mills had had the gray tinted out and her hair shaped into wings and cemented by lacquer. She was thin from careful dieting. She wore the sleeveless dress in antique sand she had put on for dinner at the hotel, and smart costume jewelry, which, as she moved, clacked like a chain of bones.

There was a strong fragrance about the dressing table which harmonized with her own. The girl had been spraying Amanda Mills's perfume.

Amanda checked her jewel box. It was spread with the expected items. Not a thief then, or had not had the chance to be.

At Timothy's door Amanda did not hesitate. She went straight in.

Timothy's bed was as it always was, except on the days the cleaning woman made it, flung wide, disemboweled. Multiple rape might have taken place there always. But going close, Amanda Mills found no trace of the giveaway perfume. There were no long black hairs. And the odor of the male, which in any case she recoiled from, was muted.

Probably nothing had happened. Coming back as they had, they had been in time to stop it.

Coming back of course had been bad enough, without finding *this*.

Clive had ruined the weekend. It had been spoiled swiftly by him. Friday night was pleasant, almost romantic; the stroll in the hotel gardens, the candlelit dinner. She had had a little too much wine and had felt rather good, rather young. But in the large hotel bed Clive had been his usual self. He was so selfish. She would not deign to protest, could not, had never been able to find words to explain . . . Irritable and nervy she had lain awake listening to him snore. The noise made her ears ring.

Saturday morning had been all right, though he had made the normal cracks about her shopping trip, as if he would not be the first to complain if she failed to appear groomed. She had warned him not to have the roast beef at lunch. Red meat was venomous and at his age he should watch what he ate.

He was grumpy all afternoon, reminiscing constantly

about his days as a young man, before he met her, as if
that was the golden part of his life, now over.

Amanda Mills had been looking forward to dinner.
The hotel provided lots of health-conscious proteins and
local salads made into patterns almost as attractive as
those she herself constructed when at home—naturally,
her gifts were not properly appreciated.

Clive Mills chose veal in batter. She did not say a
word. She had brought an indigestion remedy with them.

When the veal came, Clive began on it, then laid
down his knife and fork with a clatter. With an imperious
wave he summoned the waiter. "This veal's rubbery."
The waiter expressed surprise, which was a mistake.
Other diners glanced about at them, amused, as Clive
Mills raised his voice and trumpeted so that the candle
flattened on its wick.

The veal was removed and Clive waited, rumbling.

Amanda Mills sat staring at her exquisite salad, no
longer able to eat.

When the waiter returned, there was no improve-
ment. It was the same rubbery veal, now cold.

As Clive Mills stormed, his wife stood up and va-
cated the restaurant.

Half an hour later, when he came up to their room,
they argued. What had she thought he should do?
Meekly eat the inedible veal? He should not have chosen
veal in the first place. It would have disagreed with him.
Just because she only fed him muck at home did not
mean he could not eat decently when away. She was sure
he ate "decently" every lunchtime then, at Masons, judging by his waistline.

Eventually they packed, Clive Mills paid the hotel
bill, loudly proclaiming that at such prices one anticipated proper food, and they left.

The drive was long, and accomplished in silence,
save when Clive swore at other motorists.

As they came up the steps of the house, Amanda

had seen the glow of light in the living room through a crack in the dralon curtains. Timothy was in. Thank God. She could tell him about Clive's awful behavior. Although Timothy would pretend not to listen, she knew that it was her side he would take. When he had been a little boy, how he had loved her. Sometimes he had got on her nerves, she had to admit, but children were like that. When he had been dressed in his good clothes, how gorgeous he had looked. And he had held her hand so tightly.

The instant after she called his name, he sprang out into the hall. She had just noticed the flowers she had left dying by the mirror, but Timothy's face made her forget the flowers.

"Here we are," said Amanda. "Your father made a scene at the hotel. There was no point in staying. So much for the weekend."

"Ah—right," said Timothy.

"What's the matter?" said Clive.

"Matter?" asked Timothy.

He seemed to want to demonstrate, by the angle of his body, that the living room did not exist.

"You've got some of your mates around," deduced Clive.

Amanda knew a surge of fear, beer cans on the carpet, perhaps cigarettes.

"That's all right," said Clive. "I'm going up to my den. Your mother probably wants to sulk."

Amanda moved past Timothy. He did not try to stop her but fell away like a spent petal.

"And who is this?" said Amanda.

The girl was sitting on the couch, barefoot with bright red nails. She looked about twenty, the way they all did from thirteen upward. Her face was expressionless, like a bad painting. She was ugly, amid a tidal wave of blue-black hair.

"Oh, this is—this is Ruth, Mom." Timothy smiled.

His eyes were set like jelly. "You remember? I met her months ago at Jake's party. She comes up to visit—to visit her—grandmother." He did a sort of pirouette. "We met in Marks and Sparks. So we had—dinner."

"I'm glad someone did," said Clive.

"Ruth," said Amanda.

The girl did not really respond. She did not speak. Her black slow gaze had roamed from Timothy to Amanda to Clive, as they talked. But when Amanda said her name, Ruth looked back at her. The look was closed as the eye of a camera. Was she on drugs?

"Well, Ruth," coldly said Amanda, "how do you do?"

"Now come on, Tim," said Clive Mills, "this is a bit much. We come back and find you parked in here with some girl we've never seen or heard of."

"But I told you about Ruth months ago," protested Timothy. He looked very sincere and slightly outraged as always when he was lying.

"Give me a bit of credit, Tim."

Amanda turned to the doorway. She felt a kind of hormonal boiling. "I'm going upstairs for a minute," she said. "Clive?"

But Clive did not join her. He had planted himself like a tank in a suit on the rug before the fireplace, the teasels in their vase outlining him oddly.

Amanda went out and up the stairs, to see what had happened, and if they had used her bed.

When she came out of Timothy's room, her husband was standing in the passage outside. He regarded her, sneering slightly. "Snooping? Well, *has* he?"

"Don't be crude," she said. She shut the door.

"What do you mean, crude? What have I said? I asked you—"

"I don't think so."

"No, he didn't have time. We messed that up for him good and proper."

"How can you be so flippant. Do you want him bringing sluts in off the street to sleep with?"

"Now who's being crude." Clive Mills waited for her returning blow, which did not come. He sighed. He wondered if the girl was a slut, or just impressed by Tim, his big mouth and his car and the Italian dinner they had apparently had while he, Clive, was driving back dinnerless.

Clive sensed himself vaguely, tallish and heavy, in his expensive lounge suit with a spirit of mauve, the lilac tie —but not the matching handkerchief which his wife had told him was vulgar. He doubted this. He had seen TV news presenters in just such ensembles. She was always getting at him. She drove him mad, with her "Living Room" and "Loo," her white meat and fish, her nouvelle cuisine salads, her endless tirades on social propriety and constipation. Amanda. She had been easy on the eye once. Now the rigid diet had made her face a skull, and had left the skin of her arms rather too loose, but he was too tactful to tell her. Not like her. She was quick enough to criticize.

That bloody veal. He wished he had never ordered it. Had the sodding diet plate. Then there would never have been all this.

Old Tim, eh. What could you say? He must have had girls before, not still a virgin for Christ's sake.

This girl was a bit bizarre though. Clive had told them both off fairly soundly. And Tim had gone red. But she. She was cool as a cucumber. No, not a cucumber, a smooth, white grape.

Below there was a sort of crash. Probably Tim dropping something in his scurry to clear up.

Amanda bounded down the corridor. She half screamed from the bannisters into the well of the house: *"I don't like this!"*

Stupid bitch.

"She'll have to stay the night, you know," said Clive. "That girl." Amanda stared back at him as if he had announced their divorce. "It's after eleven. Apparently her gran's had to go into hospital. She's nowhere to go."

"You don't *believe* that?"

"Well. Maybe not. But you can't put a teenage girl out on the street at midnight."

Amanda was rigid. She charged to the bedroom, and from a closet began to tear out a duvet for the operational spare room.

Mothers got jealous when their sons showed interest in other women.

Perhaps if she paid Clive more attention, she would be less sensitive.

In bed, Amanda sat up, her face like half an egg spread with oil, reading an article on fiber.

Clive lay with his hands behind his head watching the papered ceiling.

"Let's make up, shall we?"

Amanda did not reply.

Clive thought of the girl with black hair, over in the spare bedroom under the duvet. She had no pajamas. Would probably sleep in the T-shirt. Or in nothing. Bet Tim wished—

Clive turned his mind to tomorrow's dinner. Amanda would have to make it now, and he had already seen the selected fish emerge from the freezer, and the mushrooms and carrots put out to soak. Tomorrow there she would be with her flashing knives, slicing up salads wafer thin. The fish would be full of bloody bones, it always was. Bony, like Amanda.

The girl was slim. But a large firm bosom.

Think about something else.

"You know, Mandy, never go to sleep on a quarrel."

Amanda rustled her magazine. He had betrayed her.

He had spoiled their weekend. He had let the girl stay the night.

The girl . . .

"Ah. Call of nature," said Clive guiltily. "Must be your magazine."

He went to the bathroom and shut the door. He turned on the taps in the autumn leaf washbasin that changed water into blood. He stood over it, and thought about the girl sleeping naked, and opening the door, going in softly. And she was awake, smiling up at him in some dim half-light of the imagination. "Shh," she said playf··lly, and she put his hand over one of her big young brea.._. He masturbated roughly, hard on himself, and came with a lunge, noiseless and hygenic, into the running water. Then he dried himself, flushed the toilet-loo, splashed around the taps, turned them off.

The bedroom was in darkness. He stubbed his toe on the side of the bed. His own bedroom, and he did not know it yet. Amanda lay like a stone, pretending to sleep. But he knew she was awake, for always she snored when she slept.

CHAPTER 4

✥ *SHE WOKE AT SEVEN, AND IN THE* chintzy window was a thick summer mist. When she stood there, she could just see to the edge of the pub wall, and over to the road beyond. And as she watched, two lighted eyes, strange as a dragon's, stared through the mist, and a dark shape glided out of it. Then another. Two black Rolls-Royces slid down the road and melted to a stop below the wall.

Twenty minutes later, Cheta came with breakfast from the bar kitchen.

The Scarabae were moving on.

At half-past eight, Cheta and Michael got into the second Rolls. Eric, Sasha, Miranda, and Rachaela entered the first car. The windows were polarized.

The nice young man came rushing to the car door. He had brought them a hamper, and more champagne, unsuitable for a journey. He fawned on them so desperately, Rachaela wished she might throw a stick for him to run and retrieve.

The Scarabae were not very interested. They were polite, and absent.

He gave up, and closed them in their polarized cabin.

The driver of the car was a shadow behind a dark partition, who did not disturb them with communication.

The Rolls was like a luxurious hearse.

Rachaela wondered if they would speak to each other, Eric and Sasha, Miranda and herself. But then she fell asleep.

It was a long journey. They stopped in the middle of the day, and once in the afternoon. On each occasion a different gray-suited man came decorously and ushered them into a different small, clean room of some hotel or public house, and here they were offered lunch, and later tea.

The Scarabae picked at these meals. The healthy gusto of appetite Rachaela had always associated with them was not there. Perhaps this was due to sorrow, or only the discomposure of travel.

Rachaela also picked at the food.

She too was Scarabae.

At the second halt, she said generally, "Where are we going?"

"Everything is taken care of," said Eric.

"To a hotel," said Sasha, "for a while."

"It will be all right," said Miranda.

They had all been talkative, too. But now they had lost their entity. They were soul fragments flung out into space.

No one said anything else.

After the tea, as after the lunch, they got back into the car. The champagne had not been touched, nor the hamper.

Beyond the greenish blackness of the windows, the alien brightness of the day went by. The long winding of roads up and down, once a motorway, but only briefly. The other car kept behind them, separate yet unified. Presumably Michael and Cheta had left it at the halts, but Rachaela had not seen them do so.

Hills were on the polarized skyline. Trees massed

over walls. The sun began to set, a brown roar in the window.

The Scarabae looked sad and small and isolated.

They had never upbraided Rachaela for letting Ruth escape the attic in which they had shut her. They had not said to Rachaela that it was her fault, the burning of the house, the deaths by fire. They had recognized Ruth, it seemed, as a demon.

They had not mentioned Adamus.

As the night came black on the black windows, Rachaela was wide awake, and so they reached their destination.

The hotel had been built as an eighteenth-century mansion. It still stood in its towering grounds, cloaked by chestnuts, blue larches, spread yews. A thirty-foot monkey puzzle raised its tarantula crown above the lawn.

There was the impression, probably untrue, that no one existed in the hotel save themselves, and the mysterious unseen staff.

The Scarabae occupied a vast meandering suite, perhaps half a floor. The rooms were designed to the eighteenth-century formula, almost, but not quite, exact. There were shades of azure and bronze, sugar almond and eau-de-Nil. The heavy curtains were kept drawn but here and there a piercing needle of the sun would fall through at some time of the day. Around these gold razors the Scarabae pecked with a kind of morbid ritual care. They had braved sunlight. Now they could move back from it. But like all dangers, though faced, it must not go unsaluted.

There were clocks in the rooms which kept actual time.

Cheta and Michael waited on them, as they had done in the house. The hotel staff were merely responsible for sending up to them the stacks of clean bed linen, towels and soaps, the dishes under silver, silver teapots, the bottles and decanters, and goblets of cut glass.

Fresh flowers came every day. They had been carefully chosen to echo the colors of the rooms. Blue African iris, blushing lilies, yellow roses, and extraterrestrial flowers, never seen before, without a name.

In Rachaela's bathroom were shampoos and conditioners, waxes for the hair and skin, emollients, astringents, perfumes, essences, creams, and gels.

In her room the walnut bureau was supplied with what seemed to be a ream of pale honey paper, accessory envelopes, and two sheets of first-class stamps. There were Biros in a plastic tube, and a fountain pen in a slender box. In one bookcase, rose gilded encyclopedias, dictionaries, sets of Shakespeare, Trollope, Dickens, Jane Austen, George Elliot. And in the other, pristine hardback editions of contemporary novels and short stories.

There was a well-tuned machine which comprised a radio and cassette player, and tapes of classical music in a case.

A booklet in a calfskin cover referred to the hotel library, and what tapes and books were also available.

Eric, Sasha, and Miranda perhaps discovered television at the hotel. Certainly they would turn on the big perfect screens in their rooms, and sit watching them, usually alone.

Rachaela played music. She walked in the grounds. She met no one at all in the rose garden or among the topiary snipped to resemble peacocks and pyramids. No one out among the trees.

On some fine mornings, from an upland path among rhododendrons, she found she could see away across miles of country, distantly yellow with crops, turquoise with farness, otherwise featureless, flowing into a dream.

She did not know where they were. They were not near the sea.

Rachaela did not ask the Scarabae any more questions. She was not even restless. She read the books and sent for others. She slept later, and sometimes again after lunch. At night she might sit by her window, watching the moon ride over the park.

At dawn, pigeons cooed in the monkey puzzle. Once a fox ran through the chestnuts. Then she thought of Ruth. But it was better not to think of Ruth. Rachaela pushed the thought away.

I am a Scarabae.

She did not truly believe it. Yet she could not wholly reject it, either.

Summer deepened into autumn.

Rachaela wondered if the Scarabae were now settled. She considered her departure, but to what? What had happened to her flat in London . . . ? It was too complicated. Days like falling leaves. The leaves began to parch and fall.

Being at the hotel was almost being out of time. And yet the mansion was subtly modern. There were radiators in the rooms against the coming of the frost.

Frost came.

Then came driving winds and the trees lost their leaves. The monkey puzzle now was more than ever like a spider, its legs wrapped tight. Grass blue with cold, matching the azure sitting room. Rachaela said to Sasha: "You'll spend the winter here."

"Oh, yes." Sasha added, "The house isn't ready yet."

The house. Had they rebuilt it? Rachaela could not bring herself to ask anything else.

Every Scarabae in a solitary room, TV and music and books. Rachaela felt like a child. There was no other way she could explain it to herself. Melancholy, and safe. Held fast in nostalgia.

At Christmas, literally, Michael and Cheta decked the walls with boughs of holly. There was even a tree the management must have sent, tall and resinous, hung with golden filigree balls and tied by scarlet ribbon.

The dinner was served in the evening. The main course was not a turkey but a huge roast joint presented with hot fruit and creamy, spicy side dishes, cabbage with raisins, whipped potato, and a type of black sausage. Afterward there was a pudding, sweet as an ache. They drank a somber wine that came in two bottles with dust upon them and two matted seals.

When the meal was over, Eric led them in a prayer. At least Rachaela thought it must be a prayer. It was in another language—Russian, Romanian, God knew. Michael and Cheta stood by. They too murmured the responses. Rachaela sat in silence.

When this was over, Sasha, Miranda, and Eric gave each other little gifts. These were tiny curious things, an embroidered handkerchief, a porcelain thimble; some were concealed, especially by Miranda, and Rachaela did not see. Cheta and Michael were also passed small tokens, wrapped, which they did not open. To Rachaela came a package, in due course. She held it, defiantly. She had not realized there would be presents, and had contrived none.

"You know I don't deserve this."

"Oh yes," said Miranda.

"No, I don't. I'm your failure. I let you down."

"Don't speak of it," said Sasha. "Not tonight."

Eric said, "Undo the paper."

They were not the same as they had been. They had taken on characteristics, sloughed from their entity. Sasha abrupt, Eric commanding, perhaps secretly fierce, and Miranda kind.

Rachaela peeled off the shiny white paper. She found a band of silver in which was caught a polished ruby heart. The ruby was antique, and conceivably priceless.

"You can't give me this."

Miranda's face puckered as if she would cry.

Rachaela's heart clenched within her.

Sasha frowned.

Eric said, "It was Anna's. Miriam brought it from the house."

Rachaela felt no pressure from them anymore. They were not forcing her to anything. The dark spearhead of their lust, Adamus, continuance and seed, was gone. It was only a gift.

She slipped it on to her little finger—it would not fit any of the others. Perhaps, when she was older, then.

"It's very beautiful."

Ruth would have loved the ring. The hard, cold silver, the ruby, for blood.

Eric got up. Michael and Cheta began to clear the table, leaving only the wine. The Scarabae perched on chairs about the room, and the TV was not switched on.

Something else, then, something more to come.

As he had led them in the prayer or chant, Eric conducted them to a round table by one of the curtained windows.

Michael helped them into the four chairs, Eric, Sasha, Miranda, Rachaela. Then Cheta laid out around the table's rim a circle of cards. They were made of thin wood, and on each was a painted symbol. After a moment, Rachaela realized that these were the letters of an alphabet, but not her own.

Michael put down on the table, at its center, a cut-glass goblet, upside down.

He stood back.

He and Cheta began to turn out the gracious side lamps of the sitting room.

Dark entered, on cue.

It was to be a séance.

Rachaela said, "You can't include me in *this*."

"We must," said Sasha. And then, "Anna would want it."

Anna. Adamus's mother—perhaps. Therefore Rachaela's grandmother. Ruth's. Anna: stabbed through the heart by the heartless knitting needle.

"But I can't—" said Rachaela.

They waited.

When she did not go on, did not get up, Eric put the forefinger of his right hand onto the glass, and Sasha and Miranda followed him. The rings of the Scarabae crackled in the half-dark and the last lamp went out.

A chair creaked, as Michael sat down by Cheta in a corner.

Rachaela put her finger on the glass among the fingers of Eric, Sasha, Miranda.

There was a stasis, a *cessation.*

It won't work. Why should it?

The glass trembled, and began to move.

They are moving it.

In the blackness of the room perhaps they could see, but Rachaela could not very well. Somehow she saw the glass, running like a white surge across the polished table.

Well, let them play at it. If it could comfort them.

The glass was spelling out words, of course, but—of course—she could not tell what they were. Eric exclaimed in another tongue—not that, she thought, which had been used in the prayer. And then Miranda murmured something. A name? *Stephan?*

The glass darted.

There was a vibration in it, a thrumming, as if from thunder miles away.

Don't imagine things.

Adamus had drunk her blood, in the dark, lying over her, flesh on flesh, so long ago. Adamus . . .

A pressure mounted in Rachaela's throat, like tears, or the prologue to orgasm.

She would not be coerced. Not even now.

The glass was skidding on the table, squealing.

She lifted her finger—and the glass was gone, seeming to pull the pulse out of her finger's end.

Irresistibly, she let her finger drop back on to the surface of the goblet.

The Scarabae were quiet now, only breathing, concentrating.

There was a light in the room. Someone had lit a lamp. But it was not the lamp. It was too low down.

Keeping her hand in contact with the goblet, Rachaela looked. A powerpoint was glowing fierily against the wall. And there another, slowly blooming up like a gas flame. The light switches had begun to shine. At the room's center, the overhead lamps abruptly fractured with a dull dense crack. Glass showered the carpet.

The Scarabae took no notice.

Suddenly there came the hiss of water and a loud knocking from beyond the room, a bathroom along the corridor also apparently reacting. There were faint noises of stress from every corner. Thumpings, patterings. The hotel sitting room had come alive. The carpet was shifting. Pictures tilted on the walls.

That doesn't make it real. Psychic electricity, a poltergeist.

One of the chairs was rent as if by a blade and stuffing jetted up in a cloud, coming gradually down again, like dandelion fluff.

The glass had stopped.

Rachaela was shaking. It was not fear or nerves. Something had been leached from her.

She took her hand away from the goblet, and getting up, she went to the dinner table. Michael was there before her, pouring her a glass of wine. She took it. Not meaning to, she laughed. To her surprise, she heard Sasha laugh, just as sharply, randomly. Then they were silent.

Rachaela stood by the cleared table where the old

wine remained alone. She watched the Scarabae file out of the room.

Cheta switched on a lamp. Slowly, slowly, the powerpoints were losing their radiance.

"Quite a lot of damage," Rachaela said to Michael. "I believe the hotel will clear everything up, no questions asked."

"Yes, Miss Rachaela."

No questions.

The bronze clock had lost its hands, they had flown off and landed on the floor. Its face was empty. Rachaela remembered all the broken clocks of the Scarabae house, the clocks which had gone too fast, or run backward.

When she reached her room, she found the pictures had crashed from the walls, the mirror had shattered making a rain carpet on the ground.

In the bathroom, judging by the mess, the wonderful shampoos and gels must have exploded. The tops had come off the taps and water had erupted at the ceiling, next, just as irrationally, miraculously losing force and falling back, now only trickling like weeping in the bath and basin. The toothpaste had made long white snakes, looping crazily, decoratively.

She investigated without panic or surprise.

In the drawer of the bureau the paper and stamps were torn into confetti. She opened the little sewing kit. The two needles had sewn through and through, then curled up like springs or the shells of snails.

On the table by her bed, the flowers were straight and dewy. The buds had opened wide as wings, giving off a rich pure scent.

CHAPTER 5

 RUTH HAD NOT SLEPT IN THE T-SHIRT.
She had not slept at all.

The Millses' operational spare room was done in coffee and milk, with hint-of-pink walls. There were a coffee washbasin with milk towel, a milky reading lamp beside the coffee bed, magazines, a cupboard for (nonexistent) clothes. On the chocolate and rose rug, Ruth's white and red feet lay still as she watched them.

She sat on the bed, motionless, until all the human sounds of the house had ceased. Then she turned out the lamp and allowed her eyes to get used to the dark. This was easy. She was a Scarabae.

In the dark, she moved out of the room, and along the passage, slim and agile as a ferret. She went downstairs.

A faint unearthly glow shone into the hall from the glass window in the front door, the streetlight over the road.

Ruth did not need this beacon to find the kitchen.

The tiled floor was cold, the gadgets and fitments rose apparently impervious.

Ruth reached across the stainless-steel coffee grinder and selected, from the conveniently laid-out panel on the wall, the sharpest, longest knife.

* * *

Across the table, the girl wore a low-necked black dress. Her hair was piled up on her head, and clipped by a *diamanté* buckle. As the waiter put down the veal in front of Clive, the girl pointed at it and said coldly, "You can't expect my husband to eat that, it's rubbery."

At that moment the door opened. It was not a door in the restaurant, but the bedroom door. Clive thought it was Amanda, returning from the bathroom, she always made sure she woke him. But no, Amanda was snoring gently on the far side of the bed. For a second Clive had the idea that Tim had come in, as he used to do in childhood, seeking reassurance after a nightmare. It had been a hell f a nuisance, always. Sometimes he had insisted on climbing in with them.

But obviously it could not be Tim.

Clive raised himself to one elbow and leaned toward the bedside lamp, and as he did so, he saw the girl, Tim's girl, right in front of him, a shadow with hair.

"What—" said Clive. And the girl said softly, "No." So Clive did not finish his question. And then the girl swayed forward, her arm waved, and she had cut his throat.

Clive made terrible noises but he was choked by blood; they were not very loud. In fact they were very like noises he often made when snoring in slumber. This was probably why Amanda did not wake, only gave an irritated little muttering in her sleep.

As Clive flopped down, his head and arm and blood pouring off over the bed, Ruth went quickly around to the farther side. She raised Amanda's chin, and sliced accurately. The knife was sharp enough to cut meat and raw vegetables and it made short work of Amanda. Possibly Amanda woke up before she died, but if so it was much too late.

There had been no commotion, and the peace of the house seemed undisturbed.

Ruth stood looking at her two kills, in the dark.

She had learned butchery from horror films. It did not require great skill, only decision and some strength, both of which she had.

The Millses were not vampires, she had not had to stake them.

It was she, of course, who was the Scarabae.

She drank Amanda's blood first, daintily, fastidiously. Then she visited Clive on the other side of the bed. When she had had some from both of them, she lightly stepped across the room and came out, closing the door quietly behind her.

Out in the corridor there was the impersonal silence of comparatively modern houses, whose central heating was off and whose plumbing was reliable. This was not comparable to the notes of an old house, which shifted in its sleep like an animal, ticked and purred and sighed.

Ruth arrived at Timothy's door and opened it. She remembered the layout of the room well, but in any case could see it exactly.

Timothy lay on his back and, as she entered, he raised his heavy lids.

He thought he was dreaming. But it was not a dream. Christ, she had sneaked out after all, to join him. He had thought she was sexy, but given up. After the disaster of the evening's end, he had hoped for nothing.

Timothy was wide awake now. He sat up.

He hissed at her: *"Shut the door."*

"It won't matter," said Ruth.

"Jesus—keep your voice down."

The streetlamp shining faintly through his curtains had enabled him to see her, though not well. Now as she slid toward him he realized there was something in her hand.

What was it?

She was a couple of feet away when he understood it was a kitchen knife, and it was wet.

Instinct shot him out of the bed. But the duvet

snared his foot and he rolled onto the carpet. Before he could get his feet under him, the girl whirled down.

Timothy screamed.

He screamed loudly and violently. But it had been a rainy day and his window was shut. In the house, there was no one left to hear.

Because he tried to fight her off, he was slashed in the arm and across the face before the knife tore home through his neck. He died against the pastel wall, which he had blackened with his blood.

Ruth took only a sip of this. She had had enough.

She left the knife beside Timothy, not needing it anymore.

By three-ten, Ruth was downstairs in the kitchen again, frying herself eggs in one of the copper-bottomed pans.

She had gone through the house carefully, or those areas which might be of interest. She had put on some of the lights, for the cupboards and drawers were easier to search this way.

From Amanda's wardrobe Ruth had taken a large brown suede shoulder bag. This she then filled with other items. Amanda's chest of drawers had yielded a packet of unused cotton panties and some tights in cellophane. In Timothy's room Ruth located new jeans, and three plain black T-shirts, but left the other tops which had colorful designs. She also found a leather jacket of Timothy's. It was a little too big but not cumbersomely so. She kept the trainers.

Amanda's jewelry had no attraction for Ruth. There seemed to be no books or proper music in the house.

In Clive's wallet Ruth discovered a wodge of notes, and elsewhere a stack of pound coins. She ignored the plastic credit cards, and also the heap of small change in a dish. In Timothy's desk, too, there were some ten- and twenty-pound notes, as well as useless change and the Visa card. If Amanda had money it did not surface.

Ruth did take one small thing from the living room. This was a green glass apple.

From the main bathroom she appropriated toothpaste, Amanda's deodorant, and a wrapped tablet of soap, some tissues and cotton wool, and a miniature oval mirror.

In the kitchen Ruth switched on all the lights, and first made herself some sandwiches from the wholemeal bread and cold half-chicken in the fridge, adding pickles for a garnish. The sandwiches were placed in plastic sandwich bags and stored in her suede container, with a liter bottle of diet Coke.

Then she poured herself a large gin and added tonic.

She could find no bacon, but put three eggs into sunflower oil to fry, grilled five tomatoes, and opened a can of beans. She had watched Emma Watt, and later Cheta and Maria, and later still, others, cook—long ago —and learned the rudiments from observation, just as she had learned the methods of slaughter.

Ruth finished the wholemeal loaf with her breakfast, and then she ate a packet of dates, and the last apples from the fruit bowl. She drank some orange juice, and put an unopened carton also in her bag.

The light had not yet come, but there was an insubstantial quality now to the dark. Outside the windows, the garish streetlamps stood like sentinels, seeing nothing.

Ruth took the pan of cooling oil off the stove. She donned one of Amanda's tan washing-up gloves, and then fetched the Cook's Matches from the work surface. She lit a match, and dropped it in the oil.

The pan lit with a thin blue flame.

Ruth carried her new coat and the bag of provisions up into the hall. Then she returned for the frying pan.

She went into the dining room first, and touched the blue fire to the seats of the chairs, the fringes of the lamps.

She came out, leaving the door open, and crossed

into the living room. Here she spilled fire onto the sofa, and gave it to the curtains, and the teasels in the fireplace.

Nothing else was needed. In each room a pale animate bonfire was now in progress. Fire was very fast.

Ruth came out again, into the hall.

There she hesitated a moment. Then she walked to the dying flowers under the mirror, and offered them, too, the kiss of flame. They sprang up prettily, blue and saffron, as if all the life had come back to them, and in the mirror Ruth saw her face behind the fire.

She set the frying pan, still burning, carefully down on the hall carpet.

Then she removed Amanda's glove, put on her jacket, and took up her bag.

The house, which had once been Emma's, was full now of a textured noise, crackings and gushings, little pops and gasps.

Ruth turned out the hall light, and the light of the fire took over, ancient and beautiful, as she remembered.

She undid the front door and moved out. She closed the door gently, and went down the steps.

At the end of the street she looked back.

The house was not yet blazing, only gleaming, flickering, as if full of the beating of yellow wings. Its light, however, had begun to put out the streetlamps. False dawn.

CHAPTER 6

✣ SPRING MET THE HOTEL IN WAVES OF
acid green, in crocuses and snowdrops running
up the lawn, and daffodils under the monkey-puzzle tree.
There were squirrels in the rose garden. The powdered
bloom of jade came out on the giant chestnuts.

The Scarabae lifted their heads, as if they had been
sleeping under stones.

One morning, Rachaela met Eric under the topiary.

"There were gardens like this," he said. "Once."

As if the topiary of the mansion was just an illusion,
a memory.

They walked down to the pond, where floated the
ghostly ectoplasm of unborn frogs.

"We shall be going to the house soon. We've had to
wait a long time."

"Do you mean," she said, "the house by the sea?"

Eric looked away through the wild spring morning.

"Never go back," he said. *"Never."*

Not that house, then.

Rachaela said, "This is a new house."

"An old house, of course. But in London."

She was startled.

"But—will you like it there?"

"It will be ours."

"Does that mean I'm included?"

He glanced at her. "Things occur," said Eric. "Time erases deeds."

"No it doesn't. But then, the *deed* was yours. I mean, it was the Scarabae's. Mating Adamus to me. Producing Ruth."

"Don't speak of Ruth."

He said this without anger, almost without expression.

She said, "Surely in London I should leave you."

"We wish you to remain. If you won't, well then."

"I'll—we'll have to see."

Eric nodded. He looked into the pond. The ghostly life trembled between the lily pads.

After a while he left her, walking off under the pyramids.

A week later the two great black cars, the Rolls-Royces, appeared at the hotel.

The Scarabae departed in the afternoon, and Rachaela with them.

She felt disconcerted, leaving the hotel. She thought irresistibly of the morning after the Christmas séance. She had gone out into the gardens and, coming back, everything had been tidied and put right. Magicians had cleaned the walls, hung up the pictures, put back the mirror glass and taps. Even the toothpaste, the needles, and the notepaper were replaced.

They had been safe here, safe from themselves.

She had been one of them, or had she? Out in the world, she must be herself.

The journey was not as long, on this occasion, as she had anticipated. The Rolls ran over motorways into the capital, and they were there at sunset.

So she saw the common on a flaming sky the polarized windows could not completely withhold. The trees and sweeps of earth inside the drum of the city, wild land inside a bottle.

She was surprised by the comparative nearness of a

road. She stared at them, Eric, Sasha, and Miranda, Michael and Cheta. Below, beyond the houses of rich people (less rich, evidently, than the Scarabae), lay the London village with its shops and supermarket, its library and pubs, and the quills of the churches, and beyond, the smoky back of London. But London was old, too. Remember that.

It was not like the first house at all. Yet it had been *made* like it. Only the windows were tarot windows instead of puns upon the Bible.

Over the pillared hall were wonderful women in robes, with harps, and rose-red hair. The stairway parted and ran up in two opposing flights, and there the windows had minstrels and flamingo skies.

There was no one to welcome them. The Rolls had driven away. Yet in every room, the machines, the TVs. And in the huge main chamber, white and gold below the stairs, was an ivory telephone.

Rachaela walked boldly to it and picked it up. There was a dialing tone. But who, *who,* should she call?

Miranda followed her to her room. Miranda made her shy. She had wept with Miranda.

"Look, Rachaela. You'll like it."

The room was the shade of a dove. Soft sweet gray lit with hints of amber. And then the bed and chairs deep green like the pines of the common. And beyond, the white bathroom with its antique finish and viridian window.

But the window in the bedroom, which showed a snowy woman with golden hair and wings, holding up her hands to the doves which had created the room, was not the picture of that other room, the Temptation, with its armor and apples, its Eve, its snake. This was a luminous romantic window, without significance, perhaps. And, it stood open.

"The window—" said Rachaela.

"You can see out over the common," said Miranda.

Sasha had appeared in the doorway.

"You must be careful at night," said Sasha, "of bats."

And this absurdity, these bats of vampire myth, improbable in a London park, made Rachaela laugh aloud, and then Sasha laughed, as once before, and then Miranda. So they all stood laughing.

"Do the colors please you?" asked Miranda.

"It's wonderful, yes."

"Do stay," said Miranda.

As if there had always been free choice.

Of course, actually, there had always been.

The Scarabae had snared her, made her live with them. She had always thought so. But in fact they had *invited.* That too was a trap, a web. Adamus had waited for her, in it. And she had been seduced by Adamus. And she had birthed, from that union, Ruth. The web had then rent itself to pieces.

At the hotel, she had played chess with Eric. He had taught her how to play, although she never properly understood, but the pieces intrigued her, the carven kings and queens of black and white, the knights and castles, and the ill-fated pawns.

They had put the board and the chess pieces on the table, so at first she did not recognize it. Then one evening she came down from a long day-sleep, and found Cheta polishing the table. It was the furnishing from the hotel which they had used in the séance, its surface scratched into a peculiar pattern.

Cheta stood aside.

Rachaela poised by the table, staring down at it.

The séance glass, in rushing from letter to letter, had ripped a path upon the table. And yet she saw now—the reason they had kept it—the scratching also spelled a word: *zegnajcie.*

"Cheta," Rachaela said. "This. What does it mean?"

Cheta said at once, "Good-bye."

Then they carried the chess board, loaded with its figures, back between them, and set it over that good-bye.

When Cheta had gone, Rachaela was alone in the room. The Scarabae dinner would not be for another hour, for afterlight still lingered through the glorious windows of walled gardens, roses, palaces upon hills. And through this window above the table, where the knight kneeled before the forest and the burning tower.

Good-bye.

Now she had glimpsed their true power. Oh yes. At last.

They could command things and elements, and people. The cars in the mist, the vast hotel, this house, prepared for them against their coming.

And yet, they beat like moths against the tempest of life. Strong, thin, black moths with eyes of obsidian. How great the storm, how small, how small, the Scarabae.

CHAPTER 7

✤ ON SATURDAY MORNINGS, ABOUT TEN-thirty, the milkman always came. And so, although she was hoovering, with music turned up loud, Julie Sawyer heard the knock.

The problem was with the milkman; if he failed to rout them out on Saturday, he would return at six a.m. on Sunday and bang and shout. Julie tried to avoid this, but sometimes she overslept on Saturdays. Terry was useless, naturally, he just pulled the covers further over his ears and burrowed down into the pillow. He was up there now, asleep overhead in the larger of the two small upstairs rooms. And although Julie had beèn making as much noise as she could, she knew in her heart he could slumber through the disco beat and Hoover, even when she cleaned the carpet around the bed.

She could create a noise cleaning the bathroom too, of course, and this sometimes did disturb him, unrhythmic crashes of shampoo bottles and Jif falling in the bath, the Niagara of water and chug of the tank.

Saturday was the only day she had time to clean, and then she sometimes left it, what with the shopping and the launderette, or if they went out. Today the chore had to be done, because Terry had asked Blackie over. Blackie was all right. But Lucy and Jenny would come too. Julie had mixed feelings about it, she always had.

Generally, when things got going, it was not so bad. In fact, she liked it, sometimes. But then, again—

At the thud of the knocker—the bell no longer worked—Julie switched off the Hoover and pushed her short black hair back. She was slim and small breasted with rather large feet, and she wore stained jeans and a cotton top. She let the music center go on playing, a reassuring *thump, thump, thump,* and went out with her purse into the narrow hall.

Through the wavered glass of the door she could not see anyone. Had the bastard already gone?

Julie flung the door open and there was the milk sitting on the doorstep. There was no sign of the milk float. She had missed him. Sod it.

Outside the front door of the end-of-terrace house, was a five-foot patch of weeds, and a dustbin. Just inside the gate stood a girl, about ten years younger than Julie. She had a lot of very black hair.

"Mrs. Watt?"

"No," said Julie flatly.

"Yes," said the girl, quietly and distinctly, "she lives with her daughter."

"You've got the wrong house," said Julie Sawyer. She jerked her bitten thumbnail at the next house along, the first of the adjacent row beyond the gap. "Try her. She might know." Knock the old cow up and waste *her* time.

Julie was going to close the door, but the girl walked forward. Her clothes were good, particularly the leather jacket.

"I've come a very long way."

"Have you? Well, I've never heard of any Watts."

"I came into London, and then out here."

"They must have given you the wrong address."

"This is the house."

"No," said Julie, trying to be strong, "it isn't."

And then the sash window went up over their heads.

Terry peered out, his face sallow and his hair looking tangled and greasy. What the droning Hoover and beating music had not been able to achieve, their steely voices under the window had.

"What the fuck's going on?"

Julie gazed up at him in exasperation.

"She's come to the wrong place."

Terry's eyes had cleared. He stared at the girl.

"No she hasn't." He smiled. "Who did you want, love?"

"Mrs. Watt."

"No Mrs. Watt, I'm afraid. But come in. Make her some ⌐ffee, Julie. We can sort it out." He added to the girl: "I'll just take a leak and I'll be down."

Julie stood rigid. Her mother used to say of her father, "He treats me like the maid." Maids did not live in Julie's vocabulary, but it came to the same thing. Bloody bugger, telling her to make this bitch coffee. As if she had nothing else to do.

"You'd better come in," said Julie.

"Thank you," said the girl, and slid in past her, over the threshold.

Her name was Ruth, as Terry elicited from her among the coffee mugs.

The Hoover stood in the middle of the brightly patterned cheap carpet, a fourth silent partner and stern reminder, of which no one but Julie took any apparent notice. While in the kitchen, which led off the one through-room of the downstairs area, last night's washing-up teetered above the sink.

Terry had brushed his teeth and splashed cold water on his face. He now had the pale morning-look which Julie once found very attractive, so brooding, and forlorn.

Between them, he and this Ruth ate a whole packet of custard creams, and went on to the chocolate wholewheat Julie had been saving.

Ruth had come from somewhere out in the country, by the sea. Mrs. Watt had asked her up. This was really all the information Ruth gave or had to give, for Terry quickly took over, talking to Ruth about himself, the boring office and idiotic people where and with whom he worked, holidays at the ocean, his plans for going abroad with Julie and Blackie, and the get-together he was having for a few friends tonight.

The music had been turned down, by Terry, for Ruth did not seem to like it.

"Any more coffee?" asked Terry.

"You know where it is," said Julie. "I mean the kettle." She got up, and marching to the back window, looked out on a further, longer patch of weeds. An apple tree grew at the bottom of the garden, and on a lower bough the cat was sitting, black and white as a magpie.

"Did you feed the cat?" Julie demanded.

Interrupted in a statement on Cornish cider, Terry said, "No."

"It's been next door again. It goes over the fence."

"Who cares what the bloody cat does."

"She gives it things to eat. You know what she's like."

"Well, it saves us feeding it."

"One day she'll poison it," said Julie, with a premonition of annoyance.

She crossed back to the music center, and turned it up very loud.

"For Christ's sake," said Terry. He too got up, and going to the machine switched it off.

"I like it on when I work," said Julie.

"Well, you're not working, are you?"

"I've got to finish the hoovering. Then there's the washing-up. And the bathroom. And I've got to change the bed."

"A woman's work is never done."

"You're bloody right there."

"Leave it then."

"I can't, with your friends coming."

"Coming, yeah," said Terry. He looked back at Ruth and smiled in a slow enticing way. "Like to stay for the party?"

Julie said, "That's not a very good idea."

"Yes," said Terry, "yes, it is."

"I'm sure," said Julie, "Ruth has to get on to her Mrs. Watt."

"But she doesn't know anymore where Mrs. Watt is."

"She could phone her. Couldn't you, Ruth?"

"I don't have a telephone number," said Ruth.

Julie said, "Isn't that a bit odd?"

Terry shook his head at Ruth.

"Don't worry about Julie. She'll come around."

"I could get the phone book. We could look it up," said Julie briskly.

But Ruth said, not flurried: "They had to have it changed."

Terry made more coffee, and Julie turned on the Hoover. She went around the room, moving furniture, and then around Ruth, who did not move, simply lifting her feet off the ground until the appliance had passed. Then Julie did the stairs, banging quite a lot, and dragged the Hoover off into the bedroom and the upstairs room Terry called his Lair. It was a tiny place he had managed to fill with shed clothes, half-made model airplanes, paperback thrillers, and empty beer cans. Sometimes Terry also wrote short pieces of fiction in here. Julie had admired this talent when first they met, but now she did not bother with what Terry wrote. Squashed in the corner was a camp bed. That would need to be made up, too.

Julie cleaned the bathroom, managing to knock all the toothbrushes and makeup off the shelf under the mirror.

Terry must be mad to ask this girl to stay tonight.

They had agreed, months ago, that it was just as well to play safe. They had their regular friends. But what did they know about this Ruth?

How trustworthy was Terry? There was that girl at his office, Sherry, and perhaps—

Julie did the beds.

When she came down, Terry was still holding forth to Ruth, and Ruth still listening, sitting composed in a black T-shirt and jeans on the two-seater settee. Terry sat on the floor by the electric fire and his mug had made a wet ring on the top of the surround. There were biscuit crumbs on the carpet.

While Julie washed up, Terry went out to get some wine and cans of Carlsberg Special Brew.

The cat appeared at the kitchen door, and Julie let it in.

"I suppose I've got to feed *you* now."

She opened a can of cat food and put it down.

The cat approached the food, and ate, standing up, tail laid flat to the floor as if to earth itself.

Ruth came into the doorway of the kitchen.

"You have a cat."

"Cat? Yes."

The kitchen was unwide and Julie found herself hoping that Ruth would not enter it, for then they would brush against each other, something she did not relish. The cat saved her from this by looking around from behind the cooker, and then walking straight up to Ruth. "What's her name?" asked Ruth.

"Mohawk," said Julie. Terry had called the cat that, and she had thought it clever, at the time. But it was a stupid name, typical.

And Ruth did not employ the name. Instead she got down on her knees and held out her hand for the cat to sniff. The cat inspected her fingers, finding something fascinating.

The cat's face was coal-black with one white dot, like

a speck of paint, on its forehead. The yellow eyes shone like lemon fruit-drops.

" 'Dark they were and golden eyed,' " said Ruth.

"Pardon?"

"It's Ray Bradbury," said Ruth. "The Martians in the short story."

"Oh. Terry reads sci-fi," said Julie, dismissively.

Ruth did not respond. She had picked up the cat, and held it in her arms, her cheek against its sleek black back. The cat purred with a high grasshopper whirr.

Julie felt annoyed, as she did about that Macdonald woman next door, the one who had complained about her music and who stole her cat. Julie would often shut the cat in, but then the cat would shit in the bath.

After all, Julie pushed by Ruth with an aggressive "Excuse me," and went to the music center. She selected one of the most vibrant tapes, put it on, and stepped up the volume.

The beat came, and she moved to it for a moment, knocking against a toffee-wood table by the settee.

When she glanced round, Ruth had gone with the cat out of the back door into the weedy garden.

Usually over the weekend Mrs. Macdonald tried to keep to herself as much as possible. It was at these times that she felt the most threatened. Weekends, and in the evenings, when the loud music was played and the noisy visits went on. Her house was separated from the house of Julie Sawyer and Terry Purvis only by the width of the wooden door, which was joined onto both their properties, and led into Mrs. Macdonald's back garden. The two gardens ran side by side.

She did not go into the garden at weekends or in the evenings, once the better weather came. Julie and Terry, and sometimes their friends, were often out there, and then they took a portable tape machine out with them.

Occasionally, on Saturday nights, beer cans were thrown over her fence by the one they called Blackie.

Today Mrs. Macdonald had risked going out quickly, because the cat had drunk all the water she put out for the birds.

It was as she was coming back between the hydrangeas that she saw, over the low fence, a girl with long black hair and red lips, standing holding the cat in her arms.

Mrs. Macdonald hesitated. The way the girl held the cat was benign and pleasing to the eye. She had never seen Julie Sawyer, let alone Terry Purvis, hold the cat in this way. It was the manner in which cats should be held.

The girl was looking at her.

The girl said, "You're Mrs. Macdonald."

Mrs. Macdonald felt threatened again. She tried to frown, but she was only nervous. She was sixty-five, but appeared much older. She secretly thought the proximity of Julie and Terry had worn her out. On their other side, the house was empty. Another aggravated neighbor might have assisted Mrs. Macdonald.

"You feed the cat," said the girl. Then she said, "I came out because of the noise."

Noise she had said. Not, as Julie had, *Music*. It was even now clearly to be heard.

Mrs. Macdonald said, cautiously, "It's not your cup of tea, then."

"Oh, no. I like Prokofiev, and Rachmaninov. Mozart."

The cat was purring. Mrs. Macdonald reached over the low fence and stroked the cat's silken head. The cat, delighted, purred louder.

"I asked her once," said Mrs. Macdonald, clandestinely, "if she'd turn the volume down. But she didn't want to."

"I don't know them," said Ruth. "I was looking for the lady who was here before."

Mrs. Macdonald's troubled heart skipped a beat. Before Julie and Terry, her friend Mrs. Weeks had lived in the house. But Mrs. Weeks had died one afternoon, sitting in her quiet summer garden.

"Mrs. Weeks?" asked Mrs. Macdonald.

But the girl disappointed her now. "No. Mrs. Watt."

"Oh, dear. It sounds as if you've misremembered the address."

"Yes," said Ruth.

"I shouldn't," said Mrs. Macdonald. Her lined, papery face blushed hotly. "I should be a bit careful," she said. "I perhaps shouldn't say this. But if you don't know them, Miss Sawyer and Mr. Purvis, it might not be—what you'd like."

And then she was mortally afraid, for the girl might be a liar, and a bit unbalanced, as Julie Sawyer seemed to be, and she might tell them all she, Mrs. Macdonald, had said, and then—

"But it's not my business," blundered Mrs. Macdonald.

"You feed the cat," Ruth said, once more.

"Oh, the cat's lovely. They call her something funny. But I call her Victoria. She's so like my last one. My Victoria Plum, I used to say. So glossy and plump, she was. This one's rather thin. But you're still my Victoria, aren't you?"

The cat, amused by its second name, swam like a snake from Ruth's shoulder, and alighted on the fence, where it raised its tail like a lamp for all the world.

Suddenly the music fell down like a lift.

Through the open windows, the voices of Terry and Julie were audible. "Where the fuck is she?" "In the bloody garden."

"Oh—I'll just—" said Mrs. Macdonald. She turned and ran up her path and in the back door of her house.

Mohawk-Victoria stared into the sky at a traveling sparrow.

* * *

Terry had brought in fish and chips. He told Ruth how much her portion had cost, and said he expected she would like to help out with the wine, too.

Ruth opened her big bag, and presently handed him without flinching a ten-pound note.

"Oh, I'll find you some change," said Terry, but he did not. Ruth did not remonstrate, or later remind him.

During the afternoon Terry, as Julie said, "made himself beautiful." When he had finished, the bathroom was soaking wet and a pile of soggy towels lay on the floor. Terry took a deck chair and the portable tape machine into the garden to dry his hair in the sun. He played the same music Julie did, and fell asleep.

Julie got ready later. She was swift. She came down at six o'clock in a short green and orange dress and very high-heeled green shoes. She wore earrings like sunbursts. She seemed to have accepted Ruth's presence, and asked her if she would like a bath. Ruth agreed.

The water was not very hot, but it was a warm afternoon. It was difficult to shut and lock the door, but Ruth succeeded. There was no curtain over the small bathroom window so Ruth hung her T-shirt there.

Julie was trying to locate the cat, on her high heels, in the garden. She wanted to shut it in, because, later, when things got going, she did not want to have to worry about the cat being in with Mrs. Macdonald. Normally the cat would hide in the wardrobe when there was a party.

A notion had come to Julie to comfort her. Lucy, she knew, had a thing about Terry. Lucy would not like Ruth's being there. And Blackie could hardly fancy Ruth, who was not good-looking and had too big a chest. Blackie did not like bigness there in girls, he had told Julie so.

The cat was nowhere to be seen and Julie gave up, going back past the sleeping Terry. His hair had dried in waves, he would look handsome by evening. Perhaps it was all right. Maybe she should open some wine early? She wished one day he would cut the lawn.

In the kitchen the cat had manifested and was eating the last scraps of cat food. She picked it up, without waiting for it to finish, and carried it to the bedroom, where it leapt onto the windowsill.

Ruth was standing in the door of Terry's lair. It almost seemed she might be searching for something with her eyes.

"Have a nice bath?"

"Yes, thank you."

"Shame you haven't any other clothes."

But Ruth did not seem to mind.

CHAPTER 8

 THAT SUMMER, A DRAGON ROARED ON the common.

It was the sound of a motorbike, but not on the road below. Rachaela got up and went to open her window, and behind her the Rachmaninov concerto was vanquished.

Late afternoon had laid a bronzy sheen across the slopes. The sun, hard brilliant marigold, flashed low between the oaks and pines to the left of the window.

Down among the deep bed of trees, the roaring moved and idled, then suddenly gunned.

Across the shallow glade there rolled a blot of black, and lightnings happened as the sun sideswiped bright metal.

Then out tore the mechanical thing, and flew up the hill, nearer and nearer, and ever more extraordinary.

It was a huge black machine with extended fork and thundering wheel, in the stance, even running, of a black Egyptian dog, which stretched. Its rear end, however, was not a bike but a curved carriage, like Cinderella's, made from a crow-black pumpkin. Something burned in the back of it like a colored lantern. Two massive chariot wheels propelled it after the fore-wheel of the bike.

The rider of this anomaly was black leather and silver fireworks of light. On his head the sun lit short spears of white hair.

Close to the house, the bike which became a carriage, reared up. It had the prow of a skeletal horse. It plunged in a circle and over the cannon of the engine came soft shrill cries like those of startled pet birds.

Beneath the wall of the house, under Rachaela's window, the orbit stopped. The creature drew to a standstill and the roaring smoldered out.

The rider straddled his mount. He was spiked and studded, ringed and buckled and chained with silver.

The double seat of the carriage behind him was lined with damson velvet, and in it now, not one, but two Cinderellas were wriggling. They were almost identical dolls, dressed in little bands of black, tiny wrappings of leather skirts, broad ribbons that just covered their breasts. They too had been spangled with silver. But one had long golden coils of hair, and the other coils of hair of a gold which had rusted.

The lantern in the carriage back was a stained-glass window, vitriol blue and poppy red and crème de menthe and purple.

The rider of the bike poked his head suddenly up at Rachaela. He gave a soprano laugh.

"Horsy!" he shouted. "Sugar for the horse!"

In the past, she remembered, they had always quickly known, and came together like raindrops running down a window. Now, the same. Even as she started down the stairs toward the hallway, Michael and Cheta were there, and Sasha and Miranda, and Eric stood by one of the big pillars that ran around the wall. In the white drawing room the television twittered, forgotten.

The engine of the black machine rumbled as it rode around to the front of the house.

Michael went swiftly and opened the two doors.

The light had darkened there, and up from the beer

brownness of it, the leather rider walked, inky and glittering, and at his back the two beautiful Cinderellas in their little black stiletto boots and anklets of silver and steel.

In the hall, the rider stood, and looked about him.

None of them spoke.

Then he said, drily, "Here I am, after all."

His face was not young, like the thin shape and feral movements of his body. But it was the face, now, of an ancient boy, with black Scarabae eyes, and framed with short white dreadlocks in which beads were plaited, the colors of his carriage window.

On his hands there were more than three rings, and they were silver skulls and swords and spikes and roses, like the decorations on his leathers.

On his breast was silver chain mail, and across his ribs, decipherable gradually as he moved, in letters of flame, the words *Burn Out*.

Miranda said, "Uncle Camillo."

He nodded to her. "Miranda. Sasha. Eric. Michael and Cheta." He looked up the stairs. "And herself. The Rachaela."

Dust, which had been gathered on all of their eyes like the powder of time, had been scorched away. His eyes too were vivid. Had he come back from the dead?

Behind him, the golden Cinderella giggled lightly. The other one, of the gold which rusted, said, "Cami, I want the toilet."

"There will be a choice," he said. He turned to Cheta. "Will you show Miss Lou and Miss Tray the easements, please."

Miranda moved slowly out across the hall before Cheta or either of the Cinderellas—Lou, Tray—had taken a step. Miranda went to Camillo and quietly put her arms about him.

"I'm so glad," said Miranda. "This is so wonderful."

And then Sasha came, and Eric last of all. They

touched Camillo, his shining carapace and knotted hair, little weightless touches.

Camillo suffered it. He was a prodigal. But then, he had always been.

"Come out," he said, "come and see my trike. Can't keep it waiting. My fine horse."

"We'd like the toilet, please," said the rusty golden Cinderella to Cheta.

Cheta led the Cinderellas both away, into the passage where the downstairs bathroom was.

Camillo went back out into amber shadow, and Eric, Sasha, and Miranda followed him. Rachaela went as far as the house porch.

She watched as Camillo showed the trike to the Scarabae. Between the handlebars the burned frame of the horse head, set with two eyes of Sauterne crystal, stared fiercely, not incongruous but perfect. The bodywork was shot with silver rosettes, streaks of fire in vermilion paint. It was a beast.

Camillo activated a CD player raised like an altar over the velvet seat. Deep pouring Gothic rock swelled up like an organ, and in the trees the birds fell silent.

"Daisy, Daisy," said Camillo. There were spurs on his boots. "Give me your answer do."

There was a celebration dinner, roast chickens stuffed with oranges and basted with honey, Duchess potatoes, boiled chestnuts, asparagus. They ate at midnight.

Camillo was, as the Scarabae would once have said, "naughty." He ate the potatoes and asparagus only. Lou, the darker and more coppery girl, Tray, the golden, ate nothing, toyed with the food. They were exquisite children, perhaps twenty-one or twenty-two. Their bodies were tanned seamlessly like the honey chicken. Lou wore sequins and Tray tassels, on their black. Their limbs were garnished by silver beads and blossoms of bone. They sat either side of Camillo.

Rachaela thought of the story, the legend of Camillo. How he had killed his bride, the broken vase of neck and all the blood. But that had been a century at least ago, and now the necks of Lou and Tray were marked only with beads or, in the case of Lou, a tattoo of a rose.

The joy was muted, but it was present.

He had come back to them.

How?

He did not say.

"Oh, Cami, can I have another pink squirrel?"

And Camillo got up and mixed it for them, the two little flawless girls. While the Scarabae sat about the table like open flowers. And the Scarabae ate. They ate heartily.

"Aren't the bones pretty?" said Tray, when the chicken had been demolished.

Camillo had an earring in his right earlobe, a silver snake holding a moon in its mouth that was also a skull.

There were no questions. No answers.

Camillo and the girls went up into one of the outposts of the architecture, on the third floor.

The trike was stabled somewhere in the lower house.

It was four in the morning.

Eric sat playing chess against an invisible opponent.

Rachaela said, "How did he survive?"

"We do," said Eric. "We do survive."

"No, not always."

"Yes. I concede."

"How then?"

"One day, he will tell us."

"Why didn't you ask him?"

"Or you, Rachaela, you could have asked."

"He'd talk nonsense."

"Yes," said Eric.

Miranda and Sasha had gone away, perhaps to their rooms or only to another part of the house.

Rachaela contacted with one finger the elegant telephone, which never rang.

"Can you survive death?" she demanded futilely.

"You've seen us die."

She was tired, her body not accustomed yet to the altered hours, wanting to sleep both day and night, and to be awake then, too.

"I said I should go away, and perhaps now I should. Now you've got Camillo back." She waited, and then she said, "Does he sleep with those two girls? If so—if he can—is he fertile?"

Eric did not reply. Rachaela recalled the sexual reticence of the Scarabae. The Scarabae who lay son with mother, daughter with sire.

"Will that continue the line?" she said.

But Lou and Tray would be on the pill. And Camillo —Camillo was old.

Rachaela felt old. She felt desiccated, and yet curiously immature, a child again among the family.

"Anyway," she said, "he's found a horse to ride."

Camillo, the outcast. He had given Rachaela the key to the attic when Ruth had been shut up. He had wanted Ruth taken away. And with the key Rachaela had let Ruth out.

Rachaela had known Camillo was burned to cinders.

She imagined him lying on a bed with the two girls like limpets, showering him with hair.

She felt far older than Camillo.

CHAPTER 9

WARM SUNSHINE STILL HOVERED HIGH up over the street; it would be light for another hour. No one was about. In the five-foot front garden of the empty house adjoining Julie and Terry's, dusky opium poppies had sprung wild between the old concrete paving. The nettles around Julie's dustbin were gilt-edged. It was a peaceful scene spoiled only by sound effects: the music center was playing loud enough to be heard fifteen doors away.

Joseph Black and Jennifer Devonshire walked up the road. He was dressed very casually, but Jennifer wore a short pink flowery dress and twenty bracelets. She carried a carrier bag with a bottle of wine in it.

"Here we go," said Blackie, swinging through the gate in front of her. He rammed the knocker against the front door and shouted through the letter box: "It's a raid!"

It was Terry who came to the door in an orange shirt and very blue jeans.

"You're late."

"No car."

"Where's Lucy?"

"She's got a cold," said Jenny.

"She says," said Blackie. "It's a cold *sore*." He

smiled at Terry and punched him lightly in the chest. "Worried?"

"Nah," said Terry, grinning. He looked worried.

They went in, and the great noise enveloped them. They seemed to like it, loosening and expanding like plants in refreshing rain.

"Someone to meet," said Terry.

Ruth was sitting on the settee in her black T-shirt and jeans. She had had a glass of wine but she had drunk it, now she only had the empty glass.

Blackie looked at her. "Who's she?"

"That's Ruth. This is Blackie."

"Everything they've told you about me is true," said Blackie.

"Hallo," said Ruth, but they did not hear her. Unlike the others she did not shout effortlessly above the music. She had taken some cottonwool from her bag and put it in her ears.

"Where's the frigging booze?" asked Blackie.

Julie appeared out of the kitchen with a wine bottle and a glass for Jenny, and one for Lucy who had not come.

"Where's Lucy?"

"She's got herpes," said Blackie.

"Don't tell lies," said Jenny.

Terry took cans of beer out of the fridge, and he and Blackie opened them, in a spray of fizz.

Julie filled Jenny's glass and her own. Then, reluctantly, Ruth's.

"Who's Ruth, then?" inquired Jenny. Ruth watched her, perhaps reading her lips.

"Better ask Terry."

"Oh."

There was a crash from the music center and then a silence louder and more painful than the noise. The tape had ended.

"Put on some reggae," said Blackie. He gyrated his

hips and waved his arms in unsuccessful imitation. "Cool, mon."

Julie hurriedly selected a tape and put it on.

"Look, a bird that can drink," said Blackie. Ruth had drained her glass again. "Like a beer, darling?"

"All right," said Ruth, soundlessly under the music.

"Eh?" said Blackie.

Ruth held out her hand, and he playfully put his can of Carlsberg into it. Ruth handed him the can back.

"She doesn't want to drink yours," said Terry. "Very sensible. God knows what she might catch." He went into the narrow kitchen and got another beer from the fridge, replacing it with four others.

When he came back, Blackie was sitting beside Ruth on the settee.

Julie and Jenny were dancing to the music, ignoring Blackie and Ruth. Julie's high heels kept catching in the carpet, but it was too soon to take them off.

"Guess what line I'm in," Blackie was saying to Ruth. Ruth looked at him. God, what eyes she had, Terry thought, like bloody Greta Garbo. And black as tar.

Ruth did not guess.

Terry said, "He fixes cars."

"Yeah," said Blackie. "Nothing I can't see to. That's how I met our Julie. Fixed her up. 'Course, they ain't got a car now. Old Terry splattered it, didn't you?"

Terry drank down his beer. "It was a fucking drag. Always going wrong. You never fixed it. It got worse after you had your paws on it."

"Secret of my success," said Blackie.

"You've buggered yours up too. Now my Morris," said Terry. "Did the whole of Cornwall in that car."

"Yeah, place called Mousehole," said Blackie to Ruth.

"It's pronounced Mowsel," said Terry.

"Oooh," said Blackie. "Well, fark me. *Moosil.*"

He looked up at Julie and Jenny disco dancing awkwardly on the catchy carpet. "Come on, show a bit of whoopsie."

Julie glanced at Blackie archly, but said nothing.

Blackie shrugged. He got out a packet of cigarettes and a big gold lighter. He showed the lighter to Ruth. "See this? Present from a grateful customer. A bird." He put a cigarette in his mouth, flipped the lighter and raised the yellow petal of flame. When the cigarette was alight, he flipped the lighter over. "Look, it's inscribed to me. *B to B.*"

"Don't you believe it," said Terry. "He fucking knocked it off. Or someone left it in a car."

Ash trembled from the cigarette to the carpet. Blackie rubbed it smartly in with his big black shoe. Julie gave a grunt and broke off from her dance. She went to the fire surround and picked up an ashtray, which she then set down by Blackie on the toffee-wood table, moving the tape player to do so. "Use that."

"Use that. Yis, Modum. Lovely."

"You brought the stuff?" Terry asked Blackie.

"I might."

"Where is it?"

"Easy, man," said Blackie. "I got it." He patted his hip.

Ruth stood up.

"You know where it is," said Terry.

Ruth moved out of the room. Terry watched her.

"Nice arse," said Blackie. "Don't say much. Fine by me."

Ruth went up the stairs, visible from the open door of the through-room. Terry went on watching her, out of sight.

Jenny broke away from the dance now. "I think I'll just go up, too."

Julie refilled her own wine glass. Blackie laughed.

Ruth was standing inside the tiny bathroom trying to shut the door when Jenny called, "Can I come in," and came in, so Ruth was forced back. Jenny squeezed past Ruth through the two and a half feet of space between the bath and the wall. "Don't worry about the door. You can't ever shut it. The guys won't come up while we're here. I'm dying for a pee. Mind if I go first?" And she raised her pink skirt, lowered her white pants, and sat down on the lavatory.

Ruth froze. Over the *thump, thump* of the music, there came the plash of running water.

Ruth turned and went out of the bathroom.

Through the open door of the bedroom the double bed lay dressed in red and gray triangles. The black and white cat crouched at its foot, ears laid back, eyes wide.

Ruth went into the room and knelt by the cat. She smoothed its fur and kissed it between the ears.

The cat got up and went to the wardrobe, and scratched at the panels. Ruth opened the wardrobe door. The cat darted inside. Ruth left the door ajar.

The lavatory flushed.

Jenny had come out of the bathroom and now stood in the bedroom doorway.

"Julie gets fed up with that cat in her wardrobe." She forgot the cat. "I'd like a really big house, wouldn't you? Three or four bedrooms. And a swimming pool. Have you known Terry long?"

"No," said Ruth.

"He's not bad," said Jenny. "Better than that Blackie."

Ruth stood against the hard forms of the bed, in her long, long hair and silence. There was something . . . childlike?

Jenny frowned. "How old are you?"

Ruth said, "It's none of your business."

"Oh, you're going to be great, you are," said Jenny angrily. She turned and went away down the stairs, her bracelets clashing.

Ruth looked at the bed. The duvet was folded back.

Downstairs they all laughed suddenly. Ruth intently stared at the floor, as if she could see through it at the top of their heads.

At about nine, when they had drunk quite a lot, Jenny and Julie were sent out to the Indian in the high street for a take-away. "Go on," said Blackie, "you're liberated. You don't need us to hold your hand." "Bring back some more beer," said Terry.

Ruth did not offer to go out with the girls.

After some argument, Jenny and Julie went.

On some level now alone, the two men formed a sort of conspiracy, sitting on the floor and letting one of the beer cans spill over, and chuckling. Ruth sat above them on the settee, with the last of the wine.

"Let's have a smoke now," said Blackie. "Before they get back."

He drew out cigarette papers and some loose tobacco, and another substance, sweet and grassy smelling, in a cellophane packet. He began to make an untidy brown cigarette.

When this was lit, the men passed it back and forth, drawing on it deeply, with half-closed eyes. A foreign scent, like the musk of ancient temples, filled the room.

Terry offered the remaining half of the joint to Ruth. She shook her head.

"Go on. It's good stuff."

"No, thank you."

"It'll make you feel good."

"Perhaps she feels good enough," said Blackie. He tore open a beer can, showing her the raw edge. But his voice had slurred now, his eyelids were at half-mast, he looked sleepy.

Terry was brighter, energetic. He pushed the joint at Ruth. "Haven't you smoked before? I'll show you how."

"Stop pissing about and pass it here," said Blackie.

"I fucking paid for it," said Terry.

"And I fucking got hold of it."

Terry gave the joint to Blackie, who finished it off.

"The girls'll smell it when they get back," said Terry like a naughty little boy who had been reading in bed after lights-out.

But when the girls came back they too were high, for they had had a couple of gins at the restaurant while they waited. Jenny sang the praises of the Indian waiter she fancied. "Oh, his *eyes*. They're *beautiful*."

"Not so beautiful as Ruth's," said Terry. He lifted Ruth's hand and kissed it, but Ruth neither pulled away nor seemed pleased.

Julie picked up the torn can and took it out to the bin in the kitchen.

The aluminium dishes were opened up and another foreign fragrance filled the room. This time it was Julie who asked Ruth for the money for her chicken tikka.

They had not brought back any beer, only two more bottles of wine.

Julie and Jenny began their prawn curries, and Terry forked up a lamb passanda. Blackie, who had ordered a tandoori mixed grill, potato bhajee and vegetable curry, had spread his dishes out along the carpet, dipping in naan bread and splashing.

They all ate hungrily. The music, now habitual as air, blared on, ignored.

Jenny wiped her lips and fingers on a Kleenex. She looked across at Terry. "Would you like to see my new bra?"

"Black lace," said Terry.

"Wrong," said Jenny. She stood, a little unsteadily, and, unzipping her dress, pulled it up her body and off over her head. "What do you think?" She was not wearing a bra. Her two breasts stared at them like eyes with round beige pupils. Jenny shook herself, and her breasts wobbled.

"And what bra is our Julie wearing?" said Blackie.

He had taken out the paper and tobacco again, and among the empty smeary dishes, was constructing another joint.

"You'll have to guess," said Julie. "I'm not sure you're really interested."

Blackie nodded. "Maybe not. I bet Ruthie's got a good one on."

"Well," said Jenny, "I bet you won't get to see it."

Blackie lit the joint from his gold lighter *B to B,* and drew on it as if performing a yoga breathing exercise. He passed the joint directly across to Jenny.

"Ruthie'll show me." He looked up at Ruth and bared his teeth. "Won't she, eh?"

Ruth looked down into Blackie's face. Her eyes were the night of temples far, far to the east, a night deeper than the neon dark which had settled on the house. Terry stared at her long mascara lashes. He realized he had not felt anything like this for a girl for half a year.

"You stay here, Ruth," he said, stumbling on his words, on the taste of curry and hash and beer and wine, and on the chill-sweet bottomless aroma of desire. "You stay with me."

But Ruth got up, and Blackie had got up from the floor.

Julie said loudly, "Blackie, you cunt."

"Dead right," said Blackie.

"Don't use the fucking bedroom," shouted Julie.

"We'll use the camp bed," said Blackie, with kindly reassurance.

Terry tried to stand up. Jenny pulled on him. He sank down and Jenny put her hand possessively over his fly.

Thump, thump, went the music, and the house went on thrumming like a space ship, *thump, thump, thump.*

Blackie walked in front of Ruth into Terry's lair and turned on the light. The curtains were drawn. Blackie sat down on the camp bed, bouncing once, to test it. Then he undid his trousers. His penis burst free.

"Take your clothes off," slurred Blackie. "And then come and try this. It'll taste of curry. Wait and see."

Ruth had shut the door behind her.

She poised in the small room, looking at Blackie, and at his penis. Her face was whiter than the rice they had eaten but her lips were scarlet and he would be a lovely fit.

Her eyes were funny though. Who cared?

Ruth ran her hand lightly over Terry's table, among the books and spent cans. She took up a Biro and drew off the cap.

Blackie was not concerned with the pen. Everything was in a wonderful slow motion. He was looking forward to the T-shirt coming slowly off. Ruth was a big girl, better than that bloody Julie, like two gnat bites, stupid mare.

Ruth came toward Blackie, slowly, slowly, and he took hold of the edge of the T-shirt. But he had slowly raised it only half an inch when she stabbed him quickly and thoroughly through the windpipe with the Biro.

Terry and Jenny had had sex, on the carpet. Julie had been expected to join in, but where was the fun in that, making it nicer for them and nobody bothering with her?

Now Jenny was asleep on her back on the floor wearing only her shoes and her bracelets. Terry was probably finished. He had taken out the Polaroid camera, the flash sparking white in the sixty-watt lamplight, and was snapping Jenny with her hair in the curry dishes.

Julie went toward the door.

"Let those two get on with it. That bastard. That cow," said Terry.

"They can rot," said Julie. "I'm going for a fucking piss."

"Bloody bitch," said Terry. Perhaps he meant Ruth.

They had certainly made a noise up there, rolling on the floor, judging by the way the ceiling rocked, even over the music.

Julie went out and up the stairs. Halfway, she paused and took off her high-heeled green shoes, allowing one to drop back into the hall, carrying the other up to the bathroom, then aimlessly letting it fall outside.

While she was in the bathroom, she listened. Not a whisper from the lair.

That Blackie. That was the last time. They were going to stop all this. She did not—had *never* liked it. And Terry. He had drunk far too much, he would be sick in the morning. And the bloody milkman would come at six o'clock. Well, he could wait.

Julie flushed the lavatory and walked from the bathroom. As she came onto the landing the light went out. Julie swore, and then Ruth stabbed her in the throat with one of her green high heels. Rather as Blackie had done Julie tried to throw up around the obstruction. And died.

Terry put on another tape. He turned it up, but the volume control was at its limit. He could not see why old mother Macdonald had complained. It was not very loud.

The room was a mess. Julie would be ratty. He felt a little queasy. Must have been something a bit off in the curry.

When Ruth came in, he took a Polaroid shot of her, and the flash exploded. Terry laughed when she jumped. She held one of Julie's shoes in her hand, in fact the one from the bottom of the stairs.

"Got ya."

Ruth turned to him.

"You are a bitch," said Terry, weaving on his feet.

Ruth ripped out the side of his neck with the metal point of Julie's heel.

Terry squealed, and as he went down, the Polaroid photograph ejected from the camera. He lay on the floor, trying to get up, his neck all wet but not hurting, and saw Ruth lean over and pick up the tape player from the table. She brought the machine down on his head, with enormous strength and great attention.

When Terry was still, Ruth took one of the empty beer cans and tore it open as she had seen Blackie do. And moved to the sleeping Jenny.

When Ruth had let Victoria from the wardrobe, she fed the cat in the kitchen. Victoria had come out quite willingly once the music was switched off. She sniffed the body of Julie on the landing, and next Terry's body briefly, below, but the corpses did not hold her interest. When she had eaten, Ruth carried Victoria back upstairs. The cat sat on the side of the bath as Ruth washed off the ejected blood.

The bed in the bedroom was clean and they slept there, the cat on Ruth's pillow, Ruth's cheek in the cat's soft fur.

Ruth had a lie-in in the morning. About midday, she got up, fed the cat again—the last tin but one of the cat food—and made herself beefburgers, peas, and oven chips from Julie's slender stores.

The milkman had not roused her. He often could not rouse Julie and Terry.

When she had had the food, Ruth checked the house for anything useful, and took some T-shirts of Julie's and Terry's, and a small amount of paper money which she found in a drawer.

At two o'clock, Ruth, carrying her bag and Victoria on alternate shoulders, used Blackie's lighter to set a small fire in Terry's lair, utilizing some of Terry's short fiction for the purpose.

The cat glared at the fire, and when the door of the lair was shut, Ruth carried the cat down and out of the house. She put Victoria by Mrs. Macdonald's door, separated by the safe distance of the garden passage. Ruth left Victoria on the Macdonald doorstep, eating her last tin of cat food off a saucer. Before she went away, Ruth rang Mrs. Macdonald's bell.

From farther up the street Ruth witnessed Mrs. Macdonald coming out, and Victoria trotting into her hall.

Smoke was already issuing from the top of Julie and Terry's house, but Mrs. Macdonald did not seem to notice it yet. She would say later the silence had puzzled her, for by eleven on Sundays Julie normally had the music center going.

The music center blew up at three o'clock and the top floor fell through into the downstairs room, precipitating all that was left of Blackie and Julie onto the cheap carpet, which was by then also on fire. By then, too, Mrs. Macdonald, with a purring Victoria in her arms, had called the fire brigade.

CHAPTER 10

BEYOND THE CONSERVATORY THERE WAS a terrace laid with peach and terra-cotta tiles. A statue stood on it, a draped stone woman with a stone basket on her shoulder. As summer had begun, red and wine geraniums had come from the basket.

Under the terrace six steps went down into the garden.

The garden had high walls of sepia brick, up which wisteria, clematis, and ivies grew, and other climbing plants with tendrils and heart-shaped leaves. Over the wall tops the trees of the common massed thickly. Trees had assembled inside also. It was a dark, overgrown, and in parts sunken garden, into which the sun pressed sharply in two or three places.

Lou and Tray were on the terrace, on long garden chairs. Their golden bodies were metallic with sunscreen. Each wore a tiny black bikini, Lou's with one diagonal strap. Tray had a small tattoo of an orchid around her navel. Their hair had changed as the days passed and Camillo let them, or ushered them, out and about; Tray's gold was streaked with white and Lou's was rose-red like the women in the hall windows. They were painting each other's toenails black with little stenciled designs in silver.

"Hi, Rach," said Lou.

"Isn't it lovely and warm," said Tray.

In the house, the Scarabae had gathered, as they sometimes did, to watch the TV news in the drawing room.

Lou pointed her flawless arm. "Cami's down there."

Tray smiled at Rachaela with flawless teeth.

Each girl was adorably beautiful, as if they had been fashioned out of some material, custom made, like Camillo's trike. There was not a pore in their skins, not an imbalance in their bodies. Their hair was silken floss. Lou had hazel eyes but Tray's were smoky blue. They could never conceivably age or deteriorate.

They had infiltrated the house more and more. Sometimes they even watched television with the Scarabae. But both girls were in a sort of dream that had only to do with their own perfection. They seemed to think Camillo was a film director or perhaps an elderly rock singer. Being dolls, they apparently expected to be often set aside, picked up again when required.

"You've got lovely hair," said Tray as Rachaela crossed the terrace.

To them she would look about thirty, therefore past her best. Tray was being kind, genuinely good-hearted, in offering the compliment.

"Thank you."

Rachaela went down the steps.

She followed the path into the thickets of oak trees, and came to what seemed a grove in a forest. Here an apple tree grew tall and bent and wild, fruitless. The terrace, the house, were invisible. A fountain in the form of a twisting fish rose from a mossy bowl. A little water still dripped from the jaws of the fish. On its head now was a straw hat with enamel cherries.

Camillo sat on the ground, cross-legged, watching her.

She had been able to find him in the past. She had found him now.

"Can't get up," said Camillo. "Too old."

He wore, as usual, his leathers, and a T-shirt which read, under the chain-mail, *Wild Thing*.

"It's time you told me," said Rachaela.

"Told you what? How impressive you are?"

"How you survived."

Camillo said, "Do you like the fish's hat? I found it in a jumble sale. Too good for a woman."

"You gave me the key," she said, "which let Ruth out. They won't talk about Ruth. Ruth burned the house. Did they tell you about Miriam?"

"They don't tell me things, they never did."

"But you're resurrected, Camillo. That must make a difference."

He did not look like Camillo anymore, not with the dreadlocks and beads. His old forearms were muscular as steel. Hair grew on them, steel colored.

Yet since he had come here, he had grown introspective. He had shut himself away, sending the two girls out alone with handfuls of money so they could have their hair done, and could buy countless almost identical tiny black clothes, and silver for their golden limbs, and bags of chips and ice-creams, which was all they ever seemed to eat.

On his new music machine above in the house, Camillo played The Sisters of Mercy, Carter U.S.M., and Iron Maiden. Rachaela heard the murmur of these musics, like the sea in a cave.

Sometimes he cleaned the trike in a large utility room beyond the kitchen. Sometimes he and the two girls went riding it. The stuffed horse's head attached between the handlebars had once been scorched to the bone.

She did not know why she wanted to hear the story of his escape. Perhaps only because, in a curious way, Camillo had been bound up for her with Adamus. And there was no way on earth Adamus, hanged by the neck and devoured by flames, could come back from the dead.

"They don't open doors, here, after dark," Camillo said. "Very wise. London was always a jungle."

Once before he had told her a story of an escape. She had wanted him to stop. She had thought he might be dying, that time. He was almost three hundred years of age. Or was he only a terribly crazy, normal old man, insanely sane like the other three gray hamsters watching TV.

"Down on the beach," he said, "that's where I was. I'd gone to make a fire."

His words pulled her back. She stared at him.

"To make a—"

"A fire. Like the time Sylvian was cremated."

The Scarabae burned their dead. Who had *this* fire been for? For Ruth? For Anna's memory? Or for himself?

"Go on," she said.

"Little Miss Muffet sat on a tuffet."

Rachaela said, "The hat suits the fish. It needed something."

"Then I saw the house catch alight," he said. "It was a vision."

"Like the burning town, when your father and mother fled in the sleigh."

"No, not like that. That looked real, convincing. The house looked like a stage set in a bad film. I watched until it had all come down. Then the daylight broke."

"Why didn't you—" she said "—why didn't you come up from the beach?"

"I couldn't," he said. He said, "I cried for the rocking horse. She burned it."

"And the Scarabae, did you cry for them?"

Camillo gave his high mad giggle. It was like the other times, as if he had left it too long without a sign of mental instability.

"I climbed up later," he said. "Nobody there. I went through the ruin. I found some strange things. Do you remember my horsy? I found the head. It's on the trike now. My horse."

He got up, and walking over to the fish, he took a lipstick out of his pocket and began to crayon the round lips. "Maple Kiss," said Camillo. "One of Tray's. And where did I meet Lou and Tray? But that comes later." He stepped back from the fish. "What do you think?"

"It's very attractive."

"When I came away from the house, I walked across the heath. I walked above the sea. I walked for days. I caught a rabbit once, to eat it. But I couldn't kill it. It was so alive. I ate grass. The rabbit ran off and told the other rabbits old Uncle Camillo had taken a bite out of it, but the rabbits didn't believe it. One evening there was something on the beach below. So I climbed down again. It was another fire. What do you think I found?"

"People," said Rachaela.

"A road ran through to the beach. There were ten bikers like soldiers in black leather, and the bikes shining in the firelight."

Rachaela saw in her mind's eye the fire and the dark sea, and the bikes and the black-clad men, and Camillo gazing like an eldritch boy.

"They said," said Camillo, " 'Hallo, Granddad.' I said, 'I'm too old to be your grandfather.' That made them laugh. They gave me some of the beer they were drinking and a pork pie. They asked me if I had escaped from somewhere. I said I had. They laughed again and said, 'Good for you, you old cunt.' I slept on the beach and in the morning I got up on the back of one of the bikes. We roared off along the road and into a town by the sea. They were like Cossacks. The roads cleared and everyone ran. The young girls looked after them."

Camillo put the lipstick away.

He said: "We had steaks at a pub. Then there was a fight with some other customers. I fought alongside the Cossacks. They were surprised. They said, when we had got out, 'This old geezer can handle himself.' They asked my name. They always called me *Camillo* after that. I got some money later, and made them rich. Then they bought me the gear. We parted the best of friends. They wouldn't have stayed rich long. The drink, the black metal horses."

Rachaela did not ask about the money. The Scarabae could command funds, certainly she had seen that by now. The story was as much a fairy tale as the other, the story of the flight by night over the snow. Both probably were true.

"The lipstick compares favorably with the cherries," said Camillo.

"Yes."

"And I met Lou and Tray at a concert. Not Prokofiev, of course. A gig. They attached themselves to me like pretty flowers to a gnarled old branch. They think I'm some fallen star. And do I sleep with them? What does Rachaela suppose?"

"You like to ride things," Rachaela said, bleakly, "why not Lou and Tray?"

"Superb," said Camillo. "Now you can go away."

"I'm thinking of it," she said, slowly.

"Your former plaint, that you would leave us all. That you would take the nasty Ruth and vanish."

"Ruth *has* vanished."

"Like a demon," said Camillo. "Gone, yet not exorcised."

"Do you believe," Rachaela said, "that she—"

"No, I won't talk about Ruth, either. Or even about you. When I learned that I wasn't the last, that they were here, in this house, I came back to them. Scarabae. We always come back, even if we have gone away. Let that be a lesson to you."

Lou and Tray were sunbathing on the terrace, while the gray woman stood over them with her basket.

In the drawing room, the Scarabae had finished with the news and were watching an action film. A man hung from an American building one hundred floors up. But did not fall.

There was never a hint of restraint now. It was easy to come and go.

Rachaela left the house.

The day was hot, with a pale dusty sky like India.

She walked down past the great houses with their timbered fronts and bay windows and triple garages, and wide green lawns, down through the semidetached villas where there were children playing noisily in gardens, and cars filling the air with the smell of burned macaroons.

In the London village there were cake shops and boutiques, a florist's, and a hair salon, Lucrece, to which presumably the gemini of Lou and Tray had come.

Rachaela moved along the pavement, which was full of a glitter like chips of diamond. The cars snarled by and the people swung past, their hot flesh and summer clothes, polished dogs with strawberry tongues, and kids on bicycles.

How much longer would she want to be out by day? (That had been her name once, *Day*.) How long before she kept indoors, behind the syrupy-colored windows, whose stained lights seemed sunk into the furniture so far that, even if the windows should be blasted out, the colors must remain?

And that policeman on the corner, what would he know to do, or not to do, if she went to him and said, *I am a Scarabae*?

For she had overheard a flutter of talk between Lou and Tray. That time, they said, Cami had been stopped on the bypass, because he did not have a helmet on. And there had been a scene at the side of the road, and suddenly, over the walkie-talkie had come some garbled message, and the police officers had backed away, telling

Camillo how sorry they were. Leading him like a king to the trike. Wishing him a nice journey.

Of course, Camillo was a film director. What else?

But Camillo was not anything of the kind, and any way, such men were fair game. No, it must be because Camillo was *Scarabae*.

Rachaela passed the policeman, who followed her only appreciatively with his eyes.

She bought complex cakes in the shop, for Sasha, Miranda and Eric, Michael and Cheta.

With a sensation of defeat, that was only the veneer for some other, deeper, darker, more arresting, more peculiar emotion, like *waiting,* she went back up among the villas and neat streets that led toward the common. Home.

CHAPTER 11

✥ WHEN THE YELLOW DOOR OPENED, A
black woman stood there, fat, and fragrant like
apple blossom. She smiled at once and behind her black
eyes were blue seas. Her black eyes were bright and lit,
and there were depths to them, soul-windows. Unlike the
paint-black eyes of the girl outside.

"Mrs. Watt?"

Delilah Trinidad eased her bulk a little, from one flat
shoe to the other.

"No, pet. Mrs. Watt? I never hear of Mrs. Watt."

Down by the curb, James, Delilah's son, was cleaning his Datsun, his slim body moving to the tempo of his
pride.

Delilah looked at him, and wondered if he had
heard of a Mrs. Watt.

"This is the house," said the white girl with long
black hair.

"No, pet," said Delilah, "if she ever here, she gone."
But Delilah was troubled.

"I've come a long way," said the girl. "Into London."

Out of the cool blue hallway behind the yellow door,
another girl appeared. She was the shade of dark chocolate, and where Delilah was fat, she was slender, like a
young tree. She had the beauty of a model, an icon of

high African art. Unlike Delilah, too, she had an English
voice, but not the voice of the street. This was RADA.

"What is it, Mom?"

"Dis young girl, she looking for a Mrs. Watt. She
better come in, have a cup of coffee. She come all the
way to London, Pearl."

Pearl slipped her arm around her mother's cushion
shoulders. She did not know it, but by doing so, she had
filled up the doorway now, like a fence, the big woman
and the slender woman as one.

"I'm sorry," said Pearl. "You seem to be lost. Have
you tried next door? They may know."

And now a dog came up from the blue hall, a black
dog, black as the Trinidads, and with a carven head, and
it put itself into the space where the women's bodies had
left a little gap.

Ruth looked at the dog. "May I touch him?"

"Oh, he's fine," said the beautiful girl.

Ruth put out her hand, and the dog permitted her to
stroke his forehead. He gazed at her, but that was all.

James had left the Datsun all soapy. He walked up
the path, grinning and friendly.

"What's up, Pearl?"

"You come in now," said Delilah Trinidad to Ruth.
"Come in. We think about it."

The two women leaned together unconsciously.
Their bodies had once been one, and not forgotten.
Love. There was love.

And the young man on the path, with the sponge in
his hand, amused, tender. Love, also.

Somewhere in the house a child happily laughed.
The dog smiled and panted.

"There go the baby," said Delilah.

Ruth took a step back.

"I made a mistake," said Ruth.

She turned, and walked away from them. She looked

very small, and truly black, the black of the dark and the shadow and the night.

Delilah watched Ruth go, her eyes wide and sad.

"Poor chile," she said. "Poor little girl."

Something like Ancient Egypt, night river water, and fire. But it was only the Thames at its most muddy, and a bonfire of refuse up on the bank, under the derelict warehouses, keeping three tramps warm.

The sun had died on the river like a broken egg. The barges passed, and miles up were the rusty docks, and farther the big white ship with the fancy name.

But here it got cold.

There had to be a fire, even in summer.

"Look," said Jimbo, "poor little bird."

"You let it be," said Sedge.

And deep in his drink of sour red wine, Baldy said nothing at all.

But Jimbo had had a daughter once, in another life, and finally he got up and crept along the bank toward the small dark girl.

"Here," said Jimbo, "here, girlie. D'ya want to come down to the fire? We won't hurt ya."

The girl turned a white face with dark lips and eyes. "No, thank you."

"It's warm. It's better. The fire keeps the rats off."

"No."

And down the incline, Sedge stood up by the fire in his cardboard raincoat, and he bellowed. Sedge was a devil. He would not share.

Jimbo left the girl and went back, and Sedge seized his arm as if he would kill him.

"Leave her alone I said."

"But she's just a kid."

"The streets of London," said Sedge, "are paved

with child." He sometimes said these things. He pulled Jimbo down. "Bad. She's bad."

And Baldy hiccuped, and passed the wine.

Ruth sat above the river, listening to it. At a distance, far enough, the tramps' fire crackled. After a time, she went through the contents of Amanda Mills's bag. There were T-shirts and clean underclothes, Kleenex, makeup, toothpaste and deodorant, and money.

Ruth was hungry, although she had gone to a burger bar for a double hamburger and french fries, fruit pie and cream. She was always hungry now. Sometimes she bought Kit-Kats and Mars, and ate them, or bananas and apples off a stall.

That had been the first thing, after the fire. Hunger. She had gone over the heath away from the sea, and her face had hurt very much, where he—Adamus—had struck her, her eye swollen and her mouth bruised. But she had still wanted to eat. She did not look back. She had killed all the Scarabae. Burned them up. Only she remained.

And Rachaela. Probably Rachaela—Mommy. But Ruth did not think about this.

She was like a butterfly freed from a chrysalis. A hungry butterfly.

The night heath was familiar, as if she had been out on it before. Things moved about in the undergrowth and she hoped to see an owl. But she saw nothing.

She came to a road, and she had known it would be there.

As Ruth stood looking at the road in the dark dimness of early morning, a car spun out of the blackness behind two beams of light. It was going very fast, and Ruth stepped aside. The car flashed by her. Then pulled up with a complaint of brakes. It sat on the road, and Ruth did not move. Then the car reversed slowly back toward her.

"My God, I thought I was seeing things."

The man was middle-aged, plump, with a shiny-clean face and black line of mustache.

Ruth, in her dress which had been designed in 1910, her sensible school shoes, her skeins of hair, looked in at him.

"Your face—" said the man. "What's happened?"

She had been told not to speak to strange men. But all that had changed.

"My boyfriend," said Ruth, "hit me."

"The bastard. My God, I'd better get you to a doctor. You'd better get in. Do you live round here . . ."

"No," said Ruth. She went around and opened the door of the car, a Ford Sierra. "I don't want a doctor."

"All right. We'll see."

Ruth was in the car, and the man reached over and shut her door.

"Do you want to go home?" said the man. He sounded coaxing, but this was a constant tone, with him. He was a rep, it was his business always to persuade, to something.

"I can't," said Ruth. "Where are you going?"

"Gavil Mount," he said. It might have been a crater on the moon, and in any case it would not matter, since they would not get there.

"That will do," said Ruth.

"Right you are, then."

He started up the car and they raced forward, parting the night.

The man was Tom Robbins, so he told her. At the moment his line was excellent little traveling packs for young ladies. She could take a look at his supplies, and see. Ruth did so. Each pack was in a floral case, and comprised a toothbrush, comb and brush, cleansing tissues, manicure scissors, nail file and emery board, and matching nail varnish and lipstick, eyeshadow and mascara, these last four varying from pack to pack.

"Go on, take one," said Tom Robbins, who had never been able to get over a weakness for young pretty girls, although it had sometimes caused him bother at home and on the road.

Ruth selected a pack with black and mink shadow, and Red Hot lipstick and varnish.

"You'll look good in that," said Tom Robbins, "once that nasty bruise goes down."

From one side she was a stunner, from the other like a horror film. Luckily one of his contacts at the Mount was a pharmacist in a chemist shop.

As they drew nearer the town, they moved onto the motorway, and signs came up for a Happy Eater.

Ruth said she was hungry.

When they had pulled in, caution made him keep Ruth, her bruise, and her outlandish dress, in the Ford Sierra. He brought her out a cheeseburger with an egg, fries, and a piece of gâteau, and a Coke. She ate greedily, as if she were starved. Perhaps she was, she was slim as a wand.

It was getting light when he drove off down the side lane.

He had plans for Ruth, but these involved a nice little discreet hotel, a bottle of wine, and before that a visit to the chemist's shop, which would be open by the time they got there, and, along with the potion, a packet of three.

Tom Robbins pulled into the lane in order to relax and have a smoke, away from the motorway, before driving on to Gavil. That was all.

But when they were there, the red of the car blooming up in the dawn like the free lipstick he had given her, Tom made the error of rubbing Ruth's knee. It was a friendly gesture, nearly avuncular. He meant it to say, *If you're willing, let's*—but Ruth punched him hard in the genitals. And as he was leaning over the wheel crying, she

got out the metal nail file from the kit and stuck it
through his neck.

She drank a little of Tom's blood, when he was dead.
She did this because she knew she was Scarabae, a vampire. She did not actually enjoy the blood. It was a sort of
duty.

When she had run away from the car and Tom, carefully carrying her makeup kit, Ruth became lost in the
English countryside, which was like a wild garden with
roads, hills, and fields.

At midday she came on a camper out in a meadow.
No one was about but the door was unlocked. Ruth stole
bread, Spam, cheese and tomatoes, a bottle of mayon-
naise, and a carton of milk.

These provisions did not keep her going long, but
then it was not long before she found something else.

The travelers had come off the highway and parked for
the night by a wide stream. In the little wood, the birds
were fluttering and shaking off their final songs. One
edge of the sky was still gold, but dusk was rising.

There were two ancient post office vans, painted
black, and a battered Volkswagen. Thirteen adults, and
four children between the ages of four and ten, had come
out. A couple of the women were cooking on Primus
stoves. They wore, male and female alike, the uniform of
the summer road, bristle-cropped hair, cotton vests, army
trousers, Doc Martens. They had lit a fire, and one man
played the guitar beside it.

Through the shadows into the firelight, Ruth moved,
out of the dusk. With her puffed sleeves and long ebony
tresses, she was like a modern picture-book version of
Snow White. Except for the bruise.

The travelers accepted her coolly. But they let her sit
by the fire without argument. And when she said she was
hungry, they gave her a portion of the Primus cooked
food, nectarine-colored baked beans, and from the black

wok a dollop of crisped oily peppers, tomatoes, lentils, peas, onion and rice. Some wine was opened and of this too they gave Ruth a mugful.

They spoke in university accents, had tattoos on their arms, shoulders, and breasts, done with ink and a pin.

After an hour or so, someone asked Ruth what had happened to her face. Truth had overturned fantasy by then. She told them her father had struck her. This they absorbed, wordless, as if, with her couth voice and tale of generation violence, she had passed some test.

A spot or two of blood on her antique dress they ignored, although, in the days to come, Susie would sell Ruth's dress in a town. By then they had dressed her like themselves. They advised her to cut her hair, it would get dirty. But Ruth managed to wash her hair and her body at the sink in the back of the Volkswagen, which the rest of them used occasionally. They gave her strict privacy for that, as they did each other.

Two of the girls, Susie and Clare, were sleeping with two of the men, Mike and Colin. Only one of the children came of these unions. The others had sprung from earlier attachments. In a way, the children were held in common, as in a wolf pack, although they did not get the care or affection wolves lavish on their young. Ruth had no time for the children at all. The travelers thought her sixteen, but in fact of course she was not even twelve, too close to childhood herself.

They would take turns with the driving. The others sat or lay in the backs of the vans, amid the bedding, buckets, boxes, and bags.

At night, Ruth slept in the back of the "girls' van," with Jane, Pat, and Chloe.

They were vegetarians. They told Ruth how much better this was for the spirit and the bowel, but Ruth missed meat, and now and then they indulged her with ham rolls or fish and chips.

Chloe and Ron had credit cards, and in the towns, where often the travelers were refused service, Chloe and Ron would queue up in the street at cash machines. Conversely sometimes, Peter, Susie, and Mike would take the children and go begging.

Their life was aimless, that was, literally without aims. This was what living was about, they said. Not to join in, become imprisoned by rules and inhibitions. One should simply exist.

Ruth, because she had lawlessly, liberatedly, come to them, and perhaps because, as her injury faded, she looked unusual, they had kept. But she never fitted in with them, her hair in a long plait, her hands without tattoos, her ears unpierced, her shoes too big, her face like porcelain.

At night Allan would play the guitar, or they brought out the radio tape machine. But the music they produced did not appeal to Ruth. She thirsted for Prokofiev, and Beethoven, as she did for the meat.

Ruth contributed nothing, although now and then she joined the begging parties. She bought a skirt and T-shirt in an Oxfam shop. Chloe gave her the money. Ruth had not thought to take anything from Tom Robbins, beyond the makeup kit he had given her. The methods of the travelers taught her what she should have done, as once in the street Roger found a wallet. They shared the money equally between them.

The summer died around them as they traveled up and down the roads. Smoky mornings, trees like bonfires. Frost on the vans, with their scratched painted dragons, and on the loads that were roped to their tops. The clothes altered a fraction. Heavy jumpers, thicker socks, gloves and scarves, for Ruth a dilapidated raincoat. The quarrels began. They were always squabbling, but this was harsher. They quoted Shakespeare and Nietzsche. Susie threw a saucepan.

As the cold shut down, the group began to break up.

Peter and Allan, Mitch, Roger and Tony went off together. Susie and Mike left separately. Then Pat was gone, then Jane. They would be back, apparently, in the spring. The children were abandoned, at least one by its parents, but desertion seemed to make no difference.

Ron and Colin, Clare and Chloe remained. And Ruth. Ron and Chloe became close. Ruth slept alone in the "girls' van," at first with the children. But the children were afraid of Ruth, and in the end they went into the Volkswagen with Chloe and Ron.

The remaining travelers overwintered above a village built of gray stone, under rounded, louring hills that eventually were marbled with snow.

The cottage in which they lived was the summer retreat of Ron's elder brother, who perhaps did not know that they were there. Certainly they treated his furnishings with scant care, and used his electricity generously. There was no central heating, but electric fires were in all the rooms, and in the living rooms they burned wood on the open hearth.

They shopped in the village without problems.

The winter was a confinement. They all grew to hate each other deeply. Initially Clare sided with Colin against Ron and Chloe. Then Chloe and Clare banded together. One early morning, when the snow had begun to melt, Ron drove off in the Volkswagen, leaving Chloe's things in a pile on the cottage floor.

Chloe mourned, and in the end Colin went to bed with her. This caused an ultimate estrangement of which, oddly, Ruth was made the scapegoat.

In the spring, they cast Ruth forth. They had found out from her that she had a friend in Cheltenham. They gave her some money to get there.

Ruth was not sorry to go. But as she walked along the village lane toward the highway, she felt a sense of something left undone.

Emma Watt had lived in Cheltenham, with her

daughter and her daughter's husband. Ruth recalled perfectly the number of the house, and the road. Emma, physically, she recalled less well. Emma had been Ruth's mother, although not in name—"Mommy" was Rachaela. Emma, however, had brought Ruth up, taught her to read, cooked for her, made her world. And then Emma's daughter had wanted Emma. And Emma left Ruth at once. Ruth had been seven.

Ruth was twelve now. Unmarked, her birthday had gone by just before Christmas, when the travelers had been organizing nut roast and carrot cake to celebrate.

Emma would not recognize Ruth. But Ruth, who had forgotten Emma's face, would know Emma at once.

There was a deep animal excitement about going back. Ruth did not analyze it, was not even entirely aware of it.

But on the journey, as she put on her skimpy skirt under the old raincoat in the station lavatory, Ruth remembered she was Scarabae.

On some amorphous level, she had noted what had been wrong in her parting from Chloe and Clare and Colin. The thing she should have done. The thing she could do.

That she had not thereafter found Emma did not count. She could go on looking for her. And she could look anywhere, anywhere at all.

At the tramps' fire, Sedge stirred as Ruth walked past above him. The other two slept.

Sedge got up and stumbled after Ruth.

When she turned, he plucked out the silver cross he still contrived to wear, unknown, about his neck, and jiggled it at her.

Ruth showed her teeth like a cat, and ran away into the darkness.

CHAPTER 12

✣ *DURING THE LONG SUMMER EVENINGS,* the Scarabae still dined after sunset. They would gather beforehand in the white drawing room, in front of the white television, to watch the late news.

Eric came in first; sometimes he had been there most of the afternoon. Then Sasha and Miranda. Now and then Rachaela would join them. Why? The terrible events of the world did not truly penetrate her mind. Powerless, she was uninterested. To be with the Scarabae then, maybe only a courtesy, before dining.

Camillo was absent, with his handmaidens. They had gone on the trike to the Round House.

And the Scarabae women had come out of mourning. Tonight Sasha wore lavender and Miranda indigo. They were new gowns, styled after the 1940s and '50s. Eric wore a correct evening jacket, perhaps from the 1930s.

Rachaela had put on the gray silk dress she had selected from a catalogue, and on her hand the ruby ring they had given her.

An hour before she had been naked in her bathroom, having slept all afternoon.

She had tried not to look at her body, but there was a long mirror opposite the bath, its glass clear with only a little flotation of enamel water lilies. This might be a concession to her fleshly youth, as the windows which opened were the consolation of her waywardness.

The mirror had made her look, and see.

Black fleece of slightly curling hair, from the head and from the groin. Creamy skin without a touch of her proper age. The slim firm body and immaculate breasts of a woman of twenty-five or -six. Beautiful. Yes, she was beautiful. And once, she had felt so—one night. By the sea. With him.

But he was gone, and she was here.

She had dressed quickly and come down, down to the Scarabae and their television, to elude the dark ghost of Adamus in her bedroom, who sometimes, even now, would approach her in dreams. The wound of pleasure, which surely his death should have cauterized, even if the birth of Ruth had not.

Something political was on the TV screen.

"The Prime Minister said today that she . . ."

Michael and Cheta were serving drinks. Miranda drank gin and tonic now, surely that had never been so, before. Sasha took a cerise kir. And Eric had black brandy, as Stephan had done. Michael brought Rachaela a glass of white wine. She noticed its peculiar freshness, an undertaste of apples. She was about to ask Michael its origin, when a dire picture darkened the screen. It was the frame of a burned house.

Not, of course, like the Scarabae house, not remotely. This was the remnant of a terrace dwelling, and it had not, for example, collapsed. Yet the windows gaped in on a rabid, empty blackness.

". . . The latest fire, which also occurred in south-east London, has now definitely been linked to the series of other fires police have been investigating since April of this year. The circumstances surrounding the first of these fires, which took place in Cheltenham, were quickly believed to be suspicious when the remains of a frying pan were found on the floor of the downstairs hall."

A shot of another burned ruin, in a different sort of terrace, with tall pillars now black and smoking. A fireman stood in his battle helmet, smudged and very tired.

"We don't like the look of it at all," he said. Under his chest appeared the caption of his name and rank and an April date. "There was no toxic material in the house, and the fire seems to have started downstairs. Two of the people don't seem to have woken up, and you'd expect they would. The third man looked funny. I mean, he looked odd. You get to know—the way they look. And it wasn't right."

To another angle of this blackened house, the announcer went on in the voice he reserved for ill tidings short of war and famine, "Two similar fires a few days later in the Oxford area alerted police nationwide."

And another view came up, another house, also charred and inimical. Followed by others. All were different and all had been rendered to a dreadful sameness.

The ruins were followed by montages of scenes, happy family groups, confetti weddings, school outings, such jolly, such ordinary occasions, days of roses and daisies the participants had not known would end in this. Names were read out, but they were gone in a flash.

The announcer resumed in his tragedy voice:

"A chain of fires in Oxford, Reading, and Guildford were soon firmly connected to the Cheltenham case. Forensic evidence, where available, revealed that all the victims had died before the fires took hold, of lacerations and punctures to the neck and throat. In the second of the Guildford fires, three small children were among the dead."

More photographs, three little unlived-in masks, like unbought toys.

Another ruin and another fireman, face congested, nearly desperate. "We see some things. But this little kiddy. No, she was already dead. There can't be any doubt. The fire didn't get up to her." Picture and sound were abruptly cut off.

"Two fires in southeast London, the most recent of which took place during Sunday afternoon, are now believed to be the latest of the arson attacks. Four people lost their lives. Names are being withheld until relatives have been informed." The announcer rallied like a warrior. "Police now say they have an important lead."

A police officer appeared, in a suit no one had warned the producer would pixilate, so rainbows zigzagged over the screen.

"A very curious incident was reported at the scene of the latest attack. A young woman left the pet cat with a neighbor just before the fire broke out. A similar event occurred in Guildford. A pet dog was removed from the arsonist's target and placed with an animal shelter. The dog was quite unharmed and has now been found a new home."

The police officer cleared his throat. "The owners weren't so lucky. The important thing is, apparently, in both cases, the animal was rescued by a young woman answering the same description. The animal shelter don't have a record of her, and unfortunately the neighbor who took in the cat, although she had quite a long conversation with the girl, was unable to give a detailed description as she wasn't wearing her glasses. However, we do have a description which matches a Polaroid photograph found in the second south London house."

The rainbows were replaced by a blurred, inadequate picture, its edges unevenly trimmed with black burning.

In the silence, the world hung in space.

Miranda gave a sigh and her glass fell on the white carpet, letting out the bloodless gin.

"The girl is believed to be aged between sixteen and nineteen, is white, with very long black hair worn loose down to her thighs. She is thought to be wearing jeans and a black leather jacket or a black T-shirt. Police say she should not be approached by the public, but anyone seeing her should contact them immediately."

From such a functionless image, no one on earth could know her. But to everyone in the room she was known at once.

Rachaela had turned to ice. Sasha did not move, nor Michael, nor Cheta. Miranda did not move again.

But Eric had stood up.

Eric strode to the white television and lifted it up on his left hand as though it were made of paper.

Eric screamed.

And with his right fist, ringed and old and hard as iron, he smashed in the TV screen, and with it the blurred unrecognizable face of Ruth.

Before midnight, in a large somber van, all the papers came, several with their ink still wet.

Every paper conceivably in London. Presumably. The great stern sheets, the rags, some with colors and some without.

She was there in all of them, somewhere.

She had a name, not the name Emma had chosen for her.

They called her The Vixen. Tally Ho, Hunt The Vixen. The Vixen—has she gone to earth? The Black Vixen, where will she strike next?

It was probably the telephone which brought the newspapers to the Scarabae. Eric standing over it, the wreckage of the TV behind him, pushing at the rest of the instrument with the receiver in his hand, trying to get the operator, as perhaps he had sixty years ago. And then, turning round rigidly: "*Michael.* How do I make this work?" And Michael coming to him and taking the receiver quietly. "It's all right, Mr. Eric. I will dial."

Rachaela had left the room. She had gone up to her apartment and opened wide the windows.

The moon was high and wetted the trees of the common with milky white. The owl hooted in the air.

It was impossible to stay.

Eventually, she went down again.

After the papers came, the Scarabae investigated them. Rachaela too.

Dinner was not served.

Twice more they watched the news, now on a set which Michael had brought up into the room.

Eric did not strike the screen again.

At two in the morning, the dragon trike came roaring up the road. Camillo entered the house with Lou and Tray, and Eric sent Michael out to bring him in.

Camillo walked into the drawing room in his black leathers and his silver adornments, and Lou and Tray stood in the doorway like nymphs.

"My ears," said Camillo, "are full of the beat of enormous musical machines. Drums, guitars, synthesizers, voices."

"Forget them," said Eric. "Ruth is in London."

"Ruth," said Camillo. "Ugh."

Sasha went to him and gave him a paper, the *Independent*, Rachaela thought.

"Read. They call her The Vixen."

"Yes," said Camillo. "For centuries in this English tongue Vixen has implied a wicked woman."

He glanced at the paper, then put it down.

"Cami," said Lou.

"Hush," said Camillo. Then, "Go up to your room."

Lou shrugged and Tray pulled a tiny little face, then they were gone, obedient as golden greyhounds.

Miranda said, softly, "It's horrible."

"No," said Camillo. "It's what we are."

"Liar," said Eric. But his violence had dissipated. "Michael," he said, "I must use the telephone again."

"Yes," said Sasha.

Miranda put her hands to her lips.

Rachaela stood in stasis. What new demonstration of their dominion was to come?

She did not learn. For Michael dialed a long while, and when Eric spoke into the phone, it was in another language.

CHAPTER 13

✤ PAMELA BELLINGHAM FELT RELIEF AND
pleasure when she opened the front door. She
had thought Trevor would forget, again, to call the
agency. And even if he did, they would just go on being
dilatory.

"Mrs. Watt?" asked the girl.

Pamela laughed. "Oh, they always get the name
wrong, don't they. No, actually it's Bellingham, but
Pamela will do. Come in. I saw you with the policeman.
Were you asking the way?"

The girl paused. She looked very self-contained.

"Oh, yes."

Pamela had gone up into the children's playroom;
they were making so much noise, perhaps they had spotted the damn fox again. The house was on a corner, and
looking out beyond the garden wall, Pamela had seen this
young girl with long black hair in conversation with two
uniformed policemen. The dialogue seemed completely
ordinary, and it did not occur to Pamela that the police
might have stopped the girl rather than the other way
about. In any case, a police car suddenly pulled up, and
another uniformed officer jumped out and ran across.
They left the girl abruptly. All three men got into the car
and drove off.

The girl did not appear either surprised or annoyed,

although Pamela, in her situation, would have been decidedly irritated.

Then the girl came in through the gate, and Pamela realized that Trevor had got on to the agency at last, dealt with everything, and they had sent the au pair.

She was certainly easier on the eye than the previous one.

Pamela buzzed her through the hall into the kitchen.

"Would you like a coffee? As you can see, we've got most of the gadgets, it shouldn't be too awful for you. Washing machine there, dishwasher, microwave. We'll have a drink and I'll take you over the house. It is honestly just light work—making the beds, a bit of dusting, Hoover once a week or if Trev's got someone coming. Help me with a dinner party now and then. And, of course, the brats. They did tell you about the brats, didn't they? The last girl didn't realize we had two. It was a bit of a shock." This girl nodded, obliquely.

"They're super kids. Really bright. But they are a handful sometimes. Dominic goes to school usually, but it's one of their holidays. Violet's only three. And what's your name?"

"Ruth."

"Mm, lovely. Biblical. I like the old names. That's why I chose Violet. I try to dress her in violet, too. Did they tell you about us at all?"

"No," said Ruth. "They didn't tell me anything much."

"Your English is awfully good," gushed Pamela, preparing weak instant coffee. She wondered to what ethnic group Ruth belonged. Probably Slavic, although there was a delicacy, a small-boned, fragile endurance that reminded her only of the Chinese.

When the kettle had boiled and hot water had gone into the cups, Pamela put them on a big pine table with a bowl of sugar and a carton of single cream. Feeling expansive Pamela also brought the biscuit barrel, which was formed like a pig, and contained the luxury biscuits with apple, raisins, and icing sugar.

"Help yourself. I feel we're going to get along fine. I'm an artist, that's why I need some help in the house. I work full-time at home. Book jackets mostly. I'm working on something at the moment. Absolutely dreadful, some fantasy book. But I always do my best, even when I don't like the material. That's one thing I have to make plain. When I'm in my studio, I'm afraid it's a no-go area. I mustn't be disturbed. Unless something dire happens with the brats."

Pamela noticed that Ruth had taken her sixth biscuit. She might have to be firm, there. It would be a shame for Ruth to spoil her lovely figure.

Pamela sighed inwardly. She had been eight stone when she and Trevor got married. But after the children she had put on weight. Of course, her shape was still all right, but she was three stone heavier. Ruth made her feel it, although Pamela did not acknowledge this. She shut the stomach of the pig and stood up.

"Well, I expect you'd like to see what you're in for. Bring your coffee."

"I've finished it, thank you."

The tour of the house was quite brief. Pamela would walk into a room, wave her arms artistically so her large breasts gesticulated in her cotton shirt, and then lead Ruth out again. Downstairs was a brown room with two large modern paintings, Trev's "study," which was done in beige with a poster of Corfu, and a small dining room with a chandelier and orange walls.

Upstairs on the second floor were the bedrooms and two bathrooms, one black and white with sepia photographs, and one yolk yellow, with a red abstract, and Pamela's studio, a large chamber in vermilion. On the vermilion were the large framed paintings Pamela had done for particularly successful books, and framed letters from authors and publishers thanking her. On an easel was an unfinished oil of mountains, towers, a girl and a winged horse. On several tables lay tubes of paint and brushes, bottles of turps, rags, various implements.

When they reached the third floor, there was a very small room which had been varnished purple. This was apparently to be Ruth's.

"I can't stand all that pink and chintz," said Pamela.

There was also a small bathroom. Across the landing were the children's bedrooms, and next door, their playroom. Quite an amount of noise was still coming from here.

"Isn't it ghastly," said Pamela, with a strange pride, "so much energy. We put them up here out of the way. Trev says we should fit them with silencers."

She opened the door. The room was white, and all over the walls were the drawings Pamela had encouraged her children to make, so the immediate effect was one of dangerous lunacy.

Violet was sitting in her violet frock and mauve tights on the carpet. She was holding her doll, whose head had just been pulled off by Dominic. Her expression was of surgical interest, interrupted.

Dominic was hiding behind the door. He burst out on his mother with a yell. She caught him laughing and held him off.

"Now don't be naughty, darling. Look who I've brought up to see you. This is Ruth."

"Wooth," said Violet. She widened her eyes, and dropped her headless doll. Standing up, she raised her skirt. "Ook. I've dot villip panties." She had.

Dominic pointed at the violet panties. *"Rude."*

Violet came slowly and determinedly across the floor to Ruth, staring at her. "Do you wand teer my song?"

Pamela said, "Not just yet, darling. You can sing to Ruth in a minute."

Dominic shouted, with great force, "Ruth! Bloody old Ruth!"

"Darling!" cried Pamela. "They pick up this swearing," she added. "Now you mustn't say things like that."

"Bloody!" shouted Dominic. He beamed at his mother. "Bloody old Ruth!"

Pamela ignored him. Violet had gripped Ruth's hand.

"Luff, luff medoo," sang Violet on one note.

"She likes the Beatles," said Pamela.

"Luff, luff medoo," sang Violet. "Luff, luff—"

"Actually," said Pamela, "Ruth, do you think you could hold the fort here for a minute? There's a phone call I should have made . . ." She backed into the doorway and Dominic said, "Bloody phone." "Now, Dominic, I've told you not to use that word." Pamela was gone.

Dominic looked up at Ruth.

"Who the hell are you?"

Ruth did not answer.

Violet said, "She's the opar." She seemed to be making a concentrated effort to speak in an odd, cute way.

"She's ugly," said Dominic, "and she's stinky. Stinky Ruth."

Ruth looked down at Dominic.

Dominic held her gaze for perhaps ten seconds and gradually his own flattened out. Then he turned away and punched Violet briskly on the arm. Violet fell at Ruth's feet. "He hid me." She took hold of Ruth's leg. "I wan Mommy. Mommy pud me terbed. I wan my doll. My doll's called Penny she's god real hairan she widdles bud he pulled haheadov."

Dominic went to the window and Violet sobbed but without tears, looking up to see if Ruth would respond. Ruth did not respond.

At the window Dominic tensed.

"There it is." He glanced at Ruth. "It's a fox. Mommy says the council men will come and poison it."

Violet said, "Smelly old fogs. It goes in the dudspin."

"Mommy put out some poison," said Dominic, "but the old fox didn't eat it."

"Kill the fogs," said Violet.

Ruth walked over to the window and Violet let go of her jeans perforce and sprawled on the floor.

Dominic had eased open the window and was leaning out.

Like a premature autumn leaf, the fox was in the garden. It had jumped catlike over the wall, and now doglike it nosed about a tub of geraniums. Its tail had a white blaze. It was young and whole, vital and mysterious. Dominic went over to a child-sized chair and raised the seat. He took out a catapult and some small sharp stones.

"Mommy says," said Violet, "you musson have a cadapull."

"Be quiet or I'll kick you. I'm going to hit the fox."

"Hid it," said Violet. "Hid it in the eye."

She too came to the window. Violet and Dominic stood there, he in his Lilliputian trousers and shirt and she in her violet clothes, and the little boy took aim with his catapult, and the little girl squeaked excitedly, so he had to tell her again to be quiet.

The catapult was homemade from a strong twig and a strong elastic band. As the elastic tautened, Ruth leaned across and drew it further back, past the child's ear, so the band snapped. The whiplash caught Dominic on the cheek and he yelped with pain and amazement.

Violet screamed and Ruth slapped her face.

There was, finally, true silence.

And out on the lawn the fox, perhaps sensing some feral current more intense than poison and stones, sprang away over the fence and into the adjoining row of gardens.

"I'll tell Mommy," said Dominic, "what you did."

"And I'll tell my father," said Ruth, "about you. My father only comes out at night. He's tall and pale and his eyes glow in the dark. He's dead. He can do anything. He can walk up walls. He'll walk up this one. He'll break the window without a sound. He'll come in and drink your blood."

Both children stared now. Violet whimpered, and was motionless. Tremulously Dominic said, "You're a bloody old liar."

"Wait and see," said Ruth.

Dominic said nothing more.

A minute later, Ruth came out of the playroom and went down to the second floor. She could hear Pamela talking animatedly on the phone in the first floor hall.

Ruth went into the studio. She passed the gaudy, unmagical canvas of mountains and winged horse. She unerringly went to one of the tables where, bright as silver, a scalpel blade lay shining like a star.

Trevor Bellingham worried all the way home, about how Pamela would go on. He had forgotten to keep after the agency and probably that would mean another week without an au pair. They never stayed anyway, daunted by the stacks of boring domestic chores Pamela left them, the snack meals, the troublesome children . . .

Trevor worried all through the late-afternoon traffic, which presently became complicated by fire engines.

Then he reached his street and could not get through.

Standing irate by his car, he soon discovered that his chore-filled house, Pamela, Dominic and Violet, had all ceased to be a worry.

CHAPTER 14

✤ *A DAY LATER, THE IVORY TELEPHONE*
rang. The notes of it passed through the house
like awls.

Presumably it called in answer to the use Eric and
Michael had made of it. Presumably one of them lifted
the receiver and spoke.

Rachaela did not go to see. She did not ask.

And a day after that, two days after the Scarabae
had used their telephone, Malach came.

The sunset had been hot and threatening, fires,
blood. The Scarabae kept to their rooms, and if they
watched the news there Rachaela did not know. From the
upper apartment leaked the dim organ wash of Camillo's
new music, but perhaps only Lou or Tray was playing it.

After the sunset came the night.

Rachaela sat in her window, and watched the common alter. It became a stage set for *Swan Lake*, which
once she had seen danced. The great trees were stroked
with platinum by the early moon. Only the lake was miss-
ing; instead the clearing, the glade, lay down the slope
where by day dogs were walked and bicycles wheeled.
Camillo had come from this direction, northwest.

A swan did not fly over to alight upon the lake of
glade.

It was a helicopter.

The stammering drone of it pressed up over the house, growing too large, as the noise of Camillo's trike had done.

Then the peeled lights tore down. The moon was eclipsed.

Without complications, a preposterous insect, the helicopter landed in the glade.

The wind from its aerial blades poured back against the house. Rachaela felt it on her face, a dry chemical simoom.

She stood up.

A tracery of colored streaks still glimmered on the slope, reflections of the windows of the house. Michael moved out among them, and went down toward the powerhouse of the helicopter. The wind pushed at him, but he moved upright and unwavering.

She imagined all the Scarabae, all that were left, up at their lit casements, watching. Eric, Sasha, and Miranda. Perhaps Cheta. And herself.

The lights of the helicopter glared between the trees, and the blades rotated. Then it was lifted again, straight up, over the pines into the night. And was gone.

The moon came back.

They moved out from the glade between the trees. Four figures. There were two men, Michael and another, carrying four dark bags. And then two more, fantastic.

Black and white.

Rachaela thought, *Camillo again.*

But this was not Camillo.

He was tall, straight as a creature of black iron, and the moon found out the pale angles of face and hands, and the ghost-shadows of two whitish dogs that padded up the slope ahead of him. They wore black collars with silver spikes, and went unleashed, not looking back, not straying, warrior dogs marching to a drum. The drum must beat in his brain, to hold them like that.

Adamus . . .

Not Adamus, either.

As he passed between the trees, the moon took, and became, his hair. It was a mane that fell to his waist. It was white as a nuclear explosion, the blind white of a thousand suns.

Behind him walked, nonchalantly, a black-haired woman in a black velvet coat. Not Lou, nor Tray. She was not a handmaiden, so much was obvious. Nearly as tall as he, striding on her high and inky heels.

They were thirty feet from the house when the owl cried in the oak.

The man with white hair checked, and at his back the black-haired woman halted.

He answered the owl, softly and persuasively. His mimicry was passionlessly exact. Then he raised his arm.

The owl floated from the tree top like a demon on silken sails. It came to him, and settled on his wrist, a falcon.

This scene burned through Rachaela's eyes like hurt or fire. It was so curious, so beautiful, so bizarre, unsuitable and marvelous.

For perhaps one minute he stood there, the white-haired man, the owl resting on him, its wings outspread. Then it lifted up, as the helicopter had done, and soared away into the common woods.

He laughed. She heard him. It was an arid sound.

One of the dogs barked. He spoke then.

"Quiet, Oskar. You are not yet introduced."

His voice was musical, as the voice of Adamus had been, yet not the same. This voice was the color of a white spirit, some brandy distilled in the dark. It had too the faintest trace of accent, or maybe only a different rhythm.

As they moved into the reflections of the windows, he glanced up and noticed her, but that was all. She could not see him well for shadow and shine. The woman, however, smiled, raising her face which caught a pane of daffodil light. She was beautiful, extraordinary. They walked around the wall.

Then the house received them.

Rachaela came down the stairs, and, rather to her surprise, Miranda was coming down after her. They stood together on the third step up, and through the open door, out of the night, Michael had come, and the other man, carrying the bags.

Sasha and Eric were already in the hall, and Cheta, to one side.

The great rosy oil lamps, which were also lighted at the same time as the electricity, fluttered against the pillars like pink moths.

The woman entered first. Her beauty was astonishing, for it improved with proximity. Her black hair was like Rachaela's, very long and slightly curling. She was very tall, perhaps six foot in her high heels.

She stood aside like a royal herald, and the man came in with the two dogs.

"Malach," said Eric.

"Eric," said the man. He came forward and held out his hand. Eric clasped it. They stayed quite still, looking at each other.

The man was tall and spare, as Rachaela had already seen, and framed in the flood of wintry hair his face was that of an adventurer, a commander, one who fought. High cheekbones and thin muscular jaw, nose aquiline but not thin, lips inclined to refinement but perhaps of cruelty. The eyes were the pale blue of aquamarines. Not black. She had expected black, like those of the Scarabae. (But then, her own eyes were pale.)

On his left hand were four large rings of tarnished silver. He took his right hand from Eric's as Eric let him go. Turning to Sasha, this man called Malach raised her fingers and brushed them with his mouth. He indicated the woman gracefully. "Althene." And then the man who stood with Michael. "Kei." And lastly the two dogs. "Oskar, Enki." He added, "The dogs behave well in the house. I shouldn't have brought them otherwise."

"Enki howled in the helicopter," said the woman, Althene. She had a deep voice, velvet like the coat. Also the trace of accent.

"Yes. Enki howled." Malach ruffled the head of the paler dog. Both were albinos, wolfhounds tinted by a strain of something else, and both vast as lions, with long curved tails and oddly bluish amber eyes.

"You are all welcome," said Eric.

"And the dogs," said Sasha. She smiled. "We've missed animals."

Miranda took Rachaela's arm and drew her down the stairs. Rachaela had not expected this. It was a medieval scene, or something from a Renaissance film. She was led to Malach by Miranda in the lamplight.

"Miranda," said Malach. He kissed Miranda's hand lightly, courteously. Rachaela looked up at him, steeling herself. But when his blue eyes came to her, she flinched.

"This is Rachaela, the daughter of Adamus."

"Yes," he said. "And the mother of Ruth."

"And who are you?" said Rachaela.

He did not take her hand.

"Malach. Didn't you listen?"

"You're Scarabae."

"Of course," he said. "All of us. Why else are we here?"

"And why *are* you here?"

"Rachaela," said Eric, "this isn't the time for questions. It has been a long journey, over the sea."

"You told me," Rachaela said, "*they* told me. You're all the Scarabae there were. The last."

"We are the last," said Eric, "here."

"Rachaela is confused," said Malach. "I—we—are Scarabae of another branch. Still Scarabae."

Out of the lamplight, Althene said smoothly, "There are many Scarabae."

"And in necessity," said Sasha, "where else should we turn?"

Rachaela moved back a step. She was afraid of Malach. Was it the same fear she had felt of Adamus, terror of male beauty and power, the dominance of a man and all it implied, the pitfall, the trap?

But Malach was also frightening in another way. Adamus had been a priest, but Malach was a warrior.

Rachaela stood aside, and let them all move on into the gold and white drawing room from which the broken television had been removed. The dogs followed decorously.

Michael and Cheta and the new one, Kei, were serving drinks, cups of greeting. Kei set down a large water bowl into which he poured a measure from a tankard of beer. The dogs went to it and began to drink loudly and couthly. Kei took the tankard next to Malach.

Malach wore black. Black trousers inside black boots, a black shirt and long black coat.

But Althene took off her velvet wrap to reveal a dress folded about her like two leaves against a stem, the color of green Han jade. Her pale throat was bare and her long fingers, but on her left wrist was a huge sunflower of dull antique gold held on a golden band. Her oval nails were painted the same shade. Her face was exquisitely made up, her black eyes in a coffee mask, lips tawny, the hint of tawny blusher on her cheeks. Her lashes were long as those of a leopardess.

Rachaela stood in the doorway like a bad child who had crept down to spy on the grown-ups.

Cheta brought her a goblet of wine and she took it uneasily.

They were Scarabae. The Scarabae were everywhere.

They had no look of dust, cobwebs, but in fact Eric,

Sasha, and Miranda had greatly lost that look. Even the man Kei was firm and soldierly, an adjutant to Malach's captain. Like the incredible Althene he too had the black Scarabae eyes.

But Malach was a rogue. His blood, like hers, Rachaela's, must be mixed.

They had lost their champion, Adamus. They had had to borrow a new knight from another board. But it was still chess.

"Michael and Cheta will take you up to your rooms. We hope you'll be comfortable." Eric paused. He said, "Camillo . . ."

"Isn't here," said Malach. He tilted back his white head and his hair brushed his thighs. "Upstairs hiding?"

Miranda said, "Camillo is changing, like a butterfly."

"At last," said Malach. His chiseled, cruel mouth curled a moment, then relaxed. "You were used to call him Uncle."

Eric shook his head. "If you prefer—"

"Let's be young," said Malach. "You are Eric. Let him be Camillo."

Malach's was the face of a man of thirty-eight or thirty-nine. If he was a Scarabae that would probably mean that he was a hundred years old, or older. If one believed their stories.

Althene crossed her legs. Her short black boots were embroidered with jade green and golden flowers. Above showed a sheer stocking with a seam of charcoal black.

Was she Malach's? She did not seem to belong to him, and surely women would be his belongings, not his companions.

Rachaela put down her unfinished wine.

"You're here because of Ruth."

Miranda said, "It's all right, Rachaela."

"We couldn't contain her," said Rachaela. She made herself look at Malach. "White knight to take black queen."

"A traditional move," said Eric.

Malach did not answer. The two dogs, having drunk their tipple, had come to him and were leaning their large lion heads on his side.

Althene said, "What does Rachaela fear?"

"Nothing," Rachaela said harshly. "I warned them in the beginning. Ruth is a demon."

"But you don't believe in demons," said Althene.

Her black eyes had a different power. It was there nevertheless.

Rachaela looked away. "I've never believed any of it, yet I'm caught up in it."

Sasha said, "Don't be afraid, Rachaela."

Rachaela shut her mouth tightly. It would be unwise to argue. She had never been able to talk to any of them. The conversations were carried on on a plane that had to do with psychology and the spirit, bypassing conscious feeling and need. It was happening again.

What did Ruth matter?

Demon child. Black queen.

Let Malach hunt her, out in the checkered forests of London's day and night.

In her room Rachaela put on a symphony by Shostakovich, but it had too much eerie strength. She was becoming nervous of classical music, which opened so many mental doors unbidden.

Instead she switched on her television. The newscaster was speaking of a riot somewhere, and she watched with a calming sense of detachment.

The house was now curiously full.

It had been injected with new blood. The wiring sang.

Why did Camillo conceal himself, or did he?

Rachaela took off her clothes. She sat naked in a chair, brushing her hair before the blind mirror of the television.

". . . body, which was discovered in woods near the sight of the fire, is thought to be of the young woman police have been trying to trace. The girl, aged between sixteen and nineteen, was found in bracken by two cyclists. She is thought to have died during the night."

A man appeared in a blank brown suit. Someone must have told him about the pixilation of his previous garment.

"Yes, we're pretty certain this is The Vixen. No, there were no signs of violence. It seems likely she took her own life."

Rachaela's vision and hearing apparently fused with darkness, or else time jumped. Suddenly the screen was full of another event. The Vixen and her death were gone.

In a wood. Ruth . . . a suicide under the trees.

No. It was not true. No.

The telephone . . . the telephone and the helicopter. *Malach had come.* Somehow, *somehow* the media and the law had been deflected. The Scarabae—cared for their own.

CHAPTER 15

✤ *UNDER THE TREES LAY A HOT UNBREATH-*
ing shadow. The day was stormy, the sky a dense
blue-gray against which the green of the leaves became
an acid lime. The graveyard stretched a long way, broken
now and then by upflung angels and the dark lines of
conifers. Already a few cones had fallen from the chestnuts, perfect as artifacts. Flowers stood in vases dying on
the graves, a death for a death.

She had come across a fallen angel, brought down by
a gale and never tidied. Tall grass had grown up about
her and through her wings, which were broken.

Ruth studied the angel, the picture of the graves meandering away like dragon's teeth sown in a lawn.

Then the man and woman came and sat down on the
bench just beyond the chestnuts. They had not seen her.
They did not speak for ten minutes.

"I know why you do it," he said eventually. It was a
tense, low, furious voice.

"You don't. You think you do."

"I *do* know. Don't you tell me what I know."

"You imagine things."

The man grabbed and pulled on the woman's arm
and she gave a soft cry of pain.

"I said, don't tell me what I think."

He was thickset and not tall, with thinning hair and a

good-looking, tanned face. She was tanned not at all. She wore lipstick and dark glasses, two pieces of a disguise. She twisted her hands, then rubbed her arm where he had hurt her.

"Can't you leave me alone, Richard, I'm not doing anything. I just like to make a bit of money for myself."

"You don't need it. I can give you money. God, you get enough out of me."

"You want to eat, don't you?" she said.

"How many women can say they don't have to work? You don't need to. I make enough. You're sitting pretty."

"*Pretty,*" she said, with a peculiar emphasis.

"Yes, *pretty.* But you want to be pretty for him, don't you?"

"*Him.* What *him*? You're crazy."

He hit her, lightly, a tap to the side of the face that swung her head around and dislodged the dark glasses.

Ruth could plainly see the woman had a black eye.

The woman put back the glasses. She said, desperately, "I just want a bit of money for myself."

"Yes," he said, "so you can run out on me."

"I wouldn't—"

"No, you won't. Because if you ever try it, I'll find you. I'll find the pair of you. It won't be just your eye then, Linda. I'll take him out. And I'll put you in a wheelchair."

Then the silence fell again. It was like the shadow of the coming storm, the pause before the thunder.

She said, quietly, "All right. I'm sorry. I'll—I'll give in my notice. I'll do it tonight."

"Yes," he said.

"I'll have to work out the week."

"No."

"Of course I will. Be reasonable, Richard . . ." She hesitated but now he did not strike. "Just the week. Then I'll be home. We can—we'll try and make a go of it."

"We have to," he said. Then he had seized her again,

this time into his arms. A scent boiled from the bench, Lentheric for men, and an undernote, like burning insulation. "You're all I've got, Linda. My Linda. I don't mean to hurt you. You know you're everything to me."

Presently they got up. They began to walk slowly together, like sick people released from a hospital, along the path beneath the chestnuts.

Ruth followed.

The house was in a walled park, one of several, all alike. Fudge walls and a bright red roof. Through the leaded windows showed lacy curtains, a vase of flowers like the graveyard. The garden was tiny, just room enough for a barbecue and chairs.

After they had gone in, instinct made Ruth wait.

Above, the curtains in the bedroom were drawn.

Half an hour after this, a light came on in one of the downstairs rooms. It was very dark, the storm was near.

Ruth went to the door. There was an ornate knocker, no bell. Ruth knocked.

The woman, Linda, came to the door in a housecoat. She had put on her glasses again.

"Mrs. Watt?"

"Our name's Reeves. There used to be a Watt—number six, I think."

"No. This is the house."

"It can't be, I'm afraid. They all look the same, these houses."

"I've come into London. I've come a long way."

"You poor thing." Linda Reeves was flustered and contrite. "I'd ask you in, but I'm in a rush. I have an evening job, you see. And Richard. He's very busy."

Silence.

The storm gathered like a silent churning cloud.

"Can I use your phone, please?" asked Ruth.

"Oh, God, the phone. No—I'm sorry. It's broken. Richard—that is, we had an accident."

A wind passed over the garden, the wings of angels, Semitic, hot and stifling, and the little trees in the little gardens bent before it.

"Can I come in?" said Ruth.

Linda Reeves put her hand to her mouth.

"I can't—I daren't. My husband's—he's not very well."

Ruth stood below the door, the passing of the wind lifting a halo of her hair, like fragile wings.

"I've come a long way."

"I'm sorry. I'm really—I'm sorry."

Linda Reeves shut the door of the fudge house abruptly.

Ruth stood outside.

Upstairs she heard him shout.

"What are you doing?"

And the woman shouted back, "Oh *hell*, for Christ's sake—"

"Don't use that language!" he shouted. "I've told you—"

And through the walls of the house, one breeze-block thick, Ruth heard Richard Reeves descend. She heard him come into the living room and through the lace, in the lamplight, she saw him smash Linda Reeves across the face so she fell to the wall-to-wall carpet.

"Don't ever do that."

"I'm—sorry, Richard."

Far off, the thunder murmured.

Ruth knocked again.

But no one came and the door stayed shut.

CHAPTER 16

✤ *UP THROUGH THE EARTH WALKED THE*
white-haired man. It was early in the afternoon,
and the intestines of the tube had their usual smell of the
inside of a Hoover. .

A sparse crowd came and went. And through the
warm plastic air, unsuitably heavenly, ribboned the ca-
dences of a violin.

At the elbow of a tunnel, the violinist appeared. A
young girl playing, as if alone with the instrument and her
soul.

The crowd trotted robotically by and vanished.

Malach stopped to listen.

If the girl was aware of him, she did not show it. The
crowd had been aware and had stared at him, sometimes
turning a head over a shoulder.

The violin played Paganini, cunningly adapted.

After perhaps a minute, Malach tossed a coin into
the biscuit tin.

Apparently lost in her dream, the violinist inwardly
cursed him.

What had rung against the ten- and twenty-pence
pieces was plainly a foreign coin, little, thin and yellow.
Worthless. Later she would take it out and puzzle briefly
over the vague equestrian figure, before throwing the
coin away. Her forte was music.

It was true the coin was foreign. A French gold franc of the early fifteenth century.

Malach went up out of the tube station into the intensity of the late-summer afternoon. The sky was heavy, and thunder was muttering like distant cannon. A light that resembled rain, drily wet, hung on the street. Cars pushed through, and tall red buses. To every era, its panoply.

On the pavement a child eating an ice cream gazed up at Malach a mile above. Malach observed the child. It was old, imprisoned in the immature body and clearly uncomfortable. He touched its head as he passed, weightlessly, with one finger.

At the bus stop two young women saw Malach and giggled secretly. When a bus came, he got on to it.

It carried him slowly and bumpily across London, through a sea of stares.

The lines of streets curved and twisted, ebbed and flowed.

Sometimes girls walked along them, some with black hair.

He watched from the windows of red buses, with eyes like river-washed stones.

At a quarter past six, The Cockerel had already filled with young men in sharp gray suits and creamy shoes. The three fruit machines flashed, reflecting on the lagers and the gin and tonics, diver's watches, gold signet rings.

The door opened and otherness walked through, slow and still.

"Here, Kev. Look at this."

They looked, laughing, nudging each other.

At home, the obedient lacquered mothers waited with low-burning oven dinners and speedy microwaves. The girlfriends were in their showers, preparing themselves for brown smooth hands loaded by watches and rings. Outside were the paper-cutout cars, glittering in the sun, the perfect hot English summer a ruined ozone layer had allowed.

And here was this, this misfit. Something from the night. Dusty black, pale unred tan, blizzard hair.

Kev's hair was very short, half an inch. In his right ear was the hole the earring had once made before he left off wearing it. He would tell people now he got the aperture in a fight.

Kevin watched the outcast come up to the bar.

"I don't think much of your one," said Den. "She's too tall." Den was pleased by his wit and his glasses shone.

"Shhh," said Kev, "I want to hear what it drinks. Malibu and orange? Bristol Cream?"

The outcast spoke softly to the barman.

"What did he say?"

"Beer, he drinks beer."

"Nah, he's going to wash his hair in it."

They waited, as the white-haired man waited. His back was turned to them, which intuitively they took for a sign of weakness.

"I wonder where he gets it styled," said Ray.

"He don't style it, just puts fertilizer on it, make it grow."

They laughed, and the white-haired man turned. He faced them, smiling. He had the beer now, which he raised.

"Proost."

"Oh, he ain't English."

"He don't know what we've been saying."

"Here, matey, where you from?"

"Bloody German."

"Nah, they look like pigs, Den."

"Yes, he looks more like a rat."

The slow riverine eyes went over them. The smile did not lessen.

Malach dipped one finger in his beer. They watched, fascinated.

Malach drew a circle around the rim of his glass. A faint silver note came from it, irritating to the ear as tinnitus.

"Do you think it's some sexual gesture?" Kev asked Ray.

"Maybe he fancies Den."

"Take off your glasses, Den, and give him a kish."

The note on the beer glass became suddenly shrill and unbearable. Across the bar a few heads turned.

Malach removed his finger from the glass. It went on singing. He lifted the beer to his lips.

And Kev's gin tumbler broke into fragments, showering on the floor. The gin and tonic splashed across his pink shirt. Kev yelled. He had gone white. Blood dripped on his diver's watch, which he had not noticed yet had stopped.

"Christ," said Den. "Oh Christ, my glasses—" He pulled them off and one of the lenses cracked in half and fell out onto the ground. He went down on his hands and knees on the lary carpet, stupidly trying to find the two bits.

Ray backed off. He put his drink on the table. "All right, mate," he called out at Malach. Then he turned and walked quickly into the street.

Malach shrugged.

The glass had stopped singing and he drained it.

A few people watched curiously, not understanding what had happened.

Kev said, "Very clever, smart-arse."

Malach leaned forward. He caught Kev's face in his long hand with the tarnished rings. Kev's whiteness went to green.

"Tot ziens," Malach said, and Kev wet himself.

Outside on the pavement Ray was not in sight. An

old woman came past, stepping carefully over Malach's shadow.

The sun was a methyl orange star in the western sector of the sky. The storm had not broken.

CHAPTER 17

✤ GRADUALLY THE TERRACE WAS LOSING
the sun. A cool breeze riffled through the garden
trees, and Lou and Tray had goldenly sat up. Althene,
beneath her sunshade, continued with her book.

Earlier in the afternoon, Althene had disturbed Lou,
and particularly Tray, by hanging up on the sunny wall a
gas mask in which grew a clump of yellow and red poppies.

"That's really gross," said Lou. Tray cowered in her
chair, going "Ugh, ooh," as though cold slimy things
crawled over her.

"Not at all," said Althene. She towered above them
on her long legs, most of which a slit in her Mocha skirt
revealed. "A symbol of peace. After the gas, bayonets
and bombs, the battlefield is covered by flowers."

Later Lou said, "I saw a ring shaped like a gas
mask."

During the afternoon Lou and Tray went on toasting
themselves, turning to the sun like sunflowers and pulling
their chairs about the terrace.

Althene, pale as a lily, read under her sunshade.

Rachaela watched from the shadow below, where
the trees massed thickly.

The Scarabae had vanished. That was, the first

Scarabae. Only this specimen of the new Scarabae, Althene, remained, imperturbable.

In the morning, about four, the man Kei had gone to Covent Garden. He returned at seven in a car, with meat and vegetables. In the kitchen, a roll of knives and other culinary utensils lay above the sacred mangle. Cheta and Michael deferred to Kei in matters of cuisine. That was his function.

And Malach was the hunter. He was gone. A fiery tension left the house when he was not in it.

But Althene, if she was not Malach's, what was her role?

The book was an English novel. The sunshade was turquoise.

Now and then Althene would glance across the garden and Rachaela would pretend an interest in her own book. But she had lost the habit of reading, and having chosen the volume at random from the library in the London village, it did not hold her. It was only an excuse.

Once there had been a rumble of thunder, but it was a planet away.

Althene mesmerized Rachaela. Not her glamour, which was overwhelming, but some terrible quality of serenity and precision. It had awoken Rachaela to an uncomfortable interest. All these months with the family, indeed, had done so. She did not know now what she felt about Ruth. Perhaps, like the Scarabae—the former Scarabae—she wanted only to put Ruth from her mind and let others see to it. Would the apparition of Malach find Ruth? If so, in what capacity? Was Ruth the vampire and he the vampire hunter? Or was he the predator and Ruth the victim? An innocent white-skinned maiden—who killed.

She thought of Eric smashing in the face of the TV screen, the face of Ruth.

There were no answers, only interminable questions.

The breeze moved over the garden again, and Lou

and Tray twittered like sparrows. They would go in in a minute, perhaps searching for Camillo, who also had disappeared.

They had seen Malach that morning.

Rachaela had noted them holding their breath as they stared at him from the dining room, where sometimes, about eleven o'clock, they drank orange juice or Fanta.

If Camillo was the film director, what was Malach in their scheme of things?

The two wolfhounds had been exercised on the common by Kei, and then they too had gone away, perhaps to the kitchen to consort with him.

Some kind of delivery had also come. Clothes, seemingly, for Althene. Perhaps this dark brown garment, clinging to the slim, flat-bellied form, the narrow buttocks, and high, quivering breasts.

Rachaela studied Althene and her body as she descended into the garden.

"How wise to sit beneath the tree," Althene said, standing over her. "Those two awful little girls with their cooked skin. In ten years they will be withered as raisins, but not so appetizing."

Rachaela said, "At least, you come out by day."

"Oh, yes. That is their age, Eric and Sasha and Miranda. To be afraid of sunlight."

"One of them was consumed by it."

"Really?" said Althene, dispassionate. "Who?"

"Miriam."

"You mean, she caught fire?"

Rachaela said coldly, "No, that's too dramatic, isn't it? I mean she couldn't stand the sun. She fell down and then she died."

"Or perhaps it was the shock of the house burning. And of the deaths of the others."

"Are you like them?" said Rachaela.

"Yes. No."

"And you like word games, too."

"All sorts of games," said Althene.

"I mean, do you claim to have lived hundreds of years? Do you drink blood? You, and Malach."

"That is," said Althene, "a personal question. Intrusive. Do you mean to offend? What's your purpose?"

"They evade questions. They wriggle around them."

"To the family, sometimes, the question of blood, being to do with lovemaking, is considered—impolite."

"But you're young and liberated. What are you? Thirty? That makes you anything from forty-five to ninety-five, I suppose."

Althene sat down on the grass in her Mocha skirt. The grass was dry and seemed to receive her with the promise not to taint or stain. She had that casualness they can afford, those to whom the world molds itself obligingly.

"Let's say," said Althene, "I'm a little older than you. Just a very little. As I am a little taller."

Rachaela felt herself blush, mildly, almost coolly.

She thought: *Another corruption. One more inch toward the Scarabae.*

She said: "And the blood, Althene?"

"No," Althene said. She smiled. Her teeth were white, well set, even. But Ruth's had been like that.

"And Malach?"

"Is it Malach who intrigues you?"

"Malach is hunting my daughter."

"Your daughter. They told me, you didn't want the child. She was imposed on you."

"Yes." Rachaela let her hands fall on the book.

"This must take its course," said Althene. She turned her head. Her face was flawless as the still of some film star of 1915. Translucent white, her skin seemed bloodless as that of a pale, young, wondrous child. Like . . . Ruth's. But Althene was not like Ruth. The coiling of her hair, her brilliant eyes with their azure outer rings recalling those of an Indian woman. Today her lips were coffee as her eyeshadow and her skirt.

"What am I expected to feel?" said Rachaela.

"I wonder," said Althene. And then, "Did you have a wicked stepmother who never let you have emotions?"

"I had a wicked, pathetic mother, ditto."

"Ah."

"My father was Ruth's father."

"I know," said Althene. Her deep hushed voice was restful as the fur of a cat.

"My mother was used and abandoned. With me. She tried to—regiment me. Whatever I liked was wrong. Of course, I didn't have a father. And then, thirty years after, I found Adamus, playing Prokofiev, looking no older than I did."

"Adamus was spent," said Althene.

"I've been made to feel," said Rachaela, "that I helped drive him down into the abyss. That I helped to make Ruth into a monster."

"And who made you feel this?"

"I," Rachaela said. "I have."

"The family thrives on guilt."

"Scarabae," said Rachaela.

"Scarabae."

Up on the terrace the two girls were picking up their toys of nail varnish and magazines, and going into the house.

"Poor little things," said Althene. "Like pretty little flies. They'll break like sugar."

Rachaela saw a wing of darkness on the garden. It was the westering sun, nothing more. But she said, "What the family touches is spoiled."

"Then the family must remain incestuous. It's safer."

"Don't," said Rachaela. "Don't try to push me toward Malach."

"Malach?" Althene laughed. Gold brushed her now,

she was like a statue that had been given true life. "Malach is for Ruth. Are you sorry?"

"I know how they think. *Continuance.* I could still bear children. They might want to breed him to me."

"He does as he wishes," said Althene. "You'd better credit that."

Rachaela felt something relax inside her. It was a flame going out. Yet she was glad.

Malach was for Ruth.

But how? The razor or the kiss?

"It will be a wonderful dinner tonight," said Althene. "Kei is invincible."

"Pleasures of the flesh."

Like a rich nunnery—stomach for loins.

Althene turned to her. How old *was* she? Old as history, perhaps, in a young white sheath.

But then how old am I?

"Little Rachaela," said Althene.

It was like a caress. Sweet, unthinking, meaning nothing.

In the hall Lou and Tray were huddled, standing each almost on one leg, like storks.

The two dogs, of which they were afraid, were in the hall, thumping with their scimitar tails.

Camillo was petting them.

Camillo said to Rachaela, "They're his. He always had dogs like this, I remember. These two are the descendants of dogs that ran across Ireland when men wore the Eye painted on their foreheads."

"But you hide from Malach," she said.

"Wouldn't you?" Camillo grinned. More than ever he looked like a boy. The warm light of evening ironed out the lines, the runneled skin. Changing . . . a butterfly. "Horsy," said Camillo, "keep your tail up. Keep the sun out of my eyes."

CHAPTER 18

✤ *THUNDER LIKE AN EGYPTIAN CROCODILE*
circled the sky. But the storm had not, did not
break. Perhaps it never would.

Ruth had gone to a Bernie Inn, where happy fami-
lies had congregated. Amid the chatter and the laughs,
alone, she ate her meal. Steak and a jacket potato with
sour cream, a salad, carrots, peas and onion rings. Afterwards she had an ice cream. There was a sparkler in it
showering golden stars. This for a moment drew attention to her. In that moment, Ruth was afraid.

But fear was a passing thing to Ruth, like a short-
lived digestive pain, foreboding nothing.

She had drunk orange juice with her meal. She did
not consume alcohol unless it was offered her, freely
available. This was partly the instinct of survival, for she
still looked young, might be only sixteen.

When she came out of the restaurant, the day was
bleeding away, mocked by the formless thunder.

Red sky at night, shepherds' delight.

Ruth walked along the street. Red as the dying sky,
the streetlamps were blinking on.

Traffic passed monotonously, at intervals.

A silver car detached itself from the stream and
drove slowly in toward the curb. It crawled there, as if

searching for a particular address among the line of shops and stacked flats.

At the traffic lights, Ruth turned into the side road. She was moving back in the direction of the Reeves' house on the estate.

The silver Mercedes waited until the lights gave it way, then turned into the road after her.

The Merc pulled up just in front of Ruth.

She took no notice.

A man got out of the car. He was thin and wiry in a box-shaped pastel suit and silk tie. His hair was slicked back with gel. He had a face of bones and very flat bright eyes.

As Ruth approached him, he skipped forward and took hold of her without a word.

No one else was on the street. On either side the houses lay well back behind high screens of privet and old trees. From the few lit windows nobody looked.

The back door of the car stood open.

Ruth fought. The thin man spoke then. "Don't, babe. Or I'll break your arm."

Ruth stopped fighting, and the man inserted her into the backseat of the car. He slammed the door and jumped into the passenger seat beside the driver. Before his door had closed, the Merc took flight, going fast now, a silver rocket, out into the main lane of southbound traffic.

Lorlo Mulley looked at the fabulous bimbo that had just been propelled into his car.

Pure chance that he had seen her, known her. She was the one all right. The one the police wanted, and then said they had got, dead in a wood. But obviously they were mistaken there, the way the bill did get mistaken now and then.

"Relax," said Lorlo Mulley to the black-haired girl. "You're safe now. Your good luck I saw you. Got you out of a bit of bother. Lot of law around here. But I'll see you're okay."

Ruth gazed back at him.

What a looker. They thought they had a body in a wood—but he had it here, and what a body.

"I know," said Lorlo kindly, "your spot of trouble. They're after you, ain't they? No problem. You're okay with me."

Just once or twice you got a girl like this. The shape, and the hair, and a face to go with it. She could make him a bit of money. And her eyes. Was she stoned? No. She was only freaked out. A bit crazy, perhaps. Well, he could handle that. Teach her to handle it.

"Like a drink, doll?" He opened the drinks cabinet of the car. Brandy, vodka, liqueurs.

Through the glass partition, Honey and Frankie faced forward, Frankie manipulating the car effortlessly through the busy evening traffic. Good driver, Frankie. And Honey was first class, the way he had done it, just scooping her off the pavement. Even if he was a pain in the arse. "Have a Cointreau. You'll like that. It tastes of oranges."

"All right," said Ruth.

He poured a friendly measure, but not too much. He did not mean to make her sick.

Ruth drank the Cointreau without pleasure or reluctance, straight down.

"Steady, steady," said Lorlo. "You like a drink, don't you?"

His new girl did not reply to this. She said, "I'd like to get out now."

"No, no. Not just yet. The bill'd have you. You come with me. I'll show you my place. You'll like it. I can help you, you know. Help you make something of yourself."

Ruth did not protest again.

To reward her, for it seemed she could cope with it, he gave her another drink.

"I've got some stuff at my place. Make you feel good. Just relax, you're safe now."

He told Ruth she could call him "Lorlo." It was a privilege he awarded his best girls. The trash still called him "Mr. Mulley."

He asked her name. She said she was named Ruth. He liked that. It had a bit of class.

The Merc bypassed the West End, going at steep angles through brick-walled alleys and down long side roads under railway arches.

They came out into Lorlo's territory, through dereliction, to the great warehouse. On every side was wreckage, the skulls of buildings eyeless with broken glass. But the warehouse was pristine, with eyebrows of white paint, and not a scrap of paper even on the cement forecourt that stood above the narrow channel of the river.

On the concrete, Frankie parked the Mercedes. And in the holes about, maybe the rats peeked out to see. But no one would touch this car. They knew better.

In the warehouse foyer, Chas came from his cubby, and grinned with joy when he saw Lorlo. Chas loved Lorlo.

"Evenin', Mr. Mulley." He glanced at Ruth and chuckled.

Honey and Frankie ignored Chas, who was beneath them. An ex-boxer, just a touch punchy, Chas had no vices but Havana cigars and fizzy lemonade. He spent the days in his room beside the lift, among his boxing cups, smoking, and looking through the papers. From a box of dressmaker's pins with colored heads, he would select a couple now and then, and stick them through the nipples of the pictured topless girls. Then he laughed. Women made Chas laugh.

Under the battered kettle leaned an axe, the type a lumberjack would use. Chas was handy with the axe, and still with his fists.

"Hi, Chas. Got your lemonade?"

"Sure, Mr. Mulley. I got it."

Over the fire extinguisher was a sawn-off shotgun.

Honey was already summoning the lift. It came with a leisurely dinosaur rattle. The massive doors opened slowly.

Lorlo Mulley put his hand under Ruth's elbow and guided her into the big elevator, large as a room, being careful not to touch the sides or doors with his ash-brown suit.

They rose. The lift juddered.

"This outfit needs oiling," said Lorlo. "Frankie, see to it."

Frankie nodded. "Yes, Mr. Mulley."

The lift came to a halt, and the doors cracked and began to draw back.

A white carpet appeared, a plain of it, unmarked, like arctic bear fur.

"You'll like this, Ruth," said Lorlo.

He led her out. On the snow plain were scattered furnishings of black leather. On one wall stood a bank of office equipment, a photocopier, a filing system full of the names and statistics of girls and boys from thirteen to twenty-three. A fax machine sat by the telephone which was an old black model from the '50s.

Across the carpet were a black TV with video and a music center. A door stood open on a bathroom, shower and lavatory.

Over the walls were grainy photographs of cars, Bugattis, Studebakers, statically preening in forests, like Lorlo's girls.

Honey and Frankie split aside.

"Go in the kitchen," said Lorlo. "Do the chicken."

Honey went across to another door and into a white kitchen that gleamed from underuse. From the fridge, Honey lifted out a thawing chicken on a plate. Otherwise the fridge had cans of Swedish lager, two bottles of Dom Pérignon, a jar of caviar, and a Walther PPK.

Setting the chicken down beside the coffee percolator, Honey rolled up his laundered sleeves. He thrust his right hand into the cavity of the chicken and drew out a tinfoil package.

Lorlo had got Ruth across the upper floor of the warehouse, the acres of white carpet, and opened the final door.

The carpet went on being white, and the furniture black. But there was a wide bed, king size, covered by a spread of leopardskins. The skins were real, catching the wall lights on a harsh wild nap.

"Come in," said Lorlo. "Come into my parlor."

Ruth moved into the room.

She had a terrific way of moving.

She was a find.

Just get her under control. That would be simple.

Above the bed were two prize black-and-white photos; Bette Davis, Joan Crawford. They had it then, those women. But this one had it too. Something special.

Ruth looked about her. She glanced at the photographs. Crossing to the bed, she touched the spread of skins.

"Oh, you like pussies, then?"

"Is it real?"

"Yes. I don't go for rubbish. Leopard. Beautiful."

"It's dead," said Ruth. She smoothed the skins.

"Better believe it," said Lorlo. "It won't bite. I'll leave that to you." He went toward the cabinet. "Another drink?"

"Yes," said Ruth.

She could hold her booze. Where had she learned? He would swear she was tighter than Mother Teresa. He could smell it on her, virginity.

"Anyone looking for you?" asked Lorlo. "Other than the filth?"

Ruth did not answer.

It hardly mattered anyway. In a week she would be different.

He handed her the Cointreau, this time over ice, and taking his vodka he went into the bathroom that gave on the room.

"If you want anything," he said, "Frankie and Honey are outside." He meant, she was not going anywhere. But maybe she knew that and did not mind.

He closed the door and ran the shower hot. He liked to be clean. It had not been so easy in his adolescence.

Lorlo thought about Candy, under the shower. She had been his best; her drop of Asian blood had made her really something. He had controlled her by introducing her to cocaine, but Candy had become too dependent too quickly. In the end she had only been the habit and he had had to get rid of her.

He must be careful with Ruth. Ration her. Keep her nice. He rubbed himself vigorously with coal-tar soap.

After the shower he rinsed his mouth with Listerine, pushed a little baby oil through his hair and over the hairs on his chest.

He liked all this. It helped to put him in the mood.

He patted his face with aftershave by Pierre Cardin. No rubbish.

When he came out, he was warm and naked inside the black silk kimono, on the back of which was a rippling scarlet dragon. Across the pocket in white were the initials *L.M.*

"Nothing like a shower," he said to the girl, who was sitting on the leopardskin bed. Her glass was very full. Either she had not drunk it or she had finished and poured herself another. "You like a drink," said Lorlo. "But I've got something even better." He opened the outer door and Honey came immediately toward him with the cellophane packet, fresh from the tinfoil in the chicken, washed and sealed.

And who should it be tonight? Froggy, Lorlo

thought. He took down the photograph of Bette Davis, with her beautiful frog eyes. Unsealing the packet, he scattered the cocaine across her face and breast and hair.

Ruth was watching.

"That's right. See what I do."

He cut the powder with a gold-plated, cutthroat razor. Then he took the silver tube, and snorted up the drug. He made the noises of a man trying to shift heavy catarrh.

Lorlo raised his head.

The cocaine was at once singing in his blood, the wonderful clean high, not like alcohol at all. Nothing was like it. Candy had been a fool, greedy, abusing little bitch. The partition of her septum had disintegrated. She had been ready to snuff up the dross of the streets, cut with bleach and talcum.

"Now some for you," said Lorlo to Ruth, generously standing away and offering her the tube.

"No," said Ruth.

"Yes. It's great stuff. The best. Have some. Then you can take a bath. I've got some pretty things for you to wear. You're a lovely girl, Ruth." He picked up the photograph with its remaining lines of powder, and went toward her.

"No," said Ruth. "I don't want it."

"It's easy. Just use the tube. You'll love it."

"No."

Lorlo stopped. "Okay. Your loss." He put the photograph back on the table. Lowering his face he slid the silver tube up his nose and snorted the last cocaine noisily.

Ruth still watched, stroking the dead leopards on the bed.

He would give her some later. There was the other packet. She would need it then.

"Okay, Ruth. Go and take a bath."

When she had washed and donned the lace and rubber undies, he would fuck her. The cocaine would make him potent but quick. So then he would strap on the dildo, and do it to her that way, until he was ready again. He would play '80s Sinatra on the music center. The greatest.

No girl who came in here stayed unbroken, or unlearned.

He would know Ruth, by the time he had finished. She stood up. She said, "I want to go now."

Lorlo laughed good-humoredly. "Can't oblige. Come on, why waste yourself?"

"I want to go."

"Can't, doll. Tell ya. We can do it nice, or do it rough. Honey and Frankie can come in if you want and hold you down. Yes? You want that? Or you and I can have a party. Just the two of us. You ain't going nowhere."

The girl's face did not change. He had seen it all, and now he expected something. But there was nothing.

She said quietly, "My dad will come. My father will come and find me. You'll be sorry."

Lorlo laughed again. He felt clean and young and fit, and ready as a donkey. "Don't think so, doll." He glanced at Bette Davis on her back with the dust of cocaine in her hair. "Now go and wash. Don't be too long."

CHAPTER 19

✤ *THERE WERE TWO PEOPLE DOWNSTAIRS* on the late bus, and one of them smiled as Malach got on. The smile was not for Malach. It was a twisting up of elderly male lips that showed stained, smoker's, bad false teeth bathed in Steradent once every seven or eight days. The eyes were shiny with venom. The smiling man angled himself a little to the aisle.

"What do you think of that, then?"

The elderly woman, nothing to do with the elderly man, stretched her mouth subserviently. "Ah." And looked away.

The bus started off into the Martian-lit darkness.

Malach sat about halfway down the bus, in his black, his long legs edged a little out into the aisle. His white hair lay back behind him, gleaming like a sheet of ice.

"Get to Woolworth's soon," announced the elderly man. "Knock 'em up. Get some scissors."

The elderly woman giggled. If she had been young, she might have liked Malach's hair. It sparkled, was tactile, and savage as fur. But she was getting on now, and the wicked crime of youth was, it was wasted on the young. The man spoke again. "Yes, some good sharp scissors. That's what he needs."

Seen from the front, Malach's eyelids had lowered

themselves a centimeter over the pale lapis eyes. That was all.

The bus lurched around a corner. The smiling man got up. His stop was coming. He edged past Malach, and stood near the doors. He peered back.

"He's like Goldilocks," said the man, " 'n' he?"

Malach looked up at him.

"And are you one of the three bears?" he asked politely.

But the elderly man was too entrenched in his poison to hear.

"Six years I served my country," he said. He stood straight, muffled in his dirty, musty garments of faded sick yellows and browns. On his head the properly short hair greasily coiled, laved with soap once a fortnight, otherwise washed in ashtrays. "Six years, for the likes of this."

The bus had been caught at the lights. It had halted and the man stared out into the orange dark, gathering himself. Then he turned again and looked sidelong at Malach, not quite into Malach's face. "Six years I served. So he can go walking about with his hair down to his bum. Disgusting."

No, he had not looked into Malach's face. Had not seen it. Like the face of a stone angel, and with the hair of an angel.

The bus bounced and started off again, and so reached the stop.

The elderly man with the short hair got off.

Malach rose in darkness, and went after him.

"Ooer," said the elderly woman, softly.

At first, as he walked along, Arthur Simpkins was not aware of any pursuit.

He was thinking of soaking his feet.

It had not been much of an evening. He had won nothing at Bingo, he should never have gone. Waste of money and there was little enough of that. These blacks could get it, with their whining and jabbering. These queers and freaks. But it was different if you kept to yourself, got on without complaining. Still, the government was tougher now. Trust Thatcher, she had the right ideas. Not like the usual stupid woman.

And that one on the bus. God almighty. That was what they were like now.

They needed a war to sort them out.

He had had that, and it had done him no harm. Best years of his life, in a way. The companionship of real men, knowing you were someone, that you counted, what you said carried weight.

As he turned down his road, Arthur Simpkins felt a primeval need to look over his shoulder.

He did so.

There behind him, about forty feet away, a tall black figure in a slim loose coat. The Martian streetlamps caught the yard of hair.

Arthur Simpkins felt his belly gurgle and a sour taste came into his mouth, through the familiar pall of fags and dentures.

He speeded up, walking quickly now. Not far. Soon be indoors.

He got to the low wall and went through the gate. A strip of cement was there which an Irishman had laid cheaply three years ago. The front door needed paint. Arthur Simpkins unlocked it hastily. As he slipped inside he saw his pursuer standing motionless under a lamp.

When he bolted the door on the inside the elderly man had a strange sense of siege which was not happy. But he shook himself. What could that namby-pamby do? Trying to frighten him, but he was a soldier.

He went to check the back door was bolted, then put the kettle on.

* * *

Twenty minutes later, when Arthur Simpkins brought his tea, and the steaming bowl of hot water, with a dash of Fairy Liquid, into his front room, he saw through the window, whose curtains were not drawn, the white-haired man sitting on his garden wall.

He should go to the window, bang on it, and shake his fist. But Arthur Simpkins decided not to. No, better just to let him get fed up and go. Probably on drugs or drunk. These kids were all the same, they all had money to burn.

Arthur Simpkins took the bowl and the tea out of the front room and into the small dining room. Here he switched on the overhead light and drew the curtains, shutting out the square of Irish cement garden.

He sat drinking his tea, and rolled a cigarette, being careful not to waste any tobacco. He took off his shoes, but, with his socks still on, he crept back into the front room again, to look.

The white-haired man was still there. He was just sitting, not facing the house even, staring along the street, as if he was waiting for someone by appointment.

Trying to put the wind up. Young bugger.

Arthur Simpkins went back into the dining room, and drank the rest of his tea and finished his cigarette. On the floor the bowl steamed less.

There were no ornaments in the room, as there were none in the front room. Over the fire hung a framed photograph of Arthur Simpkins the warrior, with two of the other men. They were beaming and contented in their battledress. You knew where you were then. Under the photograph hung a medal. He had his pride.

On the dining-room table lay Arthur Simpkins's scrapbooks of the Royal Family, and the little pile of cuttings that he had yet to insert. He had been going to see to those tonight, but he could not settle.

The water in the bowl had got cold.

He would go and boil up the kettle again.

Arthur Simpkins went out, and, creeping once more, passed around the wall of the front room to the window.

Still there.

What should he do? Call the police? It seemed extreme. But then, this was a threat, was it not, implicit. He was a poor old man. He was alone.

Arthur Simpkins sidled to the small bureau where the telephone was kept. Above it hung the other picture in the house, of the Queen trooping the color. It seemed to offer slight protection, and as he raised the receiver, outside the man on the wall turned his head. He looked straight in at the window as if he had heard the receiver being lifted.

Arthur Simpkins's hand shook. And in his ear he heard a tinny silence. There was no dialing tone.

He turned on the phone, working the cradle a couple of times, without hope. You could rely on nothing nowadays. He could be dying, and the phone not working.

Then he looked up, the dead receiver in his shaking hand, and relief washed through him in a scalding wave.

The man was gone from the wall.

No trace of him.

He must have seen Arthur Simpkins on the phone through the window and, not realizing the instrument was useless, got scared.

Yellow, a coward. No backbone. That was how they were.

Arthur Simpkins slung the receiver back on the hook. The thing would probably have righted itself in the morning.

Whistling, he went out to the kitchen to boil up the kettle again.

Then he carried it into the dining room and added the hot water to the cold. He left the kettle on the carpet and slipped off his socks. Aside from a bath, which he took regularly once a week, the foot soaking was his little luxury.

He rolled another cigarette. He might watch a bit of TV in the front, after. (Though there would doubtless be nothing but rubbish, blacks and nancy boys.) It was too late to start on the cuttings now. He would do them tomorrow.

Malach penetrated the gardens, agile, like a cat. The fences were low, the ground strewn only with flowerpots and gnomes.

Even from the back, the house of Malach's quarry was at once identifiable. Its barren yard, and general appearance. Years of neglect had stamped themselves upon it. There were no plants, no garden toys, no dog food set out for hedgehogs. The man with short hair was sufficient unto himself.

The kitchen, like an outhouse, stretched from the back wall. The door was bolted and locked. Above, two unlit windows with undrawn curtains.

Malach set one foot against the brickwork. He put his hands there. He began to climb, up the wall. There were the thousand crevices of desuetude, the pointing was no more, his long fingers tucked into the gaps and the long feet followed. His spine was straight, he moved like water flowing, upward. In the lamp dark, almost invisible, but for the beacon of hair.

When he had reached the sloping kitchen roof he stepped delicately across the tiles and onto its brickwork ridge. He walked along it to the bathroom window.

Like knives, his fingers drove into the rotted frame, the crumbled, sixty-year-old putty. Dust, rot, and ancient flakes of paint fell away. Then the frame came up and out, and the window with it.

There had been scarcely a sound. A noise maybe like a cat scratching.

He lowered the window in, onto the bathroom lino.

The smells of the house pushed out of their long imprisonment. Tobacco smoke and nicotine, old midday dinners of mince, kippers, tinned peas, cabbage and spuds, the stench of the never-cleansed lavatory.

In the dark the bath glowed pale, with cracks of verdigris where the taps for ever dripped. Above the washbasin was a tiny shaving mirror, and below, on a shelf, razor and brush, the Steradent, the greasy comb, soap, and slimy flannel.

Outside, across the landing, the bedroom, the box room.

Malach did not bother with them.

He passed like a shadow down the worn carpet of the stairs.

With the years the eighteen-inch TV had grown muffled and low, and Arthur Simpkins was forced to turn it up.

He sat in the mustard armchair, his feet again in the bowl of hot water which he had carried through, a threadbare towel on the maroon carpet, trousers rolled up. His old legs were maps of veins. His mouth had dropped open in half-sleep. On the screen in black and white, tanks rolled across a wasteland. A voice boomed out of Beirut.

Then a shadow moved between Arthur Simpkins and Beirut.

Silence exploded in the room like a shell.

Arthur Simpkins awoke.

The TV had gone. Someone had switched it off.

He looked up, and for the first time he saw the face of Malach, aureoled in a cloud of burning white.

"Oh, Gawd," said Arthur Simpkins. He tried to rise and his feet slipped in the Fairy Liquid water, and he fell back. "How did you— Don't hurt me. Don't you hurt me. I'm an old man."

Malach nodded across the room.

Arthur Simpkins turned and saw, over the chair, the picture of the Queen in red.

"So," said Malach, "these are the gods you pray to."

"I'm an old man," said Arthur Simpkins. He dribbled, his false teeth slipping as his body shrank in fear. "Don't do nothing."

Malach looked down from his height like something on the wing.

And then he had shifted, and was behind the chair.

"Your hair," said Malach. He placed his hands, the left with its bracing of silver rings, upon Arthur Simpkins's head. The fingers curved, and rested at the hairline. "Your hair is too long."

Arthur Simpkins felt a sting, like that of a wasp. Eight times. The nails of Malach had torn into his flesh. Very deep. He screamed.

Before he could scream again, in two neat perfect strips, Malach scalped him.

The moon was up, a lion's mask, the same as if above a desert.

Malach came out of the front door and quietly closed it.

He was immaculate.

The street was empty in the curse of the orange light. Then a man slipped from the shade between the lamps. He ran to Malach like a messenger on some quay of the Nile; and reaching him, at the gate of Arthur Simpkins, who by morning would be dead, the man bowed.

He wore an unfashionable raincoat in the warm night, thick trousers, cumbersome shoes.

Malach looked at him, and the man spoke rapidly in an undertone, perhaps in a foreign language. He gestured, into space, and Malach nodded. He touched the man on the shoulder and went by.

The man stood, a messenger out of time who had been touched by a king who was a god.

Malach had disappeared.

Up the street, a black taxi pulled out from the curb.

CHAPTER 20

❖ *OVER THE SOUND OF SINATRA'S LAMENT,*
the knocking on the door was uncouth and illogi-
cal. Lorlo Mulley waited unbelievingly for it to end.

It did not end.

In a sweet slow motion, Lorlo went to the door.

"Piss off."

"Mr. Mulley. There's a fax."

"It can wait."

"No, Mr. Mulley. Please, Mr. Mulley. You'd better
come and see."

"You fucking mouse turd. I said—"

"*Please*, Mr. Mulley. It's from Manchester."

Lorlo opened the door. Honey stood there, dismayed.

"All right. This had better be good."

But it had come from Manchester. Nothing from
there could be ignored. Honey was right, sod him.

Lorlo was peevish. His mood was being spoiled.

The girl had gone into the bathroom and he had
heard the splash of water. He put on the Sinatra record,
tenderly. Gentled by his high, he wished he could find a
girl who would appreciate Ol' Blue Eyes. They had no
musical taste. Perhaps, Ruth . . .

She would be hot. He knew it. Once he got her going.

But now this.

Lorlo walked over the acres of white carpet. A slight leadenness was building in his gut.

Manchester—

He reached the fax and looked down at the printout neither Frankie nor Honey had had the temerity to pluck.

On it, in gray and milk dots, was Ruth's face. It was exact. Lorlo stared, bemused, his body trying to catch up.

Under the image were a few lines of prose.

White girl, hair black and long, eyes black, height approximately five feet two inches, weight between six-ten and seven stone. Age twelve years and some months. Name Ruth.

Below this were just four words:

MULLEY. LET HER GO.

"Shit," said Lorlo. "Oh, shit."

He backed along the carpet. Then he came to Honey, and clutched at him.

"I didn't know."

"No, Mr. Mulley. We none of us—"

"I didn't know. They won't believe that." And then. "I got to get her out. *Out.*"

By the time he reached the door, Lorlo had a sort of control of himself. He opened it, and went in, casually.

Ruth had come from the bathroom. She was standing by the bed. She looked bizarre, because she had wrapped herself, head to foot, in the skins of leopards. It seemed to him that this was only part of the whole. This was as it had to be.

"Doll," said Lorlo, nicely, "there's been a change of plan. Got to let you go. All right?"

Honey was in the door, and behind him was Frankie. They both looked scared.

"Now, babe," said Lorlo to Ruth, "nothing happened, did it? Didn't hurt you, did I?"

Cowled in leopardskin, a feline nun, Ruth said softly, "No."

"That's good, *good,* Ruth. Just a bit of fun." Lorlo laughed. He walked to the music center and shut off Sinatra. "You can go now. Wherever you want. And Ruth, I want you to know, if there's anything I can do—just ask."

Ruth looked by him, to Frankie and Honey.

Lorlo said quickly, "And the boys, Ruth. We're at your service, babe. Where do you want to go? Frankie'll drive you in the Merc."

Ruth gathered the skins around her.

"I'd like this."

"*Take* it, baby. Just take it. It's yours."

A white hand came out of the skin. Ruth drew up her bag, and into it, from another white hand, she dropped something she had been hiding in the pelt.

So, she had stolen something. That was fine.

"Do you want a drink? See you on your way?"

"No," said Ruth. "Thank you."

She walked past him, through the door.

"Frankie," rapped Lorlo, "take her down in the lift. Take her wherever she wants to go."

"Sure, Mr. Mulley."

Her black-haired head had come from the skin now. Otherwise clothed in it, leopardess, she glided over the carpet.

In another fifteen minutes—

But it had not come to that.

Lorlo felt disorientated and nauseous.

Frankie had pressed for the lift. The wide doors opened in the wall, and Ruth went through, and Frankie followed her, not getting near, as if she was an isotope.

In his cubby, Chas chose another bottle from the crate of fizzy lemonade, and opened it. He drank earnestly, like a child. During his fighting days, this beverage had been strictly off the menu.

Somewhere out of the night, deep in the dereliction, a car moved.

Chas listened. His left ear was not up to much, but his right was very acute. The car slid through the broken buildings like an alligator in a swamp, and went away.

Chas sat down and put his feet up on the table. His cigar had gone out and he relit it with the gold lighter Mr. Mulley had given him after that job in Brixton. He pulled the thick smoke down into the sacks of his lungs. Opening up the paper, he found a girl with naked breasts, and began to reach for the box of pins.

Maybe it was only a drift of smoke. Something had passed over the glass window of the cubby.

Chas looked around.

In the doorway stood a man in a long black coat. His hair was white. He smiled.

Chas swung down his legs and got up.

"Wha ya wan?"

"Many things," said the man. He had a dry actor's voice. His hair was very long.

"Ya wan Mr. Mulley?" asked Chas. "You tell me name and business. If I think ya need ta see him, I call him up on the internal."

"Yes, I'd like to see Mr. Mulley," said the white-haired man. He glanced about the room. "A boxer with a gun and axe."

"Ya better believe I don' need no gun."

"Why don't you show me."

Chas grinned, displaying ill-kept, well-made false teeth. "I'll show ya."

He lumbered forward with a weird mechanical speed, and his left arm reared out for Malach's face.

Malach caught the arm at the wrist in his left hand.

Chas gawped at him, rolled off-balance. The hefty blow had been checked as if by a wall. "A southpaw," Malach said mildly.

Chas lunged with a right hook.

Malach's right hand was there, pinioning Chas at the right wrist.

"Eia," said Malach.

Chas struggled, his face congested and bewildered.

Malach had stopped smiling. He straightened his back and looked into the eyes of Chas. Then he pulled smartly down on the lost boxer's crossed arms. There was a dull gristly creak. Chas howled. His eyes skidded up.

Malach let go the two wrists. The arms of Chas now hung down limp and too long, the arms of an ape. They had been pulled from their sockets.

"No axe, no gun," said Malach. He pushed at Chas and Chas fell over on his back under the table. His arms were useless, he could not get up.

Malach went to the crate of lemonade, and taking a bottle he shook it up, glancing around again as he did so at the elements of the cubby. Then he unscrewed the cap of the bottle, and poured the bubbling liquid over Chas's face, into his nostrils.

The lift reached the lobby and the great slow doors opened.

Ruth, the priestess of cats, came out. Her black hair rayed over the cape of skins. Her white face, with its rose mouth and black-shadowed eyes, showed nothing.

Frankie was behind her. "But I can drive you wherever you want. There's no strings. He gave me strict orders."

"I don't want to go in your car," said Ruth. "I told you."

"He'll create a scene."

Ruth said nothing.

Frankie called across the lobby. "Chas? The doll's just going through. No problem." Frankie stepped back in the lift. " 'S all yours."

He pushed at the button panel and the doors began to close again. They shut together like chunks of old armor and the lift slid up into the warehouse, back to the white carpet and the Bugattis.

After the lift was gone, Ruth did not move.

She stood in the foyer, seemingly waiting. She knew, had been lessoned in, the silent noise of death. Frankie, who should have known it too, had missed it.

Then Adamus came out of the wall.

He had changed, as the dead do.

"Daddy," said Ruth, clearly. And then, correcting herself, "Adam."

He was there, in the midst of the massive gray and rusty lobby, sidelit by the glare from the cubbyhole. He stayed immobile as an iron statue.

Ruth moved. She walked to him over the lobby floor, the leopardskin trailing, looking up at his face.

When she was a yard away, she halted.

"Not Daddy," he said. "Not Adam. My name is Malach. Say it."

"Malach," said Ruth.

He slapped her across the face.

It was a light, stinging blow, not wounding or violent, but sharp as a drawn sword.

She rocked, he caught her shoulder. As she regained her equilibrium, he let her go.

He said, "What floor?"

"Three."

The internal phone rang in the cubby.

Malach went without hesitation back into the room and lifted the receiver. Lorlo Mulley's voice was extruded, breathless.

"Don't talk, Chas. Go out and see where the girl goes. Make sure she goes somewhere. Then come up. I want you up here."

The connection clicked off.

Malach replaced the receiver.

Ruth had followed him. She gazed a moment at the legs of Chas sticking out from under the table. But Malach was already gone. He was holding the fire extinguisher. He crossed the lobby and stepped out onto the cement, where the big silver car sat against the backdrop of ruin and river.

The car had not been locked. It was unnecessary.

Malach opened the door and got in. He dropped the extinguisher on the seat.

He started the engine, which roused with a swift soft growl. The Mercedes turned on the spot, then came in smoothly backward, through the lobby, up to the doors of the lift.

Malach got out again. "Fetch a newspaper from the room."

Ruth returned into the cubby obediently. She took a paper from the table, from the pile by the uncapped bottle of lemonade. The gold lighter lay on its side, and in the tin which had served as an ashtray, the last cigar had gone out forever.

When she brought him the paper, Malach was in the back of the Merc with the drinks cabinet opened out before him.

He had undone the decanters of vodka and brandy, the bottles of Cointreau, crème de menthe and Tia Maria. He lined them up and stuck into their tops long twists of newspaper.

Colored pins fell out of the breasts of women.

"Get the lift," said Malach. Ruth pressed the button. "When it comes, you hold down the button to keep the doors open."

"Yes, Malach."

The lift came, grudging, as if it did not like to.

When the doors were wide, Malach drove the Mercedes in backward, until the car filled up the elevator.

Malach leaned into the back of the Merc and lit the spills of paper with Arthur Simpkins's box of Swan Vestas. "Close the doors, now, Ruth."

The papers burned bright, five torches finding emeralds and tiger's-eye in the bottles. The doors were beginning to close.

Malach was out of the car. Now he leaned into the front. He shifted the Merc into drive, and brought down the fire extinguisher hard on the accelerator, jamming it. Then he was gone.

As the lift doors came together, Ruth saw Malach slip between them impossibly, the car roaring at his back.

The doors shut and the car rammed into them from inside, and the lobby shook.

Over the row Lorlo was making, running about the white carpet like a crazy beetle, rummaging in the cabinets and files, shouting at them, only Frankie heard the engine of the car wake on the forecourt.

He went to one of the big uncurtained windows to look out. And the Mercedes had gone.

"Mr. Mulley—"

"Not now, Frankie. Jesus, Frankie, help me lift this file."

Lorlo was shitting himself, it was obvious. He had sent a message back on the fax, but there had been no reply.

He might be in big trouble. For some reason, the girl was dynamite. That meant trouble for Frankie too, but Frankie had his own contingency plans. These involved shopping Lorlo as soon as was needful.

Now Lorlo was doctoring his files, or trying to, looking up all the little fiddles and indiscretions.

Honey just wanted to get out. He edged nearer and nearer to the lift.

"Mr. Mulley," said Frankie finally, "the fucking car's gone."

"Jesus. She took my car," said Lorlo.

He darted back across the room and fastened on the internal phone. "Chas? Chas? Sod him, he's not there."

Then they heard the big thump in the lift which trembled the floor. It was often noisy. Nerves might make it seem worse.

"That's him coming up now," said Frankie.

"Stupid bastard, letting her take the car. There's stuff in the car. Maybe she's gone to them—"

Lorlo pictured Ruth driving through the night to Manchester.

While he was doing this, the lift arrived.

"Chas—"

The doors opened, faster it seemed than they had ever done before. Not Chas, but the burning Mercedes came crashing through. It bowled over the screeching Honey, bumped once, and then poured toward them up the plain of white, with fire leaping from its open sides.

Lorlo and Frankie wailed like children in the dark.

Down among the dereliction, Malach stood with Ruth, in the black night above the inky river.

Together they watched the windows of the third floor of the warehouse, behind which came a sudden constipated thunder, and then a blinding *whuff* of light and rage of sound. All the glass shot out, a rain of stars, and tiny pieces tinkled about them like hail, and small blobs of flame and scraps of burning furnishings and papers.

Then the fiery Mercedes burst from the far end of the warehouse and dived slowly down into the prolapse of the wasteland, into the black rubbish and the weeds. Redness rose from there to the canopy of tainted city sky. Reflected in the vitriol of the river.

As the glass and flaming fragments fell, Malach had lifted part of his long coat to cover Ruth's head, and shielded her face with his hand. The coat was like a black wing, under which he had taken her.

CHAPTER 21

✤ ALTHENE PUSHED BACK THE DOOR.
"Come in." The storm had broken abruptly, and
her room was lit and flickered by sheet lightning through
the colored window. This was like another scene. And
not like at all. Then, that time in the past, Rachaela had
woken to find Adamus, and the window of the Temptation flaring upon him.

Althene's window was cunningly of a woman before
a colored window, and this inner casement was a thing of
irises and hyacinths.

The room was art nouveau. The dark turquoise curtains were figured in peacocks of pale greenish gold. A
gilt shawl draped the midnight blue of the bed, and in tall
brazen urns fanned brown and emerald feathers. On a
polished table with storks' legs lay a platter of milk glass,
with three apples on it, one of rose quartz, one of
scratched ebony, and one of coal-blue crystal. The mirrors were of reflecting glass, rimmed by glass-paste fruits
and leaves. A curtain like those of the window draped the
bathroom door.

There were books strewn about. There should have
been a mandoline with tassels, or some embroidery on a
frame. But clearly Althene was a stylist rather than a liar.

"Isn't it charming," said Althene. "How thoughtful
they are."

"Does the window open?"

"I haven't tried. In the bathroom it does. An enormous tree almost brushes the sill. Yesterday a dove came and watched me brush my teeth. It was very flattering."

Rachaela would not give in.

"About the dress. It's very kind of you, but I—"

"You have no long dresses, you said. This is a special dinner. You and I are almost alike. Cheta will come and see to the few alterations. To please them. You must."

"Why is the dinner special?"

"Kei will cook it."

"And is that the only reason?"

"Imagine, if you will," said Althene, "that they want to celebrate a possibility."

"Of what?"

"Renewal, hope, the washing away of sin."

"Whose sin?" asked Rachaela. "Mine?"

"How self-centered you are," said Althene. "If you weren't beautiful, one would want to slap you."

"I'll go." Rachaela turned to the door.

Somehow Althene was past her, blocking the exit. She flicked at a fringed rope, and another peacock curtain came down over the doorway. "I've imprisoned you. No chance to escape until you've seen the dress." She was playful, and oddly dangerous. The power behind her eyes glowed out on Rachaela, a challenge Rachaela did not care to meet.

"You're making everything very difficult," she said.

"No, Rachaela. *You* are making everything very difficult. But then. Opposition is sometimes stimulating."

The lightning fluttered, and the woman at the window in the window appeared. The tap of rain came from the glass, a million dainty fingers.

"Negative ions," said Althene. "After all, let's see if the window opens."

It did.

A vein of darkness stabbed by diamonds.

Rachaela drew in a breath.

Althene stalked on her effortless high heels to the carven wardrobe. Inside, some twenty or so garments hung in suave gradations of color and texture.

"Here is mine."

Althene swept out on her arm, like a swooning princess, a thing of wine-red satin. She shook it and held it up, a dress with a deep narrow V of neck, long sleeves, a crossover bodice, padded shoulders, and sleek-waisted mermaid body. It had no ornament.

"Let me demonstrate." Althene unzipped her Mocha clothes, which fell around her like fawning dogs.

Her arms were lightly muscled, without a trace even of down. She wore a short camisole in caramel silk, with a high breast and hem edged in smoky guipure lace. She was unselfconscious to the point of parody. To be so gorgeous and not to know, was a contradiction in terms.

She slid the wine dress on over her head, receiving it like a prayer. She smoothed it down, unzipped.

"Do me up."

Like her page, Rachaela came and performed the duty. She was resigned.

Althene said, "You see. The dress I have in mind for you is the same. But white."

And from the wardrobe came the white dress, like snow, or Malach's hair. Silk, this one. From the right shoulder to the point of the V of the neck, extended a line of black embroidery, the shapes of tiny roses.

"Try," said Althene.

Rachaela stared at her. She did not want to take off her blouse and skirt before this Medusa. But then, not to do so was to back down, and they were in a sort of game, the games the Scarabae played.

And I, too, am Scarabae.

"All right."

She pulled off her top and the skirt. Althene looked at her, without any nuance of interest or committal.

And I am wearing a Marks and Spencer's bra and matching briefs, and no tights or stockings. Satisfied?

Althene did not help her don the white dress.

It fitted untightly but rather well, except for being a fraction too close at the bust. Althene, although taller, must be more slender there. And it was, of course, a couple of inches too long. It met the floor.

"Cheta will be here in a moment. She'll see to that. It can be let out an inch or so, and taken up. Then the dress will be yours. You must keep it."

"It's lovely, but it isn't my sort of dress."

"What nonsense," said Althene.

She turned Rachaela about by a slight pressure on her arm and back, and there was a mirror framed in gilt grapes and ferns.

Two beautiful women looked out at them, one a little taller and of a slightly larger frame. Both with loosely curling, jet-black hair, eyes of night or dusk, faces from a dream. Royal. One the Red Queen, one the White Queen.

"Snow White and Rose Red," said Althene. "Never say to me again it isn't your sort of dress. And you shall have a pearl necklet with a clasp of gray gold."

"And do I keep that too?"

"If you wish. My shoes will be too large for you. My big feet fill me with annoyance. Go barefoot."

Rachaela turned in a type of fury, and Althene turned too and caught her face in two large slim hands. "My beauty," said Althene. "You must cease running away from yourself. One day you'll catch up. What will happen then?"

Rachaela stepped back, and Cheta knocked on the door behind the curtain.

There were two-foot candles of parchment white burning on the dining table in bronze sconces, and eight places laid.

The table had a cloth of dark crimson, with a border of old scarred gold.

From the table's center rose a confection of plants, and a palm tree with dates of polished wood.

Miranda and Sasha wore black, heavily sequined, and Eric his black tuxedo. Camillo wore his black leathers, and a T-shirt with Harley-Davidson written over it, under an eagle, in white. Lou wore a black dress with a low neck, a steel necklace, a bridal veil dyed black which touched the ground. In her ears were tiny silver gas masks she had once found at Camden Lock. Tray had on a basque and miniskirt, black, with a narrow hot-pink stripe running through them. On her arms were black lace gloves reaching to the elbows.

At the hollow of Althene's throat lay a large polished ruby on a platinum chain. Rachaela's white dress now fitted exactly. She had not worn the pearls. She did wear Anna's ring.

The dinner came, borne in by Cheta, Michael, and Kei, who had fashioned it.

There was steamed asparagus with butter and black pepper, served with a Riesling of the Napa Valley. Then came poached pike with a sauce of cumin, honey, oil, and white wine, served with a dark rosé of Anjou. Lamb followed baked in pastry, having a filling of apple and dates, and matched to a red African wine from Mbanga. After this was bream flaked and baked with onions in sugar, and served with tall thimbles of vodka. Then strawberries in a brandy sauce, with champagne. Last arrived long plates of Camembert, white goat's cheese, and strong Cheddar, with slices of guava, raisins, and various nuts, and a French dessert wine.

They ate, the voracious Scarabae, and old memories seemed to rise. Of Russian Jewry, of Caesar's Rome, and of some land that was not named but was the country of the mind.

Lou and Tray did not eat. They pecked and pushed

aside. Their lips, tongues, and intestinal tracts were locked into the here and now. Besides, their sutured waists gave them no room for expansion.

Rachaela ate a little of everything. Inside her, too, strange nostalgias, perhaps prompted by the wealth of blending drinks, curiously surfaced.

Sometimes she was happy. At others near to tears.

Everything seemed cast away by the glory of the meal. It spoke of other days that had never been.

"Kei is a genius," Althene said to her.

Rachaela thought of Althene at such banquets. She was decorous. Inside the V of her red gown was a plaque of wine-red lace. Yet surely somewhere, once, she had let out poison from a ring at such a feast. The body had convulsed and been carried out. Another dead enemy.

Camillo ate like a boy allowed to stay up. Before the next mouthful he might be sent away to bed.

Sasha and Miranda and Eric ate hungrily, yet with a delicate reserve. Their hearts were broken, like sections of clockwork in their breasts. They must live with this. Did so.

Sometimes Eric, or Sasha, would beckon Michael and Cheta to the table, and insist that they sample something on a little side plate.

Michael wore also the dinner clothes of the 1950s, and Cheta a matte black dress with a golden brooch like a snake.

There was hardly any conversation. And yet, the brain was full of unheard noises, sounds and sweet airs, elegies, faint cries. Beyond the house, the storm had long since died.

Rachaela was amazed she had eaten so much, and thought her stomach would rebel. But it did not. She felt soothed and sad, easy, distant.

The meal was like a symphony, with themes and developments.

It too had an end.

After the symphony of meal, came actual music. It was dance music. Tangos, a quick-step, a waltz.

Eric partnered Miranda on the space of polished floor beyond the table, and then Sasha. They danced well, even glamorously, young slim beings with ancient faces and hands. Then Eric came to Cheta, and she shook her head, but as with the food he insisted. Then Cheta too danced like a young slim girl.

Eventually Eric nodded to Michael, and he went out onto the floor alone. And there he danced alone, graceful as a ghost and with a ghost for a partner.

When this was done, seen through a kind of mist—it was two in the morning, the candles had shed their leaves of light—the Scarabae went from the room, almost all of them. Sasha and Miranda, and Camillo, shepherding the two tiddly little girls, and Althene in her wine and ruby. Eric was left. And Rachaela.

Have they drugged me? I can't move.

It was only the drink. The wonderful food.

She longed suddenly to sleep.

But Eric stood in the dimness of the candles' dying. He said, "I must tell you now, Rachaela. Malach has found Ruth."

Rachaela felt as if she had been brutally struck through layers of sponge.

"I—Ruth. You're saying Ruth—"

"Malach has her."

"What does that *mean*?"

Eric stood still. They all had this habit, this immobility. She too.

"I mean, Eric, what will happen now?"

"It will depend."

"On what?"

"The decision is Malach's."

"It shouldn't be. What is he? Some hired assassin?"

"Scarabae," said Eric.

"But you want her dead, don't you? She's a child—"
Rachaela thought, *A child that kills.*

"She is ours."

"But she killed your kind."

My kind.

"She isn't given to us," said Eric. "Malach has her."

How did they know? Some messenger? Some telephone call while she was floundering in Althene's peacock room. *How?*

It did not matter how.

Rachaela was helpless. As before.

And Ruth—was with Malach.

CHAPTER 22

✥ *AGAINST THE BODY OF HER LOVER, IN* his bed in the furnished flat over the tobacconists on Park Road, Linda Reeves lay wakeful through the night. The room smelled faintly stale and socks lay on the floor, but these things, along with the flimsy chairs and creased bedclothes, were a comfort.

She had left Richard. He did not know yet. But it was done.

She had doctored her wrist with witch hazel and bandaged it. The bruises on her arms and across her rib cage would not show. He had not cracked a rib as she had at first feared. This had happened once before, and the pain had been much worse. The dark glasses hid the harshness of the old black eye, and the new one. There was not much she could do about the cut on her lip or the swelling.

She was afraid Danny would send her straight out. She looked a sight, and the customers might be put off their ale. Then again, they had seen marks on her from time to time. Probably they guessed. They were nice to her and bought her or gave her money for drinks. They were down-to-earth at the Fox and Glass.

Richard had disliked her working there. But he would have disliked her working anywhere. He wanted her to be at home, as his mother had been for his father, to "look after him."

But when she had made efforts to please him, they were never a success. She had even tried baking bread. But she had not got "his mother's touch," apparently. He had thrown the bread out. She had never learned not to argue with him.

In the beginning, the blows seemed to clear the air. He was so contrite afterward. He would bring her pot-plants which, in the strained atmosphere of their house, quickly died. She was blamed for this. His mother had been able to grow anything, including all the vegetables.

Early on Linda had hated the dead Mrs. Reeves. Later she realized the dead Mrs. Reeves was like Daphne du Maurier's dead Rebecca: the fantasy of others.

Richard had furnished the house as a "home" in what he thought to be womanly taste, the way he said his mother would have done it. Linda was not a proper woman. She could not be trusted to get it right. So there were flounces and lace curtains and antimacassars, horrible, graceless clutter. He collected Victoriana too, bulging candelabra roped with gross forget-me-nots, flowery chamber pots, fat huntsmen shooting at something.

She had met Iain Morrison at the Fox. It was on a night when her face was clear of bruises. She had felt quite happy because Richard had gone overnight to Birmingham on business.

She had drunk five gins that Iain had bought her, and when the pub closed, she went with him back to the ugly unpretentious flat, and in the unlaundered bed, for which he apologized, made love. She had experienced, in Iain's arms, an orgasm so volcanic, she screamed. And afterward she cried, told him she had been wrong, and went back to Richard's fudge house.

Since then, they had made love, Iain and she, only three times. Snatched mornings, an afternoon, when supposedly she was shopping in her incompetent, unlike-Richard's-mother way.

She had always been afraid Richard would hurt Iain.

Iain, begging her to leave Richard, had said that he would like Richard to try. He would like to give Richard back some of what he had doled out to her.

But she was so terrified of violence by then she could not face their confrontation. To her Richard was like some enormous overpowering force. Nothing could withstand it.

Sadism had become a custom. It was not that she liked it. It was only that now it ran in her blood.

Then came the evening that she had been arguing with Iain, in the room behind the bar, about how she could not leave Richard, must try to make a go of it. And she had thought, misinterpreting some gesture, Iain was about to hit her. And she had cowered.

Iain had gone mad. He had yelled so loudly at her that Danny had come around and ordered him out.

"If you think that's what I'm like, like *him*, that cretin—we're finished. That's it. So long, Linda. Thanks for all the rotten times."

After that, although she had cried a great deal on her own, locked in the bathroom with the taps turned on to hide the sounds, Linda Reeves had tried extra hard to be for Richard what he seemed to need.

But, of course, Richard only needed her mistakes, so he could punish her.

Truly, she knew. And as they walked back from the cemetery together, she had been saying to herself, *Oh God, what am I doing? Oh God, how can I get away?*

Then that strange little black-haired girl had knocked on the door, wanting—who was it?—a Mrs. Watkins?

And Linda did not dare to ask her in, although really she would have liked to. Someone new, a cup of tea and a chat. She might have been able to help, they could have tried the directories, maybe found the right house. Such a pretty girl, in a wild, unusual way, like a young ballerina. She would have been interesting.

But then the girl went and Linda swore at Richard. *Swore* at him—for God's sake, had she not remembered how he was about swearing, or "blasphemy"—and he had come down and he had laid into her.

It was a terrible beating, but not the worst he had given her. She had been in hospital once.

But somehow, it was the end. It was like a gateway, and she knew she had only to run through. Though, initially, she did not.

She put herself together as best she could, quietly, while Richard stayed downstairs, drinking whisky he bought for himself and never offered her, because it was bad for a woman to drink alcohol.

In the bathroom she fainted, but only for three or four seconds. She came to sitting on the floor, and something made her laugh at that.

When she was tidied up, she went down. It was best to act as normally as she could after an attack. He would be morose, but no longer violent, and eventually this stage would pass into the next one, of concern and contrition.

"Well, I'm just off," she said. "Don't forget the pie in the oven."

"That will have to do, I suppose."

"It's a nice pie. You'll like it."

"At least you don't try to make your awful travesties of home cooking anymore."

Her eyes were a little blurred, and her left ear kept on buzzing. But she would manage.

She had taken the whole four hundred and fifty-six pounds from the concealed store in her underclothes. She had saved from her wages and her tips, but not often from Richard's housekeeping. It was what she called secretly her emergency fund. Why she took it now she could not have said. Perhaps in case he searched and found it.

"I'll see you later," he said.

When he did so, she felt a hot twisting in her heart.

"Don't be late," he said. "And make sure you tell them this is your last week."

"Yes, Richard."

When she got outside, her legs almost gave way. Mrs. Carey from number seven was going by with some shopping and her nice big dog.

Linda waved jauntily.

She reached the Fox and Glass and Danny looked at her and said, "Christ, Linda." But when she shook her head, "I'm all right," he said only, "Go on, then. But if you want to come off and sit down, just let me know."

She had a gin and pineapple that Mary gave her. Then a high came on her, so that she felt strong, and that nothing could harm her anymore. Nothing. Not even Richard. And in those moments she knew Iain would come in, and she would be able to make it up with him.

Linda was adept and brilliant with the customers that night. She clowned and got them to laugh, so they overlooked her injured face. When they offered her drinks, she kept the money, to put with her four hundred and fifty-six pounds.

By ten, Iain had not come in after all.

Last orders went by, and then the pub started to clear. It drained like a glass of liquor. Only the wreathes of smoke, the empties, the flat packets of crisps. Let down.

Danny bolted the doors and Mary said to her, "Come and have another gin. You've bloody earned it."

But Danny gave her a brandy.

Linda downed it. And then she found herself in a chair with Danny saying, "I've never moved so fast in me life." And she guessed he must have caught her as she went over.

After that she thought of Iain and she began to cry.

How the tears hurt, gushing past Richard's gift of bruises, and when they touched her lip, they stung. When she blew her nose, that hurt too. He must have hit her there as well. Her ear buzzed. Perhaps it would never get better.

At midnight, when she was sitting with Mary, Iain appeared, hammering on the back door. Someone had told him about Linda's face.

He stood over her, wet from rain—there had been a storm—white and scowling, his own eyes full of tears, and fire. It was Richard's face, but it was not Richard at all.

"You're not going back to him. I won't let you."

At the flat, he held her so gently, not to exacerbate her wounds, but pain and mad joy kept her awake.

She lay and breathed the frowsty wonderful smell of love.

She thought, *I don't want anything of Richard's.*

There was nothing to take from the fudge house. Everything in it was his, or things he had bought her that he believed she should have, things she did not like. She loathed it all, even to the plain underclothes he made her buy and the flat, uncomfortable shoes, and the medicinal toilet waters, and set of brushes with fat Victorian maidens.

But I do have to go back. Just once. Iain will go with me. And that bastard, that bloody stinker won't touch him.

For Richard, confronted by Iain's male, six-foot, twenty-two-year-old fitness, would quail.

I'm thirty-four. I'm too old for him.

In his sleep, Iain turned a little and kissed her hair.

I can make this flat smashing. Iain won't mind. He'll enjoy it.

But I have to go to Richard, just once. To tell him I'm leaving him for good.

Her ear had stopped buzzing.

* * *

At one in the morning, Richard Reeves was sitting on the big sofa in the main room, finishing a whisky.

Linda should have been home an hour and a half ago, and she was never later than midnight.

Richard knew where she was. She had gone with a man. But the man would chuck her out presently, and then she would have to come back.

He could not call the pub, the phone was broken. It had been knocked over last week. Her fault.

He had been sorry after she left, sorry he had slapped her. She made him angry. She did it purposely. But he must try to control his irritation. He would say he was sorry, give her a cuddle when she came in.

But she did not come in, and, justifiably, the anger began to build again.

He went back to the whisky and soon after midnight he had drunk his fourteenth shot, counting the four he had taken earlier. He needed to calm his nerves. He needed to have it out with her. Who did she think she was? He worked and slaved to give her the best. But she was off with some man. He had suspected. He was never wrong.

When the door knocker went so loudly, Richard was fuzzy, and he thought that maybe Linda had forgotten her key. So he stood up and girded himself in rage, and went to the front door to open it.

It was not Linda who waited at the door.

A tall old man in a black coat.

No, a young man, with white hair . . .

"Richard?" asked this man, smiling at him.

"Yes, I'm Richard Reeves. Who are you?" And then the penny dropped. "Are you her bloke?"

Richard felt a mix of ferocity and alarm. He was not prepared. He was tired. This was his home ground. He tried to come out at the man, but the man instead came gliding in, and after him, like a creature of the night, a black-haired girl smothered in makeup.

"Where is your wife?" said the man.

"My—Linda's with you. Or she was. What do you want?"

"Then she isn't here," said Malach. "Oh, good. Ruth, shut the door." The girl he had called Ruth did so, and they were all inside Richard Reeves's house.

"Look here," said Richard, "I didn't ask you in."

"But here we are," said the man. "Go in there, and have another whisky."

"Don't you—"

The man pushed him, and Richard Reeves staggered crazily back into the main room. He thumped into a table and a large china cannister teetered. Richard held it down.

The white-haired man had also entered the room, and the girl had followed. They put wet prints into the carpet. What Richard had taken for a cheap imitation leopardskin coat turned out to be some sort of robe. Who were these people? What were they after?

"She described you well," said the man to Richard.

"Linda described—"

"Ruth. Ruth overheard your conversation with your wife."

Still smiling, kind, the white-haired man moved close to Richard. The scent of night and rain was on the man, and an odd fragrance of burning.

"I believe," said Malach, "you told her this." And then he struck Richard Reeves full in the belly. It was a soft belly and it did not resist.

Richard curved over and brought up his whisky on his carpet.

Malach stepped back.

When Richard had stopped puking, Malach kicked him in the side and Richard rolled over. Malach rested his booted foot on Richard's throat, pressing lightly on the windpipe. Richard tried to fight. Malach pressed harder.

"Don't," said Malach. "Just do as I want."

"There's money," gasped Richard. "I'll tell you where."

"Money," said Malach. He pulled a melodramatic disappointed face. "Only money?"

"Some of these ornaments—worth something—"

"Ruth," said Malach, "smash some of the ornaments."

Richard began to argue, but his voice was cut off.

Ruth took bulky china objects from the false mantelpiece and dropped them in the hearth, where they broke noisily.

Malach raised his foot.

"They're very unattractive. Better, like this."

"You're insane."

Malach leaned down and cracked Richard hard across the face. Richard's teeth cut his lip open and it began to bleed.

"But you are a cunt," said Malach. "Oh, forgive me. You don't care for bad language."

Richard coughed and was feebly sick again, his head turned painfully under Malach's boot.

As his eyes cleared slightly, Richard saw the girl hefting the huntsman figurine.

"No—no—don't—that's valuable. I swear it is."

Malach held up his silvered hand.

"Bring it to me, Ruth."

Ruth brought the statuette, three burly men in russet coats raising guns at some unseen flying things.

Malach weighed it in his palm, looking at it. He looked down again at Richard. "It's a fake." The piece whirled through the air and struck the wall. It smashed into a shower.

Richard was hurt and ill, and now he was very scared, and he began to cry. Life had long ago taught him that the tears of a strong man will bring him sympathy, or aid.

Not now.

Malach had removed the booted foot and instead hauled Richard up, helped him to stand, and led him out to the foot of the stairs.

"Yes, there's cash up there," said Richard. His nose ran and somehow Malach would not let him wipe it, or the blood oozing down his chin.

Malach took Richard up the flight of stairs, and, on the landing, Richard tried to turn to the bedroom where he kept a thousand pounds in fifties, in a marvelous find, an old box from the slave trade, ebony, showing a black man in chains . . .

"Tell me about Linda," said Malach.

"My wife—"

"Your wife," said Malach.

Malach brought his fist up into Richard's jaw, just avoiding the nerve point that would have rendered him unconscious.

Richard's head slammed back into the wall, and before he could save himself he fell, twisting and thumping, the length of the stairs.

Richard lay moaning on the carpet under the stairs.

Ruth came out to see.

Malach descended the stairs with a measured tread.

"The grand old Duke of York," said Malach, "he had ten thousand men. He fucked them up on the top of the hill, then he fucked them up again. Ah, forgive me. You don't like these words." He lifted Richard like a length of used material. This time he had to drag him up the steps.

At the top Malach brought his fist across Richard's face again and sent him down once more along the stairs.

At the bottom, Malach knelt on Richard.

He took Richard's head by the ears.

Richard was just conscious. The bleary eyes wavered, but they saw.

"Now Richard. Say Christ." Richard groaned. "Say Christ fucks, Richard."

"Nnn—" said Richard.

Malach banged Richard's head hard into the bannister.

"Say Christ fucks, Richard. Christ was beautiful and flawless and wise, but you know nothing about him. In your mouth he won't be Christ at all. Say it, Richard. *Christ fucks*." And Malach, holding Richard's head by the ears, smashed it like the china on the bannister at the stairs' foot.

"Chri—" said Richard.

"Louder, Richard," Malach coaxed.

"Chri—fuh—"

"And now say cunt, Richard."

Richard shut his eyes and snot rivered from his nose.

Malach bashed Richard's head again against the wood.

"Say cunt."

"Cuh—"

"Ruth," said Malach, "fetch some soap." He cradled Richard's head on his thigh, smiling down at him, until Ruth came with a bar of Camay from the bathroom. Then Malach gently put the soap into Richard's wet mouth. "Wash your mouth out now, Richard."

In the bedroom, Malach found the ebony box. He touched the shoulder of the carved black man. Malach said, "I'm sorry."

The money fell out and Ruth went to it.

"No," said Malach. "You don't need money now."

And so Ruth set fire to the fifty-pound notes, and let them flutter down around Richard at the stairs' foot. .

Richard was past shouting. He cried. His tears did not bring aid, or put out the fire.

* * *

When Linda came back at nine-thirty, walking with her arm in Iain's, little was left of the fudge house, or Richard Reeves, but a heap of black stuff.

CHAPTER 23

✤ *HALF-LIGHT. THE GARDEN DARKLY* glowed before the dawn. The rain had left its garment behind it, drops which hung and glistened, and which dripped from polished leaf to leaf down into the high grass that was not yet lit to green.

The twisted fish shone and its basin was deeply filled. The straw hat had been removed.

Rachaela stood in the grove, between the feral apple and the fountain. She wore Althene's white dress, the long hem of which was soaked.

All around, the liquid shadow and the oaks like a forest. And silence, plectrumed now and then by the songs of birds. But they did not really sing. Surely there had been a dawn chorus, rehearsed and almost strident. What had subdued the birds? Did they know the earth grew old?

Her mood was strange.

Hormones, perhaps. After all, she was in her forties now, whatever her body looked like.

The grove might be in a forest, and it might have been anywhere. Some other country. Some land of her genetic past.

There were memories, always on the edge of mental sight and hearing. She could not grasp them, yet she partly saw from the corners of her eyes, and nearly heard their whispering. It seemed she must stand wholly still, and then the veil would melt, and she would know it all. All there was or could be. And she was not afraid.

And I'm drunk, of course. Their dinner and their wine.

Yet she stayed on in the timeless garden, floating in space.

Scarabae. I, too, am Scarabae.

An oval melted in the veil and the shadow, and through it came a man clad in black with long white hair.

He walked toward her deftly, over the grass, and past the fountain.

Malach said: "It's true, the Scarabae women are the most beautiful in the world."

He lifted her hand quietly and kissed it, close beside the ruby ring that had been Anna's and Miriam's. Then he leaned and kissed her cheek. He smelled still of the dark, and of danger. But it was not for her, his dangerous dark.

"Why are you here?" she said. "Have you brought Ruth here?"

"Oh, no. Ruth is safe. I've come to fetch my sons, the dogs."

"Your sons," she said.

"My other sons are lost to me," he said.

Rachaela felt a rill of excitement flow through her, but it died because she made it die.

"Are you going to kill Ruth?" Rachaela said. "Or won't you answer?"

"What is death?" said Malach.

He widened his eyes and now there was enough light to see their hard sheer color. So bleak, so far, the distance inside the eyes.

"Death is what happened to Anna," said Rachaela. "And to the others. Death is what Ruth caused."

But she thought, *I believe in his age. A hundred. More. There, and there. How can something so old ever kill?*

"I must be going now," he said.

She could find no further words to say to him.

She watched him move away through the spell of the garden, and the veil mended, and a blackbird sang.

Under the electric lights of the utility room, Camillo was burnishing the Cinderella carriage of the trike.

He had brushed the damson velvet, and rubbed the stained-glass window, and now attended on the sharklike bodywork with rags.

A man was in the doorway.

Camillo's face set into a kind of doughy flatness. He stood up and rubbed his cleaner hand between the ears of the burned horse head.

"Come to see my horse?"

Malach walked into the room. But for the trike, there was little there. A few boxes, bottles, cans of fuel and cleaning agents, and the block of raw light. Malach stayed still, and looked at everything. Finally at Camillo.

"Let me tell you," said Camillo. He tapped the vermilion-streaked gut of the machine. "Harley-Davidson fifteen hundred super-charged engine converted for a trike. And here," he indicated the silvery spirals between the forward forks, "twelve-inch over-springer forks, nickel plated in twist-candy style. Yum."

Malach looked at the trike, where Camillo pointed.

"And the front wheel—the original twin-disc hub is laced into a nineteen-inch rim."

Camillo pivoted. He giggled. "The swan-neck frame has been stove enameled."

The fearful light burned on Malach's hair like white-hot flame.

Camillo said, "Cruise control is fitted. But I prefer to sit up when I ride. Methane injection built into the fuel system. That means my trike could go to one hundred and twenty miles an hour in two seconds. It would kill the engine but I'd be miles away."

He waved his hand in its skulls and rose masks at the black half-pumpkin. "A souped-up Volkswagen rear." He paused. "Do you like my horse?"

"I remember four," said Malach, "one a black gelding which threw you."

"I don't remember that," said Camillo sharply. "Only the dogs. I remember all the dogs."

"Perhaps it will come back to you."

"Too old," said Camillo. He grinned and dived behind the trike as if for cover. "Well, we've met again," said Camillo, hiding around the pumpkin shell. "You can go away now."

Malach still stood there, under the light. Cold fire.

He seemed to be examining the trike.

Camillo stole out again. He said, "You've killed someone. Is it horrible Ruth?"

"Just men," said Malach.

"I remember *that*," said Camillo. "I remember in the sleigh—"

"No," said Malach.

"Here you are," said Camillo. "What do you expect?"

Malach turned and was gone.

Camillo's face slowly sank inward. He looked old now, ancient, a poor old man with a shiny trike that could not be his.

"We drove from the outskirts of the town. There were men running with torches but the horse bolted past them." Camillo sighed. "Out into the white woods we ran . . . I sobered, thinking of sagas I had heard of wolves, but my father said, 'Men are to be feared, not wolves.' "

Camillo patted the horse head. "Good horse. We'll get away. Light the fire, we can outrun it."

But no one was there to listen.

Tray had been sick. It was the mixture of drinks and no food. Lou was affected another way. She lay on the large bed, mildly snoring on a mat of Pre-Raphaelite hair. Her head was turned, so the tattooed rose showed on her neck like a vampire's kiss.

Lou and Tray both took the pill right through the month, so they need never have a period, but sometimes Tray felt funny, as if her physical clock were trying to come on.

When her stomach was better, she had a shower and put on her little navy leather sailor suit with the corset waist and white collar. Two of her nails had broken and this depressed her, for her nails were one of her forms of artistic procreation, the tones and pictures she painted on them, and now the canvas was spoiled.

She went down through the house, looking for Cami, and in the pillared hall she saw Malach.

Malach was amazing. He was like a singer, but he did not sing.

He sat on a straight carved chair and by him were the two frightening large dogs in the spiked collars. He was caressing their heads, staring into their bluish honeyed eyes.

Tray went closer.

"Hi," said Tray. "Come here often?"

Malach looked up and saw her. He said nothing.

Tray giggled. It was a dulcet soft sound, unlike the noise Camillo made, like a horse whinnying. "I like your hair."

"Thank you."

"Do you know Cami, then?" asked Tray.

"Little girl," said Malach, gently, "please leave me alone."

Tray started. "I only asked."

"Don't ask. Don't ask me anything."

"Oh," said Tray. She did not believe he was dismissing her. Men turned their shoulders, but they did not ultimately resist. Tray was Desire.

She moved carefully closer, trying to avoid the big hairy shapes of the dogs.

"Cami gave me this necklace. It's polished chicken bones with silver. Aren't they lovely?"

Malach looked at her, past her eyes, into her brain. He said something in a language she did not understand. He said, *"Tires-toi."* But she knew at once, as if he had thrown her right across the hall.

She backed from him in terror.

At the stairs she stumbled, then turned and climbed swiftly up, away from him. On the landing she looked back. He was engrossed again with the dogs.

She ran along the corridor, and up the other flight of stairs, into Camillo's apartment. She wanted to shake Lou awake and tell her. *He swore at me. He said something really filthy.*

But it was not the words, it was the rejection.

She bit her broken nails, but only those, down to the quick.

Sitting up in the chair, she fell asleep.

When she woke, Lou was still snoring and Cami had not come up. The window, which was opaque white glass, was blazing with summer morning. The golden clock said it was nine-thirty.

Tray got up and went to the mirror. She looked at herself. She was the same. She turned about to admire her slender, incredible body, its seventeen-inch corset waist, her necklet of bones and silver wheels.

Lou had a thing about Althene. Lou had dug out her gas mask earrings and put them on because of Althene's gas mask with the poppies.

Lou was useless.

Tray went out again and downstairs.

She was afraid he might be in the hall still, but of course he was gone by now.

She had taken some money from the bag where

Cami left it for them. She would go to the shops and have her hair done. She would have it done black, like Rach's.

The cake shop was open, and Tray bought a doughnut. It had thick jam. Her dad had brought her doughnuts, and a plate of sugar, and let her roll them in the sugar until they were white. Her mom would say, "You'll get fat." But naturally Tray did not get fat, for she seldom ate anything at all.

In Lucrece, where—unknown to Tray—presumably they made you so beautiful you would be raped by a Roman, the manager came and led her to a chair. He said it did not matter there was no appointment, he would always make a place for her, she had such excellent hair it was a treat to style it. But he liked Cami's money, she knew that too. And anyway, they were empty.

Tray sat through the hairdresser's torture, which she did not mind, for two hours. And then she sat under the dryer.

She drank the Fanta they brought her.

When she looked up into the mirror, she saw with surprise what they had missed. Crystal tears fell from her eyes. They did not ruin her face, for her eye makeup did not run, and her blusher was waterproof, and she was like a doll that wept.

In the phone box, Tray inserted Cami's phonecard. She had taken it out with her, so she must have known she would need it, but not consciously.

The phone rang, and she hoped her father would answer.

If her mother answered, she would put down the receiver.

It rang a long time.

While she waited, an ice-cream van entered the street. It played its tune loudly, and Tray was afraid she would not hear properly who was on the line if the phone was answered.

Then there was her father's voice.

"Hi, Dad. It's me."

"Tray!"

"Hi, Dad."

"For Christ's sake where are you? I've been worried."

"I'm okay, Dad."

"I've been worried, Tray. You go off and get yourself in bloody bother. Where are you?"

"Just London, Dad."

"What's happened? Where in London?"

"It don't matter. I'm fine. I just . . . wanted to talk to you."

"You're daft, Tray, you are. You can always bloody talk to me. Why don't you come home and talk to me?"

She heard, more than his questions and sentences, the light that came on in his voice when he spoke to her. She could recall how he would grin when he came in at the door and she ran toward him, holding up some toy.

"Don't nag, Dad." The ice-cream van was closer.

"All right, all right. So long as you're okay. What you been doing?"

"Just the usual stuff."

"Bloody bikes and bloody bad rock groups."

"Bands, Dad."

"*Bands*. Ought to be banned."

His joke always irritated her. Suddenly she was far away from him again. She was twenty-two and he was old.

"Got to go now, Dad."

"What? Just wait a bloody minute, Tracy. Tell me where you are?"

"I said. London."

"Is it some bloke again?"

She thought of Cami, older than her dad, but Cami was different.

"He's famous."

"What?"

"Famous."

"Who is he then?"

"Can't say. Got to go now."

"Tray—"

"Got to go. Love you, Dad. Bye."

She put down the phone.

She felt relief, she felt bereft.

The ice-cream van, which had played its tune all through the conversation, had now left off.

She went out of the phone booth and bought herself a cornet with strawberry sauce and nuts and two sticks of chocolate.

CHAPTER 24

✤ *HE HAD GONE TO THE HOUSE WITH HER,* when she had told him about the man. That was the first thing she remembered, as she opened her eyes. He had said, the woman was all right, let the woman go. He had said he would kill the man. And he had killed the man. And the house burned. And then they came away.

They traveled on a late bus.

A man threw up at the back, and his vomit smelled, quite purely, of spirits. Upstairs the air was thick and blue, but they traveled below. He said he was too tall to go up there. She believed this.

There was a kebab place, and he bought her a slab of spicy lamb in pita bread with pale red chili sauce, and salad. Then, when they arrived at their destination, he led her into a room, and there he gave her a glass of wine. When she had had the wine, she found her head had dropped with a jolt, almost as if decapitated. Next she slept.

She came to on the bed. It was comfortable, and he had pulled the coverlet up over her. The pillows had feathers and, when she put on the lamp by the bed, she saw they were of sky blue. The sheets were also blue, and the blankets and cover in tones of deep green.

There was one window, and it was round. It seemed

to have a pattern not a picture. But it was of stained glass.

Everything in the room was green and blue, except the lamps, which were a dusty rosy pink. There was no fireplace, only a radiator.

There was a dressing table with two lights and a mirror that had frosted leaves coiling around it.

On a dark table were some books and other things which Ruth did not inspect.

The room had an aura of the Scarabae, and on the vanilla-green wall was fixed a black and white clock, which had stopped.

A bathroom adjoined the bedroom. It was green, with blue towels and a dark blue carpet. There was an extractor fan, but no window. The taps were gold dolphins.

This must be a Scarabae house.

The other one had burned, but as it did so, some portion of her had known there were other houses. Other Scarabae.

Malach was Scarabae.

He had trapped her.

She tried the door, which was locked, and then she waited for him to come back, for she sensed that he had gone away.

The day was in the window when he returned.

The window was not like the room. It was scarlet, amber, the blue of fire, the carnivorous rose of lions' mouths, hot and blind. Through it, dimly, she could see the lines of bars.

He opened the door and found her sitting on the bed, gazing at the window.

"Am I a prisoner?" she asked.

"Yes."

"Malach, I don't want to be a prisoner."

"Ruth, you have no choice."

"Why?" she said.

"You are a murderess."

"You killed that man."

"You killed Scarabae."

"I didn't mean to," she said slowly.

"You meant to."

"I was angry."

"You must learn," he said, "to use proper words. You do not kill your own from anger. It's *fury*, Ruth. It's pain."

"Then, from fury. From pain."

"Very well. Now you are punished."

"What will you do to me?" she said.

"We shall see."

"My dad," she said. She thought. She said, "My father, Adam. He hanged himself. Was it because—was it because I did those things?"

"What things?"

"You know."

"You must articulate. You must say what is true."

"Because I stabbed Anna and—the others."

"We can't ask him. He's dead."

"I killed ordinary people. I drank their blood," said Ruth. She yawned. "I burned their houses. That was Emma."

"You're a stupid little bitch," said Malach.

"No," said Ruth. "I'm evil."

Malach looked at her, and she at him.

"You're Scarabae," he said. "That is your name. Forget the rest. Forget epithets from horror films. Now, you shall meet my companions."

Ruth stirred. She looked frightened and then cold.

Malach called back beyond the door: "Enki. Oskar."

And they came, the two huge dogs with their coats of brindled snow, wolfhounds with the blood of mastiffs and perhaps even of wolves, stepping like princes, with amber eyes.

Ruth got up at once. She held out her hands and went toward them without hurry or hesitation. And they received her, sniffed at her fingers.

Their heads came to her breasts. She stroked the silky hair upon their hard stony skulls. She met their eyes and kissed their muzzles.

Lethargic scythes, the great tails wagged.

She stood between them, holding them against the two sides of her body.

"Oskar, Enki," he said, "enough."

And they slipped from her. Like sunlit smolders they were through the door and Ruth stood alone.

"What shall I do now?" Ruth said.

"You will be alone now."

"For how long?"

"Ah vous dis-je."

"I don't understand."

"You'll come to."

He went out and shut the door. The key turned.

After a moment Ruth ran to the door and banged on it violently.

One of the dogs barked, and then was silent.

Ruth retreated to the bed. She got up on it and sat by the pillows.

Gradually the sun moved, and left the window.

She was hungry.

CHAPTER 25

✤ NORMAN OLIVER BAILEY IVES WATCHED
the patio through the closed glass of the sliding
doors. Out there Marilyn, his wife, was pedaling slowly
and laboriously on her exercise bike.

She was five foot six, and weighed a little over eleven
and a half stone. Her tanned body bulged from the small
zebra-striped bikini. Her blond hair was tied up by a
shocking-pink scarf. Despite the careful hairdressing attentions of Jason, there was a brassy tinge to Marilyn's
hair that infinitesimally hardened between each weekly
visit.

Marilyn stopped pedaling.

She reached out to the green ironwork table and
took three or four chocolates from a dish. She crammed
them quickly in her mouth.

Marilyn was always cutting out potatoes, but she
could never go without chocolate. It gave her energy, she
said. Besides, she said, a bit of extra flesh was all right,
providing your muscles were firm. Anyway, chocolate was
not fattening, it just burned off. Poor old Marilyn.

Tracy liked sweet things too. But she never put on
any weight. She had been a slim, doelike child, and so she
grew, in perfect proportion, into her glove-fitted golden
skin.

It amazed him, that he and Marilyn could have produced between them something so lovely.

Marilyn was still quite attractive, of course, and when they went out she dolled herself up, made the best of herself. But he—well, he could never win any prizes. Stop a procession, he would. Ugly git.

He grinned, seeing a vague reflection of this ugliness in the glass. Short and squat, with big muscled arms from his days as a plasterer before he took to running the show —and he would still take a stint, liked to, if someone was off sick. His belly was large too, bulging out his white vest. He was brown, a tan that never faded, from his years of outdoor work, and his brown bullet head sat on his shoulders without the intermediary of a neck.

None of this had ever stopped him. His mother, the Old Girl (and that was how she had always been for him, an old *girl*), she had said, "You ain't pretty, but you're a good boy, Nobbi." It was she who had given him the nickname first, after his father, the rotten old sod, had landed him with that Norman Oliver mouthful.

Nobbi had liked his mother. He liked all women, and they tended to like him. When he first went with Marilyn, she had really been a stunner. The heads had turned.

Maybe that was where Tray got her looks from after all. Or from his own mother. The Old Girl had been quite a piece in her youth, he had seen the photos.

In the glass, over Marilyn's struggling reflection (she had started the bike again), the gold winked on his St. Christopher medallion, his sovereign ring, his Rolex.

Behind him was the huge room, which Marilyn had decorated, like all the house, but bought and paid for by Nobbi.

Red velvet curtains held back by satin cords, studded red velvet couch and chairs, red Axminster carpet. Two chandeliers. On the glass coffee table, a stack of Marilyn's *Vogues* and a big china doll in an Elizabethan dress and ruff of real silk and lace.

Over the gas log fireplace was *The Haywain,* reproduced to look like genuine paint. And on the other wall, which was papered in crimson damask, was Van Gogh's *Sunflowers,* a blot of yellow on all that red.

Nobbi did not bother with art, normally he did not notice. But the sunflowers always unsettled him a little, and Marilyn did not like them either, he knew, but only felt they should be there.

On the mantelpiece was Marilyn's collection of china figures, ladies from various historical eras. Nobbi quite liked those, because they were women.

Certainly they were expensive, like everything else.

Over by the large TV were Marilyn's fourteen exercise videos. Poor old Marilyn.

She was eating chocolate again, still pedaling.

Nobbi turned away. He would have to find something to do to take his mind off Tray.

It was no good worrying about her. When she got into a mess she would call him again, and he would go and rescue her. She knew he was always there.

He realized she was not innocent. She had slept with fellows. He wished it was not so, but that was the way it went nowadays. It would not matter in the long run. One day he would give her a white wedding, when she had calmed down, when there was a chap with money who could look after her, keep her happy. A son of one of the lads. Someone in the business.

He blamed that Lou. Lou had led Tray into all this nonsense, rock groups and running about. Lou came from scum, poor cow, she had never been any good. Had an abortion at twelve, he had subsequently found out. Too late now to get Tray away from her. Tray would find out for herself, and then he would be there, and then maybe he could get her to stay here, and she would be safe.

If only she would phone regularly. Even Marilyn had started to complain about it. If only he knew where she was—

Nobbi went out of the lounge, and up the thickly carpeted stairs.

He glanced into the bedroom he shared with Marilyn. It was curtained and bedspread with cotton sateen and matchingly papered in a pink migraine attack of small flowers. Ruched lace rucked up before the windows. On the bed were Marilyn's two bedroom dolls, a life-size little girl in a pink frock and a life-size little boy in blue.

Nobbi sometimes jokingly objected to the boy doll. Another man in his bedroom. He did not mind the little girl.

Marilyn had done the bathroom in piercing primrose yellow, to be cheerful. Tray's bathroom, around the turn of the corridor, was done in salmon. Marilyn had insisted. "You can spoil your bedroom if you want, but I want you to have a proper bathroom."

On the washbasin, next to the oyster-colored bar of unused soap, stood the half-empty abandoned bottle of Tray's nail varnish, black with gold specks. The cleaning woman always carefully replaced it when she had mopped the basin. The nail varnish was dried up. It had been there three months.

Nobbi tried not to, but he could not help it. He went into Tray's bedroom.

It was done in black crushed satin, with bands of gold-scrolled black dado. Black lace hung over the lamp. Before the windows were suspended sheets of smoked glass with skulls on them, and on the walls were posters of long-haired, bare-chested young males, and one of a decomposing skeleton creature with white hair and a sword. Tray had told him this was called Eddie.

The bed had four black posts, and here sat another doll. It had once been quite sweet, but Tray had awarded it spiked orange hair and black lipstick, chains and a nose stud.

There was also the stuffed lion.

He had given her that when she was six.

"Lovely animals," he said, "lions."

"It'll frighten her," said Marilyn.

But the lion did not frighten Tray because Nobbi told her about lions, how noble they were, and how the lion would look after her when he was not there.

He picked up the lion now, and gave it a gentle shake. "Bloody useless, ain't you, mate."

On the dressing table were other things she had left behind. Some beads, a string of real pearls he had bought her on her fifteenth birthday. A little bone ring. Her fingers were so slender.

Christ, she was tiny, and the world out there was full of shit.

Nobbi squeezed the lion.

On the surface of the built-in wardrobe hung a miniature dress in coral and black, and a big black velvet hat. The cleaner always carefully replaced them.

It was like one of those bedrooms you kept for someone dead. A shrine.

Nobbi went out quickly and shut the door. He had the lion under his arm.

He walked down through the large house, and went out of the side door and over the garden, behind the grape pergola to the built-on annexe, his office.

A kind of relief laved over him when he came here. It was furnished with stuff from the Old Girl's house at Clapham, the big creaky chairs, the ancient sideboard.

Above the clutter of his office desk hung his grandfather's brass telescope and a sea chart Nobbi could not read. His father had been a bugger, but his granddad was a winner. An ugly old bastard, like Nobbi, with about three teeth in his head, mouth like a sewer—his mother had screamed at the language—and a mind full of treasure. He took snuff, and Nobbi had kept the battered tin. He could recall taking those gifts of snuff and fags, the bottles of rum. The muddly house. The lovely elderly dog with one blind eye, like Nelson.

Nobbi would have liked a dog, but Marilyn had been upset by the idea of the hairs. Tray was frightened of dogs.

Bugger this.

Nobbi put the lion on the desk and gave it a pat.

Then he picked up the phone and dialed Sandy.

They were doing a job over at Richmond. It was something for the Corporation. Had to be spot on. Should have been finished by now.

When Sandy came on the phone, Nobbi gave him a bollocking.

Things had to be special for Mr. Glass. Christ help you if they were not.

But Nobbi had always kept on the good side of the Corporation, and he did all right.

Then again, his firm was raking it in. He charged top prices for his work, and something over. Some people were so bloody stupid, they had more dosh than sense.

Except now and then, he would do a job himself, like for that old bird in Kentish town. Two hundred that had cost him, but she lived like a sparrow. "Call it ten quid, love. And give us a cuppa. Or give us a kiss and we'll call it five."

Sandy took the bollocking in his stride. He promised the job would be complete by Monday morning, they would go on over Sunday.

After the call, Nobbi tried to relax. He lit one of his cigars, which Marilyn said smelled, using the matches on his desk and ignoring the gold lighter. The cigar triggered his cough.

The lion looked happier in the office.

It had been fine when she was little. She used to follow him about. He had been able to look after her.

Nobbi put out the cigar and got up. He took his jacket off a chair, and went out of the office, locking the door.

Marilyn was sitting out on the lawn now, by the saccharine-blue swimming pool.

"Sorry, love," he said. "Something's come up. I've got to go over to Richmond."

"Oh, Nobbi."

"Sorry, love. It's a special job."

Marilyn knew it would be useless to protest. She understood, although they were maintained as a secret from her, that Nobbi sometimes did favors for and always had contacts in shadier areas than plastering and decorating. She preferred not to think of this.

She said, "Will you be back tonight?"

"I'll stay over with Sandy. Get an early start in the morning." Poor old Marilyn. "We'll go up The Fantail tomorrow night," said Nobbi.

Marilyn always liked to go out, although they did so two or three times every week. She brightened.

He left her looking at the blue pool, and went to liberate his Jag from the double garage.

Nobbi drove over the river.

As he went through the winding streets, he found himself looking here and there, and once he saw a slim little girl with long curling sunny hair. But it was not his Tray.

The sun was low, slanting sherry-colored through the parched green of the trees in tiny gardens, and sheeting the dim walls with apricot. Indian summer. Why did they call it that?

The gray Jaguar turned down the road with the launderette, fish shop, and Pakistani grocers. It came to a halt outside the three-story block of flats.

Nobbi got out, and glanced up at the windows.

Marilyn always liked notice if anyone was coming.

She even preferred it if Nobbi gave her a call to say what time he would be in. Tray used to drive her mad.

But here, there had never been any awkwardness like that.

He walked up the path over the square of grass and opened the outer door. Then he walked up the two flights, although it brought on his cough.

Flat 5A had a cream door that could do with another coat, and he ought to see to that fairly soon.

He rang the bell.

He knew what would happen, but he never got tired of it.

The door opened about two inches, and a thin face peered out. The face was framed by dead black hair cut level with the jaw. It was without makeup, strained and thin-lipped, with two enormous black-brown eyes. There was nothing about the face, nothing, until it saw him. And then it blossomed like a flower. It became flushed and almost pretty, and the door and the eyes opened much wider and the lips softened and parted.

"Nobbi! It's you! Nobbi, darling."

"Hallo, Star. I'm sorry, I didn't bring nothing for you. I forgot."

"I don't want anything. Only you."

And Nobbi went into the flat, and Star flung her arms around him and kissed his face with lots of quick light kisses.

Her actual name was Stella Atkins. She spoke well, and that always pleased him. He liked that sort of accent, the kind that was without any accent at all. She was a library assistant, clever.

He supposed that maybe she never minded when he arrived because she was always prepared. She was always bathing, and never put any cosmetics on her face. Her nails were bitten down like a girl's, although she was thirty-five. She was thin like a girl, too, and not very big on the bust. But she had lovely skin, smooth and pale.

The flat was always dusty, and always cluttered, with books and records and tapes everywhere. She did not care about appearances, wearing shabby suits to work, and jeans and sloppy shirts at home. She had no jewelry but for a silver watch which had been her mother's.

She had had a cat. It had been twenty-six when it died, sleeping on her lap. She had never been able to bring herself to replace it. The cat had been before his time.

"I've got a bottle of wine in the fridge. I saved it for when you'd come."

She ran to get it, her feet were winged.

He watched her bend to remove the bottle. She had a lovely bum.

He pinched her gently, and she squeaked, and came up and around with the wine in one hand, and kissed him deeply on the lips. Her other hand cupped his genitals. There was no mucking about with Star.

"Saucy," said Nobbi. He felt himself getting hard.

He was half a head shorter than she. But that had never concerned them. He opened the bottle, with slight difficulty, as Star caressed him.

They managed a quarter of a glass each, and then she was pulling him fiercely to her clean and neatly made bed, the only neat thing in the flat, soon to be wrecked.

Nobbi drew up Star's shirt, and found her bare shallow breasts. He tongued them all over and Star writhed and wrapped her legs around him.

He got off her jeans and panties, and licked her clit thoroughly. She tasted lovely, she always did. She came as he did this, giving off wild high cries, and the spasm running through her strongly enough he could feel it in his tongue, and taste the sharp minty fragrance.

"Christ, you're fucking lovely, you are."

Then she undressed him.

She did not seem to need chocolate for energy. The only sweet thing he had known her eat was an apple or a peach. She did not like chocolates, in fact. She did like his penis.

Star finally climbed up on Nobbi's fat muscular body like a queen into her chariot.

She rode above him, her face now glorious, and savage. "Oh, Nobbi— Oh, Nobbi—"

She flung back her head and had an orgasm that shook both of them, and, as he watched her, Nobbi came, groaning.

Star went to fetch the wine. She asked if he was hungry, and when he said he was, she brought him a toasted bacon sandwich on Boursin, with green chillies.

"Can I cook for you tonight?" asked Star.

"I can stay the night."

She kissed him.

When he had rested, she lay down across his legs and began to suck on him again. Although her lips were not full, her mouth was adept and marvelous, and her tongue drove him crazy.

He came again with a shout, and Star drank him down.

"I wish I could keep some of that in a bottle."

Nobbi lay back. He felt great. He slipped asleep, thinking that he had not thought of Tracy for a whole hour.

CHAPTER 26

♣ *LIKE ANOTHER PLANET, AUTUMN.*
The oaks were gold, against which the pines stood black.

In the garden, individual red leaves, like lipstick.

Rachaela listened to Shostakovich, Beethoven, Sibelius.

She slept in the day.

The nights drew out.

She dined with the Scarabae. They were very silent. They watched their action-film videos in the small hours. Once Eric pointed wordlessly at the screen. There was an actor who resembled Malach.

No more was heard, or spoken, of Ruth.

Sometimes, often, Rachaela would go to Althene's room. She would watch Althene make up her perfect face, or brush her hair, and Althene would encourage her to try on garments. Rachaela had lost her self-consciousness, and her animosity. They drank wine, and sometimes beer.

In the beginning, Rachaela meant to discuss Ruth, or Malach. But this, somehow, never happened. Instead they spoke of music. And then of what music suggested.

They spoke of history.

Althene must have studied it. She knew a great deal. Occasionally they took to going out. They would walk over the common. Althene wore black slacks and a coat that seemed made of some black skin.

Rachaela thought, *I have never had a woman friend.*

There had been Emma, of course. But Emma was Ruth's, and eventually not even that.

The others did not count.

One evening, Rachaela heard a piano faintly, in the house.

The playing was exquisite, painfully brushing the nerves.

She thought of Adamus.

Then Althene appeared on the stairs, and said, "It's Kei. There's a piano below."

"Kei," said Rachaela.

"Not only Adamus played the piano."

Rachaela said, "Does Malach play?"

"No."

They went up to the room of peacocks.

Althene brought her a glass of white liqueur, the dry colorless blood of strawberries.

"You loved Adamus."

"No. Never."

"Are you certain?"

"Quite certain."

"Then you never loved."

"No."

"Alas," said Althene, playfully. And then, "Tell me about your awful mother."

Rachaela must have dropped hints. She had once said harsh things. She sipped the liqueur.

"My mother was mistreated. She didn't want me but she got me. She tried to—malform me, too."

"Yes?"

"I remember, in her coffin, she was all the wrong shape. They'd done something. It wasn't her."

"Fools," said Althene. "And so you never said good-bye."

"Why would I need to? I'd never said hallo, if it comes to that."

"What was her name?"

"Her name?" Rachaela felt a pressure in her head. "Why does it matter?"

"My mother," said Althene, "used to whip me. With a leather whip. Can you imagine? It hurt very much. No, it didn't induce in me sexual pleasure. I lived in terror. And then Malach learned about it. And he stopped her."

"Malach. Is he your brother?"

"No."

"What then?"

"My . . . shall I say, my uncle?"

"You're lovers," said Rachaela. She held out her glass for Althene to fill it.

Althene paused, quizzical.

"Not at all."

"And your mother?" asked Rachaela.

"At last she came to see that everything was well. Now she's my friend. She likes to pretend she never touched me in anger. I don't labor the point." She filled the glass.

"Why did she whip you?"

"Why?" said Althene. She sat down in one of the midnight armchairs. She smiled. "One day, I'll tell you."

"More secrets. *Scarabae.*"

"Scarabae."

Rachaela said, "My daughter played the piano. She used to have lessons from Adamus."

"I can't tell you," said Althene, "about Malach and Ruth. I don't know."

"Don't you?"

"Why should I?" Althene sipped her liqueur in turn. "They mix a little strychnine with this. It's what gives the wonder of the taste. Not harmful. But your heart may beat quickly."

Rachaela said nothing.

Althene said, "You are becoming yourself. You can cease succouring yourself with the nonsense that all Scarabae are one, and in league against you."

Rachaela put down her glass.

"I drink more now than I used to."

"You can drink and eat what you like," said Althene. "It won't change you."

"What will?"

Althene smiled again. "Who knows?"

The day after, Rachaela made herself get up early. She bathed and dressed and went down into the garden.

Michael and Kei were in among the trees, putting out bread for the birds.

They did not see her. They laughed together.

Suddenly Kei touched Michael's cheek. It was a gentle mobile gesture, kind, provocative. Both men turned their heads and their eyes met.

Unmistakably they were lovers.

Rachaela drew back, not to intrude on their moment. She was surprised. Almost pleased. It occurred to her that maybe Carlo had been Michael's lover, but Carlo had died, and here was solace.

Thank God there was some reparation.

Then she felt alone, partly enraged.

She stood under the terrace, looking up at the house, with its ornate windows and towers.

Leaves fell, without wind.

Then Tray came out.

Her hair was black now, curling. She had taken to whitening her face, and somewhere she had bought some long black dresses with padded shoulders and sequins.

She was trying to be Scarabae. It was blatant.

Is she like Ruth? *No.* Not in ten million years.

Why then, the cold kiss of a wind that did not pass?

She looks like a pretty vampire from an early horror film. A film where the violence is only implied.

It was autumn, and winter would come.

Tray sat down, beneath Althene's discarded sunshade. She had nothing to do, and gazed away into the trees, and watched the leaves falling.

CHAPTER 27

✤ *OUTSIDE THE SMALL BARRED WINDOW* was a brick wall, thick with ivy. Standing in the room, the wall and the ivy were all there were. Seated on the floor, a slot of gray sky appeared at the window's top, and the form of a tree, already windswept of its leaves.

But Malach sat with his back to the window.

The walls of the room were painted white. The floor was of polished wood, with one flat rug of white and gray, like the walls and the sky.

There was a long table of whitish stripped pine. There were black, mildewed books on it, some bottles of faintly green glass. The table had drawers. Before it was an upright black chair.

In one corner stood a large canvas on an easel, ready stretched and primed; blank.

Low on one wall hung a Saxon sword, perhaps a reproduction, and under it a French saber, and under that a knife of stone.

There was nothing else.

Malach sat cross-legged.

He wore a white shirt and white trousers and old white boots, soft and patchy with age.

He was looking into space, not staring, but seeing something. He had not moved for an hour.

Beyond the window and the ivy wall a police siren sounded five or six streets away.

Malach half turned his head.

A dog growled quietly on the other side of the door.

"Yes, Enki. One moment."

Malach stood up. Although he had kept still so long, his movements were fluid, coordinated.

He went to the door and opened it and the two big dogs came to him with stately eagerness, thrusting their muzzles into his hands.

"You must have the garden. It's too soon today for walking."

He crossed the large living room of the flat, with its sea-green carpet and dark green chairs. There were yellow candles before oval mirrors on the walls. There was wallpaper like ghosts of bamboo which rose up and covered the high ceiling, infusing all the room with a dim green aquarium light. Between curtains of pale yellow silk the french windows opened wide and the dogs ran out gladly, up the steps and onto the lawn.

The garden was higher than the basement flat, the old garden of the house which had been remade into four apartments. The other three stood empty overhead. Lilac trees still held a cluster of their leaves, and at the bottom, where another house had been partly demolished, and then left, tall laurels mimicked the colors of the room. On the two other sides, the ivy wall seemed to go up forever.

The dogs trotted into the laurels.

Malach appeared to be watching them.

The flat had three bedrooms and two bathrooms, and a straw-tiled kitchen that had never been finished. Food came from a restaurant, croissants, little pots of jam and butter, vacuumed hot coffee in the morning, an Italian or an English lunch, an English or Italian dinner, at various hours, pastries, omelettes, cheeses, wine.

In the refrigerator in the kitchen were bottles of Coca-Cola, cartons of orange juice, a little beer with curious labels. The ice-making compartment was full of ice.

From elsewhere came the clean towels and the sheets for the beds, the soap and toothpaste, and punctually every month a stock of sanitary protection for Ruth.

He gave her all these things, for he went into her room once every day.

When he gave her the sanitary towels, Ruth's face crushed itself down. She marched into the bathroom and hid them. When she came out, she said, "You shouldn't have done that."

"How else would you manage?"

"It isn't nice," said Ruth. She was not prim but cold.

"I'm your jailor," he said.

She had accepted that. After the first time, she had never beaten again on the locked door, except to knock and call to him that she was hungry, or thirsty.

When he came into the room she did not protest.

But now she said, "It's wrong."

"Why? You menstruate."

"You should pretend not to know."

"Very well."

It was apparently his return for her obedience, this acquiescence of his. When next he brought her the towels, he folded them in the bath sheet. The same, too, with the nightshirts and underthings, the deodorant, even the shampoo.

She no longer wore makeup. From the third day she had begun to do her hair in two long plaits.

Sometimes she asked if she could see the dogs again, and sometimes he allowed this, bringing Enki and Oskar into the room on his next visit, but never allowing them to remain more than five minutes.

She was always docile, although occasionally she made polite passionless objections.

When she was alone, she took up one of the drawing pads and the paints or pencils, and drew and painted.

She created rooms and stairways, and endless variations of colored stained-glass windows, some with pictures of knights and women with birds. She painted nothing burning, and no dead, no blood. Then her architecture expanded as the time of her incarceration did. She drew pillared porticoes and soaring tiered towers. She drew archways which gave on archways, receding to vast distances.

She did not make landscapes.

Malach would look at all her work when he came. If she was at work on something when he entered, she would set it aside.

She sat on the plushy green carpet, a different shade from that of the living room which she had only briefly seen. She looked up at Malach sitting in one of the armchairs, like a pupil at a teacher. He had not told her to do this.

Once she had cut her finger on some paper, and it bled. She hid this from him like the evidence of the other bleeding.

She never referred to their meeting in the warehouse lobby, his killing of the men, how she had subsequently told him of the Reeveses, and that they had gone there together, and Malach had killed the man. The blood and flames.

She played the game with Malach always, without demur. She never argued against it or attempted to be facetious or obstructive. She only objected to the observations he sometimes made to her. As when he had said, "Suppose, Ruth, that I keep you here. That you never go out again." Then she said, "You mustn't do that. You know I must go out." "Why is that?" "Because I have to." "Why?" "Because I walk about for miles. I look at things." "Perhaps you never will again." "Yes, I will."

"And when, then," he said, "do you think that will be?"

"When I've been punished," she said, "enough."

On the first morning, after the first croissants and coffee, he had gone into her green and blue room with the Nasturtium window, and he had sat down in the chair. And Ruth immediately seated herself below him on the floor.

"We'll talk now," he said, "but not in the usual way."

Ruth nodded. She had not yet arranged her hair in plaits but her face was washed and white.

"I will say a word to you," he said, "you will say a word back to me."

"What kind of word?"

"The word that seems to fit what I have said."

"All right," said Ruth.

And Malach said, "Egypt."

Ruth answered swiftly, "Incest."

"Father," said Malach.

"King."

"Mother."

Ruth thought. She shook her head. "I can't think of anything."

"Nothing then," said Malach. He said: "Fire."

Ruth lowered her eyes. "Nothing."

"Blood," said Malach.

Ruth said: "Scarabae."

Then Malach stood up. He had been with her only fifteen minutes. He left her without any formal expression, but half an hour later she knocked and called out, "Can I have some more to eat?"

He phoned the restaurant, and two apple and raspberry Danish came, and an ice cream. She ate all of it.

The second day he went to her in the afternoon.

"Hunger," he said.

"Empty," said Ruth.

"Empty," he said.

She blinked. "Heart."

"Ruby."

"Heart," said Ruth.

"Heart," he said.

"Window."

"Describe the window," he said.

"Red. Ruby red. Ladies in red dresses and a red horse and a red sun."

"Darkness."

"Eyes," said Ruth.

"Whose eyes?"

"Yours."

"My eyes aren't dark, Ruth."

"Yes."

"My eyes are a very light blue. The eyes often turn paler, as the body grows older."

"Ink," said Ruth, starting the game again.

He let her. He said, "Ink is black."

"Blue ink. Mixed with white wine."

"What color is the window in this room?"

"Blood color."

"Blood, Ruth."

"Yesterday."

"Tomorrow."

She looked up at him and shook her head.

They played the word game every day for more than two months. Sometimes they would play for over an hour.

He did not seem pleased or dismayed by her reactions. It did not occur to her that rather than trying to learn about her, he was trying to teach her to be herself. She performed for him, only now and then lowering the shutter of her silence, and then only to decide. Even her evasions were relevant.

"Egypt," he said.

"Kings."

"Scarabae."

"Beetle."

"Describe the beetle."

"Black, with a face carved on its back."

Autumn came too quickly now, attached to the end of summer in a sudden sickening and death.

In the misty early mornings, more often after sunset, he would walk the streets of the capital, now with the dogs, and now alone.

But Ruth strayed only in her mind. She had nowhere else to go.

The dogs were sparring under the laurels, rolling and kicking at each other, barking joyfully.

Malach went back into the whitewashed room and drew the stone knife off the wall.

Going to Ruth's apartment, he unlocked the door, paused, and went in.

Ruth was sitting drawing. It was a palace, a compendium of many differing architectural styles, Renaissance Italian, Homeric Greek, timeless Egyptian.

She said at once, "I'd like some books. I'd like some books about buildings."

"I'll arrange it."

"Thank you."

"You are always very polite," he said.

"Emma taught me."

"But you dislike Emma."

"No . . ." said Ruth. And then, "Emma doesn't count."

"What word do you put with Emma?"

"Warm."

"Warm," he said.

"Fire," said Ruth. Then she screwed up her face. It became ugly, an imp's.

"The hanged man," said Malach.

"Tarot," said Ruth.

"Which card do you think is yours?"

"Priestess."

"Why?"

"I don't know."

"Where did you see a tarot pack?"

"In the market. And Mommy let me have it."

"Look," said Malach.

He held up the knife. It was bluntly shaped, yet with the edge honed like a razor. The stone was pinkish gray.

"What is it?" said Ruth.

"A knife of sacrifice."

"Is it real?"

"Yes."

He gave it to her. She examined it, meekly.

"Imagine," he said, "you are on a high place, before an altar, with this knife. On the altar is strapped a man. He asks you to kill him, to send him to the god."

"It's not sharp enough."

"Don't prevaricate. It's sharp."

"I'd wait for the sign," said Ruth.

"What sign?"

"That the god wanted him."

"But," he said, "you've never waited."

Ruth looked up at him. She put down the knife. She frowned.

"Sometimes—" she said.

"Sometimes. But it was an accident. The priest kills for God. The warrior kills for his legion. But you."

"Please," said Ruth. "Don't."

"Ruth kills for Ruth."

She bowed her head.

"I don't want to play anymore."

"Good. That means your eyes are opened."

"I don't want to see. The sun's too bright."

"There's no sun in this room."

"There's a light."

"Fire," he said.

"The house," she said.

"Anna," he said.

"Heart," she said.

"Heart," he said.

"Needle," she said. "Hammer and needle."

"Death," he said.

"Empty," she said.

He leaned forward and seized her. He pulled her up, up his body. She had grown perhaps an inch. Her head rested on his chest. He put the knife, cool, against her throat.

Ruth was quite still.

"Can I die if you kill me?"

"Believe it. Didn't Adamus die?"

"I don't know."

"Didn't Anna? Didn't Alice?"

"Did they?"

"If they didn't, why do I have you, Ruth, by the neck?"

He heard and felt her swallow. She did not struggle to resist. She said, "Thank you for doing it in private. When you've done it, will you hold my hand? It doesn't take long, does it? Just so I know you're there."

Malach let her go.

She fell straight onto the carpet. She had believed him.

He left her.

He locked the door.

He put the knife onto a little round polished table.

Then he walked into the second beautiful modern bathroom and vomited the bitterness of centuries and two thousand lies.

CHAPTER 28

✤ *IT WAS NOT HER LATE NIGHT AT THE LI-*
brary. At a quarter past six, Stella walked out and
up the road, towards the supermarket, which today was
open until eight.

After she had met Nobbi, after Nobbi began to stay
with her for the evening, Stella had bought a big freezer.
She stocked it carefully. She liked to cook for Nobbi.

The supermarket was comparatively empty. Stella
manhandled a trolly and wheeled it up the aisles under
the hard fluorescent lights.

She took some fruit first and a can of pilchards for
her own supper, two cartons of orange juice and some
crusty rolls. Then she moved among the tins, selecting
tomatoes, lentils, kidney beans. When she knew he would
be coming, she went to the delicatessen, gathered white
gourds of garlic and fresh vegetables.

At the frozen-meat section, she leaned deeply into
the vats, drawing out a leg of lamb, fillet steaks, a wedge
of bacon.

Anyone seeing her would think she was shopping for
a family.

Well, one day. Perhaps.

She did not often think of it. She rationed her
daydreams. But there might come a time, after he had
got his daughter settled. He would leave Marilyn all his

worldly goods, and he would come to Star. She would support him until he could build his business up again.

It did not matter to her if he came to her with nothing. She only wanted him.

Stella for Star. That was the first thing he had said to her when he stepped into her flat for the first time. He was carrying a box of chocolates. Stella hated chocolate, but she loved the ones he brought. She kept them until the sweets turned white, and then she kept the box, which had kittens on it. Marilyn, apparently, liked kittens. She had been known to say, wasn't it a pity they had to get bigger.

Stella for Star. When he said it, she had exclaimed with delight. "Just some old film I seen," said Nobbi. Stella said, "It's Tennessee Williams. *A Streetcar Named Desire.*" "Oh," said Nobbi. He had lowered his bashful eyes. He was slightly embarrassed and already hard. Five minutes later they were on Star's bed.

She had met him in the library. He had not come in for a book. Books, to Nobbi, were the commodity of others.

No, Nobbi had come in about a crack in the Senior Librarian's office wall. A favor to someone, Nobbi afterwards said.

It was two weeks after Stella's cat had died. There were only three elderly men browsing among the book stacks, and Stella alone at the computer, which she disliked. It had just messed her up, and she had started to cry.

To her rage and wretchedness the door opened, and this burly bloody man was there, through her tears only a graceless shape.

"Where's—" said Nobbi. And then, in a voice so utterly gentle, so utterly kind that it made her see him, he said to Stella, "What's up, love? What is it?"

So she saw him. A short, fat, common London wideboy in middle age. Bristly thin hair and nut-brown skin from all weathers, in a vest with a jacket over it and a flash gold chain.

And in his eyes, Stella saw—

She saw that which is eternal and indescribable, what the lucky ones have all seen, once, and the very lucky twice or three times. What she had never seen before among the gropings of her youth and the frigid evenings of her maturity.

Stella blushed. It was her body's flag, raised to signal to him from a hill.

Then she said, "My cat died. She was very old. It's silly, isn't it?"

"No," said Nobbi, "no it ain't. It breaks your bloody heart. My granddad had an old dog. Only one eye. It died, and I bawled my bloody eyes out for a month. Lovely old dog, it was. What was her name?"

He knew the cat had been feminine, or else all cats were female to him. "Gertie," said Stella. "My mother called her that. For Gertrude Lawrence."

"Oh," said Nobbi. He plainly had never heard of Gertrude Lawrence, but he liked the name. It had been the Old Girl's. "The thing you got to tell yourself," he said, "is that you gave her a good life. We all got to go. It's what you get here that counts."

"She did have a happy life. She died in her sleep."

"There you are," said Nobbi, "bless her."

"Bless you, too," said Stella.

And then Nobbi also blushed, faintly but unmistakably.

He went on to the Librarian's office and the crack.

A week later he came back. The gang of three workmen had created the usual chaos. Nobbi stood surveying it proudly.

"Look here, Mr.—er—isn't there any way you can hurry it up?" bleated Mr. Rollinson. "It's been going on for a week. You really—"

"Yeah, squire, I know," said Nobbi. "Not a thing I can do."

There was an open courtyard in the library, with potted trees and a seat. Here Nobbi came, to look at the offending wall from outside. Stella was eating from a carton of salad.

"Hallo."

"Hallo," said Nobbi.

He made a couple of passes at the wall.

"Funny old job, this." He glanced at Stella. "How do you get on with him?"

"Mr. Rollinson? I wish I could kill him."

Nobbi grinned.

"It's nice," he said, "all them books. I don't get time to read. No, it ain't that. Just don't have the knack for it. I bet you enjoy it, though."

"It fills in the gaps," said Stella.

Her heart bounced in her throat. She said, "Will you have lunch with me tomorrow?"

Nobbi's mouth fell open. He looked about eight. Maybe nine.

"Well I—I get my dinner as I go. Always moving around—"

"Don't make an excuse. Say yes."

There was no one anywhere. The red walls of the library turned the courtyard into a medieval garden.

Stella got up and went to Nobbi.

She went right up to him, and softly touched his balls.

"I want to go to bed with you," said Stella.

Nobbi looked frightened.

"Hang on—"

"No, I do. I really do."

"I'm married. I'm old enough to be your dad. Got a girl of my own—"

"I'm thirty-five. I haven't made love for ten years."

Nobbi back away and the wall stopped him, Stella's friend. "But—"

"I'm telling you about the ten years," said Stella, "so you know I don't make a habit of this."

"I'm not—" said Nobbi. "You're brainy," he said, "all that."

"I'm Stella," said Stella. "I want to feel you inside me."

"Christ," said Nobbi.

He looked up into her burning eyes, and seemed to recognize her from a long way off.

"Please don't—" said Stella, "don't, don't say no."

"You're bloody scaring me," said Nobbi.

"I'm bloody scaring me."

Next day they met in the park. Stella had brought sandwiches of cold roast pork, mustard and cream cheese, and a half bottle of Muscadet.

They ate under the trees. It was spring, not very warm, and when she shivered, he put his arm round her.

"I shouldn't," he said. "And you shouldn't. A girl like you."

"I'm not a girl."

They kissed experimentally. It reminded Nobbi of former times, kissing on the grass, nowhere to go. But there was somewhere to go.

In the evening he rang Marilyn, told her he was working late over at Roehampton, and went to Stella's flat with a box of chocolates which he knew, intuitively, were wrong, but not what else to get.

Stella's love-making was frenetic but not violent. She did not grab. In his embrace she seemed to have no bones, a slender snake.

Even in the eager beginning, Marilyn had never been like this. No one had, that he could think of.

When they had exhausted themselves, Stella for Star had made bacon and egg, which she served with a hollan-

daise sauce. She did not cry or carry on when he left. She
did look wistful. She did not reckon he would come back.

He called her in the middle of the night, from his
office in the annex.

"Nobbi," she said, "I wish you were here."

"Don't wish that, Star."

"No, I don't mean . . . I just mean, if you could
have stayed the night."

Outside the grapeleaves, young and tender, rustled
on the pergola. With the year the grapes would bud and
turn to green and purple. The cleaning woman would
pluck them and take them home. By then, Star and he
would be an established thing, but he did not know this,
then.

"I just wanted to tell you," he said, "you were
lovely."

"Was I, Nobbi?"

"You was wonderful, Star."

"Was I?"

At the caress of her voice, his erection strove upward, longing for her hands and lips, the velvet tunnel of
her loins.

"Sleep tight, Star. I wish—I wish I bloody well was in
there with you too."

At the checkout was a dowdy woman with her handsome
husband. He spoke to her in knife cuts.

He's ruined her, thought Stella for Star. *So many shits
of men.*

Her own father had not been much. They had been
happier after he was gone, her mother and she.

Star had loved her mother. But she loved Nobbi
more. She loved sex with Nobbi. She loved sleeping with
Nobbi, back to back. His hard bare buttocks against her
own.

She loved his goodness. His shyness. His loyalty to
Marilyn and Tracy. Yes, she even loved that.

She paid for the food.

One day.

One day she would go home, and Nobbi would be there, working on his accounts at her table. They would have a big dog, and a cat, bought together in infancy so each believed the other was a version of itself, a meowing dog, a barking cat.

And, it might be, if it did not take too long, that she could give him a child.

Why not? It happened all the time, mothers of forty-five and more. She was fit and strong.

A girl. He would want a girl.

Another Tracy, but better. A Tray brought up to appreciate him.

She thought of Nobbi pushing a little girl on a swing. And stopped herself.

She had to wait.

God knew, she had waited long enough for love.

The bus came, and she lugged the heavy bags of food, merrily in her strong arms, aboard.

"Foggy old night," said the woman beside her.

"Terrible," agreed Star. She had not noticed.

CHAPTER 29

✤ *CROSSING THE RIVER, THE FOG LESS-*
ened. Lights hung in the night water like reflections in a mirror that had been breathed on.

For a moment it might have been anywhere. Torch
poles above the Tiber. Brands on the living bank of
Thebes. Or some stretch of medieval water lit for an occasion.

But past the river, the fog closed in again.

Rachaela remembered the days of the fog, years
ago, when the Scarabae first reached out for her.

"Of course," said Althene, "this is nothing. Hardly a
London Particular."

She sat away along the seat of the taxi, the traveling
lights catching her colors. She wore a blue velvet coat,
and under that a tunic suit of ash-blue silk. Around her
neck was a spray of green cut-glass vivid as crystallized
angelica, and on the middle finger of her left hand a large
polished emerald.

Rachaela had put on the olive-green dress Althene
had bought her. It was her concession to the evening. She
felt vaguely angry, uncomfortable. Why had she come?
Perhaps to see the film, or merely to escape the house.

But there was never any escape now, and she had
accepted that, surely.

Areas of her emotions had opened out. She seemed

to have another sense. This constant awareness of other places, times, feelings . . . different lives, previous centuries. It was insidious, and pleasing in a bittersweet way. Perhaps it had even been there from the beginning, and her mother had successfully driven it under. When she listened to music, maybe it had come then, in another form.

Althene did not say very much.

She too seemed to be deriving some sensation or thought from the foggy city. Once, she sighed. Her perfume was light yet brunette, cinnamon with something darker.

Her perfection was slightly, as always, intimidating.

I don't really like her, Rachaela thought. *She only fascinates me.*

No, she makes me angry.

Althene had said that Rachaela should come with her to see the film. An old film, made in 1916, Griffith's *Intolerance.*

The restaurant was in a tiny side street with old-fashioned lamps that gave a greenish cat's-eye glow through the fog.

Rachaela noticed that Althene did not pay the driver.

The room was small with high wooden screens. There were only seven tables.

An impeccable, short, swarthy man stepped out and led them to the seventh, behind the highest screen of all.

On the cream tablecloth a single thick white candle burned.

"For you, madame, madame," he said, holding their chairs.

Then he went and a young girl, plump and rosy in a black dress, came and brought them each a glass of palest red wine in long goblets without stems.

Rachaela made no comment. They drank the wine. It was slaty and very soft.

The meal had been ordered, apparently, already. Rachaela was not offered a choice, but she could hardly object, for everything was—naturally—perfection again.

They had a fennel salad, and then a bourride singing with garlic. With this had come a bottle of water-clear Mâcon.

When they had finished the bourride, the girl cleared their plates. The restaurant had filled up quietly and was now full of murmurs and the muted clink of glass and knives behind the screen.

An old woman arrived next, with two thimbles of some golden liqueur. She set these down, and then she spoke to Althene in a strange rounded French. Althene answered her.

Rachaela drank her liqueur, which tasted of the smell of roses. God knew what it was made from. Cyanide, perhaps.

The old woman took Althene's hand, and then she went away.

"Forgive our speaking in another language," said Althene. "Her English isn't good. It should be. She's been here since before the war."

"Which war was that," Rachaela inquired archly, "the one with Napoleon?"

"Oh, no." Althene behaved as if the question were unprovocative, ordinary. "The last."

"But you knew her then."

"Yes. She was younger. She was pretty. She still is."

"The meal was wonderful," said Rachaela grimly.

"There's just one tiny dessert which you must eat."

"I can't, I'm afraid."

"A mouthful," said Althene. She drained her liqueur in a single immaculate gulp. Her eyes were on Rachaela, intensely dark, depth under depth. The eyes of the seducer. *Is that what she wants?*

Rachaela recalled Michael and Kei in the garden. Michael had not looked elderly anymore. Was homosexual love, then, permissible among the Scarabae, with their obsessions of continuance?

Rachaela realized that Althene did make her feel beautiful in turn. And was this too the root of her unease? Even her annoyance?

An image of Jonquil barged into Rachaela's mind, her employer of earlier years, mannish and earringed in steel or bone. Jonquil had been rather fond of her, but very careful. Althene was the antithesis of Jonquil. And Althene's aura, sexual, exquisite, alarmingly unflawed, had no caution to it at all.

When she wants, she will ask me, that's all. She'll ask and I'll say no. And that will be that.

The dessert came, borne by the owner, who had seated them. Miniature tarts amber with apricots.

Rachaela tried hers, and finished it.

She was becoming greedy, like all her kind.

They had coffee in painted white cups, and Calvados in curious squat wooden goblets.

"Don't hurry," said Althene. "There's plenty of time. I hope you'll like the film. Not all of it, perhaps. But there are marvelous things. The ancient past seen through the lens of the early 1900s. Glimpses of authenticity that astound, and moments of utter abandon impossible before, or since."

She refilled Rachaela's cup from the coffeepot.

"I saw this film once, with a terrible audience. They must presumably have known when it was made, and that there would be touches of melodrama or naïveté no longer usual. They must have known too it was a landmark, the matrix for very much else. And they laughed uncontrollably. High-pitched, silly laughter, to show they knew, had grown up, progressed. Worst of all, an actress from the film had come to introduce it. She was lovely, tiny, and charming. They laughed, as she sat among them. I would have turned a machine gun on them all."

"Yes," said Rachaela. "Well, I won't laugh."

"Obviously. You have no need."

When they left, Althene paid.

The owner saw them to the door. The other diners were too discreet to stare.

Outside, another cab was waiting, which took them to the cinema.

As predicted, not all the film concerned Rachaela.

She found the biblical sequences interesting, or delightful, or remotely sad. The Babylonian scenes astonished her, the reeling walls and spinning sunwheels, the elephants and eagles of stone (which was not), the staircase of lions, where beautiful women embraced, lip to lip.

The audience did not laugh. It observed a reverential silence.

All dreamers then, those with memories.

Rachaela found the film had played upon her incoherent nostalgia, as if Althene knew, and had chosen purposely.

Rachaela felt a little stunned. It was a long film, of course. It was midnight when they emerged from the cinema.

To her surprise, no car was waiting.

"Shall we walk in the fog?" said Althene. "I know a little club, only a few streets away. We can have something to drink."

Rachaela was not sorry. She did not want the intimacy of a car. She pulled her coat closed against the thick dankness of the air. The fog had grown woollier, and the city . . . was unspecified heights and shapes of dark, with here and there a streaming diluted light that might be made of anything . . . a candle, a shallow lamp of oil—

The women on the stairs. Flowers that kissed. How had the censor passed it? Had they missed those mouths in the alabaster deluge of shoulders, arms, lily faces ringed by black curls?

They had turned into an alley. The fog pressed gray about them.

Anywhere. They might be—

Shadows massed. What was it?

Rachaela heard, after all, a laugh. Male.

Five men came out of the fog in front of them.

After the siege of Babylon, the violence of reality.

They were young, between eighteen and twenty-five. The fog dimmed them, giving them vegetable faces with paint hair and big white trainered feet. Between were quilted jackets, baggy cords, tracksuits like adult rompers.

" 'Ere," said one, "two fucking dykes."

"Never had a porking," said another.

"Like it," said another.

They hovered in the fog, stupid as the carcasses of butchered meat, but solid, alive.

Althene too had halted.

Rachaela thought, *Never before—*

"I'll have that one," said the voice in the blue tracksuit. "She looks fucking hot."

Rachaela saw his eyes, as if from miles away. They were blind, yet they could see.

Where was the road, where were the cabs and the protection now?

I was raped before.

I'll just have to put up with it.

Althene said, musically, "Run along, boys."

The boys stood there, looking at them, not laughing now, and not running.

CHAPTER 30

 ALL CITIES WERE THE SAME.
The first was the blueprint for them all.
There were the high places, lighted and mobile with traffic, the sumps of darkness where the thick mist crawled. Through them ran rivers, to which steps sloped down, and under the rivers lay the dead, as they lay under the streets.

Malach walked.

He was silent, but behind him, more silent still, the two ghosts of the dogs padded. Sometimes they would pause to examine some odor or essence. Sometimes they slipped a little ahead. Then they would wait for him, nose his hands, and fall back once more.

Malach moved out of time.

Once or twice, pedestrians passed him. Startled and wary in the fog, they stared or averted their eyes, for in this atmosphere he was even more inimical, and more correct. Dark and fog might have made him up.

The fog had crossed the river now, knitted over.

Phantom things slid along the water. Lamps like moons rose, melted, and set.

Malach turned from the bank, down among the side streets.

Beyond the last lamp, a stretch of shadow. In the shadow, a voice. Not loud, quite reasonable.

"Give us yer bag."

And then a dog barked, the noise the product of a small barrel chest.

Malach stopped, and Enki and Oskar came up to him like two drifts of mist.

Down in the shadow, a breathless woman said, "I haven't got much. It won't help you."

"What you got?" asked a second voice.

"A couple of pounds—"

"Let's see."

"No, please. It's my bag. It's private."

The dog barked again.

"Keep your rotten dog off," said the first voice.

The second said, "You scared of *that*? I tell you, lady, I'm going to kill your dog. I'll skin it."

It was possible to see into the shadow, after all.

The woman was fattish, with glasses, and not young. The dog stood at her ankle, waiting to defend her, trembling. It had a round white and tan body and pointed fox's ears.

The black youth aimed a playful mock kick at it, and it cowered away. It was in the worst predicament, the dog, a coward wanting to be brave.

The white youth spat. "Fucking ugly dog, that is, missus. Better off out of it."

"Please—" said the woman. She pulled the dog back by its lead, as if she would pull it into her fat body.

"Yeah, I'll skin the fucking white dog," said the black boy. He had a knife now, the shadow-fog reflected on it wetly.

The woman held out her lumpy handbag.

"Here. Take this. It's all I've got."

"Oh, she wants us to have it now."

The black boy said, "Now give me yer dog."

Malach touched the backs of the wolfhounds' two stony skulls.

Without hesitation they trotted forward.

The white youth danced around, alerted by some
current of new air. Out of the fog he saw something go
up and up, and on it the face of a grey-white fog beast,
long teeth and glowing eyes. It rose until it was over his
head, and then two iron paws came down on his shoulders.

He made a sound. The beast growled into his face.
Its breath smelled of meat and smoke.

The black boy, too, had turned in amazement, and at
the same moment the other pale dog reared up to meet
him. He shrieked and tried to pull away, but the sheer
weight of the animal held him pinned.

The knife wavered in his hand.

"What's happening?" said the woman. "What is it?"
The little dog on the lead was wagging its tail now.

The black boy tried to get his knife right, so he could
push it into the great stone dog that leaned on him.

Then he felt the knife drawn lightly from his grip.
He heard the knife break in two, and the two pieces clink
on the street. A hand closed on the back of his neck,
mild, almost loving. A man said softly into his ear, "Your
people were hung on a cross. You should know better."

The stone dog swung suddenly off and away.

Malach led the black boy forward to where the other
wolfhound had the white boy, blocked, shivering. He had
dropped the bag. "Enki."

As the second wolfhound cascaded away, the little
dog on the lead gave a pleased high yap.

Malach put his right hand on the white boy's neck.
He stood between them, the youths, benign, priestly.
Then he slammed their heads together. Something hap-
pened. He let both of them fall down.

"What's going on?" said the woman.

"It's all right," said Malach.

The fog and her eyesight had hidden it from her. He
picked up her bag and took it over.

The little dog jumped and panted, and Oskar lowered his head to it, licking it once end to end.

Malach gave the woman her bag.

"Thank you," she said, "thank you, Officer."

She pulled the little dog, bouncing and excited, away into the fog. Something made her hurry.

Malach stepped between the two dead muggers, his dogs running now to keep up with him.

CHAPTER 31

❖ FAINTLY A WINDOW SHONE DOWN ON them, that was where the light came from, about five stories up. Possibly someone had seen, and phoned the police. But it was a forlorn hope. More likely the light, probably of some office, had only been forgotten.

Within, immersed in her terror, Rachaela knew a bizarre curiosity. What would Althene do?

So far, she had only antagonized them.

Did she even understand that such an affront was conceivable?

A kind of electricity came from Althene. Rachaela experienced the tingling of it. But it was not fear.

Too arrogant to be afraid.

The five men were slouching there in front of them, liking their own strength, enjoying the threat more than the action. Turning themselves on. Only one of them was as tall as Althene, but in this type of encounter, that was not going to matter.

"I like the bird with the big tits," said the one in rompers.

"The other's better. Big girl."

"I bet she's got a big cunt. Take two of us at once."

They laughed again, they had overlooked Althene's patronizing remark. They began to move forward.

Althene spoke.

"Wouldn't you like to see what you're getting first?"

They checked, chuckling disbelievingly.

Rompers moved out. "You show us then."

Althene opened her coat. She started to raise her skirt, very slowly.

They encouraged her, whistled. They watched the long slim leg appear above her high leather boot. Rachaela saw, also. Just below the stocking top, was a garter of dark green lace. And in the garter, a tiny gun.

Althene had the gun neatly in her hand. She let her skirt fall.

Four of the men had stopped laughing. But Rompers was not impressed.

"Look. It's a toy. It's a fake."

The gun was silver with a white bone handle. It looked too elegant to be anything dangerous.

Rachaela said, "Althene—"

"Tell you what," said Rompers, "she's showed me hers. Now she can see mine. I've got a big one, darling. Just the size for you and your friend."

He moved forward again, and the other four were there behind him.

The gun gave a little click, like a pip breaking between the teeth. Then Althene fired into Rompers's body.

Deafening red in the smoky light, blood jetted from his genitals. He gave a shrill squeak. He flopped backward and the others split away from him. They paused in odd attitudes, half crouching, looking at him. He screamed once, and then he only lay on the pavement under the fog.

The men ran away abruptly, like a herd of animals frightened by something unseen.

"What have you done?" said Rachaela.

"Don't you know?" said Althene. Her voice sounded deeper, rougher, less glamorous. She raised her skirt once more and set the gun back into the preposterous garter. "That will keep me warm."

The man on the ground did not move. Was he dead? Rachaela glanced up. No one at the window.

"We'll have to call an ambulance." She tried to speak sensibly, as though Althene had done something normal, like twisting her ankle.

"Why?"

"You shot someone."

"So I did. Did you love him?"

Rachaela said, "That isn't an answer."

"Yes."

"He was scum," said Rachaela.

"Good-bye," said Althene, "to the scum. He will be dead in a few minutes. I shot him in his big penis, of which he was so proud."

Rachaela began to shake. She thought, distantly, *So much for rationality.*

"Don't faint," said Althene. "We'll go and find a drink for you."

"For *me*? I'm here with a wild beast and it offers me a drink."

"How complimentary. What beast?"

"That gun—" said Rachaela, uselessly.

"Custom made. A Derringer Remington. One of the smallest weapons in the world, bar the hatpin. A leopardess, perhaps. Come. The club I spoke of isn't far."

"You want me to walk into some private club with you as if nothing—as if—as if you had—" Rachaela stopped. The alley whirled, settled sickeningly, and was still. Althene had her by the shoulders.

"He would have stuck himself into you," said Althene. "And elsewhere, quite soon, into some other woman, less able to cast off what he did to her than you. Requiescat in pace."

No one had come. No sirens or rushing feet.

Althene let her go. Instead her warm and scented

mouth came like a butterfly and brushed, for an instant, Rachaela's lips.

"Walk with me as if you will live for many hundreds of years," said Althene. "Walk with me as if you have seen it all before. And as if you love and trust me."

"But I don't."

"Then make believe, little girl. *Pretend.*"

They walked.

The darkness and the lit window drew behind and the body of the dying or dead rapist was hidden by a twist of buildings. Dim notes of buses, cars, far off. Music from a cassette.

They reached a shut door under a lamp.

Althene rang the bell.

The shaking was fading off, as if something that had had Rachaela in its teeth was now growing tired.

Rachaela had a double brandy, and then they drank china tea. It was a long room with comfortable chairs and small waxed tables, a luminous bar, prints of ancient houses.

At any moment, for the first three quarters of an hour, Rachaela expected someone to burst in, crying of a corpse close by. No one did.

Althene was gracious and attentive, but she did not really speak for a long while.

In an alcove a man sat playing a guitar, softly and beautifully. It seemed he might also be one of the scatter of patrons, who simply played there to please himself.

Rachaela, an insect newborn, hardened. She felt only sad, like a child who had realized it would die. But this was the reverse of that. It was as if she had learned that death was not for her.

Finally, she said, "I suppose murder isn't anything fresh in your life."

Althene smiled in the old mysterious way. She had readjusted her voice, jettisoning harshness and banality.

"Now you think I've slain a hundred men."

"Have you?"

"I would have to count them up. Wouldn't that look like boasting?"

"With the gun?"

"With whatever was to hand," said Althene.

"The handle of the gun is bone," said Rachaela.

"Don't worry. The bone is human."

"I'm not afraid of you," said Rachaela. "I should be, probably. But I'm not."

"I should hate you to be afraid of me."

"Yes." Rachaela drank her tea. Althene watched her. Her classical face was serene, her dark eyes only like still waters, running inevitably deep. "Don't the Scarabae frown on a homosexual liaison?"

Althene lifted her eyebrows. She looked amused now.

"Not in itself," she said.

"But they want the line to go on. They want children born."

"Yes."

"Is that," said Rachaela, "why your mother beat you?"

"It was why my mother *thought* she beat me."

Rachaela looked into Althene's eyes, carefully.

"I'd rather we didn't get into some situation that you and I both would find—embarrassing."

"I become bashful," said Althene, "very easily."

"To spare me, then."

"So selfish," said Althene.

"I don't sleep with women."

"No. You are a nun. No women, and no men."

"Once. You know the result."

"The little girl who kills."

"Enchanting, adorable Ruth, yes."

"Perhaps the fault wasn't with you, but with the father."

"It doesn't really bother me whose fault it was. It was cause and effect."

"And so you'll be always celibate. How enticing."

"It isn't meant to be, Althene."

"I'm on fire," said Althene. "All I can think of is clambering up the ivory tower and breaking in the window."

Rachaela could feel her heart knocking fast in her throat. It was the brandy. The shock, and the brandy. Or just exhaustion.

"I want to go home," she said.

"Home is where the heart is."

"My heart isn't anywhere."

"So you have said." Althene nodded at the bar, and a girl came at once with a tray, the bill, a tired omnivorous smile.

CHAPTER 32

✤ MALACH UNLOCKED THE DOOR.

After the usual moment he allowed, for the sound of the key was the equivalent to a knock, he entered Ruth's bedroom. She was sitting up in the blue and green bed, with the sheet raised over her nightshirt to her collarbone. She had been drawing.

The two dogs pushed through, and went to the bed. Ruth let her drawing go and gave them a hand each to sniff. She rubbed their long heads. Enki climbed onto the bed and stood there, huge as a horse, staring about.

Ruth laughed up at him in pleasure.

The lamplight caught Ruth's treasures on the table, by the books. An apple of green glass, the gold-plated razor with which she would have slashed Lorlo Mulley's throat, a cheap floral case of cosmetics and manicure, a porcelain duck, a gold bell on a chain. Under the table lay the leopardskin, rolled up, a creature not yet become. Oskar walked over to it and growled, as a courtesy.

"Get up," said Malach, "and come into the room."

Ruth looked at him intently. She even slept with her hair in plaits.

"Are you going to kill me after all?"

"I'm not going to kill you."

He went out, leaving the door open and the dogs in the bedroom.

After two minutes, Ruth came out. She had put on a cotton dressing gown, and belted it tight at the waist like a little girl. Her body was that of a woman, but it had always been. She carried her drawing.

"Do you want to see?"

She did not look around at the room.

He took the drawing from her hand. He glanced at it and threw it down on the carpet with some curse in another language.

"Is that German?" she said.

"Latin. You're an ignorant bitch. You'll have to be taught."

"I don't like school."

"Tutors," he said. "You'll learn somehow."

"I'd get bored."

"If they bore you, we'll send them away and find you others. It's their task not to bore."

He stared at her, his face was terrible. It was full of the murder he had committed, where before murder had seemed to leave him unmarked.

On the green carpet the black and white drawing lay face up. It showed a hall, combining both a terror of enclosure and a horror of wide open space. Vast pillars held up a ceiling far above, and their reflections sank under them as if in water. Before a slab of stone a white-robed man raised high a sword. His hair also was white, and fell behind him. The figure was too small to require much detail, or any real features.

"Do you want me to go back into the bedroom?" said Ruth.

"No. Go into that room over there." He pointed.

She crossed the green living room, and opened the door of the room with whitewashed walls.

"Here?"

"Go to the table. Open the left-hand drawer."

"All right."

She obeyed him, but as if reluctantly.

With her hand on the drawer, she said, "What is it?"

"Look and see."

She opened the drawer. Inside was a pile of sketches, some of which had been torn from books. On the top was a watercolor painting recently done, perhaps a few days old.

Ruth drew it out.

A wide hall, red, red pillars large as houses, holding up a mile-high roof, and reflecting in the floor like monstrous candles. There was no sacrificing priest. Otherwise, it was the same.

"It's like mine."

"And where is yours meant to be?"

"Egypt." Ruth came from the whitewashed room. "Do you want to do the game, now?"

"No. Sit there."

She sat in the green armchair, her bare feet just reaching the floor.

"Who are you?" he said.

"I'm Ruth."

"And who is Ruth?"

"Scarabae."

"And who am I?"

She lowered her eyes. "Malach."

"And who is Malach?"

Ruth folded her hands.

"My jailor."

"Why?"

"I have to be punished."

"Why?"

"I hurt Anna, and the others."

"Why?"

Ruth looked up. Her eyes were alive and fiery black.

"Leave me alone!" She stood up and screamed at him. "Leave me alone! I don't want to. I won't! I want my dad! I want my daddy! I want—"

Malach laughed. Ruth became silent.

"You break so simply. Your father's dead."

"I know," she said.

She cried.

Malach walked into the white room and shut the door, leaving the rest of the flat before her, vast, enclosed.

Presently the two dogs came, and pressed against her, and Ruth kneeled down with them for comfort.

When she had been kneeling there, weeping on their coarse fur for a few minutes, Malach returned. He sat beside her, and held her in his arms. She did not see his face, which was old. The dogs lay over their feet, waiting patiently for the enormous pain to pass, like night.

CHAPTER 33

✤ AS THEY WALKED UP TOWARD THE
house from the road, loud tuneful music ran
down to meet them, the Stranglers playing from
Camillo's trike. A few colored windows gleamed above
like sweets on the darkness. Electricity burned out of the
open door, lighting the trike, its own green-blue-poppy-
purple casement. Lou was sitting on the velvet seat. She
wore a short black dress over long black tights painted
with red roses. Around her neck was a ruff of silver wire.
Her red hair had been streaked with mauve. She seemed
demure.

Camillo was standing by the horse head, and Tray
was on the path below the door.

Tray wore one of her long dresses, 1920s shoes with
straps. Her long black hair framed her pale-powdered
face.

"No, you're not coming with me," said Camillo.

Tray inclined her head to one side, plaintively.

"Cami . . ."

"Not like that," said Camillo.

Lou said, "Come on, Cami. Let's *go*."

"I wanted," said Tray.

"I don't want you," said Camillo, "like that." He got
into the saddle of the trike. "You look like my mother."

The engine gunned. The trike turned effortlessly and soared off down the hill, Lou sitting in the back.

Camillo stared at Rachaela as he passed her, and he grinned contemptuously. Speed, darkness, light, made him appear about thirty-eight.

Tray went on standing by the door, looking like a flower on a bruised stem.

As Althene and Rachaela reached the bottom of the path, Miranda came out of the house.

She appeared, also, too young, in a dim white dress. She had taken to wearing her gray hair loose, and it fell down her back in thick waves. She touched Tray's shoulder.

"Come in, dear, and watch the film with me."

Tray looked at her shyly, perhaps stupidly.

"There are some chocolates," said Miranda. "Marzipan ones, and strawberry creams."

Miranda led Tray indoors, and when Althene and Rachaela went into the house in turn, the two long-skirted women, young and young-old, had disappeared into the white living room where the TV fluttered.

"Is Miranda kind?" asked Rachaela. "Or playing?"

"Or something else," said Althene. She shut the house doors.

The oil lamps were out and only the electric light filled the hall.

Rachaela looked up the stairs. She felt inert. As if she had been stretched to some breaking point, and so broken, and now nothing could be done to her or with her, or expected of her. Safe. Dull. And wide awake.

"I'm going to the kitchen to make coffee."

"Yes," said Althene. "It's that sort of night. Then again, in an hour, it will be sunrise."

"Time to burrow into our coffins," said Rachaela tartly.

She knew, ironically, she would find it easier to sleep once the sun had come up.

They walked through the side passage of the house, and down into the cream and black tiled kitchen.

The dishwasher was gurgling quietly, and on a chair under the mangle, Cheta sat, embroidering in gold a pair of cucumber-green shoes.

"It's all right, Cheta," said Althene, "we can manage."

And Cheta got up and went away.

"How extraordinary," said Rachaela. "I mean, even if she'd been darning a sock. But *shoes*—"

"They were Maria's," said Althene. "Do you remember Maria?"

"Of course." Rachaela digested this slowly. Another gemini of lovers? Cheta left behind alone at Maria's death. And where had the shoes come from?

She took the coffee jug and a filter paper, virtually her own, for no one else seemed to use them, and set the contraption to work. The rich deceptive aroma of coffee bloomed in the kitchen.

Althene had sat on the table. She had crossed her legs and the smooth skirt ridden up a little to show the silky length of leg. But not far enough to reveal the gun.

"I have the sensation," said Rachaela, "that I imagined everything. Perhaps not the dinner and the film. But the other thing."

Althene shrugged lightly, as if slipping a gossamer shawl from her shoulders.

"If it makes you happy."

"It's made me decide."

"Oh, what?"

"Tomorrow, I'm going to make arrangements to leave here. I really am finished with it now. I mean, the Scarabae. No, don't tell me that I can never finish with the Scarabae. That I'll always be part of them. I know that. But I'm going to make my own way. A flat somewhere. A job. My old unimportant, lazy existence. This is too—taxing."

"Yes, coming back to life is very tiring."

"How would you know," said Rachaela. "You've always been wildly alive, haven't you?"

"One day, I'll tell you."

"One day you won't know where I am."

"The Scarabae can always find their own. Hadn't you noticed?"

In the jug the coffee glowed. Rachaela took milk out of the fridge.

"Do you want some, Althene?"

"Perhaps. What I really want is you."

Rachaela felt a plunge of panic. It surprised her, for she was past all that.

"We discussed this. I said no."

"There was no discussion. You did say no."

Rachaela lifted the jug before it was ready and filled a cup. Her heart was thudding against her breast, her legs felt heavy. Somewhere in her brain tears were trying to rise like fish out of deep water.

To her consternation, she heard the silky whisper of Althene's garments as she left the table. Althene came up behind her, very close. The subtle perfume wrapped around Rachaela like a veil.

"One rape per evening is enough," Rachaela said. "Isn't it?"

"Were you thinking of raping me, then?" Althene asked.

Rachaela put down the coffee. She was frightened, her nerves alight.

"Please don't crowd me."

But Althene's body was against her now, Althene's breasts pressed into her back. And Althene's hands circled around her cupping her own breasts, covering them, stroking.

Two thrills like fire shot through Rachaela.

She tried to resist. She pulled away and came about,

and Althene caught her again, as if it had been choreographed.

Althene placed her hand behind Rachaela's head. Althene's mouth came onto hers. The scented taste of lipstick . . . Althene kissed her, the long cool tongue moving in her with a passionate stealth.

Rachaela thought how it had been when Adamus kissed her. The whirling and the fall. This was not like that. Nothing could ever be like that again. She gave up. Gave in.

She did not put her arms around Althene, only let Althene move her body as she wanted. A dizzying arousal saturated Rachaela. She did not care anymore.

When Althene drew back, Rachaela was angry. She had not wanted it to stop. If it stopped she would have to think about it again. Then it would be unacceptable, maybe ludicrous.

Althene looked cruel, but still flawless. Not a smudge. Only her lipstick had vanished away.

"Yes?" she said. "Or no?"

"I suppose yes."

"You suppose. What a nasty virginal little bitch you are."

"No, then," said Rachaela.

"Be quiet." She took Rachaela's hand, and they walked from the kitchen.

Out in the hall Sasha was standing by a pillar, as if waiting for them.

She must see it all. The bruised ripened mouths, the hands linked, emerald and ruby rings.

Sasha smiled. Nodded.

It was all madness. Rachaela laughed.

Althene led her up the stairs and her legs were so heavy now she could barely make it, her breath coming in gasps.

In the corridor above, Althene pushed her firmly to the wall, and kissed her again. Her large sensitive hands were inside the neck of the dress. They burned on flesh. Rachaela was overpowered, capsizing. Falling after all.

She had been so long without sex. That was all it was. And Althene was clever, of course.

It was Rachaela's room they came to. Rachaela checked. "Don't you want—"

"The little nun will be happier in her own apartment."

Rachaela had a vision of two nuns writhing together in union in some shadowy place.

"You'll have to forgive me," she said. "I don't know what to do. I mean, in this situation."

Althene had shut the door.

"Take off your dress."

Rachaela unzipped the dress and dropped it on the floor. She undid her bra and let it go, next her pants and tights, unrolling them from her body without artifice.

Althene watched her nakedness. She said nothing. Instead, more deftly than Rachaela, she undid the blue silk and the two pieces slid from her like a wave.

As usual her underclothes were astonishing. Dark holly-green satin, the high bodice trimmed with dark green lace, a corset that nipped in her waist, french knickers also trimmed, the gartered stockings with their stalks of butterflies.

So she came to Rachaela, and drew Rachaela's nakedness against the glide of fabrics.

Rachaela rubbed herself on these limpid textures. In the middle of lust, she felt a curious comfort. She buried her face in Althene's neck.

They went to the bed. It was a relief to lie down. Althene made warm circles on Rachaela's breasts with her fingers and her tongue. Her black hair mingled with Rachaela's, and all over Rachaela's body her perfume had anointed, so now they were scented the same.

Althene raised Rachaela's legs onto her shoulders.

She bowed her head to Rachaela's sex, and the wonderful tongue trembled there like a flame.

"Don't stop," Rachaela said.

"Just for a moment. Now do you want me?"

"Yes."

Althene kissed Rachaela's mouth. She drew Rachaela's hand steadily along her own belly. Rachaela reached out to feel the soft mound, the moisture and pliancy, the inverted lily of a sexuality like her own.

Instead a golden wand was put into her hand. Alchemical. Impossible.

Rachaela thrashed away. Before she knew what she was doing, she had jumped off the mattress. But her legs gave way. She fell on the carpet by the bed.

She could say nothing. She half lay on the floor. She was shocked as if she had been scalded.

The trap—

Althene kneeled on the bed, harmfully beautiful and clad in satin and lace. And from the center of her slender female body there rose the dark tower of male potency. Indeed the body was not female, it was possible to see that now. Slim, depilated, lightly muscled like the physique of a girl who swam and rode horses, smooth and almost poreless, blessed by sweet false breasts, by wonderful hair, and a face like a jewel. But still it was a man's body. It had a man's power now, and a man's penis, erect, and demanding.

So that was why—

That was why it did not matter.

It would not be two women in a sterile embrace.

Sasha, nodding and smiling . . .

"No." Rachaela tried to get up.

"Yes." Althene stepped off the bed. The grace was catlike, wolflike. Not female or male now.

"Yet more *lies,*" said Rachaela. Her voice was hoarse, as if she had been screaming.

"No lies."

"Yes. You were a *woman*."

"I am a woman. In a way."

"Your mother," said Rachaela, "hated you, until she found out—"

"Until she found out that, although I liked to *be* a woman, I also liked to make love with women."

"Christ," said Rachaela. She managed to get to her feet. She felt sick, sick with loss. "This family," she said. "I wish it would sink into fucking hell."

Then Althene came and lifted her up. Althene, a man, picked her up in his arms—in her arms—and put her back on the bed without fuss.

"You are this family, Rachaela. My beautiful, my lovely one. Lie still."

Rachaela lay still. She looked up into Althene's matchless face. The shock had only made desire worse. Inside the cage of madness, caught after all in the trap, she wanted the duality of this fabulous monster, she wanted Althene.

Althene knew. She eased herself, the root of her power, into Rachaela's body. Rachaela was so ready, there was no difficulty.

For a moment there was the shift of a kaleidoscope. The beautiful body and the face of the woman, the brush of satin, the ribs of the corset, and inside the core of her the strength of maleness, hard and pure, the rod of the tree, the tyranny of life. Then the colored panes tumbled over and the pattern was complete. Not monstrous. Correct.

She was miles out of her body. She felt Althene come with her. They were on a spiral, turning.

When Rachaela opened her eyes, the pictures in the window were growing clear.

"Well," Rachaela said, "you got your way. But the Scarabae always do."

Althene drew aside from her. There was no longer

visible evidence. Althene was only a marvelous woman, perhaps a little pale, not really disheveled.

"I'll leave you now. So you can brood on what's been done to you."

"I have some cause," Rachaela said.

"There's always cause," said Althene, "if you must have one."

She put on her blue silk. She was again as she had been.

And what am I?

"The sun's coming up," said Althene. "You'll sleep now."

"Good-bye," said Rachaela.

Althene observed her intently. Then she went out of the room, closing the door quietly, as if upon a sleeper, or the sick.

CHAPTER 34

THE PIANO ARRIVED IN THE WEEKS BE-
fore Christmas. Ruth came from her bedroom,
dressed in jeans and jumper and her black plaits, and
found it on the green carpet.

"Is it yours?"

"No." Malach stood by the french window. "Yours."

"Mine?"

"It's your birthday."

"Is it?"

She went to the piano and touched off a spray of
notes.

"It's got a clear sound," she said.

"Yes."

"Can I play it?"

"It's yours."

Normally, after breakfast, he gave her books to read.
They covered many subjects. In the afternoon, after she
had eaten lunch, sometimes he took her walking. The
dogs would go too. They went through parks and streets,
along heights and wastelands of the river. Now and then
they went shopping. At least, he took her into shops, and
there let her buy what she wanted. She bought tapes of
music and occasionally books but these were generally to
please him, as though he might be pleased, volumes with

pictures of ancient civilizations. Or she bought books
about animals.

In the shops, the dogs often caused consternation, or
admiration. But Enki and Oskar viewed the world calmly,
casually.

Ruth asked Malach questions. They were the ques-
tions perhaps of a child. Where did that bus go to?
Where did that street go? Why were they going this way?
He had answers always. Apparently, sometimes, he lied.
Or else his replies were so fundamental that they seemed
unlikely.

Ruth accepted all he said.

He was not misleading, merely leading.

Today, there were no books. At breakfast she ate
one croissant and left the rest; she seldom ate more than
one now. Then she went and washed her hands, and
came back and sat down at the piano.

There was also sheet music.

Ruth went through a Mozart sonata, and then a
Chopin mazurka, and then through some idyllic
Rachmaninov.

Malach sat in one of the chairs.

She stopped, and said to him, "Do I play well?"

"Do you think you do?"

"Yes, quite well. Adamus taught me."

"You play like a young concert pianist. But sometimes you bluff."

"Yes, he said that. I try not to."

"No, you don't try."

Ruth thought. She said, "I will try."

She played a transposition of a Beethoven concerto;
the music sheets were unusual.

When she had finished, she said, "Music is wonderful."

"Music and I have grown apart," he said.

"Why?" she said. "How?"

"There's been too much."

Ruth sat at the piano. "Are you very old?"

"Stop speaking like a small child."

She turned and looked at him. He was quite idle, the two dogs lying at his feet.

"I meant," she said, "the Scarabae live a long time. Will I?"

"You're thirteen."

"I feel much older."

"Do you. With your hair in plaits and this quaint way of talking." He did not look at her. "How old do you feel?"

"Twenty-five. Perhaps more."

"That's very young. The same as thirteen, maybe."

Ruth laughed. She frequently did this now. She kicked her bare heels mildly on the legs of the piano stool.

"What shall I play?"

"Whatever you want."

He went out into the garden and the dogs followed him.

The lilac trees were stripped and the laurels had darkened and drawn close. A bird was drinking rain from a mossy birdbath. The dogs watched it languidly.

Ruth played a strain of unearthly Debussy.

Malach, the dogs, the bird, took no notice.

The shops had put on their Christmas masks. Tinsel and silver trees with scarlet balls. Santas in grottos bribing howling toddlers, charming white bears and mice in Santa hats costing only five pounds with purchases of twenty pounds or more.

They had tea in a store. Ruth drank the tea but did not want a cake. She seldom ate more than a salad for her lunch. Food had lessened its grip on her.

She bought chemist items and hid them in a bag, and then a black velour top with a bronze-buttoned epaulette on one shoulder. The top cost thirty pounds and as Malach paid for it, they were offered a fat white mouse.

Ruth looked at the mouse. "I had a bear once."

"Lovely for the kiddies," said the saleslady.

"Which kiddies are they?" said Malach. "Do you want it?"

Ruth took the mouse and stared at it in a sort of incredulity.

Malach bought the mouse, which Ruth then carried out of the store.

On the pavement outside, harassed shoppers ran about in the rain. A child in a pushchair glared at them.

"Emma never let me have a pushchair," said Ruth abruptly. "It's bad for the spine."

The child saw the mouse and pointed and began to cry with a terrible impassioned affront.

The mother looked helplessly down.

"Oh, dear. Stop it, Harry."

Ruth leaned over and put the mouse into the child's arms. It clasped the toy fiercely, possessively, and the crying ceased.

"Oh, no—" said the woman, blushing. "No, really."

Ruth said, "I'm too old for it."

"No, but—he mustn't—I mean—"

"It's good," said Malach, "to learn that if you cry out you may be answered."

"Pardon?" said the woman.

"Please keep the toy," said Malach.

They walked on.

"That was clever, Ruth."

"Was it? Why was it?"

"Some things belong to some people by right. A gift. A caress. Or even death."

"Yes," she said.

"But you must learn which. You mustn't bluff."

"Malach," she said.

"What is it?"

"I wish I'd kept the mouse."

"No you don't."

"I do."

Enki pushed his head up under her hand.

"Enki is your mouse."

Ruth laughed.

In the park, as they crossed it, the sun came out in daggers.

"Look at the sun," said Malach. "One day it will go out."

"Not yet?"

"You know not yet."

"You don't mind the sun," said Ruth.

"How do you know?"

"They used to hide from it, at the house."

"They were more vulnerable, Ruth, than you or I."

"What do you mean?"

"We draw our personal darkness around us to keep us safe from the sun."

They were in the middle of the park, under the hill. The bare trees rose bravely against a future of gales and snow. Now a light glinted on their wetness, optimistic, clean. Far off, the city showed in riven lines, the streets and peaks, the high roofs that the day turned suddenly to gold and brass.

Malach turned. He climbed a tree, with the ease of a cat. The dogs stared, and Enki barked, but only once.

Malach swung from the high branches, and dropped back in a shower of rain.

His face was young. Ruth gazed at him. She said, "Are you going to leave me?"

"I'm going to take you away."

"Where?"

"Another country."

"Where?"

"Sing and wait."

"What?"

"An Assyrian poem. I must do with my life what I can. I must do as I must. I must love and be and kill. Sing and wait."

"What does it mean?"

"What do your questions mean," he said, "child in plaits?"

"It means I don't understand."

"Don't you."

Ruth considered. "Will I have to be punished again?"

"You must be taught."

"Will you be there?"

"Yes."

"Why?" she said.

He looked down at her. The sun was behind him, and turned the mane of his hair into a fire, darkened his face, so his eyes were the color of ashes.

"You and I," he said. "The same."

She was flattered. She smiled.

"Are we?"

They walked up the hill, and the dogs raced ahead of them. A couple coming from the opposite direction halted in fright. Oskar and Enki darted to either side and were away into the nude green chestnuts.

She asked him: "Will we have Christmas?" He did not reply, for once. Ruth said. "Emma always had it. Mommy . . . Rachaela didn't."

"You're a Christian, then," he said, "that you want to celebrate Christmas."

Ruth shook her head. "I don't believe in Jesus."

"He lived," said Malach.

"The Scarabae don't have Christmas," she decided.

That was the day they went to the museum.

They walked between the sand-polished stones, the gods with beast heads, and the pharoahs with the faces of wise girls. In the back rooms, into which they were secretively let, ancient things crouched in cases or lay about on tables, shining in the bright light.

"Here is an image of Sekmet," Malach said. The goddess stood on a shelf, dark as coal, her lion head inscribed with whiskers that made her seem playful. "Sekmet, Power of Battle. She killed without mercy and drank the blood. Only another god could hold her back."

"How did he do it?"

"He gave her something she thought was blood, but it made her drunk instead."

"Then what happened?"

"She became gentle and clever."

Ruth scrutinized Sekmet.

There were cartouches of gold, and one set with lapis lazuli. Malach indicated small statues, naming them indolently. Once he said, "And this is wrongly labeled." He did not say what the label should read.

There was a great goddess or queen by a door. He put his fingers to her lips.

Ruth frowned jealously.

In the Roman section they passed the busts of generals, golden cups, and jugs of opaque greenish glass.

"At Lupercal they looked for werewolves," Malach said. "If they found them, they sent them into the forest. See this head from Germany. It's grinning."

There was a room of open books under glass.

"If you look long enough," he said, "the pictures will move."

Ruth stared at the medieval patterns on the books. They moved. The fisher drew up a fish, a bird flew across a page.

"Why?"

"A trick of the eyes. This glove," he said, "belonged to a captain of mercenaries. Look at the embroidered key. The mark of some lord who wanted to own him."

It was dark when they came back. They traveled by

bus, a form of transport Malach seemed to favor when they did not walk.

As they entered the basement flat, the two dogs barked resonantly.

Ruth embraced them.

Malach went into the living room, stood by the window. Ruth switched on the lamps. The dogs trotted to Malach. He touched them absently.

"Are the bars on the windows," Ruth said, "because of me?"

"No. To keep out burglars. This is London."

"The long window," she said.

"Bullet-proof," he said.

"Will we go out?" she asked. Often, now, they went to the restaurant for dinner.

"Wait," he said.

Ruth waited. Then she said, "What for?"

"You ask the wrong questions," he said. "You ask about stupid little things. You've been starved of answers."

"Yes."

"Ruth," he said. Then, after a pause, again, "Ruth."

"What is it?"

"I want," he said. He stopped. He put both hands on the glass. The silver rings on his left hand burned. They were like the rings from Egypt and ancient Italy and France in 1403.

Ruth felt afraid. It was an old fear, and she knew it.

"What?" she said.

Malach grunted. It was a strange sound, coming from him as if he had been punched. Nothing could hurt him or get at him. He was too quick, too old. But now, something did.

He took his left hand, and covered the left side of his face, slowly.

"What is it?" said Ruth.

Malach shouted. Without words.

He spun around. His body whipped backward. The hand over his face had formed a fist of burning rings.

Ruth became very small. She seemed to shrink.

Malach's agony filled up the room.

The dogs dropped on their bellies, whining.

"Eyes," Malach said.

Ruth had a child's face now. A face she had perhaps never had before.

"What?"

"Ice," he said. *"Ice."*

His right eye was open, staring as if blind. He came across the room, and past her, past the two dogs. He walked into the second bedroom, the spare sparse place where he slept. He kept his left fist pressed over his left eye.

"What is it?" Ruth said again.

"Megrim," he said. *"Crier en bas."*

He slammed the door suddenly so the whole flat shook.

Inside there was a second crash, as if he had thrown himself against the wall.

Ruth crept slowly to the door. She listened. She heard him say loudly: *"In umbra erat aqua—in umbra erat aqua de petra . . . quasi sanguis ex Christo—"*

Ruth thought stilly by the door. Was this a migraine? Once at school she had heard of them.

Migraine. Half-head. A severe headache on one side of the skull. Perhaps due to an injury, a blow, or distortion in the vertebrae of the neck . . .

Ice. He had said that, ice.

The dogs were silent and almost as motionless as the furniture. Only Enki raised his nose and looked at Ruth, and when she moved, he wagged his tail, once, twice.

She walked into the kitchen and opened the ice-making section of the fridge. She put her hand on to the ice. The ice would not come away.

Ruth sobbed. Like the movement of the dog's tail. Once, twice.

She left her hand on the ice.

Her heart was racing. She was full of lights. She felt Malach's pain, a sharp instrument pressed through his skull, his eye.

Malach.

She squeezed her hand down on the ice.

It hurt terribly, a sort of burn. Like the rings—

"Don't," said Ruth.

She started to cry from the pain of the ice on her right hand. It gnawed at, ate at her.

She felt herself growing weightless and quiet inside the shell of anguish, his, hers. *Wait,* he had said.

Ruth waited. She waited fifteen minutes by the kitchen clock which worked.

By then she had completely turned to ice. The core of her, her groin, her breasts. Her stomach, heart.

Then she took her hand out of the fridge and walked from the kitchen and back across the living room.

She opened the door of Malach's sleeping place.

She seemed very tall, and to be floating in the air. She saw the chamber with its bare plastered walls, the bed, and Malach lying on it. He was rigidly immobile. He said, *"Quod natura relinquit imperfectum—"*

Ruth crossed the carpet, floating, and stood above him. Her plaits had somehow come undone, and black hair showered over her.

She took hold of his left hand and pulled it away from his face.

There was no mark on him. His face was only hard, clenched, a stone. He did not resist her. He said, *"U doet me pijn."*

Ruth put her right hand, frozen, against his left eye, forehead and temple.

Malach screamed. His whole body erupted into motion.

Ruth, too, cried out. She clamped her frozen hand against him. She forced her hand to remain on his face, which was like furnace heat.

The world seemed to crack.

Then she felt a hurt worse than before. The pain in him had come into her. Into her hand. She kindled. She was on fire.

Then it went out.

She felt bruised, perhaps smashed, but she sat on the bed. A band of flame still circled her right wrist. It was Malach's hand. He was looking at her.

His eyes were so pale they were nearly white.

He said, "What did you do?"

"You said—ice."

He said, hoarsely, "You can heal as well as harm."

"No, it was the ice."

"Once in a hundred years," he said, "it comes like that."

"Is it better?" she said. "Are you all right?" She started to cry.

"It's gone. You took it. What did you do with it?" He lifted her hand and turned it over. Her palm and fingers were burned blue, and bleeding. "Your hand," he said, "your pianist's hand." He put both of his own hands over hers.

It hurt like fire again. Ruth did not mind it. "Don't leave me," she said.

"At the gates of the abyss," he said, "there you are. Ruth in her black hair." He kept her hand in his left hand, and reached up to her and pulled her slowly down.

She lay over him, her lips on his. He kissed her softly.

"You're a child," he said.

"I'm thirteen."

"Too young," he said. "If you were fifty. Too young."

"No, I'm not young."

"No, you're not. But this is." He passed his hands, both of them, over her body and her hair.

Ruth began to kiss him. She kissed his mouth until his mouth tensed and changed and took hers. She put her arms around his neck, her live hand and her dead hand. Then she drew back. She lifted off her jumper like a wreath, and reaching behind her, clumsy from the burn of the ice, undid her brassière.

Her white breasts were full yet high, firm, with budded points.

"Don't seduce me," he said.

"Please," she said.

The tears were on her face like splashed gems. Her eyes were wide and black and crazed with life.

Malach traced her breasts with his hands, then with his lips.

"Old men," he said, "and young girls."

"How old," she said, "how old are you?"

"I remember the pyramids."

Ruth sighed. She clasped his head, the mantle of white hair, holding him to her.

But he held her away. "I lied."

"No," Ruth said. "You told the truth."

He lowered her down, until she was beneath him. Then he stripped both of them, until they were equally naked.

His body was tawny and hers white. The hair at his groin was like the ice which had burned her. She stared at him, at the weapon of his sex. She turned her head not to see.

"No," he said. "Look at me."

He stroked her. She clung to him. The entry of his flesh into hers was harsh and savage.

"You're hurting me."

"Yes."

"I don't mind it. I want to die. I want to die for you."

He kissed her, moving inside her, the pain like a

cathedral built up toward heaven, arches and pinnacles, bronze and air.

She turned her neck. "Drink my blood. Please. I want you to."

"Hush," he said.

"I love you," she said, "don't leave me. I love you."

He cried out, as he had in pain. She looked and saw his eyes, and in the depths of them, as if in polished mirrors, the ages of the earth, truth or lies, fire and darkness.

CHAPTER 35

✣ NOBBI MOVED THROUGH THE SAGE AND
gold door of Vittoria's and glanced about uneasily. It was a quarter to twelve, but the lunchtime drinkers had already assembled. He had seen plenty of them before, but they might not remember him. Mr. Glass's lads.

Luke was over by the walled pool, at the little secluded table under the yucca tree. He raised his hand. It was tanned and manicured with a plain silver wedding ring.

Nobbi, uncomfortable in his suit, went down the tessellated steps and through the wine bar toward him.

Vittoria's was in dark green, with black glass and spotlights. Tall ferns massed in tubs and stone goddesses rose from the shrubbery. The pool was walled in York stone, with boulders carved from Derbyshire, over which tumbled a small crystal fountain. Golden fish sprang through the water.

On Luke's table was a briefcase, and a green dish with tiny strips of liver. He had been feeding the Venus's flytrap in the urn.

Luke wore a silvery gray suit, a milk-blue shirt and a tie like a pale blush. He smiled a regular white smile of which three teeth were capped, but no one need ever know but Luke's expensive dentist.

"Hi, Nobbi. Good to see you. How are things?"

Luke spoke well. His north London slurs had been ironed out, about the time the teeth were knocked out of his mouth in Hammersmith.

"I'm okay. It's just the thing I spoke to Mr. Glass about."

"Right. Well, let's get a drink, shall we?" A girl came at once, maybe a mindreader. "What'll you have, Nobbi?"

"Any beer?" asked Nobbi, without much hope.

The girl mentioned some names that sounded like trouble spots in the news. Nobbi shook his head. He racked his brains, which were busy elsewhere. What was that wine Star gave him? That was all right. But no name would come.

"Just bring us," said Luke buoyantly, "some champagne. You know the one."

Champagne. Did that mean it was good news? Nobbi could tell, Luke had had a sniff of something, maybe in the back of the taxi, or the gents. He was bright and alert. One of Mr. Glass's star boys.

Someone like this, obviously unwed, and a bit younger, for Tracy. Yes, that would be okay. In the Corporation. Look after her. Make her happy. But not a user. Nobbi did not like the idea of Tray with a husband who snorted coke, even if only as an occasional stimulant.

"How's business?" asked Luke, as if he really cared.

"That's fine. Everything's fine. Apart from Tracy."

"Yes, sure. They're a worry, aren't they, girls. My kid's only three, but she already gives me sleepless nights."

"You see," said Nobbi, battling on, "she's gone off before, like I told Mr. Glass. But never so bloody long. Not a word off of her. Nothing."

"Pretty girl," said Luke, "your Tracy."

"Yes, she's lovely," said Nobbi. "That's the trouble. These bloody blokes take a fancy to her and then they drop her, and there she is, in some bother."

"You're a pessimist, Nobbi."

"No, I ain't, but I've seen what happened before. And even Marilyn, now she's started. It was Christmas. It really got her down. Tray never even sent a card. She's always been with us, Christmas."

"Well. Maybe this is something special, Nobbi."

"Is it?" Nobbi stared Luke out, and Luke lowered his gentlemanly eyes.

"Hold on, old man. Here's our wine."

The girl had come, with a boy to open the dark green bottle, which was first displayed to Luke.

The cork came out with a rich pop.

"No, I won't taste it, it'll be just fine. Just pour, and leave the bottle."

The girl and boy went away.

Luke sipped his champagne.

"Exactly what I needed. Only flew in from New York this morning. And came straight from the airport here."

"Good of you," Nobbi muttered.

"Mr. Glass was very particular. He appreciates you, Nobbi. You've done some good work."

Nobbi recalled abruptly the very first job. The patched up wall with something behind it. Working at four in the morning, plastering to the rays of battery lamps. Ask no questions.

"And Mr. Glass," said Luke, "wanted me to see you, explain things."

"Look," said Nobbi, "I just want to know where she is. My girl. That's all. And I know Mr. Glass, with his contacts, he can—"

"Oh, yes, he can, Nobbi. Now go on. Take a drink. It's terrific stuff."

Nobbi looked at the champagne. He raised the glass and had a mouthful. Like sour fruit juice with Andrews in it. Star would have liked it, though. She had taste. He was just a pig.

"Lovely," said Nobbi.

"That's good. Drink up. We can have another bottle."

"Maybe," said Nobbi, "you're going to tell me they ain't been able to find her."

"Tracy? Oh no, Nobbi. No. We know where she is."

"Thank Christ for that."

"And she's absolutely fine, Nobbi."

"Where?"

"Ah, yes. Well, Nobbi. That's the problem."

Nobbi put down the laxative wine and set his fists on the table. He felt overdressed, his tie a garrote, and his waistband pressing. He was hot under the spotlights, and outside the ferns and gilded glass the reality of January murk lay on the street.

"Look, I don't want to offend no one. But I don't want no bloody nonsense. I asked Mr. Glass if he would find my Tray, and now I want to know—"

"You see, Nobbi, old man. Tracy is with someone a bit special. And we can't interfere. Mr. Glass wouldn't like it."

"Who the hell is it?"

"Some people. Just . . . some people. Very important people. Mr. Glass wouldn't want to upset them. And with the best intentions in the world, you busting in there—"

"You bet I'd bust in there." Nobbi was red and sweating. He leaned forward over the champagne glasses, the liver. "What do I have to do to get you to cough it up?"

"Now, Nobbi. Calm down. This isn't going to help. We don't want a scene."

"You know what I want, you Brylcreemed cretin."

Luke frowned with his entire face. Then smoothed the frown away. He was good with an iron.

"I'll forget you said that, Nobbi. You're tense. Have a drink."

"I don't want no drink."

"Have a drink and pull yourself together."

Nobbi sat back suddenly. He lost his redness.

"I'm sorry. I never ought to have said that."

"Forget it, Nobbi. You're under stress."

Nobbi drained the champagne. He watched Luke fill up his glass again.

A tall slim woman with sculpted hair and dangling earrings came across the room and stood over their table.

"Everything all right, Luke?"

"Sure, Stephanie."

"Would you like some company? I've got two girls who'd love to meet you."

"That's okay, Stephanie. Not right now."

"Ciaò," said Stephanie, and drifted away.

Nobbi felt rough. The champagne had turned his stomach, and he should never have spoken like that to this ponced-up bugger.

Luke seemed to bear no grudge.

He said, soothingly, "You'll just have to be patient a little longer, Nobbi. That's all it needs."

"I don't see why," Nobbi said.

Luke finished another glass of champagne. He half turned his head, and the girl and boy began to get out another bottle.

"Did you happen to hear," said Luke, "about that accident over the river? Mulley's operation."

"Mulley's . . . Yeah. Gas main, weren't it?"

"No, Nobbi. It wasn't. And you remember Chas? Arms dislocated and lungs full of lemonade."

"Mr. Glass can't be happy about that."

"Mr. Glass believes that, in this case, it's better to turn a blind eye."

Nobbi absorbed this. He felt sore, as if he had been kicked. The world was full of shit. And she was only little.

"You mean some cunt blew up Mulley's place and this same cunt's got my bleeding daughter?"

The second champagne came.

They waited while the bottle was displayed and the cork popped and the wine poured, and the boy and girl left them.

"I don't want none of this."

"No. All right, Nobbi. Just take it easy."

"You take it easy. You fucking tell me what you mean."

"Tracy is perfectly safe. But yes, substantially. The same people. They're—strong. Mr. Glass won't touch them. That's all there is to it, Nobbi." Luke stared Nobbi out now. Luke's eyes were like brown marbles, faintly flecked with wine and cocaine. "Got to accept it, I'm afraid. Nothing we can do. Not a thing."

"My Christ," said Nobbi.

Luke leaned back. He wanted to be kind now.

"Mr. Glass realizes this has been a strain. He suggested you took a break. Take the wife on a little holiday. The villa at Malta's free, or there's Corfu if you fancy—"

"No," said Nobbi.

"All expenses paid, Nobbi. Fly executive class. Marilyn would love it."

"Yeah," said Nobbi. "I'll think about it."

His heart pounded like lead.

"But you do understand, don't you, Nobbi? I mean, Mr. Glass wouldn't like it if you hadn't understood."

"I understand."

"That's good, Nobbi."

Nobbi drank the poison in his glass. Luke smiled on him. Nobbi was a good man.

"How about some oysters, Nobbi?"

It was sleeting, and Marilyn was at the hairdresser's, with Jason. In the lounge Van Gogh's *Sunflowers* eyed Nobbi malevolently.

He went out into the garden, into the sleet.

On one side of the swimming pool, covered now, a

rock garden full of gnomes filled him with a sense of all futility. He walked over and let himself into his office.

The stuffed lion sat on his desk. It looked reproachful.

"Bloody useless," said Nobbi.

He took out one of his cigars and stood gazing at it. They *knew*. They knew and they would not say. And he had to buckle under. Because he was helpless.

He sat down at the desk, and he thought back to that day she had phoned him. "Where are you?" "London. Just wanted to talk to you . . . He's famous. Don't nag."

Some bloody rock singer. Some weird place. In London. *London.*

The conversation had been doubly frustrating too, because an ice-cream van had been there, gurning outside the box.

Nobbi stiffened. He put down the cigar and pointed at the lion. *"Christ."*

How could he have forgotten that? The van playing that tune so loud he could barely hear what Tray said to him. And it was an outlandish tune. Some classical stuff, he thought. If only he could remember how it went—

Nobbi got up again, and walked round the room, trying, trying—

He could hear it, just upstairs in his brain, just too far away to make it out.

Nobbi struggled, and his blood roared in his ears, so he could not hear the tune at all.

The sleet slashed at Stella's windows. She had drawn the curtains, a restful light brown with green leaves. There was a wonderful smell of roasting beef, slowly cooked since morning until it had the consistency of butter.

They went into the bedroom to make love.

Nobbi put his hand on Star's warm thigh. "I'm sorry, love."

"Am I doing something wrong?"

"What you're doing's lovely. But I just—can't keep my mind on it. It's worrying about her, you see."

"Oh, Nobbi, poor Nobbi."

They sat in the main room while the joint cooked, and held hands. He was glad to be near her, she was restful. Quiet.

In the background faint music played. Something classical, but not the right one.

"It's this bleeding tune. If I was to get it, I'd hum it to you. You'd know it, Star."

"I might not."

"Yes you would. I've heard it myself. Don't know where."

They ate dinner, the roast beef with creamed potatoes, Yorkshire pudding as good as the Old Girl's, steamed celery, garden peas, and fried mushrooms. Nobbi liked the food but he did not eat very much. Star gave him beer.

They went to bed early and lay in the dark, pressed close.

In the middle of the night, Star woke up. She woke because Nobbi was sitting bolt upright in the bed.

"What is it?" She was frightened.

"I got it," he said. "Star—listen—"

Star listened as Nobbi growled out the tune he had heard the ice-cream van play behind Tray's weightless voice, the unsuitable melody of that long hot summer.

"Are you sure?" said Star.

"Yeah—that's it. I know that's it."

"It seems odd—"

"Do you know it?"

"Yes. It's 'The Thieving Magpie.' Rossini."

Nobbi swore, uncomprehending, triumphant.

"They all have their own areas," Nobbi said. "D'you see? I can get a couple of my own boys on to it. I can find her, now."

CHAPTER 36

 IF SHE CONCENTRATED, SHE COULD hear him playing.

Far below.

Below even the stairs, somewhere down in the dark under her heart.

But this was not Adamus. It was Kei, Michael's lover. It was possible to tell, anyway, that the musician was not the same. There was none of Adamus's violence, or breadth. Rachmaninov, she thought. Song without words. How apt.

Rachaela walked off the staircase and into the white and gold drawing room. Premonitions of sunset soaked the windows. It was so early. The long winter-January night would soon be here.

Up in the tarot window, the knight knelt before his burning tower. The colors reflected in the scratched table which said *Good-bye*.

No one else was in the room. The television was off.

The other windows, roses, palaces, flamed softly.

I said I'd go away. Over and over I've said it. And here I am.

Rachaela sat down at the table, and put her hands on the scratches.

Somewhere in the house, probably, was Althene.

Usually, once a day, Rachaela and Althene would

meet each other. If at no other time, in the evening, at the hour of dining. At Christmas there had been a complex dinner. Everyone had sat through it, Camillo also, with Lou. Tray had been along the table, next to Miranda. She had worn one of Miranda's dresses, presumably a little taken in. Tray's tan had faded to white, where Lou's had turned a dire obdurate yellow.

And Althene. At Christmas Althene had worn a silver dress. Rachaela had never seen a silver dress before which did not look vulgar, unpleasant. But Althene's dress was exquisite, like something from a description in a fairy book . . . the silver of moonlight on waves, something like that.

Althene was trapped here, too. She must be waiting for Malach. Or some order from Malach.

She did not seem to find the situation uncomfortable. She was level and polite. Her eyes never rested on Rachaela. There was the palest whiff of arrogance, which might be the cloak of embarrassment, anger, or contempt.

And I.

Rachaela tried to examine herself frankly. She went about the house, or walked on the common, consciously avoiding Althene where possible—Oh, she has gone out, I must not; Ah, she is in the white room, I will not go down. Such things. And when they chanced to pass, greeting each other quietly, soullessly, a sting like an electric shock.

Rachaela thought, *I'm like some silly schoolgirl with a crush on the prefect.*

She dreamed about Althene. Some nights, some days when she slept, the dreams went on and on, until she would force herself awake, exhausted.

The dreams were rarely sexual. Generally Rachaela was lost. She would search for Althene in enormous frightened pain. Occasionally she would glimpse her, but always unavailably, in the carriage of a rushing train, on the roof of some high building without steps.

Then again, there was a dream in which Althene and she walked together through some amorphous place. Althene talked to her in a language Rachaela could not fathom, perhaps medieval French—but what did that matter? The analogy was clear enough.

Twice, an erotic dream. In one, Althene wore the fabulous lingerie, not green but black, and Lou's black wedding veil of long ago. In the other, Althene had pulled the sheet up over her body. "Don't look." And Rachaela pulled the sheet away and woke up. Neither was satisfying, but left her electrified, aroused.

One night, Rachaela had drunk a lot of wine before and during dinner. She wanted to follow Althene out of the room and take hold of her, her hand or waist. After all, Rachaela was the same. She was not pregnant. She thought, crudely, perhaps Althene was not particularly potent, for she was surely more woman than man.

But Rachaela did not follow Althene.

Althene, for all she was a woman, was also male.

And sometimes Rachaela only dreamed of her, not knowing what she dreamed, waking up with the memory of a dark glistening wheel which had turned forever through the daylight sleep.

And once she had imagined herself in Althene's lingerie. Would they resemble each other even more?

Rachaela had seen Althene today, from her window, walking on the common in the black skin coat.

What skin was it? Dyed human, maybe, like the bone handle of the gun.

There was a noise. Rachaela jumped horrifically.

It was the telephone. The telephone was ringing.

Stupidly, Rachaela sat looking at it, waiting for someone, Michael or Cheta, to come and answer it.

No one came, and the phone rang on.

Rachaela got up, and went to raise the receiver.

"Is that you, Gladys?" asked a quavering voice.

"No . . . This isn't Gladys."

"Is she there?"

"I'm afraid you have a wrong number."

"Oh, dear. It's me eyes. I'm sorry, dear."

"No trouble," said Rachaela.

She replaced the receiver slowly. Even the Scarabae were not immune to calls dialed in error.

But she was trembling. She felt sick. What was it? Fear? Why?

She sat down in a chair and shut her eyes. And, after a moment, steps crossed the room very lightly. As the firm cool hand touched the back of her neck, she smelled the unique perfume, cinnamon, shadow.

The fingers rubbed at the base of her skull, briskly. Rachaela relaxed.

"It made me jump, the phone," said Rachaela, foolishly.

"An instrument of evil," said Althene sardonically. "Bad news and sorrow."

"Yes, pure primitive fear. Absurd."

"You're better now."

"I think so. Thank you."

The hand left her alone.

Althene stood away, shimmering darkness. Water drops glittered on her hair. The windows had faded to copper.

"It's raining."

"At least, not frogs," said Althene.

"When I was a child I thought it rained cats and dogs," Rachaela said. She felt numb and at the same time desperate. "My mother used to shout at me. She thought I was trying to be cute. A proper child. But I was really a useless child. I always felt self-conscious in that ridiculous small body."

"Ah, yes," said Althene. She looked out into the hall. Longing to get away?

"Don't let me keep you," said Rachaela.

"I'm quite expensive," said Althene. "Do you think you could afford it?"

"I think sexual jokes are going to fall rather flat," said Rachaela. Then, "I apologize."

Althene took off the coat and dropped it on a white sofa, like a dead snake. She wore gray, a nun's color, and had masked her eyes in smoke. But her lips were rubies.

"Let's drink some of Eric's brandy," said Althene.

She went to the oval silver tray and lifted up one of the cut-glass decanters.

Rachaela sat still, obedient.

Althene handed her the black drink. It was bitter and burned like gall, whatever gall was.

"My mother's name," Rachaela said, "was Janet. Janet Smith. It's ordinary enough she may have contrived it."

"And how did she pick your name?"

"I think . . . he must have suggested it. God knows why she let him. Why she did what he said."

"Why did anyone do what Adamus said?"

"He mesmerized us all. My mother, myself. Ruth."

"I never met Adamus," Althene said, "although, of course, I knew of him."

"If the Scarabae live so long," said Rachaela, "why do they commit suicide—how can they be sure . . ."

"Vampiric resurrection," said Althene, "is that what you infer?"

"I don't know what I *infer.*"

"Are we still talking about Adamus?"

"Camillo," said Rachaela suddenly. "He's altered. He isn't just an old man wearing boy's clothes. Sometimes he looks—he looks too young." Althene did not answer. Rachaela said, "And Miranda's hair. Is she coloring it?"

"I doubt it."

"Then Miranda's hair—" Rachaela stopped.

They sat in silence, and the golden clock, which ran, ticked softly. Time, passing. Perhaps.

"Althene," Rachaela said, "nothing's happened to me. I'm not pregnant."

" 'Tis wel goed."

"I mean, Althene, I believed perhaps I was *meant* to be."

Althene shrugged.

"I mean," Rachaela said, "that was the plan the last time. I was used. Just like my mother."

"Yes, you were used."

"I don't want to be used again."

"In what sense am I to have used you?" Althene said. "By trying to impregnate you with rabid Scarabae seed? Or by masquerading as one thing and being another?"

"It isn't a masquerade, I realize that. But a deception. To make me think I was safe with you and then—"

"And then," said Althene.

She finished her brandy and walked across the room, the coat trailing from her hand.

Rachaela stood up. She said ironically, "Can I have offended you?"

Althene turned. She smiled, from a height.

"Why not persevere? Perhaps you will manage it."

Rachaela came to dinner in the olive dress with a coil of silver around her throat. She felt silly, anxious, fraught, and proud—yes, that was the word. Like a woman from a novel set in 1890.

She watched the others carefully.

Eric. Old and straight, ringed, in his brushed dinner clothes. And Sasha, her iron hair pinned up, in plum velvet. Tray came in with Miranda. Mother and daughter? No, grandmother and grandchild, for Tray had started to call her Nan-Nan. Tray was now a Lily Burne-Jones in her dark sequined frock. She wore pale makeup and dark eyes, but no lipstick or blusher. And Miranda. 1950s dress and hair down her back. The gray had mixed into some other color. Prune-color hair. Like black hair graying, but . . . the other way around.

Did Miranda's face look young? It did. Deep lines by the mouth and between the eyes. The marks of a thin woman of fifty-four or -five. But she had looked eighty, ninety, Miranda. Once.

Camillo did not come in, or Lou. Off to another gig, in the rain.

She won't come. The Scarabae game.

Adamus. With her for a night. Pinned like a butterfly, impaled on the vampire stake of the burning phallus. And then he hid himself in his tower, which later burned in fire.

Althene came in in a scarlet dress.

Rachaela felt the blood rush into her face and throat.

Burning . . .

They sat down and ate the meal. Something. What was it?

Rachaela thought of the sea gull they had eaten at the other house, before. Sufficient unto themselves, locked in time. But events had smashed open the glass case, and out they flew.

Was it the shock which made them alter? Kill, or cure.

After dinner they went into the drawing room and put a video on the TV.

Eric said to Althene, "This actor looks like Malach. Don't you think so?"

"Perhaps," said Althene. She was sitting in an armchair. On one of her fingers was a ring of twisted gold. She turned it absently.

Rachaela reached across and touched the ring.

"It's old," said Althene. "A prince wore it in fifteenth-century Italy."

"Yes," Rachaela said.

"Then it was stolen."

"By you."

Althene smiled. "No."

"If you tell me it was you, I'll probably accept what you say."

"How unwise."

Eric said, "Shhh. These films need concentration."

After ten minutes more, Althene got up quietly and went out. Sasha and Eric did not react. Miranda and Tray also sat staring at the screen, a box of chocolate-covered truffles between them.

Rachaela went after Althene, out into the hall.

The oil lamps were alight.

"Yes?" Althene said, turning to look at her.

Rachaela walked across the hall, until she was near to Althene's salamander redness.

"If it's a game, I don't want to go on playing," Rachaela said.

"Or it isn't a game."

"Your dress," said Rachaela.

"Yes?"

"Bloodred. The Scarabae betrothal color."

"Betrothal and marriage."

"Why?" said Rachaela.

"I happen to own a red dress."

"If you want me to," Rachaela said, "I'll go up with you. To your room. No more protests."

"Really? No more? But I'm a man who is a woman. Which do you want?"

"I don't know," said Rachaela. "I want you."

"Ah." Althene leaned back on the bannister. "But now, I'm not convinced."

"They get young again," said Rachaela, "don't they?"

"Do they?"

"Will it happen to me?"

"I've no idea."

"I need," Rachaela hesitated. "I can't go on with it. Something's already happened to me. I can't—you're the only one—"

"Not at all. There are many Scarabae."

"I don't want to be bred from."

Althene said, "You wouldn't be safe with me. There are things we can do to avoid it. If you want. But I'm as dangerous to you that way as Adamus. You had better understand."

"I feel as if," Rachaela said, "my body were full of doors, standing open. And my mind. I can't cope with it. I can't even run away."

"All right. Not here. You'll upset them if they come out."

Althene held out her hand. Rachaela took it. They went up the stairs, up and up, to the room of peacocks.

In the room the light was darkest gold.

Rachaela turned herself into Althene's body and looked into her face.

"Do you want me," said Althene, "to wipe the lipstick off?"

"No. I like it. My mother never kissed me."

"I'm not your mother."

Through the scented sheath of garments, educated now, Rachaela felt the restrained hardness of Althene's second self, as Althene's lips came down to hers.

On the bed, Althene wrapped Rachael's nakedness in the gilded shawl. Althene's kisses and tongue came through the eyelets.

"Is this what you want? And this . . ."

Rachaela pulled on Althene's body. "All of you."

"But then how can I—"

"I don't care. All of you. Now, now."

Love me and leave me, Rachaela thought.

"Yes, I'll leave you," Althene murmured, "but I'll come back."

Back from where, from history, from the night? Rachaela's orgasm was long and sad, sweeping like the sea, and full of tears. Something beautiful held her through the spasms of ocean, through the storm.

Althene withdrew from her gently. "The Roman method."

Rachaela thought of their kind by night, flying over deserts and the snow. Althene came silently and fiercely against her.

Life and death, day and darkness.

"I want to sleep with you," said Rachaela.

"Sleep then," Althene said, like a magician. And Rachaela slept.

CHAPTER 37

✥ THROUGH THE WOLF-BROWN DAY, BE-
tween the iron cities, they rode out of the north.
It was February, month of the Lupercal, and none of
them knew it. They were a kind of black cloud roaring
over the landscape. Over the wastelands in the rain.

As they got nearer the capital, they created pauses.
In the motorway cafés the girls in their bright slave-
uniforms treated them carefully.

On the great wide roads they burned up tarmac.
Black jets with flares of blue, crimson and silver.

At the head rode Connor. His long black hair was in
a tail, fastened by a cinch of steel. He had a big powerful
body and the beer-gut of a Viking. He liked screwing
women, but he loved Viv, who was in the saddlebag on
the left-hand side. He loved her like the bike. If ever
anything happened they would be together, the three of
them, into Valhalla.

Viv was of middle size, white, black, and yellow, with
one upstanding ear in which, long ago, another dog had
bitten a hole. Through the hole now was a silver stud, a
heart. Viv wore goggles to protect her eyes, and a scarf,
red, with silver cat skulls. This was Connor's tribute, for
he liked cats, too.

Behind Connor and Viv on the Harley Shovelhead,
came the rest of the fleet. Whisper on his black beast,

shouting loudly at every twist and turn, and Red up behind him, grinning with joy. And then Pig and Tina, and
then Cardiff, alone and looking grim, as if he needed a
shit, as he always looked. And lastly Rose, his shaven
head tattooed with a flower, his hard beefy chest naked
to the wind and rain, only the silver coins and chains
slapping it from his black jacket.

They stormed into London, no longer walled, but
clotted by dismal outskirts and high blocks of concrete,
and through its Avernal avenues, as the dusk came down
early.

At the pub, The Compasses, they pulled up and
slipped from the saddles. Red took off her helmet and
shook out her laval hair.

Connor glanced at her with approval, and then drew
Viv from her bag.

"Come and put your snout in some beer, baby."

Viv smiled and wagged her tail.

He took off her goggles and she licked him.

He carried her in the pub under one arm.

Red bought the first round. She was all right. Viv
had a pint to herself, in a bowl—the landlord knew them.

"Better get some grub as well, we don't know what
the setup is."

So they had pies and chips and beans, and Cardiff
farted loudly, so drinkers in the next bar stared across.

"You could bloody power your bike on that," yelled
Whisper.

Cardiff farted. "Yours, too, you old bastard."

Connor bought a round, and they downed them.

This was journey food. They had somewhere to get
to.

Tina and Red went to the ladies' and came back
smelling good. Red wore no makeup and needed none,
with her clear pink skin and sapphire eyes. Connor would
have liked a go at Red, but Red was not for him.

"Whisper treating you all right?"

"Oh, it's marvelous. Like chariot racing."

"Better," said Connor.

"Okay," said Red. "Better."

She kissed Viv on the nose and Viv licked her. Viv was soppy with the good ones, but she had taken a chunk out of a guy who had raised his hand against Connor. Viv was a doll.

They went out and the night was dark, the way night got to be, even in the sodium-lit cities.

Connor looked up. "Once there were stars."

"You want to tear this streetlamp rubbish across," said Red, "get at the darkness."

She was a good one all right.

They mounted up, and Viv sat in the bag and Connor put back her goggles and gave her a handful of crisps.

She liked riding.

They took off like rockets. The engine poured up its power. You grew into the machine. The body became a shaken jelly of rock and the soul slipped loose, half an inch out into the night. That was how you rode. You were the bike, and out of the body, and never so real as then.

They arrowed up the hills of London, through the lumbering cars and elephant buses, past the parks of winter grass, between the high walls flimsy as paper.

When they came up the final road, the big trees were looming above like a forest. And then there was the house. Connor had been told what he could expect.

A witch's mansion. Turrets and towers. Sunbursts of windows.

"Up there?" said Rose, coming level.

"That's the place."

They soared up the hill toward the house, and swerved to rest on the flatter ground before it.

The noise of the bikes died.

It was quiet.

They stood marshaled, and Connor reviewed them.

"Okay. Now watch yourselves. No messing about. This is Camillo's drum." Cardiff farted. "And none of that, either." Viv barked. "You're smashing," said Connor. He took off her goggles, and marched toward the door.

No bell. A knocker that was a green man head, leaves sprouting from its lips. Nice. "Hands off," he said to them, indicating the knocker. Then he knocked.

No one responded. But they waited patiently. Camillo had told Connor to come, late winter, just before the spring. "Come and rescue me," Camillo had said, and gave his high horse laugh.

Finally the door did open. A slim old lady in a black dress, alabaster and ebony, like a waxwork meant to represent an old lady.

"It's Camillo we want," said Connor, gently. "He invited us."

"Please enter."

They entered. Two doors to go through, and then the big hall, with pillars, and under the electric light, the rosy oil lamps softly flickering.

"I will go and tell Mr. Camillo that you're here."

"Thank you," said Connor, courteously.

The light was wonderful for Red. They looked like an invasion, of course. The black hard leathers. A faint whistling sounded.

"Cardiff," said Connor, "I warned you."

"Sorry."

Tina laughed.

Rose was over stroking the balustrade of the stairs. "Look at this."

Then a woman came out of a doorway below. She wore a white party dress, like something Ginger Rogers might have had, at her most glamorous. Her long dark wavy hair was great and Connor liked the way she wore it, even though she must have been fifty-five.

"Please come in," said this woman.

So they went in behind the stairs to a wide white room, Viv bustling after them.

There was a black-haired beauty sitting on a sofa, but she looked too vacuous for Connor's taste. She was eating a rum baba. Behind her on the huge TV was *Die Hard.* The sound had been turned down, but Rose, Tina, Pig, Whisper, and Cardiff at once began to watch the film, the way they did the TVs in pubs, and even through plate-glass shop windows.

Red stood in awe over a gilt table with a small green bowl on it.

"This is *real,*" she said.

She should know.

"Will you have something to drink?" asked Miranda. "I'm afraid Eric and Sasha are upstairs. And the girls. Tracy and I have been watching this remarkable film. Do you know it?"

"*Yeah,*" said Cardiff. "Can we have the sound up?"

"No," said Connor.

"But of course," said the woman. She touched Connor's hand sweetly. "I'm Miranda. Camillo will be here soon, I'm sure." She went to the TV and turned up the sound. Rose, Cardiff, Whisper, Tina, and Pig became totally glazed. And the beauty with the plate of rum baba also returned a fixated gaze to the screen. Viv sat and stared only at Connor.

Miranda made them drinks then. There was a bottle of Zinfandel two-thirds full standing in ice, and Connor had some of that. Red too. Cardiff asked for beer and Miranda went out into the hall and called softly, and someone came and she sent him for it.

Rose and Pig had vodka, and Tina had some sherry. There seemed to be virtually everything there.

"Would your dog like a drink?"

"I'll give her a drop of wine, if that's all right. She's got a good palate. Never smoked, you see."

Miranda laughed, musically, like a girl. Connor

looked at her closely. She was old, but he quite fancied her. She bent and smoothed Viv over and Viv beamed. Then Miranda took the real jade bowl off the table and put Zinfandel in it for Viv. The dog lapped. She was delighted.

Someone died on the screen.

"Yeah!" bellowed Whisper.

An oldish man came in, carrying a big tankard of beer on a tray. Cardiff grabbed.

"Watch it," said Connor.

"Thanks," said Connor to the oldish man, who was not actually really old at all, only gray-haired.

The man went out.

Connor said to Miranda, "Ever been on a bike?"

"No," said Miranda. "In my day it was horses."

"It's like a horse," said Connor. "A horse that has wings."

"Why—" said Miranda, "how exciting."

Her eyes were glorious. Black as buggered night.

She was a queen of the green hills, and he could sit at her slippered feet with his harp, if he only played one.

"If ever you want to try," said Connor, "I'm your man."

Secretively, the way the women did, she lowered her eyes, and Connor thought of riding with Miranda, and those slim pale hands around his big middle.

"The last time I rode on a horse," said Miranda, "was to a wedding feast. The bride was dressed in blue, and there was a big cake colored by saffron, the shape of a hand holding a key. The things one remembers."

"Some foreign wedding," said Connor.

"Oh, yes. In Italy. My name wasn't Miranda then, you know. That came later, from a play."

Connor felt a wide crevice opening before him, and he was almost eager to drop into it, but something stayed him. The raven goddess, the dark-eyed Morigan. Best beware.

Red said, "Connor, he's here. This is him, isn't it?"

She had confided long ago that she did not care for young men. At Cambridge she had had an affair with a scholar sixty years of age. She had wrapped him in her copper hair.

Connor looked around, and in the doorway was Camillo.

He looked young tonight. Maybe too young for Red. But no. The ancient eyes were still there, looking out.

"Here you are," said Camillo. "Is it time then? It must be."

"Whatever you say," said Connor.

Viv barked lightly. And Camillo knelt down. Viv went to him and they greeted each other.

"On your feet," Connor said to the TV addicts. They got up and clustered around. He brought Red forward. "See what I have here."

Camillo looked up, slyly.

Red smiled, showing her even white teeth.

"Not a bimbo this time," said Connor. "Red has studied history. She's ridden a long way to meet you."

Camillo stood up again. He looked at Red, with his head to one side.

"I'm an old man," said Camillo, skittishly.

"I like old men," answered Red. "They're clever."

"And grateful? I'm never grateful."

"I'd hate you to be," Red replied.

"Tell me something about history," said Camillo.

Red hesitated. She said, "There were three King Arthurs. Tribal chiefs. Three Camelots, too. Only one Guinevere. But that wasn't her name."

"Something else," said Camillo.

"Under the Romans, Britain produced some of the best wines in the Empire."

"More."

"In certain Semitic cultures, prostitutes placed gold

coins in the mouth of the cervix, after the birth of a child, to prevent further unwanted pregnancies."

"Do you have a gold coin?"

"No. My tubes are tied. I don't want children."

"But you want old men."

Tray turned from the TV and looked suddenly afraid.

"Camillo, shhh," said Miranda. She went to Tray and put her arm about her, and Tray rested her head on Miranda's sequined arm.

Red said calmly, "Old men are only young men in a different skin."

"Not me."

"Well," said Red, "you can teach me, can't you."

They made a camp, down the slope from the house, under the trees. Nobody would disturb them, try to move them on, Camillo had said.

Camillo was not ready yet, apparently. That was fine. They could wait.

The man who had brought them beer brought them down a supper from the house. Wine and beer and vodka, smoked fish and hot toast streaming with butter, wedges of yellow cheese, prawns, a dish of grapes and apples and peaches.

"He's a tease," said Red. She grinned at Connor. "I like that. I'll have to woo him."

Connor thought about Miranda. Viv settled on his chest as they lay in the tent. Viv was tipsy.

Outside, the fire burned. They were a camp of mercenaries. Camillo's now: Waiting. The rain slept. They slept too.

In the morning, early, Connor and Viv got up in the gray-tawny February dawn to relieve themselves. Viv was in high spirits despite her debauch, playing about in last year's leaves. When they came back, a man was standing under the house, regarding the camp.

"Good morning," said Connor. And took a stance on the grassy slope. Viv ran up, staring.

The man was tall and spare, with the longest, whitest hair Connor had seen. The face, Connor knew.

The man said, "Camillo's friends, perhaps."

"Believe it," said Connor.

The man nodded, and walked away around the house. As he went up, the woman, Miranda, came out and down. They passed each other with a vague acknowledgement. Miranda turned, and looked after him, her hands up to her throat.

Connor climbed to her.

"What is it?"

"Ah," she said. She put down her hands. "Some news. He will want Eric."

"Whitey," said Connor. "He's Camillo's son, isn't he?"

Miranda glanced at him. She was preoccupied.

"Oh, no. No. His father. That is, Camillo is Malach's son."

Connor looked away into the distances of the world.

"Malach. You're telling me that white one is the father of Camillo."

"Yes," she said, distractedly.

Connor felt a stirring he had known all his life. It was the oldness in him. He picked up Viv and ruffled her head. And Miranda glided by him down into the trees, as if she went to gather strange herbs for witchcraft, or to some tryst a hundred years too late.

CHAPTER 38

❖ *BEFORE THE DIM IRIS MORNING WINDOW,*
Althene's form was elongated and black. "He'll
bring her this evening. I am to tell you."

"I see."

"Not entirely. I am also to explain it all to you."

Rachaela said tartly, "Since I'm the resident imbe-
cile."

Althene laughed. She sat down on her dark blue
bed. Rachaela huddled there in her jumper and skirt.
They had got up early, to walk on the common, then
Althene returned from below with a tray of new bread
and coffee. And with this.

Malach was bringing Ruth to the house.

"Why does he have to come here?" Rachaela asked.
"Is it some sort of test?"

"Yes, perhaps."

"What will they do? Poison her with a glass of
wine?"

"No. They will formally give her to Malach. That's
all. It's a ceremony. Then they can be free of her, even
though she's theirs."

"And mine. She's my daughter. Supposing I don't—
won't—*give* her to Malach."

"She belongs to him already, I imagine," Althene
said. "That's what he will have been doing. Taking her."

Rachaela clenched her hands.

"You mean they're lovers."

"I expect they are."

"She's twelve," said Rachaela. She frowned. "No, she's thirteen. But—for God's sake. She's a child."

"Never, probably. A child in some ways, of course. But he will take care of that too. Malach is expert."

"Oh, *yes.*"

"So bitter, my love," said Althene. She stroked back Rachaela's hair. "Ruth was a burden to you you could never bear. But for Malach it will be interesting, a challenge, perhaps. He'll take her away. He'll see that she is educated, trained. She'll want to please him and so she will shine. A father and daughter, with the sweetness of sex added for spice."

"It's too easy," said Rachaela. "She's a murderess."

"The forgiveness of sin," said Althene. "What does it mean? That you are freed from evil. Though you have committed atrocious acts, you needn't continue to transgress. Change is possible. Is *allowed.*"

"All right. I've seen you kill. You'd judge Ruth differently."

"I make no judgment."

"How dare you," said Rachaela, drawing away. "How *dare* you—these absolutes—these *doctrines*—she's a monster—"

"I remember," Althene said, "you told me that, when Ruth was a baby, she almost died."

"Yes, and I wanted her dead."

"Perhaps Ruth, also. Perhaps Ruth meant to die. But you made her live."

"A hospital did that. And bloody Emma."

"How terrible to be forced to go on along a road you know is wrong."

"Oh, stop it," Rachaela said. She put her head on her updrawn knees. "Just stop."

"Very well. But there's one further distressing item. At least, I hope it will distress you."

"When Malach takes Ruth away," Rachaela said, "you'll go too."

"Unfortunately, I must."

"Yes. How convenient."

"I'll be gone a month. Maybe a little more. Then I shall return."

"Do as you want," Rachaela said.

"I must arrange my own affairs," Althene said, "before I come back to you."

"You want me to stand at my window, looking out. *Wearily*. He cometh not, she said."

"How can you," said Althene, evidently amused, "compare me to Adamus?"

"I don't, I don't. But you will go, and you won't come back. And I would prefer honesty. How can you, anyway, want me. The way you are—it must be random. A woman making love to a woman. But the woman is a man. Anyone who consents—"

"You try my patience," said Althene. "Get up and go away. I'm tired of you."

"Exactly."

"I shall cross the symbolic sea, and leave you here, and that's that. Back to my hoards of consenting perverted women."

"Yes."

"Rachaela," Althene said, "I'll say this only one time. Perhaps never again. And so listen to me. I love you. Am *in* love with you. The family have had a hand in it, and perhaps it was meant to happen. It has happened. You don't love me, naturally. You're fascinated by what I am. And I can give you pleasure. You want me to leave you, perhaps. To set you at liberty."

"I don't know," Rachaela said. She stared downward through the bed into darkness.

"I'll be gone. You'll be without me. Then you *will* know. When I come back—"

"You won't come back."

"We shall see," said Althene. She stood up. Behind her the other woman of glass stood before the iris-hyacinth window. "They'll want you to be present when Ruth arrives."

"They may not like what I say and do."

"Why must you say or do anything?"

"Yes," Rachaela said, "why must I."

She walked to the door.

"Do you," said Althene, "consider yourself to be perverted, because you've had sex with me?"

"I suppose I must be. No. No, not at all."

"Good," said Althene. "I have at least that, then, to carry into the sky, while Malach's dogs are howling and piddling with surprise, and the sea is churning far below."

"But is it possible," said Rachaela, "for you to *love*?"

Althene gazed at her. Althene's eyes were soft. They hardened to adamant. "And who, after all, could love you?"

In her white bathroom with the viridian window, Rachaela bathed and washed her hair. She shaved her legs, and the hollows under her arms, as she did every third day. Save today it was like a ritual, the taking of the Host before battle.

She sat over the gas fire. Set in a wide hearth, it had cement logs and looked genuine, and it began to seem to her again she was in the other house, the house above the sea.

She shook her hair to dry it and the fire spat.

Later she dressed in a black wool dress, powdered her face and made up her eyes. She used the light amber blusher and lipstick Althene had given her. This was the mask, the visor of the battle helmet.

Don't be a fool. Just let them do what they want. They will anyway. All of them.

She visualized Ruth coming in, holding Malach's hand. Her hair was done in plaits and she wore a school uniform. Rachaela laughed aloud, bitterly.

So bitter, my love . . .

Outside the dove window came a vague noise of music. There was a camp of bikers on the common, down the slope. Camillo's companions, doubtless. She had opened the window once, and glimpsed a fire and tents.

The threads were being gathered up, the drawstring pulled tight.

Going away.

Soon she would be alone here again, with Eric and Sasha, and with Miranda. Miranda, who was growing young. If such a thing were credible. But it was. It was. Camillo, too—

"Damn them," she said.

She put on Anna's ring, the ruby heart. And then a silver snake with a tiny tourmaline in its head. Althene had given her that.

I shall put it away when she goes. I won't look at it.

This is how they gather their rings. Heirlooms. The gifts of lovers.

He never gave me a ring. Adamus. He gave me Ruth.

She slid a Prokofiev concerto into the CD player. It had black humor, the sounds of diamond rats running about in a giant clock.

She felt a little sick, thinking of Ruth arriving in her uniform, with Malach.

At the commencement of the early dusk, Rachaela heard a car, a taxi, a way down the road.

Her heart stopped. She stood up.

Twenty minutes later, when her heart was beating solidly all through her body, Cheta knocked on the door.

"They're here, Miss Rachaela. Will you come down?"

What if I say no?

She came out and went along the passage, and down the stairs.

There was no one in the hall, but the doors stood open and Michael was closing them. Kei was beside him, carrying two bags. The lamps had been lit.

In the drawing room, unlike the usual sound of the TV, a murmur of voices.

I don't want to go in.

Rachaela moved quickly across the hall and into the large white room.

It was full of warm light, and the colored windows were giving up their very last gleams.

Eric, Sasha, and Miranda stood in a line. They had donned dark clothes, as she herself intuitively had done.

She saw too Althene was not there. Nor Camillo.

Then they turned, and looked at her.

Malach, Ruth.

Malach wore white; somehow astonishing, this second whiteness against the white negative of the mane of hair. But the power of him was strong as darkness. It had not abated. Could it be something had increased it?

Last of all, Rachaela saw Ruth. Her daughter. Did not know her.

Ruth had grown taller. She had grown older. She was a woman, twenty, twenty-five.

She wore a long, narrow black skirt that ended four inches from her ankles, and black high-heeled boots embroidered with scarlet and silver. A black velvet coat swung from her shoulders arrogantly, and under it she wore a high-necked tunic of silvery gray watered silk, its collar beaded with drops like red wine and rain, and tied at the waist by a broad black velvet belt that made her waist into the width of a stalk. From under the high, triangular black velvet hat, her black river of hair poured out. She looked like a Russian princess from some novel.

Her face . . . was not the same.

It was as beautifully made up as Althene's would have been. Pale as porcelain with a hint of blusher on the cheeks, the eyelids dark but now like smoke not soot, the lips a light clear red, flame rather than blood.

Her eyes. Her eyes were alive.

She was not holding Malach's hand, only a small black bag. She was perfectly poised.

He's kissed her awake. Out of the coma. This isn't Ruth.

But it was.

The two dogs were standing beside her. Enki, the paler one, let out a thin low growl.

"Still," Malach said. Enki fell silent.

Ruth's slender gloves were wine red, like the beads, and the embroidery on her boots.

Red. The betrothal color. The marriage color.

Rachaela stared at her daughter.

Not mine.

His.

Malach's.

He has created her.

"Rachaela," Malach said quietly, "I hope you're well."

Idiocy. The Scarabae were always well. Well, or dead.

"Yes, thank you." She could not take her eyes from Ruth. "And I see—that Ruth is well, too."

A little half glance of the raven head toward Malach. Then Ruth said, "Good evening, Rachaela."

Not Mommy anymore. Of course. We are both women now.

"Your clothes are sumptuous," Rachaela said.

"Thank you."

But she had always had good taste. Frightening insights. And she had always appeared astonishing, dressed up.

There were no rings on her gloved hands. Perhaps, inside?

Eric said abruptly, "We should all sit."

So they sat down. Malach and Ruth on one sofa, Eric and Sasha on another. Miranda in a chair. Rachaela in a second chair. Enki and Oskar on the carpet.

Michael and Kei came in. They brought a tall silver teapot and cups of transparent white china, and some liqueur in a pear-shaped crystal bottle, little glasses, a plate of tiny cakes with marvelous icing, blue and pink and white and green.

All this came down on the tables, and then the alcohol and the tea and the cakes were offered.

Malach took the alcohol and the tea, nothing to eat. And Ruth . . . Ruth took tea. No food. She had been such a hungry child. No longer.

Ah, no.

Something in Rachaela ached. It was like a muscle stretched too far. Hurting in release.

Althene was not there. Obviously. Tact or callousness? And Camillo always avoided these family gatherings. Almost always. (Standing in armor that time long ago, as she ran away.)

Ruth had removed her left-hand glove, but not the right.

"Is that an affectation?" Rachaela said.

Ruth looked at her, politely.

"Oh, no. I injured my hand."

"That must be a nuisance," Rachaela said, "especially if you still like to play the piano."

"Malach wants me to practice some music for the left hand only. Until it improves."

Malach wants. Adam says.

"And you're going away with Malach."

Ruth smiled. It was a pretty, fleeting smile. It was a true smile.

I never saw that. Yes I did. When Adam found her after she had killed them. Then. She came alive and she was lovely. But she's lovely now. She's alive now.

"Yes. We're going to Europe."

It was old-fashioned, excluding Britain from the Continent. But then. What else?

Eric said, "They will take care of Ruth."

His voice was hard, abrasive.

Rachaela thought how he had put his fist through the TV screen, striking at Ruth.

Rachaela said, "We're all being so wonderful to each other. Shouldn't we talk about the facts?"

"No," Sasha said. "The facts aren't important."

Eric said, "It is essential to dismiss such errors."

"Which errors?" said Rachaela. She swallowed. "How is it possible?"

Malach spoke. Rachaela had mislaid his voice in the half hour he had not talked to them. Dry and a little rough, its music in abeyance.

"Did you think I'd kill her?"

"Yes," Rachaela said.

"She's Scarabae," he said.

"You've given her attention," Rachaela said, "the thing I didn't give her. Or Adamus. Excuse me, Ruth, I'm speaking about you as if you weren't here. But then, are you here?"

Ruth did not look at her. She only drank daintily from her cup. The two dogs lay still.

"Malach has taught you how to behave, has he?"

"Yes," Malach said. And then, "No one here has a sword drawn but you. You are her mother."

"Yes," Rachaela said.

Malach's eyes came to hers. So cruel now. Pitiless, old, no quarter given. "She hurt you, did she, coming out? You can't forgive?"

Rachaela shivered. "What happens when you lose interest in her?"

Malach, without looking, put out his hand and touched Ruth's cheek. He laid his skin against hers, softly.

"I shall never lose interest. She is my soul."

The words burned in the room.

Fire, from some altar.

And Ruth turned to him. She looked at him speechlessly.

He has created her.

Is that *the reason for love?*

"Oh, then," Rachaela said, "I suppose it's all right."

Miranda said suddenly, "I'm a little worried about Tracy. Shall I send Michael to fetch her down? She'd like these cakes so much."

"You have a replacement, you see," Rachaela said to Ruth, "a nice little pale, black-haired girl who acts as she should."

The door opened.

But it was not Tray. It was Camillo.

He came into the room with an odd mincing step.

"Late," he said. "There you are. Talking with my Cossacks on the hill."

He glanced at Malach, and then at Ruth. Camillo froze. It was as if he had come into the arctic cold, knowing how it would be, and as he turned to stone, he laughed.

"Mama," he said. "My father and my mother."

Ruth had moved a little. She drew back against Malach.

Yes, last time he gave her a mousetrap.

"Isn't she lovely," said Camillo. "Will she sing me asleep? Will she wrap me in the fur as we run away over the snow?"

"*Tais-toi,*" Malach said.

"Mais non," Camillo said. "No, no I won't shut up. I like to say it. And I've brought a gift."

Camillo slipped forward to Ruth over the carpeted ground, between the purity of the furniture. The dogs did not move. *"Pour vous, Maman."* He held out something long and thin.

It was a knitting needle. It was burned.

Bile whipped Rachaela's throat.

"From the heart of Anna. What you killed her with."

Malach got up. The dogs stirred.

"Get out," he said.

Camillo leered at him.

"Too old," he said. "Not to be hurt."

Ruth had risen too. She put her gloved hand upon Malach's arm. He checked.

"Camillo," Ruth said.

"Yes, *Maman.*"

"Be my shame," Ruth said.

Camillo's face crumpled. He stepped back. He spoke in some other tongue.

Ruth nodded.

Camillo bolted from the room.

CHAPTER 39

JUST PAST EIGHT, STELLA CHECKED THE kitchen. The chicken was cooking juicily in its sauce of yoghurt, saffron, and garlic, and on the chopping board the primrose and iron-green peppers, the creamy banana and red apple, the onions and the almonds waited to be fried. The cannister of rice was full, but she peered into it again.

There were wine and beer, poppadums and hot chutney.

She went back into the main room and looked out of the curtains at the dark low night.

He would be here soon.

She sat on the couch and picked up a book, but she could not settle. She never could when she knew Nobbi was on his way to her.

She had not seen him since that time after Christmas. The time he had woken up in the night; "The Thieving Magpie."

Christmas was bad enough, anyway.

She bore it with fortitude.

Star and her mother had been used to celebrate. They had attached silver rosettes to the cat's collar, pulled crackers, watched the better films on television, got tiddly.

Star had never spent a Christmas with Nobbi.

One day.

Something hissed in the oven, and Star went to investigate. Then she came back and sat down again.

Perhaps she ought to have a glass of wine. It might calm her down. But she liked to drink with him.

Why was she so nervous?

Of course, he was out looking for Tray.

He had intimated, although not exactly said, that Tray was with people who were dangerous.

Obviously, he wanted to do something. That was Nobbi. But what kind of trouble was he getting into?

She could hardly say *Don't.*

As if he would listen, anyway, if she said something like that.

It was half-past eight now. He had said eight. That would have given them time in the bedroom before she finished the dinner.

Never mind. There would be hours later. He had said he would stay with her tonight.

She liked that. She liked so much waking up with him. She brought breakfast on a tray. And they made love. They had bought a plastic duck which he put in the bath with him. Nobbi called the duck Charlie.

Star went into the bathroom.

"Hallo, Charlie."

Charlie smiled, the way he always did.

Stella splashed some cool water on her face and dried it with a towel.

Then she looked at herself in the little bathroom mirror.

Her appearance neither pleased nor dismayed her. Her eyes were too big, and her mouth, but her skin was good.

She came out of the bathroom. She put Bach's *Goldberg Variations* on the record player.

She did not want any wine.

But she was so nervous.

When he arranged to come he was never late, never more than a few minutes. Except once, half an hour, and he had called her from a service station, something with the car.

It was ten to nine now.

She went into the kitchen and turned the oven down.

Star did not often speak aloud to herself. Now she said, "Stop acting like some silly schoolgirl. He's all right. You would *know*."

And then, the phone rang.

Stella flew to it.

"Hallo?"

"Star?" Nobbi asked her. He sounded very far away.

"Nobbi, love. Are you okay?"

"Sure, Star. Yes. I'm fine."

"I was—I was worried."

"Sorry, Star. Yeah, I should have called before."

She felt a crash of disappointment within her, like a broken loft plummeting to the basement.

She governed herself, and said, neutrally, "Can't you make it, darling?"

"Star . . . No. No, I can't. I'm really sorry. I know you really go to town, it's a bloody shame."

"It's all right, love. What's happened? Is it something with Marilyn?"

"Marilyn? No. No, it's not that."

Star felt sick.

She sank her bitten nails into her palm. There were enough of them to hurt.

"What is it, Nobbi?"

"I found her. I found Tray. I mean, the place."

"Oh, Nobbi, where?"

"Well, I don't like to tell you, Star."

The dark of night breathed in on Stella's soul.

"All right, love."

"It's just—from what I've been hearing, these people are pretty bloody weird."

"What will you do?"

"Don't know yet. I've been sitting in the car, just down the road, keeping an eye out."

"Oh, Nobbi," she said, "be careful."

"Oh, yeah. I'll be fine. I'll tell you, some bloke went up there with his bird. Classy stuff. He looked like the one. The one Tray went after. Long white hair. But this bird. Christ, you should've seen her. Like a bloody film star. And they had a couple of dogs with 'em. God almighty, big as horses."

"Oh, God, Nobbi."

"She's my daughter."

"Yes."

They stood in silence, he miles off in the telephone box, and she here, in her flat, with the scent of the chicken no one now would eat.

"Nobbi," she said, "I do want to know where you are."

"Okay." He paused. "Between us, all right."

"Yes, Nobbi."

"It's easy enough to find, once you know."

Then he told her.

Star took it in. She felt cold. She was quivering, hairs erect.

"I got to go now, Star. I don't want to miss nothing. Spend the night in the car if I have to. She may come out. My Tray. Then I'm here."

"Nobbi, take care. If you can."

"I will. Don't worry, love."

"I love you," she said.

"You silly cow," he said, "loving an ugly old git like me. I wish I was there."

"I wish so too."

"I'll make it up to you."
Then there was the dialing tone.
She stood and listened to it for a while, having nothing else.

CHAPTER 40

✤ *OUT OF MEMORY, THE SOFTNESS CAME,* the note of music. Benign and comforting, and proper. What she would have wanted, if she could have had it. And for a moment she was a child, wanting. And then a woman, finding gentle death sleeping beside her. Then she woke.

The cat had died long past. And now she had the sense of seeing double, and wrongly. Her brain struggled with it.

Two demons were on her bed, on her body, light weights balanced on four stems each.

"My God," Rachaela said.

The vocal cat meowed again. He was a young male, all white but for a speckle of black on his right side, and a totally black face. He put out his paw and stroked her cheek. He had black fur testicles, too.

Beside him stood the girl cat. She was almost exactly like him but the other way around. Black with a white face. No speckles, just a white corona here and there at the tips of her fur. She did not speak or touch, but eyed Rachaela demurely. *You won't be able to resist me,* said her eyes, which were blue. The male's were vivid yellow in the black mask. *Come on,* they said, *here I am. Be quick.*

She put out her hands and smoothed them both.

The male rubbed his face into her palm, the female narrowed her eyes. Both purred.

Althene was sitting in one of the green chairs.

"I did knock, but you didn't wake. Forgive my coming in unannounced. But I wanted you to see them and they were annoyed with the basket."

"Where have they come from?"

"Ah," said Althene, secretively, "I had them made especially for you."

"You mean you're giving them to me?"

"My messengers while I'm away."

"A farewell present."

"Bookmarks," said Althene, "to mark my place in your heart."

"But how can I—I don't—" The male cat was up on her breast now, rubbing his head under her chin. The female had begun to wash her paws.

"They are *not* a responsibility," said Althene. "Your windows open and they will be able to climb down the roofs to the common. They'll come and go. They'll sleep on your pillows."

"Something to love," said Rachaela.

It was difficult to be churlish with the two cats purring and washing and rubbing.

"Cheta will cook them food," said Althene.

"Caviar and dover sole with lemon," said Rachaela. "Marrons glacés."

"Nasty bloody liver, chopped small," said Althene, "boiled ox-heart, chicken pieces, occasional steamed white fish. They may eat biscuits in moderation to clean their teeth. Kei has planted catnip for them."

Rachaela laughed. The male approved and kissed her lips. The girl cat snuggled into Rachaela's side and slept.

"What are their names?"

"It's for you to name them."

Rachaela lay back, and the male came up and poured down on her hair.

"I never let myself—have another cat."

"Love is dangerous."

"Yes. Well, I've had it now. Hopeless to deny."

"Good," said Althene. She stood up. "We must leave tonight."

"Yes, I see."

"There are some things I want to take with me, so I must go to pack. One doesn't keep Malach waiting."

"Yes, of course. Thank you—thank you for these."

"They're brother and sister," Althene said. "When they're a little older, they'll mate."

"But then—kittens everywhere—"

"Delicious," said Althene. "I will supervise the kittens."

"Oh. When you come back."

Althene opened the door. "Cheta will bring up a sand tray for the bathroom. They must stay in for a couple of days."

"Yes, I'll be careful."

Althene went out.

Rachaela turned her face into cats' fur.

Can I still cry?

But the sadness was only leaden and still, it did not break in rain.

There had been a book, years ago, a character called Jacob, who wore a black mask. The male cat should be Jacob. And the demure, white-faced girl? She was like a young actress playing Shakespeare. Juliet.

Jacob and Juliet began to purr again, as if aware of nominal recognition. The vibration drummed through the bed. It was only eight o'clock, the windows gray. To the cats' lullaby, Rachaela let herself drift back into sleep.

* * *

Above, in the lofty pale room, Ruth stood below the window. It had no colors, but was of opaque white glass, incised with an intricate pattern, coiling ferns, and the head perhaps of an angel.

The light fell over Ruth.

She was naked. She slept naked now, with Malach, in their bed. With him she had lost her modesty and her evasion.

Ruth had grown taller with the winter. Her body was even more beautiful, elongated in its slenderness that flowered into lushness at the breasts. At her groin the raven's feathers, melting to a blue mist under her flat belly. There was no hair on her arms or legs, it did not grow there, and under her arms was only a shaven whiteness. The hair of her head cloaked her back down to the base of her spine.

On the table lay her treasures, her trophies.

She had brought them to the flat. The apple, the duck, the gold razor . . . The leopardskin had gone, given away. It was not a living animal but a robbery of life.

Ruth lifted her right hand, and looked at it. There was a dark scar across the palm, exactly below the fingers. Some of the nerves were dead, or temporarily impaired, and the fingers were stiff and awkward. Malach had shown her that with practice, she could write with her left hand.

She had burned her right hand on the ice. Malach sometimes took this hand, and held it against him, against his face, or his chest, as if feeding her the pulses of his body.

He slept now.

He slept like death. So silent, hardly seeming to breathe. Sometimes in sleep he would murmur words. They were the languages of other countries, perhaps of other times.

Ruth went back to the bed, and sat down on the edge of it, watching him.

He lay on a tide of white hair, his head half turned.

There were faint lines on his face, about the mouth, on the forehead, those of a man in his late thirties. But his skin was taut, the light brown of some lost summer, which had never left it.

Ruth wanted to touch him, but she would not wake him.

She wanted to touch him continually. She was sore with want, with always yearning. She relished the rare rich pain.

And now, he opened his eyes.

Their blueness always caught at her. There had never been blue eyes in the world, until his.

"You're awake," he said. "Wide awake."

"Yes."

"We are going," he said, "to a flat land with low skies crowded by clouds, and with a liquid light. Do you remember the paintings I showed you?"

"Yes."

"Like that."

"Will they hate me there?" she said. "Like here." It was not a child's question, it was uttered nearly indifferently.

"They'll judge you from what you are."

"What am I?"

"What I will make you."

"Yes," she said. "Scarabae."

She leaned forward and her black hair tented them in. She kissed his throat. He slipped his hands about her ribs. At once she was dizzy and weak, her yearning blossoming into the thorns and roses of desire.

"I wish I'd always been with you," she said.

"You always were."

"Don't lie—"

"You were with me," he said, "in black places and bright."

"Where are we now?"

"Between two devils," he said.

He was hard against her. "Please—" she said.

Malach lifted her, drew her down onto his body, filling her.

He held her inexorably, moving her body, helpless, toward the abyss.

She stared at him. She wanted to die for him. She wanted death at his hands. Death that burned—

Ruth wrapped her arms about herself and arched her back, her throat, becoming a white icon on a veil of black hair. Her scream was silent and for a moment all her body flushed as if in the light of flames, as if her blood showed through her crystal, like the light in the window.

CHAPTER 41

 SOMETHING WAS WRONG.
Everything was. And that bloody noise, waking him.

Nobbi tried to sit up, but he was sitting up. He was in the cold Jag and a cold glare came in, except where the figure impeded it, banging on the window.

It was a traffic warden in the irritant wasp uniform, a woman though, with a sad pinched face.

Nobbi rolled down the window.

"I'm afraid you can't park here, sir."

"Can't I?"

"No, sir."

"Restricted zone? Didn't see no notice."

"I'm sorry, sir."

Something warned him now, not to argue or question.

"Just got tired, needed a kip."

"That's all right, sir. But if you could move on now."

"Right you are," said Nobbi. He smiled at her. "Dull old day."

"Yes, it is," she said.

She stepped back and stood on the pavement militaristically, under the big dripping trees, as he started up the cold reluctant car, and drove off busily downhill.

* * *

The terrible thing was, he had overslept, cramped there in the car. It was nearly nine-thirty, and he had not called Star, as he had promised. (Had he promised?) God knew what she would think. He would have to call her tonight. He could never remember the library number. Look it up, maybe, if he could find a box with directories in it.

There was a posh café open in among the shops down the hill.

Nobbi went in and had a breakfast of strange herbal green scrambled egg and crumbly French roll-things. The coffee was a cup of froth.

He had left the Jag in a side street among a lot of other cars, all probably there for the day.

He went back to it, and sat in it.

He had to think what to do.

Then again, he had to be honest. He was a bit scared.

For one, he had gone against Mr. Glass, so he would have to be very cautious, not antagonize or cause bother.

But there again, if they were a dodgy crowd, he had to get her away.

As he was sitting in the Jag, smoking one of his cigars with the window half-down, the ice-cream van went by. It played to him the tune of his war, "The Thieving Magpie."

He sat very still, and the cigar burned out.

It took a long time for the van to go around, even though surely nobody bought anything from it in the chilly day. When its noise had faded, Nobbi threw the dead cigar from the window.

There were the dogs too, those big white hounds the bloke with the white hair had had. They could take your arm off, or your throat out.

Nobbi sat listening, to see if he could hear "The Thieving Magpie" again. But the van was too far off, or not playing.

Slowly, he opened the car door, got out, and locked up the Jag.

He wished again he had phoned Star. But somehow now it seemed too late for that.

Walking uphill from the shops made Nobbi a little breathless, and by the time he had come onto the road again, under the sweep of the common, his cough had started.

He waited below the house for it to ease up.

What a pile. Christ, it was like an old Hammer horror movie.

He went up the slope in stages.

There were trees, and a path. Above, the backdrop of woods seemed thick with old rains.

When he was fairly near, he stopped, and looked again.

Welcome to the Bates Motel. He could just imagine some mummified mother propped at an upper window, some guy with an axe or knife. But they were rock musicians, they merely liked old houses. Probably out of their skulls on heroin.

He did not want to think about that.

Nobbi got himself all the way to the door and knocked.

When no one came, he began to get angry after all. It warmed him up, and he knocked again, violently.

Then the door opened, and there was an oldish, thin geezer in dusty looking old-fashioned clothes. Black, black eyes.

A butler? Yes, they would have something like that. "May I help you?" A flat soft voice.

"Yeah, you can help me," said Nobbi. "I'm Mr. Ives, and my daughter's staying here. Tracy Ives. So I'd like to see her. Okay with you?"

The oldish fellow looked at Nobbi, as if through cob-

webs of time. He did not say anything. He was not tall or
burly.

"I'll come in then, shall I?" said Nobbi.

The man stood aside.

And Nobbi strutted, muscles tensed and round head
alert, into the Bates Motel.

CHAPTER 42

CONNOR WAS SPONGING OVER THE SHOV-
elhead. Viv sat by to encourage, shaking herself
when the drips hit her.

Down by the tents, Tina was darning Pig's tiger-pat-
terned socks, and Whisper, Rose, and Cardiff were in a
game of Dead Man's Poker. Red stayed in her tent.

The fire burned cheerily. Plenty of fallen branches to
make it go, and no police to kick it out.

Above, the house loomed in the rain-pent morning.

The butler man had brought them breakfast, ham
and eggs—actual grilled ham, and eggs poached in a
sauce—coffee and tea. And then another guy came out
to exercise two fantastic bloody great wolfhounds—Viv
squeaked, and Connor held her back, in case, but the guy
said, "It will be all right." So then Connor let Viv go, and
the two enormous dogs played with her, really nicely, and
then ran off down the slope into the oaks.

Connor wondered if he would see Miranda again,
but she must have come back some other way, yesterday.
Not a trace.

Camillo had come down before noon.

He sat on one of the packs, between Connor and the
fire. Viv had gone up to him and he tickled her idly, but
he looked old and fragile, the way Connor remembered
from that first time, on the beach.

Best leave Camillo alone.

Viv did so, too, all of them.

But there was a girl who had followed Camillo down. It seemed she was called Lou. She sat at his feet, on a piece of canvas. Short skirt, lots of hair, no brains.

Connor worked on a bad place near the forward wheel. Then he stood back. Water now. He picked up the bucket. The butler guy—Michael?—had shown him the outdoor tap.

Connor sluiced the Shovelhead and a gleam arose.

"My beauty," Connor said. Viv thumped her tail. "You too, you harlot."

Lou did not look at Viv. She had ignored Viv. Lou was stupid.

Red emerged from her tent.

Jesus.

She was wearing black rubber. Leggings showing every contour, down into her low black boots. And under her jacket, a rubber vest. Everything she had, and she had everything, was there to see, behind this film of glaucous darkness. And the red hair loose, back over one ear, with an earclip of a silver snake. She turned, and "saw" Camillo.

"How's your horse?" she called. She was glib, light as a feather.

Camillo looked at her.

"It bites."

"They all do," said Red. "The trick is to give them an apple, first."

"And a serpent in your ear," said Camillo. He was looking better.

"Serpent bites horse," said Red.

Camillo giggled. Red raised her long red eyebrows. They really were, and her lashes were like long shavings of new bronze.

Viv barked, and Red threw her a kiss. *"Amour jadis de moi,"* said Red, *"ah, vous dis-je."*

Someone spat, up on the slope. A rip of sound.

They all of them, arrested, looked up.

It was Whitey—*Malach*. The one Miranda had got mixed up over. Camillo's son? She had said *Father.*

He was a beauty, Malach. Like a priest-warrior out of time. He wore black, and his psyche was like an old red wine, nearly black, too. Sediment, and fire.

"Hail, Imperator," said Red.

Malach glanced at her, and away. He looked at Camillo.

He said something, Malach, in another tongue. It sounded Germanic, but possibly it was not.

Red gave a tiny gasp, then pulled herself together.

Camillo glared up. "English," said Camillo. "That's the rule. The talk of the time and the place."

"You want them to hear?" said Malach. "Your *soldiers?*"

Connor put down the sponge.

"Get off his back," he said to Malach.

Then Malach looked at him.

Connor felt the breakfast curdle in his gut. Jesus, Jesus—make him stop—Connor held up both his hands. "It's between you," he said.

"Yes, it's between us."

Connor stepped back. He was sorry for Camillo. But against *that,* there was no way to—no, there was no way.

Camillo sat doggedly in the camp. Lou had drawn away from him.

"Say what you want. Don't care."

"You will care. You are mischievous. Aren't you?"

"Too old," said Camillo.

"Excrementum," Malach said.

"I remember," Camillo said, "the snow and the horse running. And the town on fire. I remember my mother in the sleigh."

"Listen to me," Malach said. "You have your battalion here. But don't follow me. Don't follow her."

"Wicked stepmother," said Camillo.

"She goes back before your birth," said Malach, "back into the dark. Ruth."

Camillo scowled like a naughty boy wanting to spit too, but he did not. Malach had spat. That was enough.

"Past is good," said Camillo.

"The past is a chain," said Malach. "Break it. Take your historical whore with the bloody hair, and cut her throat on some wedding night of the mind. Slough her. Slough the dead."

Red's eyes were wide. She drew her jacket across her breasts and held it there.

Cardiff stood up.

"You watch your mouth."

Malach turned. He moved like quicksilver. Against the fire. There was a kind of doubled light. Cardiff was on his back.

Lou screamed. She would.

Then Camillo had Malach's arm, and Malach swung about again and slapped Camillo across the face. It was the back of the left hand, with the tarnished rings. A crimson stroke appeared on Camillo's cheek, his old man's skin.

"Laat me met rust."

Camillo shook his head. A jewel of blood flew away like a tear.

Viv hid behind Connor. He made himself extra big, to shield her.

Red said firmly, her voice shaking, "Can't you end this?"

"Yes," said Malach. "He can. You, Camillo. Take your *soldaat,* and go. Or stay. But nowhere near to her."

"We ran," said Camillo, "in the snow. Men, not wolves."

Tina was pulling a face as if she were going to cry, and Pig put his arm round her. Cardiff lay where he had fallen, frowning. Rose and Whisper chewed cards. Lou had sidled off toward the trees.

The fire crackled.

It might have been any rainy slope of the world, long ago and far away.

Connor heard the soundless step of giants on the earth.

Where the stairs divided into two, there was a window with a sort of medieval band playing peculiar instruments on a pink sky. The other windows had rose-haired women with harps. Musical windows—that made a kind of sense.

Under the stairs was a big white room with highlights of gold.

Nobody seemed to be there.

Nobbi stood on the floor, looking around at the windows and the pillars. The butler bloke had left him there and gone somewhere. Trusting. Or else every inch of the place was wired up.

As he waited, Nobbi heard a large dog bark, down in the levels of the house.

Not so good.

The sun came out, and the hall glimmered into rose colors, but then the sun vanished, and it was an area of shadow.

The anger was building up again. The way he had been left here, as if he did not count for anything, as if it did not count what he did, being helpless.

Nobbi bristled and his brown face reddened.

He let out a shout.

"Hey! *Hey!*"

He broke off because a man was coming down the stairs. He was old, older than the butler bloke, dressed in some stagy suit like something from a black-and-white film. His hair was gray. He wore rings.

"All right," said Nobbi, loudly. "Which one are you?"

The man halted on the stairs and gazed at him.

"I am Eric. And you, I believe, are here for your daughter."

"Dead right, squire. Got it in one." Nobbi was shouting again. His loud red voice filled the hall. "Where the fuck is she?"

"Michael is looking for her now. With Miranda, perhaps."

"Miranda? And where's he, the feller she come with? Yeah I know about it."

"Camillo is outside."

"Camillo?" Nobbi laughed. His fists were clenched. "Great names you go in for. Well, I want this Camillo. I'd like a bleeding chat with him."

Something in Nobbi, which strangely had the voice of Star, was trying to tell him to calm down. But it had all gone on too long. And he was afraid. Afraid of the two enormous dogs being let out on him, and of a gang of thugs being summoned up. Afraid of this bloody old weirdo, who might be anything.

Afraid of what he would see, when Tracy came.

There was a feel to this house. Nobbi could not have said what it was. It was like eyes watching from the walls and shapes behind the pillars. Bloody crazy stuff, but pressing in.

Just then two more men appeared from a side passage. It was the first one, the butler, and a bigger taller gink with black hair. They pulled up about ten feet away from Nobbi.

The one called Eric said, "It's in order, Kei. This man wants to see his daughter."

"Yes, Mr. Eric."

All right. Two of them at his left and the old actor type on the stairs. No dogs. All right.

Then two women came along one side of the stairs.

Nobbi saw them. They were old. Done up in mothy, silky dresses, faces pale as paper, with long dark hair. Two old women . . . who were also young.

He realized that one of them, the smaller one, was Tray.

Something battered Nobbi in the side. It was his heart.

There had been all sorts of trouble in the past, the people she got in with. But always she had come out to him, maybe scared, maybe defiant or weepy, but always Tray. Shining and lovely. Not like this.

"What they done to her?" Nobbi said. Then he bawled, "What they done to you, love? Come here. Come here quick. I'm here. What is it, love?"

And Tray, vampire pale in her tresses of coal, Tray all one with the shadows and the hidden eyes, shrank back against the other young old woman. And in a little voice he heard her say the precious name she had had only for the Old Girl: "Nan-Nan?"

"She don't know me," said Nobbi. Did she? His heart did not think so and it attacked him with huge blows. "What have you done to her? Eh? What you done to my daughter?" And he lurched up the stairs toward Tray, or toward Eric.

Without a sound, the two waiting men were on him. They had him and they held him. Christ, they were strong. Nobbi roared.

On the slope, Malach turned his head.

Connor had heard something, too. Some sort of engine or even music in the house, revved up loud.

Camillo giggled.

And Malach looked back at him.

High up, Ruth had also heard.

She moved slowly about, in a wave of hair.

Her dress was dark green, the mantle of a wood at dusk.

She listened.

Malach was in her body still, and in her brain. Malach was her teacher.

Now she knew what *Scarabae* meant.

She turned again, and paced across this room, pale and scarcely decorated, fashioned for him.

On the wall, the stone knife. She touched it.

And from down in the house, a kind of rumbling came, like an earthquake at the foundations. And then a man's voice again, like the roar of a bull.

Common sense, not the murmuring of Star, made Nobbi stop fighting.

He forced himself to relax in the grasp of the two men, the old one and the young one, both so *vital.*

"All right. All right."

The man on the stairs said, "You can let him go."

And they did. They released him.

Nobbi was shaking.

In the house of fear—

He had done everything he should not have done.

He looked up at Tray again. She seemed frightened now. She seemed like Tray.

Of course. It was only her hair, the makeup, the dress.

And if they had got her on to something, well, he would get her the best treatment. She would be okay.

But he must keep cool.

"Sorry," said Nobbi. "Het up. Didn't mean to come on so strong."

"She's your daughter," said Eric. He glanced back, and said, "Miranda, she must come down."

And then another figure came on to the other side of the stairs.

Something . . . Something dark.

No. Only the girl. The one he had seen before. The film-star girl.

She poised, above them all, looking down at him.

She wore a green dress and a green belt knuckled with silver.

"Didn't mean to cause no bother," said Nobbi. He was trying to be jovial.

The faces were all set, still. And Tray's face was set, but with a kind of human embarrassment now.

Only that other face, the highest one, was odd.

Yes, that girl was on drugs. Her eyes were blank and black as quags. Pools of paint. Nothing in them.

She started down the stairs.

"I've come a long way," said Nobbi. "I worry. You got to understand."

"You are her father," said Eric.

It struck Nobbi Eric was agreeing, backing him up.

"Too right," Nobbi said.

He had broken out in sweat.

The girl in green was still descending, but Tray was just standing there with the other woman.

"Come on, love."

"Oh, Dad," said Tray.

He felt himself breathe again. It was the usual voice, the whine of protest and self-justification.

"Come on, love. Your mom's worried."

The girl in green came down the stairs, all the way. She walked toward Nobbi with a sheer paralyzing grace, so he had to look at her.

God, her eyes—

"What is it, love?" Nobbi said to Ruth, concerned for her, bewildered.

He had always liked women.

Her left hand flicked out and there was a flash, like the sun again through the windows.

A spurt of scarlet burst upward and hit the pillars. It splashed over Ruth, into her hair and onto her white

face. Beads of blood on her lashes, blinked away. Red
tears.

"Oh!" exclaimed the old woman with Tray. "Oh!
Oh!"

Nobbi was confused. He tried to look around. A violent hiccup tore out of him, and there was a terrific itch-
ing in his head. He scratched, and then the hall turned
over.

Nobbi lay on the floor with the blood gusting from
the severed vein in his short, short neck. His eyes were
open. He could say nothing.

"Michael," Eric said.

Michael ran to Nobbi and kneeled down. He pressed
a wad of something white against the blood, but the white
changed to red.

"Daddy," said Tray.

Ruth stood over Nobbi, the gold razor in her fingers.

"Scarabae," said Ruth.

Nobbi gazed up at the ceiling. He felt silly. He
wished this had not happened. He felt sorry for the girl
with the paint-pool eyes. Then he was in the car and it
was sliding away downhill. The sensation was quite pleasant.

He thought, *Poor Marilyn.*

"Daddy!" screamed Tray. She screamed again. "I
want my daddy."

On the floor of the hall Nobbi's dead body with Michael kneeling there, and Ruth standing totally motionless.

And above, Tray screaming and next rushing down.
And then Tray tumbling into the blood. "Daddy!
Daddy!"

Eric and Miranda were statues.

Tray lifted her head. "I want my daddy!"

Sounds came out of her that human things cannot
make, yet do.

* * *

When the screaming sounded in the house, like a siren, Malach moved faster than Connor had ever seen occur. But Camillo cowered down, and, over by the trees, the idiot Lou-girl put her hands over her ears in her fake red hair.

Cardiff scrambled up, and Pig and Rose and Whisper all tried to bolt toward the house.

Connor planted himself on the slope above them, holding wide his arms, and Viv crouched at his feet, snarling.

"No."

They fell back, staring at each other.

"But," said Rose.

"No," Connor said. "And no. And no."

One by one they sat down.

The Lou-girl chased off into the oak trees.

The first screams had stopped.

Malach lifted Tray up off the corpse and turned her into his body. He held her as she resisted, and the touch of his hands made her give in. Then she hung against him a moment in silence.

She said, "I want my lion."

Miranda came and took Tray from Malach, and Tray explained, "My lion. He's my friend."

Tray was covered in blood, as Ruth was covered in blood. The blood had covered them, however, differently. In any case, the blood was Tray's, had made her. Ruth had no right to it.

As Miranda led Tray up the stairs again, softly, Malach looked at Ruth.

"He threatened them," she said.

"Who?"

"That man."

"No," Malach said. "You learned nothing."

"Yes. The Scarabae. I killed for them."

"You're filth," he said, "like some plague. I taught you nothing, you learned nothing."

"Yes," she said. Her eyes came slowly back to life and fixed on him, swimming, startled. "Malach—he was an enemy—"

"Only a fool. But you, with your gold claw. *You.*"

Above, miles high, Rachaela had come on to the top of the stairs, alone. Drawn by the screaming as if to some ancient rite. From a tower, she looked down and saw Malach standing, warrior in armor, priest in stone. And the child, Ruth, cringing there in her clothes of green and blood.

"But," said Ruth, "he was—"

"Nothing," said Malach.

"Then—I was wrong. I was wrong."

"It doesn't matter to me," he said.

Rachaela thought: *These words come out of vaults of time. Spoken over and over.*

"Malach," said Ruth.

"Don't say my name," he answered. He turned to Eric. "Put her into some room or cellar. Where you had her before. Keep her there for three hundred years. Like Camillo. She can learn that way."

"Malach," said Ruth. "Malach."

"Not to you."

"But I'm yours. I'm to go with you."

"You're not mine. Go into the furnace. Burn up. Finish."

Tray said, "Miranda, can I have a sweet?"

"Yes, dear," said Miranda. "Lots and lots of sweets. Hold my hand."

Then Eric must have gestured to Kei and to Michael, because they came together and took hold of Ruth in her blood.

And they began to carry her, as if to her execution, up the other side of the stairs.

They had incarcerated her before. When she killed. Then. *That time, she was silent.*

Now Ruth screamed. Not like the other girl, not like a machine. These were raw cries, to which every pore of the body responded. The wails of sacked Troy and Jerusalem, the blinded shrieks of Hiroshima.

Malach stood under the stairs, and listened.

Rachaela saw him listen, his face like a shell in ice.

And then they bore Ruth past her, and Rachaela reached out her hand— "Ruth—"

And Ruth cried, "Malach—Malach—"

Her screams went on, her cries, the repetition of his name. Up into the pinnacles of the house.

"Dear God." Rachaela put her hands to her lips. She was torn open, as if Ruth had been born again out of her body. But Ruth now, finally, at last, was dead.

CHAPTER 43

✤ *HADES.*
Through the dark a monster had passed, sucking slowly at the moistureless black milk of the vaulted tunnels. It was vacuuming up the asbestos dust that clung to the walls and roof. Secret thing of night, no one must know the poison that pollinated the airs under the earth.

Like the inside of a wine cask, a barrel, these passageways, the scattering coils of rails, like carelessly cast rope.

The Underground by night.

And now, after the monster had passed, the man came walking.

Malach moved without a sound through the labyrinth of the tunnels. He took another branch, and the rumbling of the monster died away.

Mice cheeped from their own city of holes and runnels.

The aroma of this Hell was like that of an old chimney, soot and dirt and unreal atmosphere heated too high and inadequately cooled. In places were lights, in others not. Sometimes deep-throated breezes blew, odored with distant electricity, for somewhere a train had passed, some carrier between the closed stations.

Malach's face, now lit, now lost. Impossible to read

there anything, not even when thick, choked light began to shine back on him from the darkness.

The clink of implements along the rails, like trapped miners, tapping with their last strength, for rescue, which would never come.

Malach moved down the tunnel and entered the light.

A maintenance gang in gaudy dungarees, clicketing at the coils on the ground. Heads turned. A pallid Irish face with sad and smoky eyes, a black man closed on an anger which would never speak. Here they are, trapped in the mine of life, tapping. But who has come?

"Hey, mate—"

Another man nudged the speaker.

They stood aside, to let him go by.

The black man said: "Tea urn next platform. Don't go no further."

As he passed, Malach raised his hand, and the black man clapped his own into it. It was a salute seldom shared with a white, but in this case, for some reason, permissible.

When Malach had gone by, the black man found a note of money in his palm, stuck there like a butterfly wing.

"Mary, Mother of God," said the Irishman.

They stood, looking at the note.

Out on the platform the half-orange-clad foreman in his vest, gaped at Malach passing down the line.

"Here, you—"

Malach paid no attention.

The man at the urn shook his head. "Leave it, Eddie."

Beyond the station, another stretch of the dark, and then more lights, and a group of women bundled in dungarees with silver faces gauzed in little breathing masks. One sang in a low and burning voice, "Every time we say good-bye—"

The song was stilled. As the maintenance gang had done, the gang of women fluffers stared. They were the moths beneath the earth who brushed off the dense black powder of shed skin, webbed hair, the dregs of expiry, psychic shadow and decay, pumped daily out into these curved arteries. They were a lost tribe, living by night like vampires, in the coffins of the tube.

"Darlin'," said one to Malach, "don't go on no further."

"No, lovey," said another. "There's a dead 'un."

"She means," said the singer, and her voice was honey, spoiled by rust, "the next station, it's closed."

"Since the 1950s," said another, a fat woman.

"Not tonight," said Malach.

The women drew aside. "You ain't with *that*?"

"No," Malach said.

"Scum," said the woman who had not sung. "I'd do for 'em. But we can't do nothing."

"You hear it," said the singer. "Far off."

"Tonight," said Malach, "silence will come."

They looked. The singer nodded. She sang, in a murmur, not like the sea but like some distant train moving over honey: "I die a little."

Malach took her hand. He drew close to her, and put down his head until his forehead rested on her dusty hair. She smelled of trying to keep clean against great odds. Never had a man held her, touched her, as this one did. Never such a man. And never again.

When he was gone, the one who did not sing, laughed. But then she stopped laughing.

"Look."

They looked at the note.

"Toy-Town money," said one of them.

"Must be."

The dark had swallowed him, the turn toward the ghost station.

"See what I found?" said the fat woman. She held

up a man's leg. It was artificial. "I found a hand, Thursday," said another. The women drew back along the tunnel, towards the urn of tea.

Down here they had always found things. Wine cellars and pits of plague. Skeletons. Once, a great dinosaur, removed in portions, stealthily, not to halt the work of excavation. And there had been banquets to prove the safety of the vaulted tunnels, candelabra gleaming and the chink of thin crystal goblets spangled with champagne.

And now, the chink of a goblet, up ahead, and the glow of new light.

The money had been the payment of passaging, coins for the ferryman.

And crossing over the bone-dry Styx, hell within Hell.

A reddish glare lit the closed station beyond the second tunnel, unveiling oddly the placards and the posters, half-transparent with age. Hovis, Ovaltine, Pears Soap, girls on bicycles and girls who swung from the moon. But they were phantoms now, forced to look on at changing times.

A ring of red workmens' warning lanterns, and flung up on the walls, sparking, searing oxyacetylene torches, blasting in a primitive fever.

On the platform they had formed the arena.

Men in tailored garments with elegant hand-set sleeves, Italian shoes. Eight men. One with his hair held back in a ponytail by a clip of ivory. One with a coat of fur. The glint of a couple of gold-banded cigarettes. Champagne bottles in vacuum coolers, and shallow glasses. Over the ozone, chimney scent, the perfumes of rich men. Cologne and aftershave and hair oil. And over that again, already, a meaty throbbing smell.

The two black dogs, barrel-shaped like the tunnels,

spade-formed faces, all jaws, the muzzles off, tugging and growling. The men laughed at their eagerness.

As they let them go, the man in the fur gave the nearer dog a sharp kick. It did not seem to notice as it belted forward.

The first blood came in three seconds.

Its odor went up like hot oil.

The men shouted. They had laid their bets.

The dogs ripped at each other, detached reluctantly and with difficulty.

"G'on!"

Another man, with greenish frogskin shoes, kicked the slower dog back into the center.

The dogs rammed each other, the spade jaws trying to fasten into throats, shoulders. They rolled snarling and choking against the tilework and blood blotched the poster of the Ovaltine maiden.

The man in fur slipped his hand inside his opened coat, into a pocket which parted obligingly. He was already hard as a rock. He breathed the gladiator stink of sweat and blood, the acidic peppery exudations of human adrenaline under Fabergé.

The last man at the platform's edge, standing away a little with his champagne, not liking to be splashed, saw something white below him on the line. He turned, and there was a newcomer there, standing under the platform, looking up, smiling.

"You're late," said the man above. He took in the darkness and the long, long hair. He held down his hand. "Can you make it up?"

The man with white hair took his hand, and putting hardly any pressure on it, leaped up onto the platform. An athlete. And doors not good enough for him. "Walk through the—" began the man, actually more interested in this arrival than the fight, which bored him. The white-haired man looked smiling into his face. No one else looked anywhere but at the two wrestling, bleeding dogs.

Noises of bubbling snarling, and shouts, curses, reverberated around the station, chaos of sounds.

Malach slammed his right fist into the man's body, into the spleen, which ruptured instantly. The man fell on the platform. No one saw.

The man in fur registered Malach, as Malach came close beside him.

"Pretty coat," Malach said.

"Pedigree cat," said the man. "Bred for it. Cost you a fortune." He was a little breathless, rubbing away at himself inside his trousers, not taking his eyes off the rolling mass of black and blood and teeth.

When Malach's hand come in, too, under the coat, friendly, against his side, he was startled but not displeased. He laughed under his breath, and then something unbelievable happened. He did not know—an incredible pulling, a dislocation and pain—pain—

Blood smashed outward from the wrong direction.

The other men, alerted after all, turned around.

The fur man in his coat of creatures went tumbling backward, with a great red cage stuck out from his side. Improvisation of the Viking method, if they had known it, half a spread-eagle, the ribs wrenched out and bent backward—

The sounds were different now.

Only the fighting dogs, scraping and wringing the juices from each other, did not glance to see.

The air had become an oven of roaring and blood.

Two men had grabbed Malach. He was grinning. He fell backward, pulling them with him, and as they landed on the ground he was free again. His elbows went into their breastbones and the double snap echoed up off the walls. One tried to claw after him and Malach stamped down his face like a rotten cabbage.

A small man was creeping off along the platform.

They wanted to leave it to each other, to deal with him. So now one came at him with a Buck knife.

"Here, let's be having you."

Malach dived at him, and his head slammed in under the knife-man's chin. The knife slashed, and cross-slashed over. But it was a reflex. Then the man was down, head angled impossibly, tangling Malach's legs. Malach stepped out of him, almost mincingly.

The dogs were locked now, silent. A stream of blood ran from their bodies. Blood poured from Malach's body on the left side.

The small man ran back behind him, swinging up what he had found, a sledgehammer.

It caught Malach in the back, a blow that should have cracked him in two.

Malach bowed over, the breath going out of him in a low animal grunt, like the last noises the dogs had made.

The small man let down the hammer, which was too big for him. He prepared to crow, to the other two, the man with elephant tusk holding back his thin tail of hair, the man with the frogskin shoes.

But then Malach straightened up again, he came around like a damaged engine, slow and entirely terrible. His eyes were all white, and he reached out and smote the hammer man across the head. The stroke sent him flying, screaming, back off the platform, sheer across the rails, into the farther tunnel wall, and into the gentle body of the girl swinging from the moon, which silenced him. He dropped with a rattle on the line.

The man with the ivory band held up his open palms. The other man whimpered.

"Okay. Okay."

"Not okay," said Malach. His face looked older than the skeletons they had once dug from the plague pit under the tunnels. But he smiled again a little, as if from courtesy.

The two dogs were finished, or seemed to be. One had closed its teeth in the other's throat. Both had shut their eyes.

The frogskin man started forward, and tripped over the dogs' bodies. He fell on them. And the dying dog turned its mutilated head and tore out his throat, suddenly and silently. He had no chance to cry.

"You're terrific," said Ivory. "You're amazing."

"Yes," said Malach.

"But you'll let me go. You've had enough."

"If you like," said Malach, "you can run a little way. The exercise will do you good."

"You see," said Ivory, "even if your spine held up when that guy hit you, your ribs are caved in."

"Are they?"

"Look, here's the money from the fight." Ivory cast over a shower, not red or black now, but blue and brown. "Don't feel too great," said Ivory, "I expect."

"No," said Malach.

"That's it," said Ivory. "You have the money. Bloody dog's useless anyway."

Ivory walked along the platform, to the place of exit, which had been carefully unbarred. A dull light shone beyond, less brilliant than the torches and the warning lamps.

Malach looked at the dogs.

The dead one still had its jaws fixed into the man. The other peered up at Malach, half-blinded. It growled.

Malach coughed, and wiped the blood which came off his mouth.

Then he moved quietly out of the exit, after Ivory.

The corridors were all white tiles, like some fundamental latrine. The little dull lights burned high up, and, under them, Ivory was walking quickly now, away.

Not hearing Malach, only sensing him, he glanced back. Then he ran, not for exercise.

Malach only walked.

The white tunnels ebbed upward, and came out in a hall. More posters (Bovril, Guinness), these defaced with old naïve graffiti, *Kiss me quick, Up the Spurs.*

The huge dragon-back escalators, unfurled from the upper gloom, came in motion, ascending.

Ivory had sprinted onto one. He stood, staring behind him, getting watery legs ready to run again.

Malach reached the escalators. He chose another, one which was frozen into time, like the dinosaur.

He raced. He raced up the dead escalator. And when he was above Ivory, had passed him, he vaulted the barrier between and came over on to Ivory's side, onto the moving track.

Ivory tried to go down the rocking up-escalator.

After a moment he tipped over on his knees, and the steps carried him upward again.

With no difficulty, Malach was descending.

Malach reached him.

Malach stood over him, and forced Ivory's head down onto the moving tread, so the ponytail of hair was caught inside. With a screech, Ivory was twisted around onto his side. Lying pinned, his hair in a vise, he pushed his hand up over his throat.

"Don't," he said.

Malach stood over him still, and, leisurely, once more they were carried up to the surface of hell.

When they were almost there, and the steps began to level out, Malach crushed Ivory's head over, and his face, or parts of it, were drawn into the cement with the track.

Presently, the stair mechanism jammed, but too late for Ivory.

The echoes of his anguish died slowly, as if the ancient station was unwilling to let them go.

When Malach went back below, the wounded dog, the only thing left alive, glared up at him again and growled and slavered bloody foam.

In the red and white furnace light the bodies lay,

immaterial as debris. Only the other dog, the dead one, had bulk and presence still.

Malach reached out and the live dog bared its shovel of fangs, from which ripped flesh was hanging.

But Malach's hand came down in its rings and blood upon the head of the black dog, and the dog closed its mouth. Its face was ugly with a dreadful wisdom surprised.

Presently he knelt and picked it up. It was heavy and almost inert, and as he stood with it, he caught his breath.

Then he held it against him and the dog looked stonily into his face.

"You," Malach said, *you* I can change."

He walked back up from hell, up the broken escalator, over the final body, and out of the little concealed door, into the city that was like all cities, and the time that was like all times, and the agony and tedium and loss that had no end.

CHAPTER 44

✤ FOR ALMOST THREE WEEKS STELLA
waited. She thought, afterward, that she had
probably done this because she knew and did not want
her knowledge confirmed. But then, curiously, hurtfully,
she had *not known*. There had been no sudden wrench-
ing, no sense of severence. No dream, not even that.
When he did not phone her that morning, she began to
feel slightly sick. And this sickness went on all her waking
hours, from the second she woke to the moment she
slept. That was all. Nothing else.

Nobbi was reliable. She had always found him so. If
he could not see her, and often he could not, he would
always call her during the week, once, twice. They were
sad little calls, because they were short and there was
nothing substantial in them, only voices. But she was
grateful for them nevertheless.

And if he said he would call, he would call.

And if he did not, then something had happened.

At first she reasoned. He had found Tracy and Tracy
had been in a state, which had occurred before. And
Nobbi was understandably taken up with Tracy, and he
forgot.

When four days and nights had gone by, Stella suspected something bad, that Tracy was ill or had been
harmed.

Then, she kept thinking, he would still have called her. Even if only for an instant. He would have let her know.

And Stella went on feeling sick, the way she had heard happened to some women when they were pregnant. Nausea that never went away. She lived on tea and bananas.

In the second week, she began to see that something had happened to Nobbi himself. She began to face it, gradually. But at the same time she thrust it away. There was an explanation. And, again, she kept saying to herself, she would *know*. Some spiritual psychic understanding. But she only felt sick.

She wanted to call his home. She had the number—that was easy, he was in the book, his name and the name of his firm.

First of all she was afraid of speaking to Marilyn, afraid of maybe causing trouble. Because what could she say?

But in the end, after nineteen days, she realized that what she could say was simple. She was a customer Nobbi had promised he would do some plastering for—or perhaps not for her, even, but for her mother . . .

So then, then she phoned.

After three and a half rings the receiver was lifted, and a well-spoken woman's voice gave the number.

Marilyn? Surely not.

"Is that Mrs. Ives?"

"No, it's the cleaning girl. I'm afraid Mrs. Ives can't come to the phone. At least, I don't think so—"

"Well," Stella was brisk and businesslike, "it's Mr. Ives I want really. He said he was going to do some plastering for my mother, and we just haven't heard from him."

"Oh, Lord," said Marilyn's well-spoken cleaning girl. There was a pause.

"He hasn't been in touch," said Stella.

"No, well, he wouldn't have. I'm afraid Mr. Ives died about three weeks ago."

Stella held the phone in her hand. She had one of those moments granted to human things of feeling the utter absurdity of the physical body, all physical objects, senses, space, time, everything.

She heard the words in her head in a sort of verbal slow motion. Mr. Ives died.

Who was this Mr. Ives? Not Nobbi. Nobbi had not died. It was Mr. Ives.

Stella did not speak.

"His wife's very shocked. You can imagine. I think she's going to close the business. So—there's not much chance of your work getting done. I should try someone else."

Stella said, "Yes. Oh, I will. Thank you. Good-bye."

Then she put the phone down.

She stood in the middle of the physical insanity of flesh and things, and she thought, *But it isn't Nobbi.*

Then she started to cry bitterly and violently.

And she listened to herself and she thought, *Then why am I crying?*

Two days later, Stella had a call from the library. They wanted to know why she had not come in.

Stella said that she had a bug. Her throat had been so sore she had lost her voice. The doctor said she would need at least a week off work.

They said she had caused them a lot of trouble. No one said they hoped she would getter.

Which was logical, because she never would.

She could not envisage ever going back to work. She could not picture herself ever doing anything at all.

She had felt appalling grief when her mother died, but somehow she had coped. She had gone on. Something in her had always grasped that mothers and cats perished. But obviously something in her had never understood that lovers, too, might die.

She did not dream about him. When she slept for a few hours in the early morning, her sleep was black. It was a death, and she was glad.

It did present itself to her that she could kill herself, but even that seemed too much of an effort.

She seemed to be dying anyway. Living on tea alone now and water from Evian bottles. She had stopped feeling sick.

There was a kind of pain all through her. Indescribable, unshiftable.

Sometimes she visualized the heart attack and then she would start up in panic.

But these mirages grew less and less.

She did not believe in the heart attack.

She had the radio on a lot, although she did not listen to it. The human voice was a weird unconsoling consolation, like a bandage on a cut that would never heal.

Sometimes she heard a London voice that reminded her of Nobbi's. Her tears were soft then, nearly kind.

The following week Mr. Rollinson phoned her from the library.

"This really is too bad, Miss Atkins."

"Go and fuck yourself," said Stella, "if it will reach."

When she put the phone down this time she laughed. Nobbi would have laughed too. He had said to her, "Star, if you want to jack that in, I can—well, you know, I'll see you're all right." He would have kept her and she would not let him. She valued her independence.

Well, that was that. No more library.

She had another bath. Like the tea and the Evian, this was her only nourishment; two or three baths a day. Perhaps a form of mental drowning in fluids.

The plastic duck, Charlie, sat on the water over her

breasts, and she thought of Nobbi, and masturbated in the bath, and came, and wept.

I suppose it'll stop sometime.

She thought of all the widows she had known. Cheery in their black, or not in black.

No, this would never stop.

A month after the girl told her of Nobbi's death, when he was presumably long buried—she found it hard to believe in any of that either, the funeral service, the burial—a candy-pink Daimler pulled up in the street below her window.

It was such a foolish, unlikely sight, it actually interested her for half a moment.

She was turning from the window when a youngish man got out of the Daimler, and crossed over the grass toward the flats.

Under the bleak sky, he was clad in a ghastly sort of acme of elegance, a pearly suit, a shirt of faintest primrose, and a tie one shade darker.

As he disappeared into the building, Stella knew. And when, quite soon, her doorbell rang, she went to open it in a dazed, limp fury.

Nobbi had had dealings with people like this. He had never really told her, but made no secret either.

What did this one want? To bump her off? Welcome.

"Yes?" Stella said. She was a sight. Life's playful opposite to him. Elderly jeans, jumper with a tea stain, unwashed hair, the Mask of Tragedy.

And he. A tan in winter. A silver wedding ring.

"You don't know me, Miss Atkins. My name's Luke. Used to be a friend of Norman's—Nobbi's."

"Come in," she said, "if it won't spoil your clothes."

Luke laughed charmingly. "Stella—may I?"

He entered, and, when she did not offer him a chair, sat down beautifully and crossed his legs. Hand-stitched shoes of pearl-gray suede. Pearly socks.

"Would you like a glass of water?" Stella said. "That's all I've got. I haven't been shopping."

"No, please don't trouble."

"It's no trouble. It comes out of the tap."

A ghost of distaste crossed Luke's countenance. Maybe he always got the nasty tasks.

"I'm not going to beat about the bush, Stella. Nobbi's dead. That was a rotten bit of luck."

"Wasn't it just?"

"He'll be missed. But I have to tell you, we do know that you were Nobbi's friend. His close friend."

"His bit on the side," said Stella.

"We know that he cared for you. I'm afraid we like to know what we can about—our associates."

"You're from the amorphous Mr. Glass," said Stella.

"Mr. Glass. That's right."

"He must be cut up."

Luke smiled. "Ha. Yes. Well. The reason I'm here. We wouldn't like there to be a lot of fuss, you see. Upset poor Marilyn. I'm sure you don't feel any animosity there."

"Are you?"

"You're a woman of the world, Stella. Sophisticated. No, poor old Marilyn's just gone to pieces."

Stella turned her back on Luke and his tan and his pearl gray, and looked down at his Daimler through the window. Maybe someone would come and scratch the paintwork or let down the tires.

"The thing is, Stella, Nobbi left Marilyn all the proper stuff—the house, and a large sum of money. But he also made sure he took care of you. I have to tell you, you're a lucky lady. We were able to make some invest-ments for Nobbi, you see. I won't bore you with details, although I expect the solicitor will want to. There's a lot of money coming to you, Stella. I do mean a lot. You won't have to worry ever again."

I'm so lucky. No worries. Nobbi in the ground and money coming.

"How much?" she said. She did not know why. So she could see its paltry quality perhaps, there in the wilderness.

Luke told her.

Stella looked at the Daimler. A dog was sniffing at it. But no one else had come to damage it. Probably it was invulnerable.

"Yes, that's a lot."

"I hope you're pleased, Stella. I know you must feel lousy. But at least—you'll have that."

"Will I?"

"Yes. Now that's what I want to arrange with you. When you go and see the solicitor." Luke undid his exquisite briefcase. Inside was a Filofax, a mobile phone, and a peculiar bulky package. "And there's this. It's rather silly."

"What is it?"

"Well, it was with his things, you see. And around its neck was a note that said 'For Miss Atkins.' Luckily, I and one of the lads went through Nobbi's office—an old arrangement, in the event of—and so Marilyn never saw."

"You mean he left me something?"

"Well, he's left you a hell of a lot," said Luke, clearly irritated for once.

He held out the package.

Stella took it. It felt soft. She put it against her chest. She would not open it while this disgusting, tanned pearl rat was here.

He made the appointment for her meeting with the solicitor—the solicitor Mr. Glass had chosen for Nobbi. It was all to be done so there was no scandal, apparently. No bother with Marilyn. Well, that was fine.

When the appointment—would she really go?—was made, Luke uncrossed his legs.

"Wait a moment," said Stella.

"Yes, Stella?" He was still attempting to look happy to serve.

"I want to know what happened."

"How do you mean, Stella?"

"What happened to—Nobbi."

"But surely . . . He had a heart attack, Stella."

"No he didn't," Stella said. She felt something come into her, like new blood, or alcohol.

"But he did, Stella. Poor old Nobbi. Just working too hard for a man his age."

"And screwing too hard? There was nothing wrong with him. He was strong."

"Yes, of course, Stella. But—he was overweight. He ate the wrong food. He worked at jobs he should have left to Sandy and the boys. And those cigars."

"He didn't die of a heart attack. Marilyn may think he did. Perhaps you sent him back there in a closed box. But I know—I know where he was going."

"Oh, yes?" said Luke. He waited.

"After Tracy," Stella said.

"Yes?"

"A house," Stella said, "a family. Dangerous people."

Luke looked down.

Stella moved back to the window. The dog had not urinated up against the Daimler, but it had shat on the pavement.

"You see, he told me all about it."

"All what, Stella?"

"The house, the people. Where."

"Where, Stella?"

Stella told him. What Nobbi had told her.

The last time on earth she had heard him speak.

There was quiet, and when Stella looked around, Luke had not produced a gun or a stiletto. He looked merely pensive.

"Mr. Glass," said Luke, "a very perceptive man, said

it was likely Nobbi might have told you. You being so close."

Stella gazed at Luke. "I need to know," she said. She thought, *He's not human.*

"All right, Stella. But sit down. It's bad."

Stella, not because she needed to, but because she needed words, sat.

"You may have heard," Luke said, with an odd casual coolness, "the police were looking for a girl. About seventeen. They nicknamed her The Vixen. She got into people's houses and cut their throats, then burned the place down. A sweetie."

Stella had not heard, or if she had, forgotten, but she nodded, meaning, *Go on.*

"Well, she's a daughter of the family Nobbi, unluckily, went to visit. Seems she didn't like him. She killed him, Stella."

"This girl—she cut Nobbi's—she cut his throat—"

"A neck wound. Carotid. Death's very quick. Not much you can do, if any of them tried. She's crazy. Long black hair, body like a dream, and mad as they come. And we . . . can't do a thing, Stella. Not a thing."

"Yes," she said.

"He should have left well alone, Stella. Mr. Glass— we warned Nobbi."

Stella got up, holding the parcel Luke had given her. She walked to the window.

"I'd like you to go now."

"Of course, Stella. Just make the solicitor's, all right?"

"Yes."

He went. She watched. She saw him come out on the grass, huffy at his brush with a moron who had not appreciated his glamour. As he opened the candy Daimler and got in, he trod exactly in the dog shit.

"Thank you, God," said Stella. "You are a monster, but you do exist."

She thought of the pearl-gray hand-stitched suede shoes beyond cleaning, and the stink in the car.

She did not think that, maybe, perhaps, Mr. Glass had instructed Luke, what he might say, if pressed, to this high-strung, bereaved woman. The thing the Corporation might not do. But Stella was different, a hysterical female alone.

Stella, not hysterical, opened the parcel.

She held out the stuffed lion before her, then drew it in.

"Oh, my love," she said, "my only, only love."

CHAPTER 45

◆ *WHY HOPE TO BE HAPPY?*
Before, it had been like a tide of water (life), not especially fast, passing over her. Not happy. Not unhappy. Indifferent.

There was music and there were books.

The rest was an interruption.

Live second-hand.

And then the Scarabae. Anna, Stephan. Adamus. Ruth. Miranda. Malach. Althene.

The cats sat looking at her, perturbed, for Rachaela was their priestess and had no function save to serve them.

Jacob, black on white, Juliet, a dainty monkey, white on black.

They were the salve, not the solution.

At sunset, the helicopter would arrive. Presumably.

He had come back from somewhere, Malach. Althene, with medical skills beyond belief, binding cracked ribs, stitching long cuts. And Kei had been called, for there was an animal, a black dog. He had tended to it, seemingly, and Oskar and Enki had shown no jealousy, only licking it, calming it. Something of all this Althene had told her.

She did not ask what had gone on.

Somewhere, somehow, Malach had spent his grief and rage.

But what was stupid Rachaela to do?

My daughter, walled up in the attic again, like mad Mrs. Rochester in Jane Eyre. *And my lover, leaving me.*

Sunset. They would be gone. Dogs, Malach, Althene.

Good. Let her go. Pervert. Half-thing. No. No. She was perfect. She was like something made in heaven, even if marriages were not made there. She, he. Damn her. And good-bye.

Rachaela knocked on the door of Eric's room.

Almost to her surprise, he called to her to come in, called her by name, perhaps to demonstrate he had not been expecting anyone but she.

It had been a clear day, but very windy. Through Eric's windows, which were of dense orange and green and magenta glass—a forest, knights riding, maidens strewing flowers—the light of late afternoon made colors on an overall paleness.

Eric sat by a little chessboard with tiny figures shaped in silver or bronze as animals. There were herons for bishops and squirrels and mice and pigeons for pawns. The kings and queens were not lions but cats with delicate crowns between their leaves of ears.

"Eric, I said before, several times, I had to leave you. And now I must." Rachaela watched Eric move a silver armadillo knight onto a geranium-pink square.

"No, that's wrong."

"I'm afraid it isn't."

"I'm sorry, Rachaela. I meant the move I had made."

Rachaela laughed. She had come to laugh, among them, strangely, with ease and genuine pleasure. Even now, the board of little beasts intrigued her. And stopped her concentrating.

"I have to say," Rachaela said, "this house has been my fortress. But now. Now it's a prison. With a prisoner."

"Ruth," he said.

"Yes." She thought, *I had this conversation with Stephan, the last time. But it isn't the same. And Stephan is dead.* "You see, I understand now," Rachaela said. "There's nothing to be done about her. I accept . . . what you'll do. There's no doctor on earth who could help her. Only Malach seemed—but then—" She recalled Ruth dragged shrieking up the stairs. Ruth, screaming for Malach. "And I can't do anything. I never could. I always disliked her and now there's just an emptiness in me with her name. The same as there is for Adamus."

"Yes," said Eric. His thin hand lay over the little armadillo, like the hand of a god of miniatures.

"And so—I leave her to you. That's all I can think of or decide. Maybe I'm grossly in error. Probably. God knows."

"And Althene is leaving with Malach tonight," Eric said.

"I'd like to say I was tricked there. But perhaps I only tricked myself."

Eric said, "It's difficult to have faith in a lover. They possess so much of you. You're at their mercy. How can you ever anticipate kindness?"

"Well, I haven't had much."

"None of us," he said, "has."

Rachaela felt an urge to go over to him. Instead she went to the other side of the board, and looked more closely at the tiny animals.

She remembered. Had he carved masks once? He had been so silent. A gift of feathers to dead Sylvian. How he had ordered champagne.

Eric said, "When do you wish to leave?"

"As soon as I can. But, I'll need to make some plans."

"Not necessary. We will provide all you require. By that I don't mean you will be tied to us. Go as far as you want. But the provisions of our house are also yours. You are ours."

"I have to concede that. So, I'll agree. I suspect you will anyway. You've put money and possessions my way in the past, I think. Before I even knew."

"Perhaps." Eric slid the armadillo forward. "And now I've trapped myself."

Rachaela picked up the silver cat-queen, who waited to one side. Poor thing, taken so early and bizarrely from the game.

"I feel," Rachaela said, "I want to be in London. I don't want to go farther than that. London's what I know."

"There is a large apartment," Eric said, "a third-story flat, overlooking the river. It could be made ready in three or four days."

"Thank you," Rachaela said.

"And if you should want us," Eric said, "we are here."

Rachaela looked at him and their eyes met. Dust still lay upon the vivid brightness of Eric's black eyes. No change. No older and no younger.

"I'm afraid of you, still," Rachaela said.

"Yes. That will go."

"Will it?"

"Time," he said.

"Oh, time. It doesn't heal. It spoils. Can it do anything good?"

"There's no choice," he said, "but to continue, and see."

"Adamus found another option. He hanged himself."

"But you," he said, "have not."

* * *

Out in the garden, Rachaela guided the two cats. They investigated every bush and stem, and Jacob arrogantly sprayed, marking a territory he did not realize was soon to be altered. Apparently the new flat had access to a garden below. She was planning for the cats as for herself. What they would eat and the freedoms they would need. This was helpful. She was not quite alone, for now she did not want to be. She partly feared it.

Among the windy, bare and acorn-colored oaks, she met Miranda walking with Tray.

Miranda was the young woman in her filmy dress, and Tray an elderly lady dressed in black. They moved hand in hand, so that Miranda could support Tray. In Tray's other arm was held close a brand-new bright golden lion, a wonderful velvet beast, with mane and tufted tail, and sherry eyes that sparkled. An old woman with a toy lion.

"There is Rachaela," said Miranda.

Tray smiled at Rachaela. She was innocent.

She had gone quite insane, so much must be obvious, but, like Ruth, she was not to be handed over to any authority, not even to her own mother, to whom the body of the fat brown dead man had been returned, smoothly by night.

"Tray has a new name we're trying," said Miranda. "Tell Rachaela."

"Terentia," said Tray. She smiled again and seemed pleased. She raised the lion and kissed it like biting a golden fruit.

"It's an old Roman name," said Miranda. "Ah, look." And she bent down to stroke Juliet. Still linked by hand, Tray or Terentia too, bent down. She tucked the lion under her chin and stroked Jacob who hurried up to be included.

The wind blew savagely against the garden, and the trees creaked like the masts of a ship.

Time . . . The world, a ship upon the seas of centuries, passed on.

Althene did not come to say good-bye again. Rachaela had anyway locked her door. She sat between the cats and the sunset began, cold red under a dome of alcoholic violet.

The helicopter dropped from the sky.

Out of the opened window of her unlit room, Rachaela saw the camp of bikers raise their heads to see. Two of the men got up, shouting and excited. Lou was there, in creased black rubber, and Camillo, just visible, the white dreadlocks, not turning to look.

The helicopter lighted in the glade, and from the house walked out the figures of the ones who were going away. As the dark filled the common and the lights of the house were unlit, they were like shadows she could only guess to be Malach, Kei, Althene. A white shine on Malach's hair. He moved stiffly, old now, as she had seen him last. And the two ghosts of the dogs, unsure perhaps at departure. Kei carried a bundle in his arms—the mysterious black dog, maybe. And Michael and Cheta followed with the few bags.

Althene's shadow moved strongly ahead. From the bikers' camp someone whistled. And another dog barked, and was hushed.

In a moment they would be gone.

The trees swallowed them, and then, presumably, the helicopter, which rose again like a chariot of fire.

I feel nothing, Rachaela thought. *Nothing.*

She thought of her mother's body lying in its box, all wrong, a stuffed doll of flesh.

Juliet started earnestly to wash Jacob.

How strange. I feel nothing. And my eyes are wet.

CHAPTER 46

✤ *IN THE SCENTED PALACE, WITH ITS PAGO-*
das of plants and rose-petal lighting, Stella was
remade. Recreated, as something which Nobbi would
never have recognized. An alien. Which was as it had to
be.

There was so much money it was beyond belief, and
Stella did not believe in it. She had let the solicitor, and
then the bank manager, and then the financial consul-
tant, deal with it. They seemed to enjoy this, their faces
glowing with greed. And she sat quietly and gazed at
them, from the valley of the Shadow.

And when it was all over, she came here, to this
place which promised a kind of beauty that Stella knew
to be also unreal.

With her she brought a small overnight bag. There
were only a limited number of items in it, one of them
the lion Nobbi had left for her, her true inheritance.

First there was a sauna, and then a Jacuzzi. Then the
sunbed, the massage, the facial. Then they came upon
her hair, her face, her hands. They were like flocks of
pretty birds settling on a worm to make it into an angel
with their beaks. But they were tactful too. Trying her to
see if she wanted chatter, and when they found she did
not, silent and soothing as nurses at a deathbed.

It was a deathbed. The old Stella had been killed, and now the new Stella was fashioned on her bones.

She saw it coming, bit by bit. She was not amazed.

In the end, they pulled a sort of diaphanous analogous dustsheet off her, and there she was.

Not beautiful, for Stella could not be made into a beauty even by such clever birds. But no longer a worm of the earth. Winged, now.

Her jaw-cut hair they had slashed shorter, and raised upon her head a sort of low comb, like thick fur. All hint of premature gray was gone, and the hair had the sheen of a crow. Her face was a cameo, pale as cream, lit with a tint of blusher, and with two huge black eyes in fans of charcoal and faint silver. Her lips were more full, colored like sweets the world would want to nibble. Her body was soft, taut, scented, closed against all assault and given to light. Her hands were exact as gloves. Even the nails, which for the duration of her grief—how curious—she had not bitten, were formed to ovals and painted a somber terra-cotta two shades darker than her mouth.

Stella went to the cubicle and put on the white silk underclothes, and then the dress and coat she had bought.

They were of the same fine woollen material, and a purple almost black, the tone of sharks, serpents, night-things.

She clad herself. She drew on the boots of black-purple leather.

In the long mirror she saw this other woman, the second Stella, no longer Star.

Dressed now head to toe. Dressed to kill.

The chauffeur-driven car was light gray, the color of the day itself. It glided through the streets and thoroughfares. There were crowds upon the pavements even in the thin rain. Girls with canary hair and boys like Renaissance minstrels, beggars with broken smiles.

They passed Buckingham Palace. Such an ugly building, she thought, as if it had just been built.

The parks were liquid green beneath their empty trees.

The driver of the car did not speak, of course.

Then the byways came again, the squadrons of shops, furniture and clothes, food and drink, chemists for the sick and florists for birth, marriage, love and death.

Stella saw it all as if from high above. The panoply of this city. Its grandeur and its sleaze.

The rain stopped.

They coasted along a road below a wood, the common? And all at once, she saw the house, that peculiar house Nobbi had told her of.

It too was real.

"Go back to the end of the road," Stella said. "Wait there, please."

She thought, *Will it matter?*

She got out and walked up to the house. Not thinking, *He did this.* Not thinking now at all.

When she reached the door, the slabs of the house above her with their blind, inky windows, she found a man there in the mud, standing by an unusual machine, a sort of motorbike with a carriage fixed on its back.

"Here I am," said the man.

He looked about fifty, but very slim and hard, and when he smiled his teeth were good and probably not false.

Into white hair, woven in dreadlocks like a black man's, were studded beads like brilliant ants.

"Are you one of the family?" Stella asked. The word *Family* had evolved, and stuck firmly in her head. That, and one other word. The fox word, Vixen.

"Am I?"

"I'm here to see someone."

"Are you?" said the man. He wore the leathers of a

biker. He touched the bike at the front where a horse
head was attached. It reminded her in an odd way of the
lion.

"The young girl," said Stella.

"Which one?"

There was nothing else to say.

"The one with a knife."

"Ah!" he exclaimed. And then he capered.

Puck, from *A Midsummer Night's Dream.* Or a devil
from *Faust.*

"You've come," he said, "for Ruth. Nasty Ruth. but
they've locked her up, my lady."

"I've come a long way," said Stella.

"Why?"

"Why," she said, "do you think?"

Camillo looked at Stella.

"The rocking horse burned," he said. "They always
do. The things you love. They die and burn and fall apart.
He knows that. Why did he try again? Broke his back.
Black dog, but no black-haired girl." Camillo laughed.
"We ran over the snow."

He's mad. Will that help?

"You'll bring her to me," said Stella. "Ruth."

"Nasty," Camillo said. "Take her away. She'll cause
trouble, up in the attic."

"Take her away—" said Stella. She had not thought
of that.

"Yes, you must. That's my condition." Camillo
moved over to the door, and pushed it. It had been open,
and behind it was another door, open too.

Beyond was a hall from a country mansion, the kind
the public paid to see.

Stella had not paid and barely saw. She saw a staircase.

"Up there," said Camillo. "I'll show you. But you
must take her away."

"All right." Stella closed her eyes and then widened them. "I'd like that. To take her away."

"Good. Then here's the key."

He held out to her something which had the name of *key,* and the being of *key.*

"The key to the attic?"

"One of them. I stole it."

"Yes."

"Take her away," he said. He went into the hall, and then turned back and flourished to her a courtly bow.

Stella entered the pillared space.

"This time," Camillo said. He made a gesture of cutting and chopping.

Then he scampered up the stairs.

Someone will come.

No one did.

Stella had a sense of things which hid, as if from her. Of things in chrysalis. Moths, spiders, beetles. Things in catacombs, waiting for some night or morning which might never come.

They had climbed the stairs and she had not noticed. There were everywhere colored windows, like a church.

A corridor. Another corridor. Closed doors. More stained glass.

I'm lost.

But she was not.

Through a door another staircase, narrow and uncarpeted.

"Up there," said the old man. She could see he was old, now, nearer seventy than fifty. "Just put the key in the lock."

"I can't remember the way we came."

"Tough," said Camillo, like a youth.

He turned and went away, and Stella looked up the narrow stairs.

I could do it here.

But why not take her, take her away? Would she

come? Yes, she too was waiting, waiting as the beetles
did. No one to assist her. And her name was Ruth.
Whither thou goest, I will go.
Stella smiled.
She went up the stairs.

Among the oaks and pines, Red was brushing her hair.
Lou sat with Cardiff, sulky in her black rubber like a
creased balloon. Cardiff kept tweaking Lou's nipples. She
did not like this, evidently.
Rose and Pig were dozing and Tina had been cooking beans and sausages over the fire, despite the won-
drous meals that infallibly issued from the house.
Whisper was rubbing his bike, sensuously.
Connor crouched, throwing a stick for Viv. Viv re-
trieved urgently, trying to distract him, for he was tense.
Camillo arrived abruptly.
God, but he looked old. Up from out of the mound,
and his death clothes on him.
"It's time!" he cried. He laughed as if with glee but
it might have been a squawk of pain. "Come on! Get up,
you cunts."
"Here!" howled Whisper.
"Stow it," said Connor. "Viv—bag!" Viv galloped to
the Shovelhead and leapt into the saddlebag, the twig still
in her jaws. "Camillo," said Connor.
"No. We go. We go. Red girl, Scarlet O'Hara. You
come around and get on my horse."
"J'entends, monsieur."
And Red ran, away to the front of the house where
the trike was.
Pig and Rose and Tina were already kicking out the
fire, Pig trying to eat the boiling-hot food from the sauce-
pan as they did so.
"Three minutes," said Connor.
"No. No minutes. Now."
"Okay, Camillo. Up, you bastards!" Connor roared.

But Camillo was gone, after Red, toward the trike on the front path in the mud.

"Con," Lou whined, "all my stuff's upstairs—"

"Leave it, you dopey cow," said Connor. "Don't you know he'll take care of that? He says go, we go."

"But *Con*—"

"Or stay here. Stay behind."

Lou huddled onto Cardiff's bike and he came and swung up before her, bumping her askew.

The others were mounting up. The fire was out.

The scene was suddenly desolate and ruined, the path of an army which had moved on to victory or wreck.

As they revved the bikes, they heard the trike awake.

Red was on the damson velvet, her hair bloodied by the window.

"Now we ride," said Camillo, "now we run."

"I'm here."

"Giddy-up," Camillo said.

The sound of the trike altered. It had the noise now of a rocket.

"Christ," Connor said. "He's done it. The methane—"

They heard the trike take off—a missile—gone.

Connor slipped on Viv's goggles. The Shovelhead rose up on its rear wheel, a wheelie. He plunged forward and away after Camillo up the slope. Viv yipped.

He's killed it, Connor thought. The fuel injection that would take the trike to a hundred and twenty miles an hour in two seconds, would burn out the guts of the machine. They would find it dead, but miles off.

The Shovelhead slammed down and Connor tore up and over, along the slope toward the road, the others streaming after, and the black mud flying.

The door opened.

It was not a dream attic from a storybook. Somehow, Stella had supposed it would be. There was nothing in it but for a sofa and a chair, a bed. This was only a room, with another door that might lead to a bathroom. Papers and books were stacked about. On a rail hung some expensive, beautiful clothes.

And by the window, which was of blank white glass, stood a girl, beautiful and expensive, like a final garment.

Nobbi's murderess.

The Vixen. Black fox. Death.

"I don't want any argument," said Stella, "I want you to come with me."

The girl moved from the window.

She was pale, she did not look dangerous, or mad. Under her eyes were patches of darkness. Her mouth was almost white, and very dry.

"All right."

"But I must warn you," said Stella, "if you resist, I'll hurt you."

"Will you?" asked the girl. She seemed almost interested.

Her eyes were full of wonder. It was like a black screen parting to reveal a darker, deeper black.

"Don't bring anything," said Stella.

"No."

The girl wore a white dress with a tight darted waist and a longish skirt, and pale suede boots.

"But take that coat," Stella said.

"This one?"

The girl took up the black coat from the chair back. She touched it, as if it were some dead animal which once she had loved.

"Do you know me?" Stella said. The girl was so compliant, surely Stella had been mistaken for someone expected.

"Oh, yes."

"Come along then."

They went outside, and Stella was ready for the girl

—Ruth—to make a dash for it. Stella would have broken her arms and her neck. She knew she could.

But the girl did not attempt escape. She stood quietly, attending, for Stella to lead her away.

"We'll go down now, and out of the house. Then along the road. There's a car waiting."

"Shall I go first?" asked Ruth.

"Just remember. Don't try to get away from me."

"Oh, I won't."

Where does she think I'm taking her? To safety? Out of confinement. Or does she think I'm a policewoman?

Stella and Ruth descended the silent house, and, as they did so, the noise came of the bikes flying across the slopes. But then that faded.

"That's right, Ruth."

Ruth walked before her. Her hair was like a silken mantle. Was this what he had seen, before—

They were on the staircase now. There, she had recalled the way without problems.

Below was the hall, and the two doors. And then the outside, the road and the car.

"So you know me," said Stella. "Who am I?"

"You're going to kill me," said Ruth.

"Yes. You're right. But don't try to get away. Do you know why?"

"No. I don't care why."

"You wicked little bitch. You fucking little bitch."

They were in the hall.

Ruth turned and looked at Stella. Ruth smiled.

The smile was marvelous. It was like music or a sunrise.

"Stop that," said Stella. "You have an hour or so of life. But it'll get shorter. Make the most of it."

Ruth's smile left her and she lowered her eyes.

Stella ushered her through the doors and out and under the gray sky.

"Can't you . . ." said Ruth, "couldn't you do it now?"

Stella frowned.

"You'll have to wait."

She took Ruth's arm, and together they stepped down toward the road and the car.

CHAPTER 47

❖ SOUTH-FACING, THE WINDOW WAS ALSO
clear. Only at the top, under the arch of the em-
brasure, was a slender panel in which were set faceted
glass jewels, which produced, as the morning sun passed
over in its arc, rainbow prisms which showered the living
room. With these the cats, sensing the infinitesimal
movement, sometimes played.

The flat was quite modern, with pale apple-green
walls in the large main room, and a ceiling three tones
lighter. The carpet was dark green and the drapes ivory-
white with a plant pattern in several green tones. There
were ivory-white blinds trimmed with dull gold. The furniture was in a white wood, that looked unbelievably like
the bark of birches. On the table was a huge green glass
bowl in which was suitable fruit, subaqueous apples and
pears, jade grapes, and one sportive yellow grapefruit.

The bedroom was also large, and done like the main
room, but in blues, with blue and ivory velvet curtains
and pale blue blinds. There was a double bed. In a concealed cupboard were quantities of sheets and pillow-
slips, even duvets and their covers, in contrasting blues
and ivories.

The bathroom was white with a wine-red carpet and
wine and white towels stacked in a second concealed cupboard. There were lights high on the walls, shaped like

wine-red roses. The window was in white glass with pink jewels.

The kitchen was in pine, very pale, with adventures in sunshine yellow. All mod cons. Freezer and fridge, technological oven, washing machine, dishwasher, gadgets for coffee and tea and every form of pulverizing food.

Modern, yet unmistakably Scarabae. The colors alone.

Had they, collectively, once known great darkness, that now they strove always after this richness? And was it, if so, only the dark of night?

But she tried not to think of them.

The great south window, which went to the floor, led into a conservatory, which had initially no plants, only a tessellated floor (soft emerald and charcoal), and strips of stained glass without pictures around its top. This in turn opened on a wide balcony with a high brick surround. Ivy grew over it, picturesque, and below, the house descended quietly, its two other floors, into an overgrown garden, with overgrown plum trees and a choked pool visited by frogs.

Beyond the garden walls the ground tumbled to mud flats, and then into the river, the oily gleaming Thames, where ducks waddled and swam, and now and then a speedboat would pass with a wake of Persil spray.

Along the riverbanks, on both sides, were attractive buildings, new considered blocks of flats with Roman tiles and ovals of glass, two churches, some complexes of perhaps an industrial nature, but with an art deco Egyptian look. From one, the farthest off, a plume of smoke occasionally lifted, and turned to rose at sunset. Doubtless unhealthy but undeniably aesthetic.

The middle floor of Rachaela's block seemed unoccupied. At the bottom dwelled a pair of couples in adjoining apartments. She had seen them in the hall, polite and smiling but not pushy. She heard no noises from them but the intermittent soft waft of cello music, or glimpses of a concerto by Liszt or a symphony of Mahler's.

They had made all perfect for her. As perfect as was possible.

Jacob and Juliet too were charmed. They climbed down the strong lattice of ivy and jumped to the garden wall, thence the garden. They sat in the plum trees like racoons or lemurs, tails hanging, and eyed the ducks on the mud flats.

By the middle of March, Rachaela had bought plants for the conservatory—she had never been able to grow things, but maybe now . . . ?—and added a music center and two portable radios to the flat. She had introduced green plants, too, and green soaps and towels to the bathroom, filled the freezer with exotic food and the fridge with cheeses and salad. She found an orange glass dish and put oranges in it.

The floor was scattered by cat toys, catnip sticks of "dynamite" with chewed tassels, catnip mice which had had their ears eaten off, and balls which were rattled and tinkled around the rooms at three in the morning.

One wall of the living room was book shelves, and Rachaela was filling it. Rebecca West, Jean Rhys, Lawrence Durrell, Proust, Shakespeare, Chekhov, Dickens, Hardy, Jane Gaskell, Louise Cooper.

Her taste in books had broadened, but, conversely, her desire for music had retracted like a bruised antenna.

Then, she found a solution. She began to paint, playing music as she did so.

She was not attracted to oils, and chose instead watercolors and creamy gouache. She worked with a light drawing board balanced on her knee, sometimes leaning forward until her hair brushed the paper and she must tie it back.

She suspected that her paintings were effective, if

still unformed. She tended to realism rather than abstraction, yet with meltings, hints, and candid lies.

What she painted were women. Scarabae women. Pale and gorgeous, with vast clouds of hair. In amorphous dresses from two or three eras, padded shoulders, flowing skirts. The hands were ringed, the eyes blinding with lights. They stood at colored windows or walked on heaths. One floated like Ophelia in a stream, but she was not drowning, only—floating.

There was a bank account. It had been opened for Rachaela, in the name of Day, and the documents sent her the morning after she entered the flat.

She used the money without scruple, and, of course, as she used the money, it was topped up.

Continual letters came from the bank, urging her to invest, to begin this or that enterprise with her healthy account.

Sometimes she walked by the river, or shopped in the smart streets behind the flats.

Twice, she cried, very deeply, and for a long time.

Yet, as she did so, she stood beside herself, watching.

Juliet came to comfort her, but Jacob, embarrassed, ran and hid.

"What am I going to do this time?" Rachaela asked Juliet.

Juliet had no ideas. To her it was all quite easy. Jacob and she were already showing a new interest in each other, breaking off their play to wowl softly, then washing each other vigorously.

Rachaela had known, before Althene got onto the helicopter. Not been sure, of course, but, in fact, where could be the doubt?

She did not blame Althene. It was her own fault. This time, it was.

She did not feel anything amiss with herself. The former nausea was not there, no tiredness. She felt well and vibrant.

Probably she should see a doctor. The social climate had changed, and she was in her forties now. A termination would perhaps be suggested, rather than withheld.

And that was the answer.

To be pregnant—to be released.

Not, again, even if now supported in luxury, to go through that long business of carriage, and then that disgusting pain and indignity. Worse than all that, not again to produce a child. For the last child had been Ruth.

Camillo had Ruth.

That was the incongruous thing.

That afternoon, when she had been asleep, and the others locked up in their silences, the bikers had fled, Camillo with them, and when Michael went up to the imprisoning attic, the door stood wide and Ruth too was gone.

Rachaela had thought that Camillo hated Ruth. Perhaps Malach's hatred of her had turned Camillo about.

Two mad things, out in the world.

She did not want to think of it. Mostly because she had seen what had become of Ruth, after the murder, when Malach let her fall. Ruth had died. She was a corpse.

"I'll let it go until April," Rachaela said to Juliet. Juliet stared at her with azure eyes. Jacob came back, haughty, prepared to overlook the outburst. "That will be around three months. I can't tell Eric. They'll protest and find some way to stop it."

She put her hand over her stomach.

Was it alive?

Was she holding in the core of her a living thing, planning its death, Rachaela a killer, as her first daughter had been?

On the 1st April, April Fool's Day, the green telephone rang in the living room.

Rachaela ran to it, petrified, and could not lift the receiver.

"Don't be an idiot."

As she raised the green arm the line went dead and then there was the dialing tone.

"A wrong number," said Rachaela.

Is that you, Gladys?

As she was turning away, the phone rang again, and she dragged up the receiver wildly.

"Hallo?"

"This is Althene."

Rachaela sighed. It was as if she had been holding her breath for half an hour. Her legs shook and she sat down. Jacob pranced onto her lap.

"Jacob's here," Rachaela said, "he wants to speak."

"I'm so glad. But do you?"

"Of course. How are you?"

"I am well. And you?"

"Oh, yes. Very well."

"Rachaela, forgive me. I'm old enough I hate telephones. I am coming back. That is, I'm coming back today. This evening."

"You're—"

"And if you want to, Rachaela, you can meet me. I'll see to it a car is there for you at five o'clock. It will bring you to the airport. It will wait below the flats until half-past five. If you don't come out to the car it will drive away. That will be that. This is all I have to say. Goodbye."

Rachaela sat holding the phone, which Jacob was using for a scent-marking object, rubbing his head on it so violently that it was dashed from Rachaela's hand.

Rachaela got ready to meet Althene.

When she was finished, she put down plates of boiled cod for the cats, and refilled their water bowl, as if she would be gone a long while. That was possible. For what did Althene want?

She had changed the sheets on the bed, and put out extra towels, as she would for a guest. But actually, she thought, Althene would want to take her somewhere, some hotel, undoubtedly very glamorous, and then that would be that. Meeting. Parting.

Or else, there was some message Althene had been charged to deliver. By Malach. Or someone.

Rachaela put two bottles of Californian Colombard into the fridge. It was the wine with the taste of apples.

She had put on a gray skirt and gray waisted jacket over gray silk lingerie and gray stockings whose tops were patterned with cats.

But conceivably that had been silly.

She did not think about herself and Althene making love, because when she had done this before, the intensity of frustrated need had, as the pregnancy did not, made her sick.

No, better just to take this as it came.

She ran down through the flats at a quarter to five.

The gentle young man from the second bottom flat, the cello player, was bringing his Labrador puppy in from its walk.

Rachaela stroked the puppy quickly, not giving it enough time to investigate the fascinating taint of cat.

"Have to fly—"

Outside she waited in the cool mellowness of early sunfall. And from the muslin light, the long car came, a Rolls.

She got in, and the driver, with only a mannerly greeting, drove her away.

The planes were coming down like giant winged whales.

They went nowhere near the arrival lounge, but away among some trees, to a tiny airstrip separated from the conglomerate by high barbed-wire fences.

It was dark now and cold lights pierced vision from all directions.

Like some film, she thought, when the famous spy arrives with the secret which will save the world.

Althene, the spy.

I don't feel anything.

She stood outside the car, and after a while she saw the little plane descend from heaven, onto the little runway.

It landed beautifully, as if sliding along a pat of butter.

A ten-seater, which, when it halted, let forth one figure. A tall woman in a layered devastating coat, not black like her hair, but flaming red.

Red. The marriage color.

Rachaela felt sick. She wanted to run away.

Althene, like fate, inexorably came toward her.

She was so beautiful she put out the bloody lights of the airport.

She came straight up to Rachaela and took Rachaela into her arms.

"Let me go." Althene did so. "Before you say anything," Rachaela said, "I'm pregnant."

"Ah," said Althene. "So much for the Roman method."

"I shan't go through with it," said Rachaela. "I want you to understand that. I'm too old—"

"You're Scarabae. Your body will do anything you want. You can't be harmed, or the child."

"All right, but I don't want it."

"That's different, of course," Althene said.

"You understand then."

"Naturally. Can I kiss you now?"

Rachaela looked at Althene. "I want you to. But then what?"

"My bags are coming. Quite a lot of them. More

things on their way. You have a flat. The second floor is also available to us. They interconnect."

"I see."

"I mean I shall live with you," Althene said. "I hoped you realized this, and that was why you had come to meet me. Obviously, if not—"

Rachaela began to cry. The third time. The tears flooded out, and were ended.

"I gather it will be horrible for you," said Althene.

"I love you," Rachaela said. "Don't leave me."

They did not kiss after all, only embraced each other. Beyond the chauffeur and the men coming with the bags and a couple of cabin crew, there was no one to see. And these took them for sisters.

CHAPTER 48

✤ LATE IN THE SUMMER, MALCOLM AND
Cherrylyn Lennox went cycling in hilly Covener
Woods. It was very hot, but they had missed their cycling
due to Malcolm's father's illness, from which, thankfully,
he was now recovered. As Cherrylyn had remarked anyway, with the damage to the ozone layer, summers were
always going to be this hot, and winters full of gales. They
would have to get used to it.

They strained up the slopes, bony with roots, and
free-wheeled down the other sides, sometimes laughing.
Yellowed green, the crisp leaves shut off the worst of the
sun. Birds were everywhere; they spotted jays, and even,
they thought, an escaped canary.

"Let's stop in Witch Hollow, I'm starving," said
Cherrylyn, as they came over the ridge, and saw, far off
below, the railway line which ran over the countryside
from London, city of muggers and pollution, like a
spreading stain.

Cherrylyn, despite her bicycling, was a big hefty girl,
but all her feeding had not covered over Malcolm's thin-
ness. They were an ill-matched couple, who loved each
other, and were very happy.

They rolled down into Witch Hollow, that they had
named from the Coven of the Woods. Among the thick
weave of the trees, they parked the cycles, got off, and

Malcolm began to unload the food. Large wholemeal sandwiches of vegetarian cheese and homemade pickle, walnut cake, bananas, and a bottle of apple juice guaranteed free of Alar.

"Just got to wee," said Cherrylyn, and giggled. She found most natural functions, except eating and sex, rather amusing.

She went off decorously into the waist-high bracken.

"That stuff's bad for you," said Malcolm. They had just heard that bracken was perhaps carcinogenic.

"I'll only be—" said Cherrylyn. And then she stopped.

Malcolm waited, then he shrugged, and went on putting out the sandwiches, cake and fruit, on the oilcloth.

Soon the bracken rustled, he looked around, and so was in time to see his wife emerge, her round face greenish white.

Though he was thin he was also strong, and he managed to catch her as she fainted.

When she came to, which was quite quickly, Cherrylyn was her usual sensible self, although her face was now the color of milk and she shook so hard she joggled him up and down.

"There's a dead body in the bracken, Malcolm. It's decomposed. Don't go and look."

"But I must," said Malcolm.

"Why? I've seen it. Honestly, love, you don't want to."

"Yes," Malcolm said. "No, all right, then."

"I'll be fine in a minute, and then we must cycle down to the village and get the police."

"Oh, hell," said Malcolm.

"I know," said Cherrylyn sympathetically, "but there's nothing else we can do."

"No."

After five minutes, Cherrylyn was able to stand up.

But she did not risk getting on her bicycle, so they wheeled them away through the wood.

The food they left abandoned on the grass, on the oilcloth, and presently the birds came gladly and ate it for them.

There had been no plan. The car took them to a great station of hard cement, where colorful shops in glass cubes offered chocolates and books, scarves and roses, and tables stood out on the concourse under bright umbrellas that were not needed, for in here, the rain did not fall.

· A train was leaving for the north in sixteen minutes.

Stella and Ruth went into the booking hall and Stella bought two tickets for the first-class section.

Then they walked to the train and boarded it. Stella and Ruth, with only Stella's small bag.

The train moved. It moved away. Setting out into the rain and the wide skies beyond the city.

At first there were factories and little houses and churchyards and huge yards full of lorries.

Stella and Ruth, sitting facing each other on the antimacassared seats, both looked at these.

Then, like the past, the edges of the city dimmed and went behind. The dark fields opened, lined by leafless, mourning trees.

Stella uncrossed her legs and the smart boots hissed.

"Shall we have a drink?"

Ruth turned. "Yes, that would be nice."

"You'd better understand," said Stella, "I've got a cast-iron head. I'm not going to lose my grip. It won't make any difference."

"No, I know that."

The man came from the buffet just after that, and Stella lavishly tipped him and told him what was wanted.

When he next appeared he brought a bottle of vodka, glasses, ice, and real lemons.

After he had gone again, Stella made the drinks.

They drank in silence for about an hour.

Stella could see Ruth was like her in the matter of being a sound drinker. She did not change.

And Stella thought for a second how she had got tiddly with her mother at Christmas, and how it had been infectious, that. And maybe this was too, this cold.

The landscape went by.

"Look," said Ruth suddenly, "there are cows."

As if she had never seen them. Perhaps she never had.

"We'll have something to eat later on," said Stella. "I don't know yet where we'll get out."

"We may just see somewhere," said Ruth, "that looks like the place."

We're on honeymoon, Stella thought.

We're at one.

Darkness began to come, the impersonal darkness of winter night. Although maybe it was spring.

"I want to tell you," Stella said, "about the man you killed."

She was not drunk. She could see and function exactly. Her hands were coordinated, her brain clear. But yes, the drink had made her want to speak. Or Ruth had. Confession.

But Ruth said, "I'm sorry, I'm not sure which man you mean."

"You've butchered several, haven't you?" Stella said. Ruth nodded. No pride, no complacency. No bravado. No regret. "Why did you do it?"

"It's what I do." Ruth's eyes dropped down under the makeupless pale lids. Her lashes were long and thick and black, like trimmings of her amazing hair. "But I got it wrong. And this man you mean—he was the last one, wasn't he? The one who came to the house."

"Yes," said Stella. Her voice was grit and it hurt her throat.

"I'm sorry," said Ruth, "I thought he was threatening them and that I had to stop him. But he wasn't. I was mistaken."

"That won't alter my mind."

"No, I'm not trying to alter your mind about me," said Ruth.

"No amount of pleading—"

"I won't plead," said Ruth. "I want you to do it."

"Why?" Stella said.

Ruth said nothing.

Stella refilled their glasses, replacing ice, throwing out the old lemon and adding fresh. Two-thirds of the bottle was gone.

When Ruth took her glass back, Stella noticed for the first time that she was left-handed.

"The man you killed had a nickname. It was Nobbi. Daft, isn't it. Like some sort of bad penis joke. Actually he was a wonderful lover. And anyway, I loved him."

"Yes," said Ruth. She raised her eyes. "Yes, tell me."

"I lost my mother you see—horrible euphemism. She died and my cat died—" Ruth made a tiny movement with her mouth. What they called a moue. "That can be traumatic."

"Yes," Ruth said, "my cat died, too. It was very old. It died in its sleep."

"Mine—yes, mine was like that."

Stella drank her vodka.

Ruth said, slowly, "And then you met the man."

"Yes, I met him and I was in love with him. I just looked at him and I was in love."

"Yes," Ruth said.

"He was married to somebody else, so we didn't have much time together. But what we had was delirious —yes, it was. And I used to think he'd leave her. Stupid, perhaps. Perhaps he wouldn't have. But I used to think we'd be together. And have cats and dogs. And—just be with each other."

"Yes," said Ruth.

"Maybe even I'd have had his child. It's not that I'm maternal. I just liked the thought of reproducing *him*. You see these bloody people, absolute rubbish, and they fill the earth with their rubbish, and they *breed*. But the best ones don't have children. Or not enough."

The train moved. Outside was the night. Now and then a dislocated light would gleam flickering in rain. It might be anything. A factory, a window, a beacon on a hill to tell of the coming of the Armada.

"And now there's no future," said Stella. "There's nothing."

"It will be so easy for me," Ruth said. "I've got nothing, either. And you'll put an end to that."

"Stop asking me to make you happy by doing you in," Stella said.

"I'm sorry," Ruth said again. "And I'm sorry about —Nobbi. I remember, he was short. He had a loud voice, but then he was quiet."

"Quiet forever," Stella said.

The waiter came.

"Can I help you, ladies?"

"We'd like something to eat now," Stella said. "Not the usual menu. Something light." The drink made her truthful. "Attractive."

"I will see to it," he said.

When he had gone, Ruth said, "I think he changed me. I think I can feel what you mean."

Stella thought she meant Nobbi.

They sat in silence again, and then the man came back with a tray laid with linen and silver. The plates were good china. There were leaves of green salad, endive and lettuce, yellow tomatoes and avocado, Brie and Camembert, and whorls of biscuits. In a glass bowl were seedless grapes and checkers of melon.

"That's so lovely," Stella said.

"My pleasure. Is there anything else?"

"No. Thank you."

They drank the last of the vodka and they ate all the cheeses and the delicate watery green pure food.

Ruth and Stella were hungry. They told each other so, and how much they liked what they had. They laughed. And were silent again.

The train began to slow. Outside, the darkness of the countryside.

They looked at each other.

Ruth said, "Shall we get out here?"

"Yes," Stella said. "That's best."

They went into the corridor.

When the train stopped with a long and dismal screeking, they undid the door and descended to the platform.

The electric lights burned, and, under these, skeletal hanging baskets were, without flowers.

Beyond the lighted station, on every side, teemed utter blackness.

There was no one at the ticket barrier, although it was lighted up. Beyond, a half-lit slope of gravel with a shed, itself unlit, labeled: *Speedie Cars*.

"What will you do?" said Ruth. "How will you get back?"

I'm going to kill her and she asks how I will get back.

"It doesn't matter. Don't worry, Ruth. Maybe there'll be a car. Or I can sleep in the wet woods."

Ruth nodded.

"You could take my coat. It would help to keep you warm."

"No, no, you keep it."

"But I won't need it," Ruth said.

Inside Stella the sword of pain clove sheer. But she did not swerve. That was her way.

As they walked, Ruth came close.

"Take my arm. I liked that."

"Must I do what you like?"

"Just this once."

Stella took Ruth's arm.

Below the station was a muddy road, and along this they went and into the great blackness of the night. The rain trembled.

There were no stars. But the sky had its own color reprieved from the lamps of the city. It was blue. Blue-black, or purple-black, like Stella's clothes.

There was a track, and they moved onto it. It pulled uphill, and the woods came down.

Wet woods, still but for the lilting patter of the rain.

"How many miles to Babylon," said Stella. "God, don't you remember funny things."

"I remember dragons," said Ruth.

Stella did not argue. Did not even query the statement in her mind.

Up in the woods was the depth of the night. Nothing in motion, but they two.

Ruth halted.

"Shall we do it here?"

"Is there anything—" Stella stumbled in her words, "anything you want to do—need to do—"

"Nothing."

"Are you ready?"

"Yes."

Stella undid her bag. Her fingers brushed the lion in the dark, and then she found the kitchen knife she had brought.

She could see Ruth now, her eyes accustomed to the dark. Ruth had undone her coat, and the white dress shone.

Stella stepped forward. She raised the knife, and braced herself. And Ruth smiled. Lost in the water of night like a note of music, a glimmer of day.

Stella struck with all her strength. Through the white dress, the white breast, down, deep down, carving to the heart of murder.

Black—it was red—gouted out about the blade, and Stella wrenched it back. It needed brute force.

Ruth was gone. She was down in the undergrowth of the wood, where the termites and the woodlice ran, down on the mulch of leaves, the sodden fern stems.

Stella peered after her, and saw her there.

Ruth was as still now as the night. The black blotch on her dress did not disfigure her, and only from the corner of her mouth one glowing jewel, like jet, had issued.

The downpour would wash her clean. All white. And tomorrow the sun might light on her. For now, the choir of shadow and water.

Stella placed the knife in the plastic carrier she had brought and settled it in her bag, careful not to soil the lion.

Then she turned and left Ruth there, under the trees:

The dead girl in the rain.